A BLACK AND SOLEMN SILENCE

COLOR BY NUMBERS

BOOK ONE

DANIELLE THOMPSON

Grateful acknowledgement is made to D. G. Rossetti for his 1861 translation of Dante Alighieri's *La Vita Nuova,* which is quoted in this text.

To request permissions, contact author.danielle.thompson@gmail.com

www.writerdaniellethompson.com

Paperback ISBN: 979-8-9896983-0-1

Ebook ISBN: ISBN: 979-8-9896983-1-8

Cover designed by MiblArt

For old friends, born in the month of November.

As they say: better late than never.

ONE

It shouldn't have ever happened; Jaden had even tried to stop him. *Don't do it,* he had said, followed by *leave him alone.* It had been dawn, and the *kitsune* watched as the boy knelt and took photos of the mountains. Kuro was bored, lazy, *impulsive.* He didn't want to listen.

His desire was deeper than mere obstinance; he was *sure* he had seen that boy before. He looked just like the same one from years ago...the one he had based his human form on. The boy had come to the mountains once; why shouldn't he come again? Kuro just *had* to know, for curiosity's sake...

And now the image of a demon fox was saved in that boy's camera, and Kuro was trapped, bleeding to death in a barn, the two events inextricably linked by his own colossal stupidity.

I don't want to think about what happened, he pleaded with his own mind. *Jaden, please help me...please find me...*

He hated the version of himself from an hour ago who had wandered the forest lost, frustrated. He had shed his human form and moved as himself, a *kitsune* so black that he stood out amongst the darkness of the night as an inky figure in a world of shadows. He had been deep in that dusty mind of his, struggling with thoughts too big for him to get a grasp on and wrestle into submission when he finally resolved to give up, turn back, and find Jaden.

And then the trees had cleared.

Kuro had stumbled out of the dark onto moonlit grasses near an old, crumbling fence. The wooden slats had crippled in one section, the beams covered in the moldy pepper of spreading rot. It reminded him of the rocks near his river...of home. Beyond the fence sat a square of dusty pasture that separated a squat country home from a sagging barn.

Kuro had cautiously crept forward. The moon cast a weak light on the barn, illuminating its faded, chipped paint and warped doors.

He sniffed the air, hopeful that the place was abandoned, but no; a horse was nearby. He could smell the sweaty scent of the animal's hide, and something else, too – something musky...

His thoughts left him as he looked up, searching. Kuro's tail dropped to the ground as he gazed, transfixed, up toward the roof of the barn.

He watched as a young woman sat up slowly, stretching long limbs with an unconscious grace. Brown hair fell down her back in long curls as she looked out into the night. She was oblivious to the damp rot of the barn's boards that held her weight. A strap of her overalls dangled, undone and forgotten, and she smiled like a dreamer coming out of a pleasant reverie. She was in her twenties, he thought, a young woman with flannel sleeves rolled up past her elbows. Perhaps she had been enjoying the forest on her land, the bass of bullfrogs in the darkness, a witness to the secret symphony accentuated by the cry of nighthawks and the steady hooting of hidden owls...until the world fell silent as a demon walked through the night.

Their gazes collided.

Kuro had returned to his human form in the span of a single blink.

Did she see me? He thought, their eyes locked on one another.

That could be dangerous, what with a possible picture of him out there, too. Better to be safe. *So what then – kill her?*

No, never that; *run.* Better to be a coward.

But then again...what was it that Jaden had said to him earlier tonight when Kuro had turned away, disgusted by the dried blood still on his friend's hands?

Enjoy yourself.

He saw Jaden's easy movements flash in his memory, pictured the way his thumb trailed smooth circles on a girl's inner wrist, recalled the way they all smiled at him...and the way he smiled back. A sudden hot anger welled up within him; he could be like that, too. He didn't need to fear some country girl, turn tail and run like a whipped hound, not after *today.*

He could kill.

Even now, there was a body – reeking, probably bloated with the gasses of death – sagging into the driver seat of a car on the outskirts of Asheville, the upholstery swollen like a tick with blood that had spurted out from a torn throat and a shredded abdomen. There had been glimpses of color before he looked away, his gorge rising: the plush red of a liver, the glistening, pearly pinkness of coiled tubes that had spilled forward, onto the car floor –

He hadn't killed her, hadn't even *known* Jaden was going to do it; he tried to rationalize her death for his own cold comfort: after all, was it so different, really, from killing anything else?

A human is not a mouse. Or a fish, or a bird, or a deer. They talk *to you.*

And this one was unmistakably *looking* at him.

He stood in plain view and shifted from foot to foot uncomfortably; he really wasn't good at this sort of thing – it required planning, cunning, and whatever special charisma Jaden had that Kuro seemed to lack. He would have to think on his feet, try to act more natural – embarrassed, maybe. He could aim for that.

"Excuse me!" He called up, his eyes firmly on the ground now, trying to work up a semblance of uncertainty in his voice, but he was no actor, no liar. He could hear how ridiculous and false he sounded. "I'm lost!"

No response.

Do I look up? He wondered. He'd never attempted this kind of duplicity before, even though Jaden made it look so simple. It just wasn't in him. Shame and frustration snuck up his spine, throttling his judgement. It would be wiser now to just run; what was he trying to prove, anyways?

And who are you trying to prove it to?

Forget it, he answered himself, angry now. *Just run. One person has already seen you today,* he thought, bitter. *Does it matter all that much if someone else does? No one will believe her anyway...*

His instinct sharpened suddenly with a prickling in his palms.

This silence was all wrong.

Kuro looked up too late. The girl had leaned forward on her knees near the edge of the barn, where a ladder stood. He could see now that she was tall, with sturdy, strong muscles carved from physical labor.

The dreamy smile that had played on her lips was gone; her arms were raised, elbows locked, one eye squinted.

She was aiming a gun at him.

He turned to run just as the first shot cracked through the night.

His blood hit the ground before he did, a light spray of the dark liquid sliding down a few blades of grass that suddenly curled in on themselves, dying: demon blood – dark and unnatural. The bullet had grazed across the skin of his shoulder, leaving a burning streak in its wake. Kuro shouted and stumbled backward, panicking, just as she adjusted her aim.

The next bullet found its home in his right thigh.

It felt as though he had been struck by a heated hammer. He dropped to his knees in pain, a scream tearing from him. He pressed both hands into the wound and watched as blood flowed out between his fingers, leaking up through the cracks near his knuckles, the bullet lodged deep in the flesh.

He wanted to change and run, to shift into his true form, the giant, sleek fox, the *kitsune,* and flee into the trees, but that would have been no good on a wounded leg; at least as a human he could punch with two good arms...if he could *think*, if his heart wasn't slamming in his chest, his breaths gasping and uneven. And his arms – they were shaking, overcome with horror and terror, and there was the *pain*...hot, *aching* now, radiating into his very bones, driving him from his senses.

Rage reared within him, surging upward on adrenaline; who did she think she was, shooting *him?* A dark and malicious energy uncoiled in his stomach, the same that had woken in him years ago and told him he was something more than just an animal: he was a *demon*, powerful, formidable, with knowledge in his heart. For one fleeting, pain-filled instant he was in both forms at once, flickering between them – his hands were the clawed weapons of the fox, his mouth a narrow bed of fangs, a black tail whipping the air from the base of his human spine – but a second scent filled the air, shattering the moment and snapping him back to his human form.

It was the same smell from before, the musky one...and it was running towards him, snarling.

A dog.

All the courage in Kuro's body fled; panic took hold as he scrambled away, fear tripping him as blood flowed and adrenaline failed. The pain of putting weight on his injured leg hit his mind like a sledgehammer, and through the fog of agony, he watched helplessly as the German Sheppard surged through the grass, its wet tongue lolling out of open jaws as it leapt the fence, barking.

Kuro didn't make it a step farther before the dog clamped its jaws onto his leg. He cried out and shifted before he realized what was happening; the two of them grappled in the grass, human to *kitsune,* *kitsune* to human, Kuro shifting back-and-forth in his frenzied panic, unable to control his changing limbs as the dog began to yank his head from side to side, lacerating his flesh.

And worse, every change grew more difficult; he felt as though he was being pushed permanently in one direction, his *kitsune* form resisting him.

Dogs. It was almost worse than the bullet in his leg, blinding him with white, shooting pain. Just the sight of dogs walking on leashes would send the *kitsune* detouring onto side streets; the barking alone could shatter their nerves. Even as humans, the animal instincts of a fox remained.

Kuro had feared nothing worse than a dog.

Except, now, for the girl.

Each bark exploded in his ears, pummeling his mind into desperate confusion. He curled into a tight ball and brought two human hands over his head, the dog shredding his knuckles into a bloody pulp. He curled up more tightly, wanting to scream, to run, to *escape,* but he couldn't even bring himself to breathe as the dog leapt onto his back, claws ripping gashes through cloth and flesh alike.

"Feral!" The young woman's voice cut across the night. Paralyzed with terror, Kuro could hear her footsteps as she ran forward. She was yelling at the dog to stop, and finally, with a vicious, unwilling growl, Kuro felt the last sharp jab of pain as the fangs released him.

Run! He could hear himself screaming in his mind as though he were watching himself cowering, bleeding on the ground. *Just run!*

But he could no more rouse himself to run than he could undo every choice he had made in the last twenty-four hours, every bad decision that had led him to this very place.

And the dog was still there, its heavy panting and the sound of it licking the blood from its jowls sending great shock waves of terror down his human spine. His fear competed with a sudden, maddening desire to gnaw his own leg off, anything to escape that searing bullet that was igniting his nerves with inescapable pain.

A voice unlike his own whispered to him suddenly, almost too quiet to hear over his own internal screaming.

Be brave, it commanded. *You must be brave.*

But he couldn't be – not with that dog straining for release right in front of him, snarling for another dash, another bite –

She grabbed his hands, yanking them behind his back. Cold metal was pressed over his wrists and snapped into place, his arms pinned securely at the base of his spine.

As usual, Jaden had been right; *you'll regret not coming along,* he'd told him.

Shot, bloodied, beaten, and *captured,* Kuro was indeed finding himself full of regrets.

She was yelling at him, her voice lost amidst the volley of the dog's barking. He couldn't change his form; pinned like this, his arms would snap and break behind his back the moment he shifted shape. For half a heartbeat, he was desperate enough to hope that if he shifted forms, the handcuffs would be assimilated like the rest of his clothes, simply 'disappearing' with the change, but no; a semblance of rational thought remained in his clouded mind, warning him that it took time for something to become *his*: he could take the chance, but he didn't want to risk breaking both arms at the sockets on what was surely a losing bet.

But desperation was engulfing him, and coherent thought was rapidly deserting him.

She was kicking him, yelling at him to move. He tried to stand, but the pain in his leg was too great; he buckled, gasping.

"Feral, no!" The dog lunged and snapped at his heels.

Kuro was up and stumbling again, lurching forward, the gun an inch from the back of his neck, every step a blow of fresh torture. There could be no stopping, though; he had to move faster, had to keep in front of the gun – if he thought he had problems *now*, things would only get worse if a human weapon touched him.

Much, much worse. It was a taboo a demon couldn't break.

At least, not without consequences.

The barn was up ahead, the double doors open. "Go through," she commanded.

He hesitated. *She's going to kill me,* he realized. *I'm going to die here.*

The dog snarled; Kuro dragged himself inside, the sweet smell of the hay overwhelming him. The interior of the barn spun in pale yellows and browns, dimly lit and rich with the scent of summer harvest.

An old gray mare reared in the front stall, shrieking as the smell of blood clogged the air.

The girl shoved him hard into one of the stalls in the back; he fell heavily into the hay, breathless with pain. He wanted to faint, but he knew he couldn't; in unconsciousness, he would turn back into his *kitsune* form, and his arms would break...or the girl would kill him.

He struggled to hold on as the world reeled. No choice, there – he had to endure. He was stuck like this until he could get the handcuffs removed.

He pushed himself against the far wall, kicking up the dry bristles with his good leg, and a brief thought managed to break through his agony; he hoped she didn't notice how abnormally dark his blood was. The pounding of his heart drummed in his ears, but the girl looked calm and collected. She busied herself by lighting various lamps and soothing the horse as Kuro sat, gasping and bleeding in the corner of the stall.

I should have gone with Jaden. I should have listened to him. He clung to consciousness, willing himself to stay in the moment and find a path to his escape. *What did she see? Did she see me change forms? Why did she shoot me? Focus!*

He forced himself to concentrate on breathing. His gaze, dark and cautious now, watchful for any chance at freedom, took in a thankful sight as she locked the dog outside and turned to face him.

Kuro didn't like what he saw.

She wore an expression sharp and clear with conviction, her eyes blazing.

He took a ragged breath and willed himself to be as still as possible, focusing his energies on an appearance of calm rationality.

Every nerve in his body was on fire, every instinct in him roused to run; he focused and shoved them all down into a quiet place as his death stood in front of him. She still held the gun with one hand. From the corner of his eye, Kuro noticed that the finger was still locked around the trigger, but trembling.

She took a step forward and brought the gun up, pointing it at his head.

"Change," she instructed.

He'd failed earlier at being convincing, and it had cost him. He needed to be as good an actor as Jaden if he was going to get out of this alive.

"C-change?" He stammered. The effort it took just to speak was all-encompassing. Kuro pushed through it, fighting for air. "Are you *crazy*? Please, just let me go and I won't call the police, you don't know –"

The bullet shattered the wood next to his head, showering him with splinters. He flinched away, panicked.

"*Don't* use that word – no one here is 'crazy,'" she said, her voice low with warning.

"Are you out of your mind!?" No acting required, now – just real, electrifying terror. He would readily beg, if it would win him his life. "*Please* – just let me go!"

"*Change.*" She spoke the word through clenched teeth, her eyes narrowed with a flinty, hard resolve.

"Into *what*?" He was trying to buy time, gather his wits and find a way to escape, but even as shock set in, the pain in his leg was edging out everything else besides his fear. The agony of the bullet gripped his mind with a white-hot hold. Regret cut him, and with it, a senseless, frantic wish that he could go back in time, that all of this could be avoided if he could just tell himself *stop, go with Jaden* or even better, go back to the morning and *LISTEN to Jaden! Don't go near the boy – that's how this all begins!*

He needed help; he needed to clean his wounds and tear the bullet out of him.

He needed Jaden to *save* him.

Kuro's stomach turned over with cold despair as he realized that, for the first time in his life, he would have to save himself.

"*Change* into what you *really* are," she whispered. The gun still hung suspended in the air, her finger balanced and poised to pull.

His own hoarse whisper betrayed his fear. "What are you talking about?"

She held the gun steady, lifting it with both hands now as she pointed it at him.

He looked at her with wide, earnestly horrified eyes and did the only thing he could do, the one thing that *kitsune* were designed for by whatever dark maker had brought them into being.

Kuro reached out and touched her soul.

There was something inside him, in all demons, that *moved,* and *hungered,* and *reached.* He used it now, that dark current of power, and clawed deeply, rallying the last of his strength to feed this needful, demanding force inside him. It gnawed at their insides, insatiable in its desire to drink deeply from the hearts of men and feast on the minds of women. A soul was inexhaustible, renewable, like a river that continued to flow no matter how many deep draughts were pulled from it – but no matter how deeply a *kitsune* fed, the hunger remained. The meal was never satisfying, the feast never concluded.

It could drive a demon mad.

He thought of Jaden, suddenly. *Maybe it already had.*

But in return, it gave him *power.*

He closed his eyes, concentrating, trying to ignore the gun as he reached deeper into her soul...

And recoiled back, gasping.

Her soul was nearly on fire, burning with a rage almost too much for him to handle. Inside of her moved a deep conviction that he was something evil, something foul and *wrong* that had to be killed –

He tried again, carefully, and let a tiny bit of her fury into him; it numbed the pain and allowed him to sit up a little straighter, a little more human. Human joys were toxic, their hopes and dreams lethal – but their sadness and fears, their insecurities and jealousies were empowering, delicious, strengthening…

And there, underneath all of her hate and bile that he now grasped and clung to, lay a single kernel of doubt, a seed of terror and shock at what she was doing. He grasped at it like a dying man seeking salvation, clutching it and willing it to surface in her heart, to amplify and *grow*.

"Listen to me." He kept his voice as level as he could manage, his mind clearing just a little. "Just let me go." His gaze had lifted; he could feel the seed of doubt blossoming, gaining ground as fear watered it, the fear that she had just shot an innocent person for no reason, had kidnapped him against his will and held him hostage at gunpoint, that maybe she was insane after all.

"I promise I won't tell anybody about this. Please, I just need to go to a hospital," he begged. That was a lie; he would just limp his way back into the woods and dig the bullet out with his claws and wait for the flesh to heal – or lose the leg.

And then, when Jaden found out what had happened to him, Kuro would have some justice. Jaden's wrath would be immediate and swift; he would be sure to kill the girl long before they ever tracked down Kenneth McMahon and destroyed his goddamn camera.

She would end up just like the other one (*and all the rest*), only she would *deserve it* for what she'd done to him.

"No," she said. She shook her head, but the gun lowered a fraction. "I know what you are. You changed your form – *I know what you are*," she repeated, and her hate surged forward again and washed over the seedling of doubt in an effort to drown it out with sheer conviction. Hate was a difficult emotion – Kuro could feed from it, but barely: hate gnawed at a person's soul like a cancer, consuming it like its own personal demon that seethed deep in the mind and its memories. If he could reach further into the core of her being and find enough footing to make it stop, her doubt would surge back in...

And then he would have her. He could get out of this yet.

"Just listen to yourself," he tried, his voice firm, *reasonable*. "Please, I'm in *pain*. I'm bleeding." He wanted to scream at her, to gnash his teeth and give in to the cold fire that was burning him, but he held on, fighting against the tide.

He was working as hard as he could; the effort was draining him as he reached out invisibly to her soul and gently felt for its twisting patterns, the fine, sinewy weaving of the tapestry of her emotions. He held it, slowly tightening his grip so that she wouldn't notice the tugging, the pulling in her heart. He couldn't read thoughts or see memories; *kitsune* could only feel the byproducts of those creations and guess at the reasons behind them. There was something inside the girl, something old and leaden and heavy, that was making her hate him in a way that had ripened with age, had given her the strength to lift and fire a gun...

Close, he thought. *Just a little longer now...*

Her fury blurred his vision as he pushed himself to grasp the center of it; he didn't hear the way she gasped suddenly as he felt a pain pierce deeper than the bullet in his body.

There, surrounded by her rage, was a fierce epicenter of love from where all her hate leapt out at him.

It almost killed him.

Almost.

Kuro let go and doubled over, retching.

She stepped forward, the sound of crunching hay shattering the sudden quiet that followed his heaving. She came up to him and stopped, the gun barrel hovering above his forehead, and each word she spoke was clipped with decided finality.

"Change back now, or I'll kill you."

Survival took over; Kuro reached out for a second and felt her real terror surging with her hate; her soul told him she was mortally afraid of killing another human being, but a deep-seated self-righteousness kept her grounded in her resolve. Her soul was too turbulent; Kuro couldn't tell if she was capable of really killing him or not.

His chances didn't seem good.

"Change *now*," she whispered. Her pinky trembled in the air as she took a deep breath. "I'm going to count to three."

He didn't move.

"One."

I'm going to die here. She's really going to do it.

"Two."

Why didn't I go with Jaden? Jaden help me she's going to kill me –

"*Three.*"

"*I can't!*"

The words came out before he could stop them. He squeezed his eyes shut, shaking now. Death wasn't so friendly when it stared at him through the barrel of a gun; he watched again in his memory as the pupils of a girl's eyes released into pools of death while Jaden stared, unmoved – death was more real and hateful when it came for him instead. *It's wrong it's wrong I know it's wrong I don't want to die!*

She stepped back and lowered the weapon so that it was aimed at his chest. "You can't, or you won't?"

"I can't," he rasped. "Not with my arms like this."

A heavy feeling settled on top of Kuro's shoulders, crushing him, worse than the pain in his leg or the wounds from the dog.

So that was it. Despair had won. His own tongue was his greatest betrayer.

Her soul, moved by conviction and a sudden, shocking joy, tore itself away from his defeated grasp and fled back into the secret corners of her heart.

She lowered the gun completely and set it down on the banister, next to an old saddle. "So now you're being honest with me," she said. An uncontrollable smile illuminated her face and made her beautiful, *terrible*.

"You're out of your mind," he moaned.

"No." Kuro watched in horror as she shook her head, her satisfaction apparent. "*You're* a demon."

"You're *insane.*"

"You can deny it all you want, but I saw what you are. I knew you were out there. My brother was right. You're a *demon,*" she repeated, convincing herself, "and you're going to die."

Kuro was sure he was going to pass out from the pain in his leg long before he got around to dying. He was bleeding everywhere from the dog's bites, but the gunshot hurt the most, a fiery, throbbing pocket of ache. Soon his vision would gray over; then, he would welcome unconsciousness and the death it would bring.

She leaned against the banister and crossed her arms over her chest, admiring him.

Once, he and Jaden had gone to a zoo. It had been an unsettling experience that had solidified their sense of isolation, of not belonging to either the world of animal or man. There had been a tiger pacing by a large pool, the orange of its fur so bright that it seemed to leap like fire streaked with charcoal. Eight steps to the right, turn, nine steps back, swinging its great head around and around as it moved, trapped in its circuit, confined to its pitiful enclosure. A group of onlookers had gathered. Kuro remembered the look on their faces: awe, wonder, and when the tiger finally turned with gathering, whirling force to roar at them, *fear.*

She was looking at him that way now, in that same state of amazement, but curiosity had supplanted all fear. Here was no tiger: here was only a prisoner. She cocked her head to the side and mused at him. His skin crawled.

"Tell me your name," she said.

"Kuro," he whispered. A hot shame spread across his face.

"Is that your *real* name?"

"Yes," he lied.

She was stupid and naïve if she thought he would tell her the truth. That he wouldn't do – she could cut off his limbs inch by inch and feed them to her dog, but he would never tell this sadistic and crazed human his true name.

It was something only Jaden knew.

"Okay," she smiled. Her cheeks puffed up and crinkled the edges of her eyes. It might have been endearing in another light.

If I break my thumbs, I can get my wrists through these things, he thought. But no: they were too tight, cutting off the circulation; the pain from breaking his thumbs couldn't add much more to his suffering, but it wouldn't be worth it if he couldn't even get his hands through the cuffs. He had a bad feeling that even if he *did,* it would simply rip the skin off the flesh of his hand, like pulling a glove off backwards. He didn't have the stomach to do it, let alone the resolve.

So I'll break both my arms by switching back and just leap at her throat, he pivoted. He would have to do it fast, then – the gun was close enough for her to grab, so if he missed or was too slow, he would die. How good could he jump on one back leg?

"Why are you here?" She asked. Her smile had fallen away, replaced by thoughtful concentration.

"I saw you," he answered. "I was walking through the forest, and I saw your barn. It looked old....abandoned, maybe. I was looking for a place to spend the night."

She shook her head, displeased.

"No, no, I mean – why are you *here?*"

He struggled to understand, his eyes darting to the gun. "I just told you. I saw you –"

"Why are you on *earth?*" She demanded.

"What are you *talking about?*" He groaned, a wave of nausea passing over him. Unconsciousness refused his call, and shock was failing him: his adrenaline had run out with his defeat, and pain had tightened his throat, constricting his voice with hoarse suffering. "Please, just *shoot* me!"

"Not until you answer my question."

He had no idea what answer would satisfy her. "I came from the

Blue Ridge Parkway to visit Asheville and then – and then you s-shot me." He bit back the bile building in his throat. An unsettling chill was beginning at the base of his spine, prickling through his veins like the budding ice of an early frost, sending involuntary shivers through his limbs.

"And where were you before that?"

Did she want him to draw a map? They had visited a few places in the last year. He rattled off the names of some cities and towns in confused succession, then finished by repeating, "the forest. I was in the forest." Something was happening to his thoughts; things were growing slippery around the edges.

"So you've been on earth for a while, then."

"I was *born* on earth, just like any other person!"

"But you're not a person," she pointed out. "You're a demon."

Kuro ground his teeth, twisting his hands against the cuffs.

"Are there more of you?"

"*Yes.*"

"How many?"

"I don't know."

"How can you not know?"

"There *must* be others like me – I was *born!*"

"Why did you kill that girl?"

"*What?*"

"You heard me." Her demand was cold and pointed.

Kuro shook his head; a sudden burst of dizziness sent the room spinning. The girl (*red pink and white, all the colors inside us, brown freckles across her nose...a small blue disc, fallen onto her cheek...*); someone must have discovered the body. Yes, of course; she'd been dead for...how long was it, now? Nearly an entire day. He waited for the spinning to stop before answering. "I didn't. That was –"

He slammed his jaw closed; the force stunned him. She frowned. "That was who?"

"I don't know," he lied. "I don't even know what girl you're talking about." That much was true – he couldn't remember the girl's name

(*Brittany, she said her name was Brittany*)

and maybe she was referring to some other girl who had met, much to her misfortune, a bear. A very hungry bear. One that probably looked a lot like Jaden.

She tried to read him through his pained expression.

"So you didn't murder her?"

"No," he answered, then shook his head. It was getting harder to string thoughts together now, let alone sentences. The pain; the sound; the smell; all of it was beginning to feel distant. "I mean, no, I didn't kill her, so yes."

She peered at him, suspicious.

"I'm not good with words," he tried, but stopped, sucking in his breath. Everything was becoming too hard now. His speech was as slurred as his thoughts. He bit down on his tongue to keep from moaning.

Her frown deepened. "Are you in pain?"

"You're...a lunatic..." He gasped. "If I *shot* you, would you *hurt?*"

She didn't reply. Silence followed until Kuro threw his head back in despair. "What do you want from me?" He groaned. "Are you going to kill me? Torture me?"

Her brow furrowed. "I hadn't really thought of that," she admitted. "I don't know what to do now. Maybe I should call –"

"If you take me to anyone, no one will believe you," he warned, snarling. Anger was like an anchor, the only thing left tethering him to coherence. His words were dark and spiteful as he spoke, his teeth flashing. "They'll lock you away in an asylum somewhere – you'll be all over the news, on television and in the papers –"

"Like you?"

Everything in Kuro's world narrowed down to those two words, halting his very breathing.

"*The Asheville Citizen-Times*. It's not in the paper yet – not for a few more hours, but the photo is already up on the Web site. I went to check for updates on the murder, after they announced that they found her body this morning...and I saw the photo of you. All my life my brother told me about demons...all my life I've prayed for proof. And here you are."

To his surprise, a sudden calm descended over him. The reality of his situation settled upon him with such a total sense of complete end that he gave up struggling against the pain, and with it, all fury at the girl. A curious emptiness replaced it as the knowledge of his disastrous mistake dawned on him. There was no need to struggle against anything now.

If she doesn't kill me, Jaden surely will, he thought, with total acceptance.

"You've gone very white, Kuro," the girl said. "Are you okay?"

He cringed at the sound of his name.

"So you caught me. Go ahead – kill me." All of his energy to fight was gone.

"No," she said. "That would be a waste. I want you to tell me everything about yourself – I want to know everything about you and your kind. Then, after I have all the answers I want, and *only* then, I might kill you."

Her face paled in the wan light as Kuro let out a harsh bark of laughter, wincing with each muscle contraction.

Nothing mattered anymore, not even his life – *especially* not his life. His *picture* was in the paper. They hadn't stopped Kenneth in time. That girl (*Brittany*) might never have died. *He* might never have needed to die. He was almost delirious now. "You think I'll tell you anything? Cut off my legs, my ears, stab out my eyes – from this moment on, I won't say a single word to you." He resigned himself to wait patiently to pass out from blood loss and then, with any luck, the indifferent embrace of death would follow.

At the rate at which the world was darkening around the edges, it wouldn't be long now.

She shrugged and moved away from him, walking toward the

front of the barn. He heard rummaging, some sort of metallic sound, and then she was approaching him, a tool gripped in one hand...

She held up an old, rusted saw and pointed at it, her expression a mixture of exasperation and resolution.

"You won't do it," he spat.

"You just spoke to me," she countered.

"I won't again."

"You just did."

Kuro's mouth pressed itself into a tight line as she stepped forward; before he could gather the strength to reach for her soul and see if she was serious, she stopped just above him.

"Which leg do you want to lose first?" She asked. "The right, or the left?"

"You shot me in the right," he snarled. "Try the left."

"See? Speaking isn't so hard."

He gnashed his teeth together and bit his bottom lip hard enough to draw blood.

She shrugged.

"Suit yourself."

The hay rustled as she lowered herself to one knee near his ankles.

He shut his eyes and prepared for the fiery agony to come. Would it feel worse than a gunshot? It would be slower, the sawing... Two hands lifted away the leg of his pants from his foot. *She's going to cut off my leg piece by piece,* he thought, swallowing hard. If only he had the strength to *move,* let alone fight. The flesh would be easy, but painful; would he pass out by the time she got down to his bone? *I've got – I've got to be brave – I've got to make it through this –*

He flinched as her fingers, cool and firm, pressed into his skin near a deep puncture at his ankle, a bright, fresh pain jolting through him.

"Feral really went after you," she said.

Kuro opened his eyes slowly, one after the other; the saw was lying next to her, discarded. She knelt and applied pressure to the lesion, looking up at him.

"Feral – that's my dog," she explained. "I've never seen him act that way – we named him 'Feral' as a joke, because he was so calm. He was supposed to be assigned to a K-9 unit, but he would just sit down in the middle of training, no spirit or fight in him at all. I ended up adopting him. Did he act that way because you're a demon?"

Kuro had nothing to say. *K-9 unit...a gun, handcuffs...police?* He just stared at her with wide, disbelieving eyes and gave a half-hearted nod. She looked down again, her eyes scanning the blood-stained hay.

"I thought so." She took in his pale expression and laughed; the sound was like bubbles in spring water.

"You didn't really think I was going to cut off your leg, did you? Frankly, I don't have it in me to do something like that. Shooting you is one thing, but sawing off a leg is..." She trailed off, cringing.

Because it's wrong. Why...why would it be wrong, though...?

"That's wonderful," he said, and his voice sounded so strange, as though spoken by someone else, far across the barn. "But I need you to remove these handcuffs now."

She shook her head. "I'm not going to do that."

The world around him was dimming at a rapid pace; even the sounds of the horse shuffling in agitation were slowly dampening, as though he was sinking deep into water, the night growing unnaturally quiet. The names *Jaden* and *Kenneth McMahon* and *Brittany* became whispers in the dark attic of his mind, words that were suddenly trapped in the corners he had never bothered to explore – and those corners were receding out of his grasp, elongating backwards into a place he couldn't reach, his consciousness sliding down into the blackness.

"No," he said slowly, focusing on every word in an effort to stay awake. "I'm about to pass out."

She looked surprised. "Why?" Her eyes grew large as she gasped. "Oh God, did I hit your femoral artery? I couldn't have, you'd be dead by now from blood loss –"

"I have no idea," he whispered, faint now. Even as his vision darkened, the lights – too poor to see by – suddenly seemed much too bright. There were halos around them, shining and iridescent, like floating oil slicks. His words were slow and fumbling. "When I fall asleep, I change back –" Her expression lit up "–And my arms will break if you don't take off the handcuffs. Backwards..." He mumbled incoherently. "The sockets...the joints..."

Her eyes narrowed, but her voice couldn't hide the trembling of her excitement. "How can I know this isn't a trick?"

Kuro slumped against the wall and fell over into the soft, welcoming hay.

He hoped that everything would be a dream when he woke up.

But just before darkness claimed him, that same voice from earlier whispered from somewhere in the back of his mind.

This is very real, Kuro, it said. *And demons don't dream.*

Two

The morning arrived with the rumble of a mail truck on the gravel road, the sound of its bumpy jostle waking him just as it came to a stop, the engine purring. Kuro stirred uneasily; images, places, and names floated in and out of his mind on moth wings, wraiths of consciousness that came and went.

He opened his eyes, squinting at the bright rays that filtered down from the slats in the barn. Dust motes hovered, suspended in the beams.

His whole body ached.

He groaned and examined his surroundings. Dried blood was crusted on his clothes and skin, dark in the hay that cushioned his body. Every part of him hurt.

Where am I?

A horse neighed. The sound made him wince. He tried to sit up, but a hot stab of pain in his leg cast him down again with a wave of nausea. He slumped back to his side, groaning.

Last night came back to him with a jolt of regret.

He reached down and tenderly felt for the bullet wound in his leg; it was there, buried under a mound of dried blood on top of his right thigh.

My arms, he thought suddenly, *she took off the handcuffs.*

But then why had he woken up as a human? In all his life, he was always a *kitsune* in his sleep; even Jaden had only recently begun to sleep in his human form. Jaden had guessed it had something to do with their 'unconscious,' a concept he had once tried to explain, but like so many things, Kuro hadn't been able to grasp the idea of it. It was something he'd read about in a book in some library he'd dragged Kuro to; he read with a hunger that mirrored their inner appetite, always seeking to devour more in his search to know, to understand... to conquer: the world, *himself,* Kuro didn't know.

Not that he had ever tried to understand.

And Jaden – where was he now?

He'll find me, Kuro thought, desperate. *He'll save me.*

"Come with me, Kuro," Jaden had said to him last night, an hour before a girl on a roof would put a bullet in his leg. It wasn't an order, exactly; he never ordered him to do anything, but when he spoke, quiet and calm, implications and insistences lurked behind his words, hiding underneath his congeniality. Jaden had looked at him with his level stare, the one that masked whatever his real thoughts were, and added in a noncommittal afterthought, "It'll be...enjoyable."

Why? Kuro thought now, desperate. He'd never felt this kind of pain, this kind of *terror* before in his life. *Why didn't I go with him? Why, for once in my life, couldn't I have just listened?*

Only an hour before he would be attacked, they had been standing in the forest surrounding Asheville; only an hour before (*a lifetime before),* he had been caught in a moment of indecision, resistance, even. He always did what Jaden wanted, eventually – they weren't brothers (deeper, darker ties had drawn them together since their birth), but he hadn't wanted to give in, to walk next to that man with brown flakes of blood still crusted in the bed of his fingernails...

They rarely separated, seldom moved without the other at his side; maybe, Kuro thought, it was because of that insistent, unyielding way Jaden spoke, his voice just above a low whisper, his maroon eyes unblinking, demanding obedience...

Jaden's eyes reminded him of the metallic, steaming heat of spilled blood, the putrescence of severed intestines, the gasp of a girl caught unawares.

Kuro shuddered.

"I don't want to go," he had mumbled.

Jaden's level stare had broken with a slow, deliberate blink; his voice was quiet – *pushing*. "Are you sure?"

His knees had almost buckled then; his nerves strained forward, his mouth opened to say no, he changed his mind, of course he would come – but his heels dug in. Kuro had slowly uncurled his fists at his side and met Jaden's gaze headlong, steady and decided.

"I'm sure."

Jaden shifted his weight to his left foot. For a moment, his eyes flicked up toward the moon, then back out to the soft darkness of the forest before them. "We came here for a purpose," he said, shifting tactics. A pointed accusation laced his words.

Kuro stiffened. "I know that." He ran a hand through his dark hair, and his black eyes had scanned the trees then, seeking whatever it was that Jaden saw out there. They had come to Asheville for a reason –

To find Kenneth McMahon, Kuro thought darkly. *Find Kenneth,* and then, *find Kenneth's camera.*

"It was your fault, Kuro."

It would have hurt only a fraction worse if Jaden had struck him, slashed silvery claws across his chest (*like the girl*). Jaden had never raised a hand against him, but Kuro winced all the same, cringing in shame.

"I didn't kill her."

"'*Her*?'" That slow, measured blink again, like an eagle, scanning him now. There had been a hardness in the way he said the word, an edge of suspicious probing. "*Obviously* you didn't kill her. I wasn't referring to *her*. I meant *the picture*."

Of course; the picture. Yes. It was his fault that they had had to leave the mountains of the Blue Ridge Parkway and come to Asheville. There had been a boy (*Kenneth!* His name had become a curse in Kuro's thoughts), an entirely unremarkable boy at that...

But the boy had a camera.

And the camera had 'clicked.'

And it had taken a photo of a shape, large and black, inhuman...*him*.

And using the papers that had tumbled from his backpack as he fled toward his car, they had surmised where to go, hitched a ride with a friendly young woman splashed with freckles, a girl who had smiled right up until the moment Jaden reached forward from the backseat...

"I just don't want to go."

Kuro knew he sounded like a sullen child; he flushed with embarrassment. Jaden smiled, but it was lop-sided, and it never quite reached his eyes. "I know you feel badly about it. The *picture*. It's okay. We'll find him – tomorrow, in the *daylight*. We won't get anywhere right now, so we should reward ourselves for getting this far, take a moment to enjoy the evening...now that we've come all this way."

He would much rather have tracked Kenneth down *now*; the night had just begun. They had plenty of time, and if they acted fast, they could head back to the Parkway come morning. The delay frustrated him; Kuro dug his fists into his pockets in a senseless effort to hide his tension. He had closed his eyes, breathed in the night air, the smell of wet pine, the spice of the sap of summer. He'd been gulping down air for a while now, trying to drive those other, lingering scents from his memory. He tilted his head back into the secret shadows of the early fog of night, and for the third time, refused his friend.

He was met by no outburst, no anger even. Jaden merely slumped; he was as tall as Kuro, with a lean, athletic build, well-toned for a young man in his early twenties, the age he was most comfortable in appearance. He could push himself up to twenty-five with ease, if he wanted; his jaw became stronger as he adjusted the years, his shoulders grew broader and imposing, like a lean boxer coming into full form, but some things never changed: his hair and his eyes, for instance.

They remained the color of deep, venous blood.

"Well. Do what you want," he said, and suddenly the young man was gone, replaced by a maroon fox as large as a lion. Its slender legs stretched, the silver claws retracting as it yawned wide, the fangs glinting under the thin moon.

You'll regret not coming along, he said.

You always have to have the last word, Kuro thought, but he replied, "I only have one regret. I shouldn't have snuck down the slope. I should have left the boy alone. Are you happy now?"

Jaden had let out a bark of wry laughter then, the shrill, chilling gekker of a fox. *You're upset that we had to leave those empty, insipid mountains to come to an actual city, a real place with living, breathing people. Oh, Kuro – get over it. We might as well have some fun while we're here. We'll find the boy in the morning – we'll get the photo he took of you. Until then, however it is you plan to spend the evening...try to enjoy yourself. Meet me here in the morning.*

Jaden had turned around and dashed away into the trees, the sound of his footfalls absorbed by the soft dirt of the forest floor.

And then he was gone.

Enjoy yourself. The words had echoed in Kuro's mind. He couldn't; he hated the city, and more and more Jaden had been dragging him out of their mountains and throwing them into the path of people. He only wanted the quiet now.

Kuro had turned around and leaned despondently against a tree.

Lately he hadn't felt like doing anything...or doing any of the things that Jaden wanted to do. Kuro's idea of enjoyment was leaping on top of unsuspecting titmice and batting them between his paws. He liked running through the trees, pressing his nose deep into the underbrush, standing high on his back legs and peeking into the cubbyholes of squirrels and raccoons. He liked to watch the foxes and see some ancestral trace of himself in them; they were miniatures, but many-hued – orange, black, white, gray, unlike the flat, unvarying single color of the *kitsune*. He liked best of all to stand in the direct gust of a strong blast of wind, his whiskers pressing back against his fur, and lift his nose high, breathing deeply, holding still.

Jaden enjoyed coffee shops, the pleasant hum of people, the swirl of a design on the foam of a latte, the clink of a spoon against a mug...and Kuro, too, could have learned to like those pleasant things, if not for what came after.

It hadn't bothered him at first; he felt, in a confused sort of way, that it was probably wrong to kill a human...but he wasn't sure. He'd killed lots of things, after all; hadn't he eaten a rabbit just the other day? Once, the two of them had even had a nasty scrap with a wild hog that had nearly gored them both (to say nothing of the deranged badger whose den they'd stolen three winters ago) but in the end, they had feasted on its flesh. Things died every day.

...Didn't people count as things?

Maybe. Maybe not. Jaden was far more clever than he'd ever be; maybe Jaden knew the answer. It was wrong for a person to kill another person, because people had laws that said so. They had discovered this early on in their forays into human affairs: humans had *many* laws, many of them perplexing, and you needed to know the important ones in order to not attract any unwanted attention, to fit in and hide amongst them.

But it wasn't against the law, say, if a *wolf* killed a person, and although he wasn't a wolf...he also wasn't a human.

So maybe it's not wrong.

But it hadn't felt *right*, what Jaden had done to that girl, the one who had picked up a pair of hitchhikers, one with black hair, the other with maroon, and driven them out of the mountains. No; it had felt *abhorrent*; Kuro fought the urge to heave every time he pictured her. She was frozen in time now, her strawberry blonde hair hanging limply over vacant eyes.

Blood had foamed at the edge of her lips. Her eyes had rolled backward in empty surprise, her entrails spilling out in front of her, steaming, the membranes glistening as her life poured out, red and thick, in the quiet insistence of death.

The smell had nearly suffocated him.

A quiet choking sound now escaped him.

Kuro didn't often wander into the back of his mind; there were a lot of cobwebs back there, dusty, dark spots that needed sweeping out, clearing. He wasn't a thinker – that was Jaden. *His* mind was like a brilliant library, illuminated well and updated often. Kuro agreed it was best to let him do the thinking for them both, because underneath Kuro's black eyes, buried above his scowl, was an attic.

An old, unused attic.

And Jaden...where was he, right now? Was he with someone, amusing himself? When would he get *bored* of people?

You know what he does when he gets bored of people.

He'll come save me, Kuro thought, but his mind was fogged and heavy.

The sounds of the morning kept him from sinking back into sleep. He could hear the mailman opening the mailbox down at the end of the gravel driveway now, the creak of its tin door cutting through the clear day. Kuro instinctually reached out to him, trying to find his soul and feed, to pull from it and find new strength –

But there was nothing.

He tried again, searching, reaching out with the unseen hand of the power within him, the *holy dark* they called it, to touch the edges of the man's soul, but the distance between them was simply too great.

A pang of panic returned, and with it, a trembling at his finger-tips. He cleared his mind and tried again.

Nothing.

The mailman was getting back into the truck now, the door hinge opening with a loud screech before slamming shut. Panic won. Kuro jolted upward and promptly sank back down in pain; there was no fighting the bullet in his body, no swimming against the weakness from blood loss that took over his vision, the colors blurring and running together.

Panic gave birth to fear, and the two began to compete, his pulse racing now. He frantically tried to switch back to his *kitsune* form and dash outside, run for the trees and safety and Jaden –

But the change wouldn't happen, and the pain in his leg chained him in agony to the ground.

Fear bludgeoned his mind with cold senselessness; he tried over and over again, imagining the way it felt to be in his real skin, to walk on paws and snarl with fangs, to balance with a tail and see with nocturnal eyes, but the form never came.

Instead, he merely sat, dazed, helpless...and human.

"Jaden," he croaked. This had never happened to either of them before; he felt cut off from the very thing he was, suddenly uncomfortable in a body he didn't want to be in and couldn't escape from. *Is this how humans feel every day?*

Shock took over. Kuro lay on the ground, unable to control his breathing or his thoughts. His hand began to itch at the wound on his thigh; his mind wandered off away from himself as he choked on his own fear, desperate to return to the forest and feel the glint of sunlight on his fur. Without realizing what he was doing, his nails began to dig first past crusted blood, then into his flesh.

He was trapped. It was the one thought that kept coming back to him as a sharp pain began again in his leg, fiery and spreading, his nails digging inward, his actions distant to his reeling, numbed mind. *Trapped in this place, trapped in this body...*

He felt the warm flow of fresh blood again and a stinging pain work its way up to his chest, but he ignored it, far past caring in his disembodied state of panic.

His mind reeled in confusion. *Why did she shoot me?* He hadn't been doing anything, hadn't been hurting anyone... *She called me a demon.* He was; they had discovered it for themselves when they'd come crouching out of the woods more than a decade ago, seeking answers. *The library – Jaden read it in the library...* A memory came back to him, a memory of Jaden's eyes, searching for something, anything, that would tell them who or what they were, as pages tore under his hands. He'd been turning the pages too fast, his arms shaking, and his eyes had been shining –

Why did she do it? He could smell his own blood now. Sharp explosions of pain were sparkling in his vision like white fireworks, then disappearing into gray haze as his human nails clawed their way down through soft fat and torn muscle and nerves in a bloody mess, digging toward the bullet.

Why did he *do it? Why had Jaden killed that girl...Brittany, she said her name was Brittany...*

His thoughts staggered onward, lost in the maze of the past in order to avoid the horror of the present. He squeezed his eyes shut; the sunlight seeping through the cracks in the barn had grown painfully bright.

Is there any answer to that question that would justify 'why'? Is there any answer that would make it acceptable, or right?

No no there isn't it wasn't right she shot me –

She shot you because you don't matter to her, just like that girl didn't matter to him. She died, and you're asking why, as if THAT matters –

I don't want to die, he thought, gasping now. *I don't want to die here!*

He was shaking, trembling, trying repeatedly to change his form, but he couldn't – no matter how much effort he put in, no matter how much he was bleeding, he remained a fragile human, lost down a tunnel of jumbled thoughts. Pain, fresh and heavy, had put a stranglehold upon him, narrowing his existence down to a fiery point of pure torment.

Through a mist of thoughts he heard the barn door open; light came flooding in now, stabbing at the edges of his vision. He closed his eyes tighter against it, terrified.

"Kuro!" A voice called. "Are you awake?"

And then suddenly she was kneeling next to him, yelling at him, pulling his hand away from the mutilation of his leg, slicking her hands in his blood. He collapsed back down in the hay and cried out, wrenching away from her until he had pushed himself against the wall of the barn, as far from her as he could get.

With a wordless choking sound, she ran out of the stall, leaving him to his misery. At last, he opened his eyes and stared up at the ceiling, where a small loft was filled with hay, and searched for the strength to run. The barn door was open – if he could just move, crawl even, he could escape...

The memory of the gunshot echoed in his head just as the scent of the dog was carried on the air through the open barn door. Even if he could somehow haul himself outside, he could neither outrun the beast nor a bullet. Kuro huddled further against himself, despairing.

The young woman was back suddenly in a bustle of noise. Kuro looked at her, white with terror, and found himself unable to breathe again.

She came forward and knelt in the hay, a bag clutched in her hands. "Why would you do that to yourself?"

It took him a moment to understand. He looked down briefly at his leg, then at his hands; blood was caked deeply under the nails from where he had dug into his own flesh, clawing for the bullet. Distantly, he realized how his hands now looked like Jaden's.

It was a disturbing thought.

She began to rummage through the bag, pulling out a first aid kit and a black bottle. "I could have taken you to a hospital." She sounded...frightened? Horrified? Kuro didn't understand her tone, her look, the note of alarm in her words. "Your leg...you're going to have nerve damage. That looks painful...*awful*."

His thoughts sharpened, pulling back from clouded confusion just enough for him to focus. Kuro looked her full in the face now. Her eyes were wide, her bottom lip trembling. Her knuckles were white from the force of gripping her bag. She took a deep breath and opened the first aid kit, a shaking tremor traveling all the way up her forearms.

"Let me help you."

"*Get away from me!*" Kuro pressed himself tighter against the wood. She had reached forward to touch him, but she withdrew her hand quickly, as though he had burned her with his words.

"You look like you're in pain. Please let me –"

Kuro moved to lunge at her, but the pressure he placed on his leg sent an iron spike of agony through his skull; he cried out, crumpling. Gasping, he drew his leg up toward his chest; the colors in the barn began to spin horribly again, whirling in the morning light.

"If you'll just let me, I can help!" He wasn't imagining it; there was genuine panic in her voice. From somewhere within the spinning world, a hand reached out and touched him, cool and slightly clammy.

Kuro instinctively jerked away. He shut his eyes against her, waiting for the world to stop its spin. The nausea lessened, but not the pain.

The smell of blood filled the silence between them. She sat back, staring at him, unspeaking. The minutes passed until at last he risked slowly opening his eyes, focusing on keeping his stomach from heaving.

She remained across from him, one hand uselessly on a small white box. Her eyes hadn't lost that wide, staring quality, but streaks of wet tears had leaked out from each corner and carved two dirty streams down her face. There was no sobbing, no gasping...just the long, unblinking gaze of regret.

"I'm so sorry." She spoke in a horrified whisper. "I don't know what to do. I didn't think..." She swallowed, her voice insistent. "I'm so sorry..."

"Why?" He bit down hard on the word, wincing under the effort of speaking. The hot ache in his leg had spread to everything now. "*Why* did you *shoot* me?"

Things were different now in the daylight. The radiant confidence that the night and shadows had given her had fled by the light of the morning sun, and now, as she looked on at the young man in front of her, bleeding and gasping, her mouth opened ineffectually, then closed again.

"*Why?*" He repeated, desperate. He needed an answer, needed to just *understand* why Jaden did it, why he was able to reach forward and rip that girl's life away –

"Because of what you are. I shot you because...because I saw you..."

Kuro lay before her, the side of his face pressed down in the hay and the dirt, looking up at her through his bangs. He curled inward now, closing his eyes as he gave himself up to his own personal hell. Maybe he deserved this; he had turned away from all the suffering Jaden had caused, all the death Kuro didn't want to acknowledge... and now it was his turn to feel his life slip out of him. "I don't want to die here," he whispered. His dignity crumbled away under the weight of cowardice.

He didn't know how many minutes passed until he flinched under the cool, hesitant touch of her fingers once more. This time he didn't lunge or even fight; he breathed out a long, pained groan, and waited, his eyes shut. He didn't think he could stand to look at her face again.

"Oh my God...I can see the bullet..."

Her hands pushed him onto his back, but he could feel her arms trembling. She began to talk to him, low and quiet, as she explained that she was going to try and extract the bullet, because *oh my God, I can see it...how could you do this to yourself...*came her faraway voice. He thought he heard the words *just hold as still as* *possible* in a tone that aimed at confidence and fell short into anxious fear.

He opened his eyes then, both hands clenched at his side. She leaned over him, staring down at the wound he had torn into his flesh, and suddenly, they were both aware of how close they were to one another. Kuro needed only to unclench his fists, reach up, and both hands could close around her throat.

She looked up, their gazes locking, and Kuro realized she had just arrived at the same realization. She froze, staring...waiting. Kuro knew the look well; it was the look of an animal, perfectly still in the approach of headlights, a mouse paralyzed by the cry of a hawk. She held herself motionless that way now, caught in the moment of death, unable to flee.

He could feel her fear.

The realization struck him; her soul was suddenly all around him, a raft thrown to a drowning man.

He didn't stop to question why he felt her soul *around him* instead of *inside her*, didn't even stop to think – he reached for it and *gripped* it like a man clinging to a cliff's edge, dangling above his certain death. Something flashed in her eyes, some new terror, and he allowed himself to breathe out, relaxing as he held himself perfectly still, anchored by the sense of her fear.

His voice was hoarse, but stronger as he allowed her fear to flow into him. He closed his eyes again, his fists tight against his body. "Please," he begged into the quiet, "take it out."

The moment broke. She leaned over, one hand resting her weight flat on his leg, and a sharp, burning pain invaded him. He arched unwillingly into it and clenched his jaw, clutching her soul so tightly that she shivered above him, twisting the metal inside of him with something cold, gripping.

"I almost have it – just hold on..."

He gasped as it came loose, fresh, warm blood flowing out of him, hot and cold all at once. A strange, tingling numbness crept out from the wound in a spiderweb of sensation. His blood flowed fast and thick now, pooling on the ground beside him.

"I've got to stop the bleeding," she said, but her voice sounded distant. "But – your pants, and – oh my God, your *blood*..."

Kuro opened his eyes, watching as his own life poured out of him, darker than the deepest red wine...and every piece of hay it touched, once golden and fresh, turned brittle and dead.

"Is it...is it supposed to do that?"

Kuro closed his eyes and let out a long sigh. A chill was creeping up toward his chest now. Dimly, he thought he should stop the bleeding, but the cold was growing almost comforting, like a soft blanket or a bed of moss...

"Don't pass out! Stay with me!" She dropped the tweezers, and with it, the bullet. Her hands were on him again, pressing something under his leg and pulling him up. She packed gauze deep into the wound, and then there was the feeling of pressure, tighter and tighter, growing as she continued to shove her hand under his thigh, then back up. He watched as she tied a bandage around his leg, over the torn pants, in her effort to stop the bleeding.

"You're lucky," she was saying, and then, shaking her head, "I mean, *I'm* lucky. I'm lucky I didn't kill you. If it had gone deeper, it could have shattered your femur, or struck your femoral artery. I'm really worried it might become infected, and it's bleeding a lot, but it's not *hemorrhaging*, and I...I think this will stop the blood flow, I really do –"

Her nervous words rattled on.

Kuro laughed, bitter and coughing.

She stopped her movements, staring at him. He used the last of his strength to lift a hand toward his face, pushing his bangs away; she recoiled protectively despite herself, startled. Red, lacerated flaps of skin hung from his torn knuckles, the result of the dog's attack.

"You're 'lucky you didn't kill me,'" he mocked, sneering. He felt no gratitude towards his captor, only cold hatred. "I remember what you said last night. You plan to keep me here. You said you were going to keep me alive until I told you everything...everything you wanted to hear. You're so *lucky*," he growled, his hand falling away. He chose his next words with spite. "You're *fucking crazy*."

She wore that same startled, wide-eyed expression from earlier, but a new, hot anger flared in her soul. "I was in shock when I said that was my plan. I didn't really understand what I'd done. I just knew – I just knew what I was looking at, I knew I had to do something, and I..." She stopped herself suddenly, forcing herself to regain her composure. "But I don't know what I'm going to do now, because I meant what I said: I'm lucky I didn't kill you. I couldn't have lived with myself if I had."

He laughed again at the absurdity of it. "Is that why you're helping me – so you can feel better about what you did?"

She drew herself up straighter, forcing a note of self-assurance he didn't believe she really had. "Yes."

"It won't help you."

"It might not," she agreed. She reached for the first aid kit and the black bottle, drawing out a bag of cotton balls. "But it might help *you*."

He lay still for the next few minutes, neither speaking as she dabbed the wounds on his hands with a liquid that stung and frothed into angry white bubbles. A pile of cotton-balls that looked as though they'd been used to soak up liquid rust grew in the corner next to her as she worked. Occasionally he stole a glance at her, noticing new details: she had loose, wavy hair that tumbled in tangling curls down her back, the soft brown of doe velvet, matching her eyes. She was tall and strongly built, and she wore the same jean overalls she had had on the previous night. Swaths of dirt were ground permanently into the denim at the knees, and they smelled of sweat and labor.

He could almost hear Jaden scoffing in his mind: she was unremarkable, a 'farm-girl.'

Her soul was far more interesting, though: it was in a state of uproar.

Emotions buffeted him, wild and intense. Self-righteousness and assurance fought against revulsion toward his injury...and revulsion was winning now that daylight illuminated the consequence of her actions and made her confront the suffering she had caused. Every time her eyes slid to the blood on the ground, it twisted within her, and from its fertile soil sprang up shame, doubt, confusion, and fear...and every time she looked down at him, pity.

The pity he could do without. The higher the count of cotton balls, the more it grew. It was like tasting the burnt bottom in a pot of stew, ruining the delicate flavors of her turmoil. He winced.

"Please stop feeling that," he groaned. "It's making me sick."

She stopped, puzzled. "What did you say?"

"I said, I feel sick."

"Oh." She continued gently, working until she had run out of supplies. She sat back then, resting against the side of the stable wall. Kuro remained lying down, but his gaze slid sideways, watching her warily. They sized each other up, each remaining unnaturally still, waiting for the other to say or do something.

"Your blood." She broke the silence first, and even her whisper sounded like shouting. "The color...is it like that because you're...a demon?"

There it is. There's the word. Her soul was heaving with the effort of fighting against doubt, but doubt had a way of spreading and infecting everything. He could see it in her eyes.

Kuro stared at her, silent. She bit her bottom lip when he didn't reply.

"You lied to me," she pressed on. "About your hands – nothing happened when you passed out. Or maybe it did, later, but I stayed for a little bit, looking at you...and then, I left. I was frightened." Kuro noted that she babbled when she grew nervous. "I had a real good look at you, then, and I thought...what if I was wrong? And then you didn't change. Nothing happened. You just lay there, yourself."

"Myself?"

"Like you are now."

"This isn't the real me."

He didn't know why he said it; he could have let her doubt grow and fester, but the words escaped before he could stop himself.

They stared at one another hard now, the truth laid bare before them. The blood, the admission. He glared at her, watching thoughts play across her face, feeling them crawl and shiver in her soul. Doubt had snaked around her, unhinged its jaw, and reared back, ready to consume her, but courage – just enough to keep the beast at bay – was still there, armed with confidence and...something else, something shining, something poisonous that was fighting back against all the rest.

Faith.

"What are you?"

Her words came in a breathless, rushed demand. Kuro stared at her, taking the full measure of her now. The pain and blood loss had numbed him, but it was the slow feeding on her soul that had brought him back from the dark brink of the void he had nearly toppled into. He looked at her now in fuller, more complete understanding. He realized that what *he* was paled in comparison to what *she* was capable of doing: would she kill him now? Hurt him? *Could* she? He remembered that core of love that had cut him so deeply the night before; something old and powerful inside of her had compelled her, weak-willed and frightened as she was, to take arms against an enemy she should have had no rational belief in.

But there was kindness in her, he could feel, and she had misgivings, suspicions that she could be wrong... and therein lay her weakness. Her resolve had crumbled with the dawn, and from the ruins had sprung a deep, terrified regret that Kuro could feel undermining her faith. He touched it gently in his invisible way, letting it fill him. She blinked rapidly, sensing something, but remained still.

"What do you think I am?"

"...A demon."

His voice had grown thick. "Do you really believe that?"

She opened her mouth to speak, then shut it again. She looked down at the hay near his leg; the blood had dried to a shade so dark it was nearly black.

"I do."

He smirked. He wondered what Jaden would do in his place – had he ever met a girl like her? *No, of course not, never like this.* He closed his eyes and breathed in her scent: cornflowers and lavender, and the wet, heady scent of freshly tilled dirt...

"What are you thinking?"

Her voice cut through his thoughts. His eyes, dark and heavy, opened to stare at her in silence.

Her soul trembled.

"What do you think I'm thinking?" He asked. A steady calm was coming over him as he regained control of himself.

She began to shake, so slightly it would have been impossible to perceive if not for the quavering of her inner being. Her soul moved, curling and writhing, grappling with a fear that told her to run and a courage that burned with the firm desire to confront him.

She senses danger, Kuro thought. He increased his grip on her soul, tightening it by just a bit. The fiery pain in his leg grew numb again as he fed from her.

He sat up now, slowly, testing his weight and strength. The world pitched for a moment, but his vision held steady. She watched him move; Kuro swept his gaze around the barn and noticed that the gun was no longer on the banister. It seemed she had left with it last night and, as far as he could tell, had not thought to bring it back.

She followed the path of his eyes. Her hand reached for the first aid box, fumbled inside for something, anything...and finding nothing, fled back to her body.

He held on tighter now. Her alarm transformed into uncertain confusion. He'd seen this look before, just as Jaden tightened his hold as crushingly as he could manage on a soul already firmly in his cold, invisible grip.

Instinctively, her arms came up, wrapping around herself.

He spoke quietly, firmly, with a tone he'd heard Jaden use often, but never before used himself, one that was demanding but calm... one that threatened without any allusion to violence.

"What's your name?"

"...Caroline. Caroline Lahey." She was blinking quickly now, appraising her situation. "I work at the police station. If something were to happen to me..."

The threat hung unfinished, cut off by a gasp. He'd been digging into her soul while she spoke, and like a wanderer lost in a dark forest, he had stumbled upon a deep well of sadness, buried beneath the surface. He plunged into it now, a long smile stretching across his lips. She sucked in her breath again, and one furtive hand shot up, scrubbing away at a tear that had escaped from the corner of her eye.

"What are you doing to me?"

He deflected, savoring the moment. "Are you afraid?"

Oh, but she was defiant, this farm girl. Her eyes flashed, and anger spiked. "...I think you already know that."

He laughed, throaty and delighted. He understood now that killing had little to do with *why* at all, and all to do with *without:* without sympathy, without caring, without pity, without concern. She must have been without *any* of that when she shot him; he was devoid of those feelings now himself. He held onto her soul with everything in him, giving himself the strength to slowly stand and walk one, two, three steps over to her. He knelt then, and though he could see the blood blossoming under the white bandage on his leg, he could feel no pain. His own physical body seemed worlds away: there was only the realm of the unseen and the palatable, and inside of him, the *holy dark* moved and took away everything else as it fed.

She sat frozen as they looked at one another, each waiting for the other to make the first move. He was drinking her all in now, filling himself with her terror and wrapping it around him like an embrace, drawing it out in great draughts of sorrow and fear. He reached forward and passed a hand through her hair, cupping the side of her face, and squeezed, his thumb pressing against the bottom of her chin; he had seen Jaden do this same gesture so many times that it was easy to mimic. Her pulse skittered just beneath his hand. A sharp bolt of her panic sent a pleasant buzzing in his head; he was moving in now, stalking her soul into the last, safe corners of her heart.

He thought of Jaden and his latest goal. Here, like this, Kuro almost believed he could do what his friend had yet to accomplish; he felt so confident, so utterly assured that if his hand slipped down, if he gripped her throat and strangled the life from her body, then her soul, like a wind-fallen apple, would loosen, twist... and release altogether. He would hold it, then *consume it* in its entirety.

And she would deserve it, he thought. He would sink into it with his jaws. It would leave him so satisfied and sated that it would have made the whole ordeal worth it. Jaden would look at him with newfound appreciation and admiration for having done what the other demon had yet to accomplish.

"Please." Her plea was quiet, frightened.

It sent him over the edge.

Kuro smiled, his hands moving toward her throat –

"Hail Mary," she whispered, the words so soft Kuro strained to hear, "full of grace, the Lord is with thee."

"What?" The words meant nothing to him, but they had a peculiar effect on her soul: the roiling ocean began to smooth, blowing over into a strange state of tranquility, a benign acceptance of her fate that spread like a balm over her desperation.

It burned him.

"Stop," he commanded, but still he could feel her soul slipping away, receding from his grasp. The pain from his wounds was returning, sharp and stinging, and she was staring at him with an expression of fearful resignation. With a start, he realized that *he* must have looked like this the night before, with eyes that had accepted death and refused to struggle against its inevitable outcome.

She had realized what he was about to do; she believed she stood on the threshold of life and death. A wave of horror and revulsion crashed over him; no one had ever looked at him like this...like he was a murderer.

Like he was Jaden.

"Hail Mary, full of grace, the Lord is with thee. Blessed are thee amongst..."

The ache in his body was coming back to him as she spoke, the pain sharpening. "*Stop.*"

"...pray for us, now and at –"

His hand twitched, but instead of closing around her throat, he crushed his lips against hers, smothering her words away.

All the movement in her soul came to a total, halting stop; for a single moment he thought he had shattered her composure and regained control, and then suddenly her soul did something that he had felt no other do before.

It reached out to him.

Kuro wrenched himself backwards.

He felt *violated*, shocked.

Caroline gasped and scrambled away.

"What did you just do?" He demanded.

"Get away from me," she whispered, her eyes dangerous. She frantically spilled the first aid box and grabbed a small pocketknife, finding it now when it had remained stubbornly buried before.

Her soul lashed at him.

He cried out and fell backwards, his tail snapping back behind him for balance, disappearing just as quickly as it appeared.

My tail! His mind reeled. He couldn't change back earlier – why now, why suddenly...?

The bullet. The bullet is out of me. There were taboos they couldn't break, things she couldn't know about, like touching weapons. Maybe the bullet inside of him had stifled his ability to change, and now that it was out...?

He looked up at her, his teeth on edge. It was possible to be in two forms at once, but it was painful, barely controllable. It happened now in his rage, his tail whipping behind him again as human hands clenched with silver claws. He just needed to dart forward, slash her throat open, and take the soul he had nearly claimed.

"Hail Mary," she said again, the knife held out at arm's length, "the Lord is with thee –"

He moved to strike, and the image of a girl, her arms limp, eyes empty, her blood soaking into the seat of her car, flashed in his mind.

I'm lucky I didn't kill you, Caroline had said. *I couldn't have lived with myself if I had.*

Could *he*?

With a snarl, he turned away and shifted forms, feeling the familiar firmness of the earth beneath his paws. He rushed toward the door, his back leg throbbing with a stabbing pain, his long tail streaming behind him. He ran forward in clumsy, desperate movements, past the fence, back toward the clearing in the woods, and only once he was firmly in the shadows did he pause long enough to throw one glance behind him.

Caroline stood in the doorway of her barn, watching as a black beast disappeared amongst the trees.

THREE

Kuro and Jaden had once gone to the movies, though neither enjoyed it very much. In the film they watched, an action hero was shot by the men he was fighting against. The hero staggered back for a moment, braced himself, then kept going, slightly inconvenienced and momentarily winded, but otherwise fine.

At the time, Kuro hadn't realized how inaccurate that was. He was aware of guns and had heard poachers firing them off, but their deadliness was strictly theoretical – he'd never even come across a discarded, bullet-ridden carcass.

Now, each step that he took felt like a hot poker had been plunged into him; fresh drops of blood fell onto the leaves, leaving a stilted path of dead vegetation behind him. This was no minor inconvenience: this was pain, searing and spreading.

The throbbing was almost unbearable; the blood was attempting to clot, but his movements forced the torn muscle to work, and even his pitiful, limping pace sent lightning bolts up his spine. It was already mid-afternoon; every few minutes Kuro would raise his head and let out a melancholy, desperate bark. He hoped Jaden was in the forest and could hear him.

He dragged himself on for another hour, weakened from blood loss and shaken from the pain. Next to a giant pine, Kuro at last sunk to the ground and hoped that no one would take a brisk afternoon walk through the trees.

He drifted into a fevered, fitful sleep. A dream flitted past his sleeping mind – always the same recurring images that Jaden claimed Kuro imagined ("Demons don't dream," he once told him, and Kuro, who knew he was right despite the dream he nevertheless had, never argued). Between the dream floated peaceful bouts of black nothingness. He'd wake from those moments and bark pathetically into the air, high-pitched and needful, then fall back into disturbed slumber.

Hours or minutes might have passed; Kuro could feel hands shaking him, waking him. *Human* hands.

Instinct told him to bolt up, slash at whoever it was, and run.

The best he could manage was a pained whine and a twitch of his front leg.

"Kuro," Jaden was saying, "Kuro, wake up!"

He struggled to open his eyes and exhaled; each moment brought another sharp jolt of agony. Jaden was kneeling in front of him, his red eyes wide with surprise.

"How did this happen? Who did this to you? Kuro, *speak to me.*" He was gripping Kuro's fur tightly, tuffs of the black hide sprouting up from his clenched fingers, his face drawn with panic and concern.

Kuro's chest swelled with grateful relief, and for a moment, he could feel the story ready to rush out of him: he would tell him of the girl in the moonlight, the dog, the crack of the bullet in the night... and then he suddenly remembered the way her lips felt, pressed against his. He shivered.

A hunter, Kuro lied. He felt strange; he never lied to Jaden, and wasn't sure why he did so now. *A stray bullet hit my leg.*

"Where did the bandage come from?" His voice was shaking,

scared. Kuro had never seen his perpetual sense of calm shattered like this; he hadn't even thought Jaden was capable of feeling fear. He looked down; the bandage hadn't assimilated like his clothes did when he shifted forms, and it hung half secured, trailing down his leg.

I broke into a house. I thought I was going to die...

Jaden knelt and pulled away the bandage; it was soaked through. Under the stiff gauze, buried beneath the fur, the ragged display of his marred flesh was revealed. He reached forward and touched it. Kuro recoiled, a thin wail escaping between his teeth.

"What happened...?"

I dug it out...with my hands. His black eyes rolled to look at his friend. Jaden had turned pale, his lips pressed firmly together into a single thin, white line. *It lodged in my leg, and then I couldn't change back to myself. I was stuck as a human.* His head sank quietly back down into the earth, and his tail curled in toward his body.

Jaden ran his hands over the rest of him, fingers passing through fur caked with dried blood, his eyes narrowed in dangerous appraisal. "Did something attack you? You have scratches, cuts – puncture wounds..." His voice was shaking with anger.

A dog. He had a dog. He sent it to track me. Kuro winced. *Jaden, don't be angry at me – I tried to get away, I didn't want to die...*

His head snapped up. "Angry at *you?* I'm not angry at you, Kuro." But his eyes were shining with vengeful malice. "I'm angry at the person who did this to you. What happened to the dog?"

I killed it. One lie came fast on the tail of another. He groaned.

"And the hunter?"

He never found me. I ran.

The human in front of Kuro disappeared; a giant maroon fox suddenly stood over him and leaned down, his jaws snapping at Kuro's leg.

Are you going to gnaw it off? Kuro asked, sick with fear.

The demon looked at him with an almost amused expression; some of his anger dissipated into kindness. *I might have to if it becomes infected,* he said, and one hind leg came down squarely on Kuro's snout, pushing his head back into the earth. *Be quiet for now and rest.* He leaned down and began to lick at the blood from around the wound, cleaning it as the black *kitsune* hissed and whimpered underneath him.

When he was done, Jaden sat back on his haunches and looked at his friend; his long tail curled along his body in a moment of thoughtful grace...and then he was a human again, his eyes narrowed in cold opprobrium, tense forearms folded across his chest.

"I want to find the hunter."

Kuro moaned. *Just leave it be, Jaden.*

"I won't."

I have no idea where he could be. I never even saw him. I just heard the gunshot, and then I ran.

Jaden looked at him levelly for a minute before speaking again. "What did the bullet look like?"

The bullet?

"Yes."

Small. Metal. Crumpled.

"That might give us something to go on." Kuro could see his mind working, already bent on revenge. When Kuro was agitated, he paced; when Jaden was roused to fury, he became very, very still...like now, as he stood nearly statuesque, concentrating. "I don't understand much about guns, but – you said it was small? If he was a hunter, was he using a rifle or a shotgun?"

Jaden, please. Let me be... He had to get him off this topic. *What about the boy?* He asked, panting from exhaustion. *What about Kenneth? What about the photograph?*

A momentary unease flashed across Jaden's expression; he unfroze, his posture softening, and Kuro braced himself for what could only be bad news. "There's been a change in the situation."

If he was referring to the picture on the Web site, Caroline had told him as much, but he tried to hide the knowledge, waiting for Jaden to speak again.

"I was in town this morning, and...I saw it. The photograph. There was a segment on the local news. It was playing on a television when I got breakfast at a café. Evidently the photograph was published on the Web, as well."

A rushing sigh of abject misery escaped his jaws at the confirmation. The Web site was bad enough, but the *television*, too?

"I listened to the story – they don't know what you are, just what you're *not*. After I saw the segment, I found a library and read the news. The paper ran the story next to a report about that girl who gave us a ride down from the mountains...and they played up the details of the slash marks on her body. Apparently there were animal prints near the car, as well. The police are emphasizing there's no connection," he said, snorting, "which just makes it sound like there *is*. They even did a follow-up press conference earlier today, which will only convince people they're lying and trying to keep the community calm. We should have taken the time to hide her body," Jaden sighed, shrugging. "It's no surprise they found her right where we left her."

Where YOU left her, Kuro wanted to correct, but his stomach turned over; he could protest all he wanted, but he was an accomplice in her death. Her dangling arms flashed again in his memory, but suddenly, he pictured another girl

(*Caroline*)

who knelt in a barn, staring at him, horrified. He imagined what her eyes would look like in death (wide and empty), and shuddered.

Jaden cleared his throat. "We might have a problem. I'll find a way to get you help for your leg, but I need you to push through this and assist me with something tonight."

I want to lie here. It hurts to move.

"I'm sure it does." His voice had softened to a whisper; he knelt and placed a comforting hand on his back. "But Kuro – listen to me. I don't think you appreciate the seriousness of the situation." His jaw was firmly set as he reached towards his back pocket, drawing out a folded piece of printed paper.

Pain or no pain, the black *kitsune* sat up. Kuro shifted to a human and reached out for the paper, unfolding it and staring at the photo...of himself.

There he was, just as he remembered it. He was fleeing the camera – he had just turned away, but the side of his snout was visible, if slightly obscured. The black form, the ears, the graceful legs – and most importantly, the long, flowing tail – were all there.

"People will think I'm a wolf," he said quickly, but his hands had begun to shake. He looked up at Jaden for reassurance, his voice suddenly on edge. "And they'll believe the police, that there's no connection with that girl's death. Won't they?"

Jaden emphasized his words with slow precision as though he were speaking to a child. "There are a number of people – important people from other agencies – who *don't*." He pointed at the story next to it. Kuro tried to read it, but the words blurred and jumped in front of his eyes. It wasn't until Jaden reached forward and grasped his wrist, then gently removed the paper from his clutch that he realized he was trembling from adrenaline. "They might try to track us down. I think the best thing for us to do is leave. Go somewhere far away, somewhere we could get lost in a crowd. A big city. But before that..."

No, this couldn't be happening; they had followed Kenneth to Asheville to stop this exact scenario from playing out. They had feared that if the photo got out it might spur hunters to invade their home, to find the mysterious animal, and now Jaden was telling him that it was too late, they had failed, the situation was even worse than they had feared, and they needed to flee...?

Kuro looked up at him, trying to control his breathing. "What do you think we should do?"

"We should go to Kenneth's house tonight to pay him a visit." The words came out in a dangerous hiss. "We're going to have a talk with him about publishing photos in newspapers. Kuro, do you understand what's happened?" He lowered his voice to a deadly stillness. "He's taken our home from us."

The earth seemed to fall away beneath him. If the police came to believe they were connected to that girl's murder, they wouldn't be dealing with casual hunters: there would be a manhunt, an organized, systematic search...and Jaden was right: they wouldn't be able to return to their home.

"But – how do you know where he lives? Do you think –" A sharp wave of pain stole his breath for a moment; he snapped his jaw shut, willing it to pass. "Jaden, please, I need *help* –"

"I'd do it by myself, but...I think we'll need your... *trick*." His words were brought up short by a hint of indignity. Jaden was ashamed and frustrated by the delay in the development of his own unique *kitsune* ability; every demon fox could produce fox fire, the blue flame that burned souls, but each demon was equipped with one singular, unique talent.

Jaden had yet to manifest his. To compensate, he had practiced creating fox fire with an intensity that Kuro had never achieved.

And Jaden could be relentless.

And cruel, Kuro thought suddenly, watching his friend's fists. They were opening and closing rhythmically, betraying the barest hint of his agitation.

But Kuro *had* developed his own ability, and it was something Jaden asked him to use on occasion. Just a small trick, really, but it was enough to make Jaden jealous in a way he never dared to confront. Kuro had noticed it once in the way his eyes had flashed, the way the corner of his mouth pulled downward in stern envy, his gaze narrowing.

"Please do this for me, Kuro," he said. "And then we'll get you help for your leg, and we'll go somewhere we can be safe. We can go somewhere much, much bigger than *here*."

I just want to go home, Kuro moaned, shifting forms. He didn't want to leave the mountains; surely they didn't need to abandon their forest? Denial warred with rationality: it was so far away...these people wouldn't follow them all the way back there, and if they did, so what if they engaged in a manhunt? They would never find them in the vast expanse of the wilderness, even if they began their search right where Kenneth took the photograph. *Jaden, who cares? So what if they come searching – they won't find us. We can hide. I just want to sleep...*

"You can sleep for now." Jaden's voice had grown firm. "But tonight, we're going to go find him, when he's sure to be home. I think I know how to find out his address..."

Jaden stood up and shifted his form, his maroon head dipping low in a cautious nod. *I'll be back shortly. Stay here.* And then, softer, *try to rest.*

The afternoon slumped onward through the muggy August heat; between the mosquitos and the throbbing in his leg, there was no respite.

Kuro had refused to stay behind in the forest; rest eluded him.

"Jaden," Kuro groaned just as sunset began, "I think it's infected." Kuro passed a hand over his pants and flinched. "It *burns.*"

Jaden's voice was not without sympathy. "You'll have to push through the pain."

Kuro felt a muscle in his jaw twitch with frustration.

The two of them had left the forest hours ago to escape the bugs and were seated on a bench in a mostly empty park in Asheville, the tall pines shading them from the heat. Jaden had gone to a pharmacy and returned with peroxide and ibuprofen. A bandage, he reasoned, wouldn't do any good: it wouldn't stay on between forms unless given enough time to assimilate, and Kuro needed to be able to shift back and forth. The ibuprofen hadn't done anything to dampen the pain, and dumping the peroxide on the wound had been a *horrible* miscalculation. It had exploded with fire and frothing anger, the pain driving all other thoughts from his mind until a red mist hovered over his vision.

He needed some kind of powerful painkiller or medication...and stitches.

He could have neither.

It was a problem that Jaden didn't know how to solve. He wasn't used to not being able to fix things, and Kuro found himself more and more afraid: he had implicitly trusted in Jaden's ability to heal him, to somehow make him right...but now Jaden was telling him he didn't know how to do that, and his injury was only growing worse. Urgent Care or a clinic could be a last resort, but a wound like that would raise questions, to say nothing of the *blood*.

"Depending on whether or not that becomes infected, you may need antibiotics...and I don't know how you could get them. I've been thinking for a while now that we need a more integrated approach to life... A paper trail: fake IDs, a bank account. But how...? As for the antibiotics, they would be hard to steal. More importantly, I don't know what they would do to your body. Our blood is different, but how much else is the same? I would be worried it could do more harm than good, even if I could get some for you...And if it does become infected, and if it were to spread..."

Jaden's musings did nothing to alleviate his fears.

Kuro had developed a severe limp, but he was determined to be rid of it. He tried walking as straight as he could, stopping when he could take it no longer. White-faced and gasping, he would pause for ten minutes, shake off Jaden's hand on his shoulder, and stumble onward. Thus they had eventually arrived at the park, stretching less than a single hour's walk into many.

"You can't go with me to the campus, Kuro." Jaden finally grabbed him by the shoulders and forcibly shoved him onto the bench. "You're covered in blood, your clothes are torn – your *leg*...well, it is what it is. You need to wait here."

He watched as Jaden drew a contact lens case out of his pocket, frowning at it. Kuro felt all the air rush out of his lungs; there was still a small fleck of blood in the righthand corner. He knew where it had come from, and he felt no sympathy for Jaden as he grimaced, forcing the blue contacts on. Maroon hair was perhaps eccentric; he could get away with it in public, though the way people stared drove him mad.

But maroon *eyes?* That could not be borne.

Kuro focused on breathing while Jaden left to find the admissions office of the Asheville Buncombe Technical Community College.

It was their one lead, and a good one: after Kuro had startled Kenneth, the boy had scrambled for his car, grabbing his open backpack. Papers had spilled out and fluttered away in the gravel as the boy sped away, and one of them was a current Fall 2011 syllabus to a class at the college. Thoughts competed against the pain in Kuro's mind, guilt climbing up his throat.

If he hadn't been curious to know if Kenneth was the boy he'd based his form on...

If he hadn't gotten so close, hadn't almost touched him when he crept up behind him...

If the papers hadn't fallen...

Then that girl with the freckles *(Brittany,* he thought, trying to forget her name, her face, the way the car filled with the stench of her death) would still be alive. They wouldn't have known to come to Asheville, wouldn't have hitch-hiked here, and her body wouldn't have been discarded like a husk on the side of the road.

Kuro chose to focus on the pain instead of the guilt.

It hurt less.

Jaden returned a half hour later with two addresses for Kenneth McMahon. One was in California, the other here in Asheville.

He found Kuro slumped outside of the building, clutching his leg.

"I told you to wait!" Jaden lowered his voice and gripped him by the elbow, steering him away across the street, fast, despite Kuro's groan. "Kuro, you're a stubborn *idiot.*"

Back under the trees, Kuro pushed damp hair out of his eyes. His sweat was chilling him; he was shivering despite the swelter. "Did you get his info?"

"Yes. I told the secretary I found a notebook that belonged to him that I wanted to drop off. She gave me both addresses," he said, putting the paper away. "You know, what she did was illegal – she shouldn't have released his private information." Jaden tried to grin; he took pride in his ability to navigate the human world, but his expression fell away.

Kuro was pale and sweating, his breathing labored.

"That's great," he panted, furious and unamused. "Now what?"

"We'll need to wait – he's probably not at home. Most students take classes during the day, and it's wiser to attack at night. Just *sit down* where I tell you to," he suddenly snapped, his patience gone. "Keep off your leg as much as you can."

They returned to the park; two hours had since passed, but Jaden had remained seated with him, waiting, his brow drawn down in a half-frown.

Kuro knew that expression: Jaden's face twitched; it was as though he were biting down on words, trying to chew and swallow them. His eyes were still hidden behind the contact lenses, which had transformed them into a peculiar shade of blue. He looked uncertain as he spoke.

Jaden had never looked uncertain before.

"I've been doing a lot of thinking," he said, "about what I want from my life." His words came out halting, jilted, not with his usual smooth composure. "How I want to live, what I want to achieve. Who I want to be. Who I am. It's all mixed up." He sucked in his breath for a moment, glanced at Kuro, then continued. "Not to mention, what I'm going to do with you."

"With *me?*"

"You wouldn't make it on your own. You're hopeless." He gestured to Kuro's leg. "You and me, we're like...brothers."

The raw admission quieted them into an awkward silence. Kuro had felt the same way for years now but had never been able to voice it. He turned Jaden's words over in his mind, trying to look under them. He had the sense that Jaden had never revealed so much of himself before, and going by the twitchy way his face moved, that he didn't like doing it; and yet, the meaning, the *importance*, was obscured, hidden behind and underneath whatever it was he was trying to say. He had the distinct impression that somehow, for some reason, this was Jaden's form of an apology.

But the fire spreading from his leg stole away his concentration, rerouting his thoughts.

"I've been thinking about what happened." Kuro cleared his throat, bridging the silence. "When I was shot, I thought I was going to die."

Jaden regarded him seriously. "You would have never been shot," he said, "if it wasn't for that boy – the photographer. If not for him, we wouldn't have been here. The hunter pulled the trigger, but that boy brought you within the range of his gun. Every time I picture you, alone, bleeding..." Jaden bit down on the thought. For a moment, the flicker of a tail snapped, and silver claws appeared and then winked out of existence. He took a deep, steadying breath. "But what's done is done. We can't change what happened to you...but we can still do something about *Kenneth*."

Kuro let his head sink into his hands, grinding his palms into his eyes. "What are you suggesting?"

Jaden settled back, folding his hands together neatly, the fingers laced into a cage. "We should kill him."

Kuro's heart sank. "Kill him?"

Something in his tone caused Jaden to quirk his head to the side, regarding him in a curious, appraising way, as if he had never quite seen him before. "Yes, of course; we go to his house, and we kill him."

We. Kuro shuddered. "I...I don't think that's a good idea." He hated the boy for photographing him, but his mind was racing, trying to put something together that was only visible at a distance. If only he could think through the cloud of agony that was suffocating him. What was it that was needling at him? Was it what Jaden had said earlier, or was it his tone? Or something new, something he forgot? "The newspaper article – they connected the picture to that girl's...death," he faltered. The word *murder* had been on the tip of his tongue. "And...if the person who took the photograph of me ends up dead in the same way as that girl, and the police or the paper or *whoever* thinks there might be a connection, that would just bring *more* trouble down on us. It would look suspicious. It would confirm that we were dangerous. They'd have people combing over the entire mountain range to track us down. It would be like hunting season."

"*Possibly,* but by their reckoning, they'd know that the 'beast' had come to Asheville. That would solidify for them that the threat was *here,* not hours away. We could go back up to the Parkway, where the picture was taken, and be left alone, and that boy would be long dead."

There was an insistent thread of persuasion in his words, but Kuro resisted that cajoling tone, shaking his head. No – no, something wasn't right...and while he wasn't as intelligent as Jaden, he knew he needed to *think.*

"I don't think it would work out that way." Kuro's head was fuzzy, and the pain in his leg kept trying to fog his thoughts with its hot insistence. His skin had begun to grow clammy as the fever found its hold. "The police would investigate. They wouldn't give up...the killings would go unsolved, and the people would always wonder. They'd go up there, where the first picture was taken. Trucks with headlights, shining into the forest. Hidden cameras. It could go on for years. They'd want to find us." They could go back, but it would be a life of hiding and crouching in the shadows; true peace and freedom would be gone.

His mind struggled to put it together. The pieces fell into place with a sudden, heavy weight, and he looked up, staring at that inscrutable face before him. "If you hadn't killed that girl, the police wouldn't be investigating *anything*." Not hiding her body hadn't been an oversight; it had been by design. *Killing her* had been intentional, not the impulsive madness Kuro thought had overcome his friend. "Maybe either way the boy would go to the paper or he wouldn't, but if she hadn't died, they probably would have never published that picture. They ran it together. And if we kill the boy... we'll have to leave. Not just the city – the state. We'll have to go somewhere...somewhere we can completely hide..."

Like a city – exactly the sort of place where Jaden wanted to be.

And Brittany was hardly the first; there had been the two backpackers, and the hiker – not to mention the campers from nearly two years ago...those girls... The police might become interested in previous attacks, re-examine old cases. They would have to *run*.

"You've been driving us away." His mouth felt suddenly dry. "Killing Kenneth would just be the last step toward that. You've been waiting for an opportunity." He was going to be sick. "Jaden..." His voice cracked. Jaden had told him not to approach Kenneth... but only after he had drawn Kuro's attention to the boy in the first place. "You insisted we leave to track him...and then when we got here, you said no – let's wait. You said *enjoy yourself.* I didn't even question it...but you were giving him time, weren't you? We could have stopped him; you would have found him some other way...but you made sure he had enough time to do *something* with that photo."

Kuro pushed back against the bench, bewildered. He felt manipulated, duped...stupid. All this time, and the answer was so clear, so obvious.

Jaden had seen an opportunity, and he had seized it.

Kenneth hadn't taken their home away from them.

He had.

The demon regarded him as if he couldn't quite believe Kuro had managed to put that much thought into something. The corner of his mouth tugged up into a gratified smirk.

"You just figured that out?"

Kuro turned and suppressed the dry heave that came upon him. He felt a hand on his shoulder and jerked away, hissing. Jaden settled back and sighed.

"Would it be so bad, Kuro? You and me, in the city? Picture it: *New York City*, the lights, the crowd –"

"I'm not going with you." This was an old argument, but this time, Kuro was prepared for more than just casual resistance.

"Kuro, listen to me."

Kuro turned on him in a rage. *"I won't go with you!"*

Genuine shock crossed Jaden's face. His eyes widened. "Kuro...if I had known you were going to be hurt, I would have never let you leave my side. Is that what this is about?"

It wasn't; it was the first time in the last twenty-four hours that he *wasn't* thinking of the bullet wound in his leg. He couldn't change anything that had already happened or erase the deaths already piled at his feet, but he would stop *this*. There was no hiding the resentment in his voice. "Why do you even want to go to that boy's house now? What's the *point?* To make things *worse?*"

Jaden frowned. "He saw you, Kuro. Regardless of what you think I want...why would I let that boy live? He *saw* you," he stressed again, but Kuro only shook his head.

"If you're going to kill that boy tonight, you're going alone." Kuro was gasping from the pain now, his words breaking off between gulps of air as he clutched his thigh. "And if you do kill him and the police investigate, we'll have to leave – but not together. I won't go anywhere with you if you kill him."

Jaden's eyes narrowed. "Kuro, you won't make it very long without me."

But another thought had formed in the darkness of Kuro's mind, something previously unthinkable, unearthed by his talk of being 'brothers,' and it came into focus in his heart with sudden clarity. For years Jaden had wanted to leave the mountains, to live in the larger world of human civilization; he could have left him any day he wanted, but no: he had architected this scheme to ensure that Kuro came with him, patiently waiting for a suitable opportunity to put events into motion. Nothing was holding him back except *himself*. He hadn't stayed with him for *Kuro's* benefit.

Kuro forced out a lop-sided, bitter smile. "I think it's the other way around, Jaden."

The blood drained from Jaden's face. Without responding, his eyes slid away, staring out at the sidewalk in the distance.

The anger seeped out of him; they were all they had in the world, and in some ways, this revelation of Jaden's manipulation was neither surprising nor unexpected. It was simply who he was. Kuro did not rage nor run; he merely sighed with weary resignation.

When Jaden spoke again, his tone had changed to a placid indifference. "...Alright, Kuro. We won't kill Kenneth. I won't lie; I had hoped to make another attempt at eating a soul, but since we're being so honest with each other, we both know that wasn't working, anyway." His voice dropped to an annoyed mutter. "I've tried everything I can think of to get a soul completely out of the body. I thought death was the obvious solution, but it's no use – I keep trying to grab the soul when it leaves, but that's as senseless as trying to grab air. I've begun to think that perhaps you can only get at it while the person is still alive...but never mind. As for *Kenneth*, instead of *killing* the boy, then *what*? Just go over there and give him a good scare?" He scoffed. "Because regardless of what we decide to do, or where we decide to go, we should probably do something to discourage the publication of any more photos."

Kuro slumped, defeated. "Possibly, but Jaden..." He braced himself for what he was about to demand. "*Promise me* you won't kill him."

There was a beat of stunned silence, and then Jaden's eyes flashed. "You want me to make a *promise?*" The word came out as a snarl.

"I trusted you."

"I haven't betrayed you."

Kuro took a deep, patient breath; it was his turn to play the parent. "I know you don't think you have." It was the closest to censure that he could come.

Jaden regarded him again; Kuro felt uneasy under the weight of that impenetrable gaze. Thoughts unknowable were moving behind Jaden's eyes as he constructed a new understanding of who Kuro was...and what he was capable of. He would not be so easily manipulated a second time.

"...That's a heavy promise to make."

"I know."

"You know what would happen to me if I broke a promise like that?"

Kuro set his shoulders back and held his ground, silent.

Jaden stared at him levelly as he spoke, his voice even. "I promise not to kill Kenneth McMahon."

Kuro let out a sigh of relief, and Jaden looked away in disgust. A promise was a powerful thing, and although Kuro had come to realize that Jaden was a liar, this, at least, was secure. He would have to figure out what to do about all the rest of it, later, but for now...

"As for what to do about the photos...Jaden, I don't know if I have the energy to do *anything*. My leg..."

The demon rolled his eyes in exasperation; his sympathy had been exhausted in the wake of the promise. "Just feed off someone and forget about your pain."

But he couldn't.

Something was wrong with him.

He'd been trying to feel the souls of passerby all day, to reach out for those strands of emotions that would feed and sustain him; they needed food and water to survive like any other living creature, but more than that, he needed to drink deep from the fount of human life. It didn't hurt people, and most of them couldn't even detect the invisible touch of a demon...unless they were particularly harsh in their touch.

Or unless they were haunted.

Panic was building alongside his inner hunger, a hunger whose sightless maw gaped, demanding food. It was as though the whole world had shut itself off from him; he could feel *nothing*, not a single human soul...and yet he still groped blindly, desperate for a relief that wouldn't come.

He remembered the way Caroline's soul had reached out and touched him. No human soul had ever done that before; as far as he knew, they *couldn't*. If he closed his eyes, he could still remember its sudden, forceful grip. He blanched.

Unless he was wrong, then it was after that touch that he couldn't feel – or feed – from anyone else.

No, not quite...

Anyone else other than *her*.

He was pulled out of his thoughts by a crumpled bit of newspaper that Jaden tossed into his lap.

"I wasn't going to show this to you," he said; there was still a simmering anger in his voice. "The printout was from *yesterday*. This clipping is from *today's* front page. I didn't want to upset you more while you were in pain, but since you can *clearly* handle yourself, have a read."

Kuro smoothed out the paper and felt as though he had been shot a second time.

Jaden couldn't even hide his sneer of satisfaction. "Do you regret making me give you that promise *now?*"

The headline – NO NEW LEADS IN ANIMAL SLAYING – had run tandem with a *second* photograph of him. Forced to respond to law enforcement and emboldened by comments from both local animal control and now two Fish and Wildlife officials, the newspaper no longer skirted around 'implications.' They were running with the narrative.

And worse: the police had admitted that they would indeed follow up on leads at the public's insistence and at the advice of interagency counsel, even though they stressed there was no need to panic.

Yet.

In the photo, he was caught turning and running away from the camera, his long black tail swinging just out of the shot; it looked as though it were taken less than a second after the first published photograph. An official quoted in the story had used context clues to estimate his size and approximate weight, and further, had commented that the paws (the two back ones were clearly visible) looked to be a good match for the imprints found in the dirt near the victim's car. The public was advised to be on the lookout and take extreme precautions.

Kuro slowly crumpled the paper, his fists balled with rage.

Jaden eyed him with some amusement. "It's actually not a bad shot of you."

Bits of newspaper drifted down as he shredded the clipping, barely able to speak through his clenched teeth. "You made this happen," he cursed. "You got exactly what you wanted – now do the same for me: *make these photos stop.*"

"Well, it's not as though I can break *my* promise..."

With a start, Kuro realized what Jaden was implying. Of course. He made the promise under the assumption that it wouldn't matter, that as soon as Jaden revealed the second photo, Kuro would kill the boy *himself.*

Would he always be one step behind him like this?

He shook his head, nauseous. "*No.*"

There was a moment where Kuro thought Jaden was going to protest, but the finality in Kuro's tone brokered no argument. "*Fine.* If you won't kill him, we'll just scare the shit out of him and get him to stop publishing any more pictures, make him call the newspaper, demand the files are deleted...whatever it is he has to do. I can't make any *promises* as to what he'll do, Kuro," he added pointedly, a new venom in his voice, "and I heard the camera click a *number* of times. How many more pictures do you think they'll print?" Jaden paused, a cruel grin slicing its way across his features. "Do you think he snapped one of your *good* side?"

When Kuro didn't reply, he laughed.

There was something especially callous about his laugh.

FOUR

The sun had set, leaving streaks of gray light and murky pools of darkness within the cabin. Kenneth McMahon stirred slowly out of a nap, stretching; his stomach complained about being hungry in one long, uninterrupted rumble. A clock on the wall ticked away the seconds, obtruding upon the evening quiet.

He yawned and sat up, his feet hitting the rug, and the first thing he thought, before anything else, was a name that wouldn't let him go: *Jacqueline.*

For a moment, he considered going right back to sleep. That would be easier. His thoughts were unkind and unrelenting, though; *don't be a coward for once,* he told himself. *Just get this over with. What do you think she's thinking, knowing you're here?*

It'd been two years since he last spoke to her. *Two years.*

Going to class should have been easy compared to the events of the day before, what with the animal up on the Parkway... It had been good to step out of the cabin's musty interior and out into a world of sunlight and fresh breeze; Albert's place was up on a mountain ridge, right along the edge of the crest that peaked before dipping back down toward the city.

Not Albert's, he had to keep reminding himself. *Mine.* His uncle had died and left what little he owned to his only nephew. Sure, Albert was a perpetual drunk, eager to escape sobriety at all costs, and even though he was usually three whiskeys in by eleven in the morning, he made the best pork chops of anyone Kenneth knew. Everyone loved Albert; he possessed a sense of humor that could undo anyone's scowl. He nearly shot his left foot off when he attempted to go deer hunting exactly once, just so he could say he'd done it, but he knew his limits: he'd thrown his truck keys under the couch years ago and never retrieved them. When Kenneth spent the summers with him, there wasn't a week that went by when a neighbor didn't drop off a bag of groceries, a casserole, or a bunt cake with a note pinned to it that read "Just thinking of you," and there wasn't a weekend without an invitation for Albert to come down to so-and-so's and shoot the shit.

Kenneth felt his heart sag at the thought of never seeing him again.

They were separated by a continent and two generations, and yet Kenneth had felt like his uncle had understood him. Albert had also been a photographer at one point; he had closets filled with outdated equipment that ached to be used once more. Once, he had squinted at Kenneth, put a clammy hand on his shoulder, and said, *You only get the one life, son. Spend the time doin' what you love and to hell with everyone else.*

Albert had then blinked his watery eyes and coughed. *Unless you love being an accountant and workin' for the IRS. No nephew of mine ever better work for those fuckin' bastards.*

At twenty, Kenneth hadn't been doing what he loved. He hadn't even been *happy.*

It'd been two years since he'd gone back to visit his uncle in North Carolina after spending every summer with Albert since he was ten years old. He'd gone silent, retreating into himself, and meekly went off to college at the University of Southern California because it was expected of him. He couldn't bring himself to text Jacqueline, to phone Eric, let alone Albert or even his parents – though Albert didn't expect anything of him and didn't mind his silence during the school year.

Kenneth wasn't sure how he even got into college; his grades were mediocre, and he'd never done a single extracurricular. A week in, he went by the registrar office to adjust his schedule and noticed one of his father's sculptures in the lobby with a value nearly double that of his first year of tuition.

Oh, he had thought, sickened by the confirmation of his own worthlessness and the sense of a privilege he didn't deserve and hadn't earned. *That makes more sense.*

And then Albert had died, and for the first time in his life, Kenneth saw a path open up...like the path between Albert's house and Jacqueline's, the one that cut up through the woods: dark, but passable, with the promise of something inviting at the end. He refused his parents' offer to have a lawyer take care of selling the estate, placing the money in an investment account or whatever it was they wanted to do.

Instead, he moved across the country, quietly enrolled at the community college, and desperately sought for the courage to call Jacqueline...and then, *she was there,* in his Myth in Human Culture class, and Kenneth, a perpetual coward, had skipped the second lecture because he was too afraid to face her after *two years* of total silence.

She knew he was in the class, knew he was in Asheville now – she *had* to.

Professor Schiller had walked in with a dazzling smile and a bright attitude for a man pushing into his mid-forties; he had a way of compelling others to smile back, his tie crinkled up against his chest from the large stack of books in his hand. He let them fall with an audible 'bang' onto the table in front of him as he surveyed the class, beaming with the enthusiasm of someone who loved their subject, and worked his way through roll call.

And all the while, Kenneth had felt like a man nailed ramrod straight to his seat, because he was *certain* that the petite girl with the heavy sheet of dark hair in the front row was Jacqueline (and it was; her name was second on the list), and *please skip my name, please skip my name* –

"Kenneth Mic-man?"

"Mac-mah-hohn," he'd corrected in a voice that sounded half-strangled, his face burning. "Sorry," he added, stupidly.

And then he waited till everyone else had left the class (including Jacqueline, who did not so much as turn to look at him, let alone wait for him afterwards), and fled.

Anxiety drove him into inaction: he neither dropped the class nor called her, and he knew he had to make a move soon. She had heard his name; every moment of silence after that was so much worse than the last two years.

But Kenneth had only ever run from his problems, and he fell back into his old pattern with shame. Two days later, instead of attending class, he was up at four in the morning and driving out to the Blue Ridge Parkway to try and get some photos for his portfolio; his photojournalism professor had promised that for every published picture, they could receive an extra point on the exam.

He needed every point he could get.

Nothing in particular compelled him to pick the spot he ultimately chose when he pulled off the road at almost seven a.m. He knelt down on one knee in the dirt, listening to his camera shutter click and whir as he snapped photos; he felt guilty in a way, unmoved by the scenery. He wanted to stare out at those mountains and that great expanse of open air and feel awed, but instead, an aching, sad loneliness grew heavier and heavier in his chest.

How could he just pick up the threads of the relationships he'd abandoned?

The truth was that he avoided reaching out to Jacqueline and

Eric because he was terrified at the thought that they wouldn't care. After all, he was just some kid down the road who visited once a year. He had looked inside his heart one day and discovered that his exactly two friends meant entirely too much to him; what if he only occupied a small space in their world? Better not to know...but his own mind was too cruel to spare him the feeling of inadequacy, the constant refrain of self-criticism that whispered insidious taunts in his heart. He *knew* why he hadn't reached out to Jacqueline or Eric, and the picture wasn't pretty: he was a coward, fearful...pathetic.

And alone, now.

He was so lost in the mire of his self-abasement that he never noticed the animal that snuck up behind him, curiously sniffing at him squarely behind his shoulder blades.

Kenneth had yelped with surprise and whirled around.

In front of him, the largest animal he had ever seen up close blinked at him for a single heartbeat, its dark eyes like pools of shadow above its long, angular snout. It looked like a giant, pitch-black fox with a long, flowing tail that swayed behind it before a barking noise suddenly caused its ears to prick up. The creature instantly turned and fled, revealing itself for the whole of less than three seconds to Kenneth, and scaring the shit out of him in the process.

But during that final second, as the animal fled, Kenneth lifted his camera, the whir of the shutter burst just audible over the sound of the beast disappearing into the brush.

The animal was gone so quickly that for a moment, Kenneth thought he had imagined the whole thing. He looked down at the white knuckles of his shaking grip and scrambled away. If the creature was real, he had caught it on film; regardless, he wanted to get the hell off the Parkway.

His backpack was near his feet; he grabbed it, hands trembling, and papers tumbled out – syllabi for classes, notebooks. Blood hammered in his ears, and too frightened to turn back, he abandoned them and jumped into his car, slammed the door, and took off.

It was only later in the day that Kenneth realized that that moment had been his lucky break.

And Kenneth was *never* lucky.

God, he prayed out of formality (Kenneth didn't believe in god, but on the off-chance...) *give me a break on this one.*

Two hours after he got back to Asheville, he was missing another class and sitting in a small conference room of *The Asheville Citizens-Times,* a manila folder open with large, glossy photographs lying on the table, printed in haste. He had explained to two different people that he was a student at the community college and that yes, he realized that he could just e-mail the photographs, but this was important. He wanted to speak to someone in person. He knew that e-mails were routinely ignored or, at best, were replied to with a cursory "Thanks, but no thanks" note. It was harder to turn away someone who was willing to beg in person.

Especially someone who looked as desperate as he did.

He waited an hour for a meeting to end, then another fifteen minutes for an editor and another photojournalist to agree to see him. When he entered, thanking them profusely for their time, he saw by their expressions the tide he would have to swim against.

Editor Lisa Cantrell and a photographer whose press badge identified him as Mathew Langton looked down at the photographs, studying them.

"I can't remember the last time someone brought in a hard copy of a photo." Kenneth looked up abashedly, studying Langton's face. The man was probably in his late thirties; the very first few streaks of gray had appeared in his otherwise boyish hair. He wore a flannel shirt with jeans, and the man looked at Kenneth with the paternal condescension of someone willing to humor a kid for a few minutes if it meant a break in his morning routine.

"This is astonishingly bad," Cantrell remarked. She was older, a petite woman approaching fifty, with the faint edges of laugh lines around her mouth, but there was no humor in her words now. Her hair was pulled back in a ponytail, and when her nose wrinkled in dislike, her glasses slipped down. The sleeves of her blouse were stained with ink smudges. Next to her, Mathew scratched the stubble on his chin and pulled another picture toward him, shaking his head.

"Real crap," he agreed.

"That's much too harsh," Cantrell amended. "It's a good attempt for a beginner."

"It's just...I don't understand the angles. It has an 'I'm running' kind of feel, but at the same time, it has an 'I'm falling and taking pictures' aesthetic and...it's just not working for me," he finished.

"But more importantly..." Cantrell straightened up and looked at him with a penetrating, hard stare. Kenneth squirmed. "Do you think it's appropriate to waste our time?"

He started. "I didn't think they were that bad..."

"Bad?" Langton snorted and leaned back. "Come on, kid. Come clean. Who put you up to the prank? Or is someone down at the college hazing you?"

He could feel Cantrell studying his face. Flustered, he gestured ineffectually at the photographs, then composed himself, trying to keep from crawling under the table.

"I don't know what you mean."

"I mean these are stupid fakes," he said flatly. "That's why you brought in hard copy, right? So we couldn't check the data – it's Photoshop, Lisa." He pointed to the clearest picture and snickered. "It's not real."

"It *is* real." He was surprised to hear his own voice rise; he didn't think he had it in himself. "I brought in the physical photos because I didn't think anyone would talk to me otherwise, and I didn't want to risk emailing them because I figured no one would reply. I don't know what it is, but it's *real*, and I'll send you the digital files to prove it if you want to publish it."

Cantrell had continued to appraise him. She pursed her lips, then looked back down at the picture, then back up at him. Her gaze was shrewd and evaluating, and she was decidedly displeased.

She spoke in an even, measured voice. "If it's real...then what *is* it?"

He didn't have an answer for her. He had asked himself that the first time he looked at the photographs; the longer he stared at them, the more convinced he was that he had taken a photo of something unusual...something worth publishing.

Something that could get him extra points on an exam.

"It's a bit like a wolf..." Langton poked at the animal's head. "But its snout is thinner, longer... and the ears, too – and the tail, come to think of it. It's a bit like a...a really big fox."

"But look at the perspective." Cantrell pulled another photograph over and slid it next to the other. This shot was blurry, capturing only the animal's hindquarters, but half of the car was in the shot. "This gives you a clear indication of its size. It's bigger than a wolf, but leaner; the legs are longer, for one. No one would mistake this for a wolf. Especially with that tail..."

Kenneth watched the two of them and held his breath. As they shuffled the photographs back and forth between them, they forgot all about him; he became a silent background figure as they pointed to new details in the photographs that he had missed.

"Look at its claws, here, in the bottom left corner –"

"You can see it's about to run..."

Cantrell turned to Langton, tapping the table with the tip of her pen. "The sell of the photo is its novelty; we don't know what it is, and the two best shots are just good enough to have a clear, visible perspective of it. Not perfect, or even good photography by any measure, but good enough to play upon people's curiosity. That being said, Mathew...you've photographed plenty of wildlife. Would you agree with me that it's most likely just a starved wolf? Do we have on our hands a chupacabra, some mange-ridden animal? I'm not in the habit of publishing bunkum zoology – not even for the clicks."

Kenneth waited, watching the photojournalist. Langton crossed his arms over his chest and stared back down at the photos. One arm unfolded itself, roughed up his stubble, and returned to its original place. He turned his head to the left, to the right, slid another photo over, and finally let out a troubled, perplexed sigh.

"I would want to ask a couple of people for their opinion," he said. "For starters, Jeffery Rose, from Animal Control, and Carol Minden up at the wildlife refuge, for identification purposes...and I think the only species of wolf up there is a red wolf, which doesn't look a damn thing like *this*. So if you're asking *me*..." He licked his lips and sighed again. "I would say no. Even when I try to convince myself that it's a wolf, I can't make the details stick. The shape of the head is completely wrong, as are the legs, not to mention *that tail*. We did that story last year on the wolf-hybrid breeder, and I remember standing next to those things...and this just doesn't scream 'wolf' to me. I'm not saying it *isn't*," he added quickly, "but I'm not convinced by any stretch that it *is*."

Kenneth's words came out in a rush of air. "So you'll publish it?"

Cantrell started, surprised that he was still there. She opened her mouth to form what was clearly the word 'no' when Langton stood up and hurried to the door, poking his head out into the newsroom.

"Bernard!" He shouted. "Come in here for a moment."

When he returned to the table, he was followed by an older man who stopped next to Cantrell. He nodded to Kenneth with a friendly smile and a head of thinning gray hair. He had the air of a man who had grown comfortable over the years, and having found the niche of contentment and fulfillment, somehow still managed to be at ease in a profession that ran its best workers ragged, right down to the quick. He lifted his coffee mug and sipped after a brief greeting to Langton.

"This is Bernard Wallace, our metro editor," Cantrell said. Kenneth had no idea what a metro editor was and knew that was something that had been covered way back in one of his J-101 courses the previous year; the time to ask had come and gone, so he nodded, feigning understanding of newsroom hierarchy. Cantrell introduced him dismissively as "a student."

Wallace took a seat and swiveled his chair around to face Kenneth. "I saw you get here earlier – it's rare for a student to come by. What can I help with?"

Langton slid the photograph over to Wallace and studied his carefully blank expression.

"Have you ever gotten any reader call-ins about anything like that? All of the other shots are more out-of-focus," he said, and here Langton nodded at Kenneth, much to his annoyance, "but this is a decently clear photograph of it. This kid took the photo up on the Parkway."

Wallace lifted an eyebrow. "The Parkway? That's *way* beyond our range of coverage. You'd have been better off driving to Roanoke."

Langton saw the pained look on Kenneth's face and took pity on him, clearing his throat. "Sure, but lots of people pass through here, move on through Pisgah and the Cherokee National Forest on their way up to the Parkway, and you know we publish local reader photos from the Parkway all the time. If you're asking my opinion –"

"I'm not."

"I don't think it's a wolf."

"Hmm." Wallace tapped the photo before settling back in the chair, one leg propped up on his knee. "Well, that is certainly...*something*. When I look at it, my first guess is a wolf, but that would be one exceptionally odd wolf. The proportions are off. The more I look at it..." He turned it to a different angle. "...The more I tend to agree with you. It's too bad the head is turned around, or else we could get a clear look at that face...Oh, this picture here, we can see that. It's very angular. Hm. Is it fake?" He looked at Kenneth with the bald expectation of the truth.

"It's not," Kenneth answered.

"Well, I'd like to look at the meta-data on the photos before I take your word. Got to do our due-diligence and all. I tend to not believe everything I see in the digital age. But, Mathew," he said, placing his coffee on the table. "An unusual photograph, all by itself, isn't a story, and Lisa looks like she's ready to bite your head off for wasting her coffee break with a Reader's Photo. What are you angling at?"

Across from him, a sly grin grew on Langton's face as he swiveled to Cantrell. "Lisa, what do you think about pairing this with that story Meihui's working on?"

Lisa stared at him as though he had suggested she resign and give him her job.

Wallace rubbed his temple. "Mathew, are you serious?"

"Look, I've been assigned to provide a photo for the story, and the pickings are slim," he said. Kenneth's heart leapt into his throat at the word 'story.'

"Wait," he interrupted, "I took the photograph, you can't just steal the story from me, that's not ethical –" He protested, but stopped. He was aware of how immature he sounded. His face began to grow hot with embarrassment. He swallowed and tried again. "I know it's not a – a great photo. I almost dropped the camera when it came up to me, but...I would like to see my work published. Even if it's just a Reader's Photo, that would be great. Unless...are you thinking of something more? Is there a way that I can be involved?"

Wallace smiled at him, kindly. "What's your name?"

"Kenneth."

"Kenneth, we all started somewhere. We all like seeing our names in ink – you can relax. We're not going to steal anything from you. We're not going to pay you," he added, laughing, "But you probably knew that. Lisa, what are your thoughts?"

Cantrell considered; Kenneth watched her mind work like clockwork behind her eyes, all precision and calculation. "Have you seen the update on Meihui's assignment? There was an animal attack this morning, circumstances unusual, just on the border of Asheville. A young girl, local, killed in her car – could be a murder faked to look like an animal attack, but from the way the police were calling it over the scanner, it sounds authentic. They had a ranger out there earlier to try and match the prints. The only information they're releasing at this time is that the wounds go *backwards;* in other words, it's as though the animal was *behind* her and attacked by ripping *back* toward itself. We have the officer on the record using the phrase 'like an embrace' to describe it."

Wallace whistled. "Some sensational language there – great quote! So the police think what, exactly – she put a bear in the backseat?"

"Despite the fact that she was shredded, they don't think it was a bear... There was some discussion of a wolf, but that would be extraordinary: all we've got is the near extinct population of red wolves. We're waiting for an identification for the headline, but the last we heard, they were calling in for a second opinion. Meihui has two officials on record reporting the preliminary findings: the wounds were made by an animal, but don't match for either a wolf or a bear. They found tracks in the dirt near the road's edge, but they stopped once the animals entered the field."

Wallace scratched his chin. "Plural – *animals?* Did I hear that correct?"

"The prints in the dirt indicate two sets, so yes, plural. Carol Bridgewater, from Buncombe County Animal Control, consulted and is on record stating that the puncture wounds began in the abdomen and then tore backwards...that's unusual enough to lead with. Strike two for novelty: there're two sets of prints. And finally, unless I hear otherwise within the next four hours, we've got a quote from a ranger stating that the prints in the dirt also don't match a known animal 'at this time.'"

Wallace nodded. "So either a mysterious animal attacked her from the back seat, which is a story in and of itself, or else this is an elaborate staging for a murder." He lifted his eyebrows in appreciation. "This is gonna be a big one."

Cantrell tapped the photo. "Police are leaning animal but have a healthy dose of skepticism regarding the whole thing."

Langton butted in. "And here we have an unidentified animal. Kenneth," he said, and his heart leapt, "How far away was this photo taken from Asheville?"

"I'm not sure about the exact distance. I could check my GPS, but it was about three hours away. I just chose a turnoff that had a good view of the mountains."

"And when did you take it?"

"Just before dawn."

Wallace paused, musing. "...And the girl is killed in the animal attack around noon. Could an animal cover that much distance in... six hours?"

Mathew snorted. "It could if it was in the backseat of a car, and still have three hours to spare."

Wallace leaned back and sighed. "We'd be implying something way beyond our scope, Lisa. You run this picture with that story, it's clearly indicating a connection when there's no proof of one. Mathew, I like your ambition – but no."

Kenneth saw Langton and Cantrell exchange a glance, and Langton spoke up again. "Would it change your mind if I told you that police contacted the victim's family...and that she had been driving *from* the Parkway to Asheville that morning?"

Wallace's fingers unlaced, rewrapped themselves around his coffee cup, and returned it to his lips. After a thoughtful sip, he looked back at Cantrell. "I understand that it could make for a good package – mysterious animal, girl attacked...the circumstances make the radius of the distance *plausible*, though improbable. On the other hand, I'm concerned that it would appear that we're trying to create a narrative where there is none and being overly alarmist. It would be hard not to read the story as suggesting that the animal – or animals, if they're interpreting the prints right – moved down from the mountains toward Asheville and are responsible for that girl's death. If you run that picture and that story together, the implication is clear and indefensible. It could start an unnecessary panic among people out on the outskirts of the city. It would be irresponsible. Not to mention it would be extremely embarrassing for us if it blew up in our faces. It would be tabloid trash."

Cantrell grimaced. "On the other hand, what if there *is* a

connection – it wouldn't be a bad idea to warn people to keep a close eye on their livestock over the next couple of days. Especially if there's a second attack...because whatever killed that girl is still out there."

"Possibly," Wallace agreed. "But my greater concern is this: I don't want to be accused of sensationalizing the death of a young woman to sell some papers during a slow news week."

Kenneth's heart sank.

Cantrell nodded, but something in the set of her shoulders, all business now, kept his hope alive. "I don't disagree, but how about this: we've already got plenty of officials weighing in on the girl's death. We can't release her name yet, *but* we can be very, very careful about the wording and any implications that may arise. Meihui is one of our best writers; she's competent and careful. We currently have no photo to run with the story, either, unless you want to publish a picture of a taped off crime scene and that girl's car in the dirt. And just so you know, there's blood visible on the windows. You'll get hate mail."

"You know I won't publish that."

"Then I think we should go for it. The story is running tomorrow; we need something visual for the centerpiece, and in the meantime, we can get it up on the web. We'll share the photographs with the officials we've talked to so far and get them to weigh in on it. I think we keep the photo and the story separate, have the design department even border it off from the print."

Wallace stared at her; Cantrell's face had hardened into a firm decision. He nodded. "Okay, but if animal control sees the picture and they tell us it's a wolf – and therefore couldn't possibly, even in the slimmest chance, have a connection – we kill that angle. If just one of them gives a positive ID, it's done. I still want to go on the record stating that I think we're overstepping some boundaries here."

Cantrell set her eyes on him, her lips firm. "I understand, but Bernard...my gut is telling me that we've got something here. We're ahead of the story right now, and I want to keep it that way."

They stared at one another for a moment until Wallace gave a deferential nod. "Your professional judgement has always been better than mine. Okay." He turned to Kenneth and gave a wan smile. "I'm older, but don't be fooled – she's got an extra fifteen years of experience in the industry on me. Which is why, of course, I look forward to forwarding her all of the outraged hate mail to respond to. And before we waste any time, I want the digital files so we can make sure we're not being set up for an elaborate prank."

"You're not –" Kenneth tried, but a sharp glance from Langton cowed him into silence.

"So, that's the plan. Kenneth, we'll temporarily plan to print your picture with a credit to you as a stringer – no payment, freelance." Cantrell's tone was final. He nodded solemnly. "That's contingent on the things we discussed here. After you send us the digital files, we'll be in contact. Get them to me immediately; I need to get them to animal control and law enforcement for comments."

Wallace stood up. "I've got to get back to work – Kenneth, it was nice to meet you. We'll be in touch."

Cantrell turned a photo over and tapped it. "Contact info?" She asked. He scribbled on the back of it, handing it to her. She nodded, thanked him for stopping by in a business-like manner, and walked out.

He was left with Langton, who let out a low, appreciative whisper as the door shut.

"Good cop, bad cop – mom and dad," he said. "They work well together. Make no mistake, Lisa is crossing her fingers on this one. I know that look in her eyes: she's on to something. I think she thinks you're a windfall and that this is going to turn into something big. I've worked under her for eight years now, and she hasn't been wrong yet; she's got an intuition that's damn near supernatural. Bernard has to be more cautious: he's made a few bad calls in the past. But hey – aren't *you* lucky!" He smirked. "No, seriously, you're lucky as hell. Once we had a bear mauling and the bear was still at large – guess who they sent to take photos? I was supposed to show up and take some pictures of knocked over trashcans, nothing big – just filler for a side-story – and the damn thing came out of the woods where it was hiding. Charged right at me. I won't let pride get in the way of telling you that I pissed my pants," he said. "You're lucky whatever that thing was ran *away* from you."

There it was again: *luck.* Kenneth couldn't believe it. Sure, his father was a famous artist who had bought his son's way into college, but good things didn't happen to Kenneth: he didn't make friends, didn't possess any real talent, and routinely failed at everything he attempted, be it academics or just being normal, *happy*...hell, he would have been the first to admit that he wasn't worthy of the oxygen he breathed.

But for once, he was lucky.

Despite himself, Kenneth smiled as Langton laughed. The photojournalist reached into his pocket and drew out a business card, handing it to him. "My cell number is on there – if you get anything else, give me a call *first*," he said. "You got away with getting the editors to humor you this time because you're young, but that good will runs out *quick*. I remember being young and breaking into the business; it sucks. Just keep at it, if you love it. Hopefully, we'll chat again." He stood up, paused, and grinned. "You haven't met her, but Meihui, the reporter who's covering the story, is an absolute stickler when it comes to grammar: she would have snapped at me for using 'hopefully' as anything other than an adverb. *Hopefully* they'll print your work, and you'll get to meet her yourself. Have a good one," he said, and headed out of the room.

His head popped back in a minute later; Kenneth had remained seated, too stunned by his good luck to even move. "By the way, Lisa is on the phone with the Asheville Police Department, and it sounds like they want you at the station with those photos *now*. One call from a newspaper and they get all up in arms over there...they'll want to interview you, so unless you want law enforcement banging down your door, save the trouble and just drive over now."

At the station, the name plate for the receptionist read 'Caroline

Lahey,' but a middle-aged man with a graying mustache sat behind the glass and asked if he was Kenneth McMahon. Wordlessly, he nodded and followed the man into the back once the door buzzed to let him through, only reluctantly surrendering the camera's storage device at a sergeant's prompting.

It was almost two hours later when he walked out. Two officers had grilled him on the photographs and his involvement with the newspaper in short bursts, leaving him alone for long stretches of time. They were frustrated, angry; they asked him the same questions over and over again, trying to trip him up: why did he go all the way to the Parkway for pictures? Did he fake the photos? How did he fake the photos? If he didn't fake the photos, what did he think he saw? A wolf? He repeated his story half a dozen times: he was trying to get a jump on extra credit, trying to snap some blasé photos of the sunrise over the mountains. No, it wasn't a hoax. No, he didn't think it was a wolf. No, he wasn't lying. No, he wasn't paid by anyone. No, he didn't know anything about a dead girl in a car on the outskirts of Asheville.

By the time he was driving home again, he felt embarrassed and somehow guilty, as if he had done something wrong and, if he could just confess to it, he'd feel better.

He checked his cell the moment he walked out and felt a brief spark of elation at the sight of a text from an unknown number: *Kenneth, this is Mathew from the Times. Check the Web site. Congrats, stringer.*

And there was his picture.

FIVE

He should have been thrilled, and for a brief moment, he was, but Kenneth was an expert at self-criticism, and seeing it now published, he saw just how bad it really was. Something inside him always had a way of robbing him of joy, but usually, if he slept, the feeling went away...for awhile.

But not this time.

He couldn't bring himself to leave the house the next day, not even to go and get a newspaper and see what the print version looked like. The heaviness in his chest was back again; it made his brain feel sluggish, his breaths shorter, and every task required an inhuman amount of effort. There was a name for this – this *demon*, he sometimes thought of it, this thing that lived inside of him and constricted around his lungs, this darkness that kept him from replying to any of Jacqueline's texts...but Kenneth didn't want to name it, let alone face it. He just had bad days, that was all.

Bad days that had stretched into bad months, and bad years.

He hadn't gotten any new calls from anyone over at the paper yet; if there were any developments, he wanted to know – *so maybe there aren't any,* he thought. It had just been a day; what exactly did he think was going to happen? He had to have faith that Bernard Wallace had promised to include him on the story. He sighed as he fell despondently down on the couch.

His heart was bursting. He wanted to tell someone about everything that had happened, maybe call his mom and dad –

Or Eric. Or Jacqueline.

Instead, he remained home in the dark, the dust, and the loneliness. The thing inside of him that pressed his heart down until it felt like a sodden lump of coal, that sapped all his energy until all he could do was lay there in the gloom, tried to crush him down into sleep.

He fought it, rising.

And now, here he was, standing on *his* front porch, staring out at Asheville. At night, it was all twinkling lights with pockets of darkness in the rising mountainsides, spare the strips of lights where the chalets and hotels nestled quietly in their relative solitude.

He wanted to call Jacqueline, pretend that the years of silence had never happened, and tell her a story of the one time in his life that he was lucky...but no; he understood what he *really* wanted. He wanted to replace the shame of failing to even say hello to her after nearly two years of *nothing* with the fantasy of sharing his published photographs with her, because it would serve as a distraction from what a colossal failure he was as a friend.

I'm so selfish. The thought sunk down into the marrow of his bones, slumping him. *All I can think about is myself.*

So don't think about yourself. Extraordinary things had happened in the last two days – what could be more extraordinary than for once in his life finding the courage to do what scared him most? *Call her. Apologize.*

His hand was trembling when he reached for his cell phone; it was effortless to tap her name, and yet somehow it had taken every ounce of his will.

"Hello?"

It was the same voice from class that answered Professor Schiller that yes, her last name was pronounced "Bay-roo," all self-assurance and poise. Somewhere on the other line a small young woman was brushing heavy strands away from her face, perhaps adjusting a head-band and drawing her legs in close to her chest, listening.

"Hello," he croaked out. He cleared his voice and tried again. "Hi. It's me."

Silence followed. He tried to move past it, but the emptiness was like a prison cell.

"Jacqueline," he said, and suddenly his throat was too tight, his voice too high, "I'm back. I'm back in Asheville. For the fall. Hello," he repeated. He fought off an impulse to punch himself in the face.

"Kenneth..." The fuzzy silence of doubt, hesitation...and then the bright, joyful voice he remembered, the voice that always sounded like wind chimes. "*Kenneth!* So it *was* you!"

He let out a rush of air and laughed too loudly. His hands were sweating; he tried to wipe them against his pants and discovered he was shaking with adrenaline. "Yea," he said, "It's me."

"You should have sat by me, I didn't think – well, I thought, how many Kenneth McMahon's could be out there, and it sounded just like your voice, but I thought I misheard, and what would be the chances, and – I...I didn't think you were ever coming back. And that's okay, it's just...you never called. Or emailed. Or anything. And it's been...awhile." There was a raw hurt in her voice. Kenneth heard it and felt a hot shame spread across his face.

"I was going through some things," he said. "Personal stuff..." He didn't think he could come up with a more stereotypically *awful* excuse if he had pulled the line straight from a movie script.

"I know." It sounded as if she did, sincerely. Nothing in her voice said that she required further explanation, or that he needed forgive-ness. He didn't know how much of her tone was real, how much of it was an act. "Kenneth, this is wonderful – we have to tell Eric, he'll be so happy. Well, as happy as Eric ever gets, anyways. When can I see you? You're at Albert's, right? Can I come over now?"

Now? Kenneth blinked, suddenly nervous. Her house wasn't far away – he'd made the run himself plenty of times, and so had she. He remembered the way she would sneak out her bedroom window and run through the forest on a clear, moonlit night to get to him. She said it was fun, and it was often too late for her to go back home. She would curl up next to him on the couch and they would sleep together, side by side, and Albert would roar with laughter in the morning at a joke Kenneth was too young to understand, until suddenly he did.

But they had been nine, ten, eleven, then; she had to be at least nineteen or twenty now – did she plan on spending the night?

"Hello?"

"Not now," he said too quickly. "Give me a half hour to clean up." He hadn't meant to say the last part, but the words spilled out before he could stop them.

"Okay. I'll walk...for old time's sake. That should give you time. See you then?"

"See you then." He hung up the phone and held his breath, but it was no use; he let out a rush of air that turned into wild laughter. She wasn't mad at him, then, wasn't faking – she was just happy to hear from him. He felt so stupid and giddy, so relieved...and so, so undeserving of her forgiveness.

His momentary joy was snuffed out. She would be here soon, and he would need to find the words to explain himself. *I'm sorry, something inside of me is strangling me, and I'm afraid to tell anyone and I don't know if I can fight it anymore* didn't feel adequate, because *nothing is wrong, I have no reason to feel this way, but I can't help it: every day I feel like I'm drowning, and I have never been good enough for you.*

Kenneth froze mid-spiral. He hadn't turned any lights on in the house, and the interior was dim with the last remnants of dusk, but something was happening...

The shadows were moving.

At first, he thought he was hallucinating. He blinked hard, rubbed his eyes, and stared.

No, he was sure of it: *the shadows were climbing up the walls.*

They writhed across the ceiling like snakes, coiling in and out of each other and combining until they formed one large, terrifying serpent that opened its mouth and vomited more of the twisting bodies. The tiny black tendrils of shadows multiplied and expanded, crawling down toward him and slithering in his direction before bursting into millions of deformed, grotesque chimeras with fangs, monsters with shapes that changed and claws that slid across the floor to him.

He jumped up and knocked over the coffee table, scrambling to turn on the lights.

A figure stood next to the switch on the wall, grinning at him.

Kenneth gasped and turned around, ducking low to grab the legs of the coffee table, then lifted it over his head to fling at the intruder.

The wind was knocked out of him suddenly; he fell heavily onto the floor, landing on his back as a weight pressed him onto the rug, the table crashing to his left. The glinting eye of a strange, black beast hovered above his face, the jowls pulling back as it growled, exposing its fangs in one long, threatening hiss. Its paws were large and heavy against his chest; he could feel the points of its claws through his shirt. Kenneth could smell the rich scent of blood and prayed it wasn't his own.

He panicked and wrenched himself to the side, freeing himself as the beast snapped its jaws and let out a short bark. It staggered forward and made a feeble slash at him with its front leg, but either Kenneth was just out of reach, or the animal didn't intend to actually maim him. There was something odd about its movements; they were jerky almost...limping.

His heart racing, Kenneth sat terrified, watching. The familiar beast lurched again, its grace gone. *It's hurt,* he realized. Something was wrong with its back right leg. Maybe he could aim for its weak spot...

Too late; the person who had been by the light switch appeared in his peripheral vision and kicked him squarely in the chest, doubling him over.

Kenneth clutched his stomach and tried to breath. He was certain: it was the same animal from the Parkway, he was sure of it, which meant *it had followed him*. He gasped and struggled up, staring at the beast in the fading twilight, when suddenly it was gone.

Kenneth felt all the blood in his body freeze, even his terror skidding to a total halt.

He was staring at *himself*.

It took a moment for his mind to catch up with what he was seeing. Even in the dim light, it was like looking into a mirror...but a cruel mirror, one that had twisted his image. This version of him was taller, leaner, muscular; he was handsome, a better, perfect copy of the slouching, miserable version of himself.

The other version of him *snarled*. His hair was plastered to his face from sweat, and his eyes were bright with sickness and rage.

The person who had kicked him suddenly hauled him into a kneeling position, yanking his head backwards by a fistful of hair, exposing his throat. Kenneth reached up and tried to fight him off, but another kick to the base of his spine left him momentarily stunned, white lights exploding in his vision.

"Now *listen to me*." The not-him staggered forward, his fists bunched, and a voice almost like his own but much deeper spoke. "Those pictures. *Where are they?*"

Kenneth struggled to speak. "The computer," he gasped. "They're d-digital!"

From behind him, the voice of the one restraining him was calm, but annoyed. "That means there're copies," he said. It sounded as though he was explaining it to the other one, the other *him*. "Destroying one set won't matter. Even destroying the camera won't matter." He let go of Kenneth suddenly and came around, kneeling down to look him full in the face. His eyes were a deep, impossible maroon. "So, let me be clear, then: don't share any more of those photos. Don't *publish* any of them anymore."

He tried to back up, but there was nowhere to go. His voice trembled with panic. "I gave them to the newspaper. The police have them, too. If you do something to me –"

Maroon eyes rolled with amusement. "Like what? This?"

Kenneth felt as if something inside of him, something he didn't even know he had, was grasped and twisted viciously within him with a force so powerful that it left him winded. He tried to scream but had no air with which to do so. It felt like hands, cold with dagger-tipped fingers, were somehow inside of him, touching the raw places of his heart and stabbing at all the softest parts of himself. Tears slipped down the sides of his face, and still it felt like something was ripping at him, *tearing*. It burned as if his very heart was being torn in two and forced through the slats of his ribcage.

Maroon eyes gleamed above a slow, delighted grin.

"No more photos," his double growled, panting now. The man looked like he was ready to collapse. "Tell them to *stop* printing them!"

Kenneth swallowed, and despite the piercing violation he was enduring, he threw himself forward at his double's legs. The double cried out as Kenneth barreled him flat to the ground. With everything he had, he pulled back his arm and aimed for his face.

Instead of a human skull, his fist collided suddenly with black fur. Beneath him, the animal writhed, twisting and hissing.

The grip on his heart was suddenly gone. A hand grabbed him by the shoulder and flung him backwards, and the red-eyed human turned to glare down at him, but he had changed before Kenneth had managed even a gasp. The same beast from the mountains stood over him, only this beast was the same color of his eyes, the deep maroon of *blood,* and its silver claws slashed forward to cut open his chest and spill his organs –

In an instant, his double had reappeared and flung himself on the hindquarters of the other beast, pulling it down to the ground as it snarled. Kenneth squinted and could see now what he already believed: it was no wolf.

It was a giant, slender fox, and its teeth were sharp and hungry for death.

But then it was gone again, and the red-eyed human was back. He glared at Kenneth. "He just saved your life," the man jeered. He kicked Kenneth hard in the stomach a second time, then turned him over and pressed his heel down onto his throat, hard enough for him to fall still. Staring up into those unnatural eyes, Kenneth couldn't see his double, but he could hear the labored panting across the room.

Suddenly the pain was back, the hand around his heart had returned, and he couldn't breathe or think –

"Now, listen. Call the newspaper and tell them you don't give them permission to publish anything else. Call the police and tell them you staged the photos, and they're not even real. You might get in some trouble, but compared to what will happen to you if you don't..." Something twisted and pierced deeper inside of his heart. He found the wind to scream as the young man above him laughed, crushing his windpipe and cutting him off. "If you don't do both of those things, we'll know. We'll be keeping an eye on you to make sure you do. And if you don't...we'll kill you. Do you understand me?"

The twisting, yanking feeling inside of him stopped. The world began to come back into focus as he struggled for breath. "Who – *what* are you?"

He leaned down and gripped his shirt, dragging him upright. Kenneth could see his double behind him but couldn't understand his expression – fear, worry? No, that didn't make sense, but he reached out as if to stop the red-eyed one, but the young man held up his free hand and smiled.

His smile was *terrible*.

"Look at me, hard. If you don't do what I said, then *I am your death*."

He released him. Both humans were suddenly gone, replaced by two animals with long, foxlike tails. They moved past him and out the front door of the cabin, the maroon one slinking with grace and power, while the black one limped after it.

Kenneth collapsed against the overturned coffee table and inhaled slowly as he slipped into a state of shock, his body shaking as the adrenaline failed. He didn't know how much time had passed before he was able to stand up and put the coffee table back in place, switching on all the lights in the cabin. Closing the front door, he checked the locks, his bones nearly rattling as he picked up the phone.

He stopped, his thumb hovering over '9' for the police, his vision blurry with fear.

What will I tell them? He thought. Breaking and entering, maybe – two men, his age – and...and two animals, just like the one he had seen on the Parkway.

And one of the men, he was almost certain, had looked a lot like him.

Too much like him.

He set the phone down and sat, trying to breathe slowly and calm his racing heart, but the blood was roaring in his temples. The harder he tried to relax and get his thoughts together, the more his anxiety soared.

Kenneth crossed his legs, uncrossed them, held his head in his hands, sighed, huffed, tried to close his eyes, got too scared and opened them; he paced, moved in circles, but nothing worked. He was terrified.

Should I call Mathew? He thought. And tell him...what? *Prep a follow-up story: the animals are here in Asheville. Two of them, confirmed, and they threatened to kill me. They might be hard to spot, though, because they also look like people, because they can TURN INTO PEOPLE.*

That's what it was, what was bothering him: there hadn't been two people *and* two animals.

There had been two...two *things*. That was the most sense he could make of it.

Kenneth stopped pacing and swallowed. *Oh my god,* he thought, his stomach turning over, *they'll put me in an institution.*

His rational mind fought for control. Maybe he *had* imagined the whole thing. He had seen the shadows moving, but now they were still, exactly where they should be, plastered up on the walls. Stress could build up in people and then come crashing down upon their sanity, making them think they saw or heard strange things. Maybe it had been the stress of calling Jacqueline...

Jacqueline. He halted, panic freezing him to the spot. *If she's out there in the woods –*

If those strange beasts were real, there was a chance they were out there even now – the woods Jacqueline would be walking through at this very moment.

He called her twice, his heart in his throat, each time fighting the urge to groan in frustration as it went to voicemail.

He couldn't bring himself to wait – he needed to get out there, to find her. He was a coward, but he owed her that much.

He grabbed his keys and cell and found a flashlight in the front hallway closet; the light was weak from the dying battery, but it would work.

Kenneth ran out the house; he didn't bother to lock the door or turn out the lights, to call the police; it didn't even occur to him to grab something that could be used as a weapon. His focus had narrowed down to the singular thought that if she was out there – if *they* were out there – he had to get to her first.

He was heading out into the woods.

SIX

Kuro sank to the ground not far from Kenneth's home; his leg was unbearable now, and cold sweat stung his eyes.

Jaden knelt next to him and examined the wound; fresh blood had broken through the epicenter again, and the skin surrounding the area was puffy and hot to the touch.

"Jaden..." Kuro gasped. His voice was quiet, his skin pale and damp; he was gripped by desperate uncertainty and a need for reassurance, but he was no fool: if he didn't address the wound soon, the infection would spread. It had taken a great deal of effort for him to twist the shadows in Kenneth's apartment; it nearly drained what was left of the *holy dark* inside of him, and now, he was both fevered *and* hungry, despite his best efforts. Kenneth had looked utterly terrified, and Kuro had tried to feed from the boy's fear with no success; the cage of silence was secure around him. He was certain now: he could touch no one's soul.

He was going to starve to death.

Jaden frowned at the wound. "Some of it looks inflamed..." He leaned over and pressed his hand against Kuro's forehead, pushing the hair out of the way, his expression darkening. "And you have a fever. You need to stay here and rest." He stood. "I'll go into the city and bring back what medicine I can."

Kuro shifted forms and rolled over, burying his face into the gnarled roots of an old tree.

Jaden sat with him quietly for some minutes, waiting for him to say something. When Kuro didn't, he broke the silence.

"That boy – Kenneth. Did you see the expression on his face when he realized you looked like him? You were right: he's the same one you saw when we were young."

If he wasn't contemplating the possible amputation of his leg, followed by death by starvation, Kuro might have been gratified to hear Jaden use the phrase 'you were right.' Kuro had known it from the moment he saw Kenneth again on the Parkway: he was indeed the same boy he'd seen when they were just kits. Back then, when they changed their form for the first time, Jaden had had enough imagination to create his own human likeness.

Kuro lacked such creative faculties. He had based his form on a young human he saw, a boy who had crossed a shallow river, one who had looked up at the sound of a rustle in the trees and perhaps glimpsed a pair of black eyes hidden in the shadows, then turned and fled, running back the way he'd come.

And then, not much later, Kuro had used the boy's likeness as the basis for his human form. He had put little effort and less thought into it, never imagining he would see the boy again. Kuro dug his claws into the dirt now, hissing with pain.

Jaden watched him for a moment before kneeling again. "Do you want me to pack the wound with moss before I go? It might help."

The only reply he received was an angry tail lash.

Jaden sighed. "I thought the shadows you moved were particularly well done."

Kuro was in no mood for this olive branch; he lifted his head, his ears flattened against his skull, and bared his teeth. *You tried to rip his soul out; I saw the look on his face.*

"So? I didn't promise you I wouldn't."

And what if you finally succeeded? It might have killed him. You PROMISED –

"'Might' isn't a certainty. We don't know if humans need their souls to live."

Kuro rolled his eyes and seethed, the fever driving him to distempered sarcasm. *If I ever find out, I'll let you know.*

"*You?* Why, Kuro, are you planning to finally learn how to use your claws?"

Some of the anger from earlier returned to him; all of this was Jaden's fault – the photograph, the bullet, the torture in his leg, and now he had to endure mockery, as well? He lashed out in imprudent, unthinking anger. *If I do, you'll be the first person I test them on.*

"Are you threatening *me*, Kuro?" Jaden's voice dropped to a low, dangerous whisper. Kuro fell silent, retracting his claws. He'd never said anything like that to Jaden before...

I'm sorry, he muttered. *I'm...not thinking. I just want to rest. You should go; I know you'll be restless if you stay here. I don't need you to watch over me.*

The tension in the air melted away. Jaden sighed, appraising him. "What if you get worse?"

Have some faith in me, Kuro tried. He attempted a grin and only managed a ghastly grimace of fangs. *I could also get better.*

Jaden rose to his feet, wiping his hands on his pants. "I'll be back in a few hours with something for you. Just stay still; there's always a chance the fever will run its course and break. Kuro..." His words stumbled to a halt, as though he were unsure of how to go on. "I'll go by the hospital and see what the situation looks like. We'll go there if your fever doesn't break by the morning, okay?"

That turned his stomach over with cold dread; if Jaden was suggesting he needed to go to a hospital and risk all the questions that would raise, then the prospect on his future recovery looked dim. He grunted but didn't reply, and soon the sound of Jaden's footfalls disappeared into the night.

But underneath the fever, another torment was growing. The

hunger gnawed at him now, aching like the pain in his leg. If he could just *feed,* the *holy dark* would strengthen his body: it wouldn't miraculously heal him (would that it could), but it would push the pain and suffering away so that at last he could *think* and not have to clamp his own jaws shut to keep from moaning in pain.

The girl.

He remembered the way her soul had snuck around him in the morning, the sweet taste of anxiety and fear, the gentle touch of her fingertips on his ankle...

Kuro stood up on shaking legs; he wanted to find a quiet, soft place to sleep and sleep, Jaden be damned.

Without realizing it, he began to limp in a familiar direction.

Jacqueline Beirioux stood in the doorway to her home, one hand on the brass doorknob that led out into the night, and paused.

What am I doing?

She hesitated, glancing at herself in the hall mirror. At just over five feet, she was petite, "like a river reed," her father had once said. Her dark hair hung straight and heavy, down to her mid-back. Her father had descended from a long line of French Canadian trappers who had traveled south, mingling with the Chinook of the Pacific Northwest before moving eastward toward an eventual home in New Orleans, then onward over another generation or two to the mossy swamps of Georgia. Her father said she had inherited his nose and his hard stare; her mother was Cherokee, from North Carolina, and she had gifted Jacqueline her hair and her indomitable spirit.

She straightened her collar, suddenly nervous. The blue of the old chambray shirt she'd thrown on reminded her of larkspurs.

Kenneth had once waded across a river, all to pick her a batch of wild larkspurs.

They'd been just little kids then; Albert was still sober enough at the time to still drive, and he'd taken them both camping up near the

Great Smoky Mountains for the weekend. They'd eaten hot dogs charred to hell and back from the campfire, then snuck off when Albert fell asleep in his chair.

The river had only been ankle deep, but at the time, it had seemed like an adventure, and Kenneth was off as soon as she pointed out the flowers on the opposite bank.

When he returned he was shaking, flowers in hand. He said he had seen something over there, but he wasn't sure what; some sort of animal, he claimed. Something dark. Whatever it was, it was gone.

She had kissed him on his cheek to thank him. It was the only time she had ever kissed him in their lives.

And now he was back.

Growing up, Kenneth never called or wrote while he was away during the school year; he would just come back each summer, as though life happened only in some faraway place…as though he could just pick up where he kept leaving off, expecting no change. For Kenneth, her life – and the life of his best friend – was encapsulated in frozen pockets of time. Things that had happened to Jacqueline and Eric that were commonplace stood out as vivid recollections for the other boy; how often had he said, "Remember last summer when…?"

But no, they usually couldn't remember; it had been just another day to them, when to him, it had been significant. If she added all those summer hours up, how long had Kenneth *really* known them? A few months more than a year?

How long did it take to form a bond, a closeness, a friendship…?

How long did it take to fall in love?

And then he had left again, like he always did… Whatever happened to him across the country was his own story: private, unshared. There were no phone calls; no letters nor emails; no texts. It was as though he simply vanished each year, then rematerialized mid-June.

Except for the year when he hadn't, and the silence stretched on, doubling upon itself. Graduation came and went; *he went to college,*

Jacqueline thought. Kenneth had no social media accounts, so it was only a guess. *He's moved on with his life.*

She had felt bad for Eric, at first; Eric worked so hard...he didn't have many friends: his exterior was too cold, his smile too empty and rare. And yet, he and Kenneth seemed to understand each other so well; they shared a connection that was born in their comfortable silences. In his absence, Eric became secluded. Two years older than them both, he earned his A.A. degree and went straight to work to support himself, absorbing himself fully into his jobs.

And then Jacqueline had been left alone. Her father had died years ago, and by the time her senior year of high school rolled around, her mother had decided to move back to Savannah.

I want to go back to where I met your father, her mom had said... *even though he's gone, I want to walk and feel some part of him with me.*

She knew what her mom meant; her parents believed in "strange things," Eric had once mocked, and Jacqueline had been raised to hold those same values. Her family believed in spirits and ghosts, in guidance and intuition, and they practiced habits that Jacqueline only half understood.

Mom... She had said. The word came out slowly, like a calf bleating at the thought of separation ...*I don't want to go.*

She *did* want to go; she'd heard so much about the city of squares in the South in the weeks moving up to their departure. She heard about the giant oaks, the cemeteries on the river, the waterfront... But it was May, which meant that June was coming. June was when Kenneth came, and it didn't matter that he wasn't responding to any of her attempts to get in touch, that he wasn't even returning Albert's phone calls...she wanted to wait for him. After all those years, something in her heart had fallen into place and clicked so soundly that she was startled to realize, with a horrible, aching tug, that she missed him.

That she loved him.

Her mom had stopped and stared into her daughter's brown eyes with that deep, piercing gaze of hers.

"Why?"

"Because...I don't want to leave my friends." It was a wretched, flimsy lie. She fumbled for something a little more believable and had absolutely nothing to say.

Her mother looked at Jacqueline and pursed her lips.

"I'm not stupid. I know what's going on. I didn't raise you to pine after some boy. I raised you to be stronger than that, not to be a girl who – a girl who *waits*." Sophia Beirioux liked Kenneth, always had; she was kind to the boy and had practically raised him every summer in the absence of any real parenting from Albert...but Jacqueline saw that her mom felt she deserved better than a boy as inconsiderate as him.

Jacqueline had looked at her and smiled, but her heart had been heavy. "I don't feel weak. I feel strong. And I want to wait."

Her mother didn't argue, though she might have, if grief hadn't robbed her of resolve; at last, she gave a tight nod. "Every woman deserves a chance to make her own choices," she had said. "I don't agree with the choice you're making, but I won't take it from you. You're too young to know better and too old to be persuaded otherwise."

Jacqueline turned 18 in August, right at the start of her senior year. Her mother hadn't sold the house, and Jacqueline remained in North Carolina...waiting.

She spoke with her mother all the time over the phone, listening to stories she had heard from the Southern genteel society and the adventures her mom was having in the swamps. She was running a boutique in the Historic district, and for the first time since her father's death, her mother sounded happy.

And all the while, Kenneth never came back, never returned her texts. She had even managed to get in touch with his parents, but it had been an awkward phone call that yielded no results, as he wasn't speaking with them, either, and she didn't attempt it again.

Her mom drove up for her high school graduation and decided to further delay selling the house when she learned that Jacqueline planned on enrolling at the community college.

And eventually, at some point during her freshman year, Jacqueline's heart broke.

It was a quiet, crumbling process; she hadn't even realized it was happening until it did. Resentment had crept into her spirit and knocked a few cracks into her confidence, stripping away her romantic notions of waiting for a boy to return to her and instead filling her with the shame of being a hopeless, deluded fool. Her cheeks burned the day she realized her mother was right: *she deserved more.*

She deserved better than this. She had made her choice and learned a hard lesson.

And she moved on.

Eric was still there, even if he was hardly available; still, he had reached down, picked up her pieces, and kept them organized and cleaned while he waited for her to put herself back together again, which she did with swift, firm resolve. She was like her mother: no tears, maybe even a little too hard for her own good. For a brief moment, their friendship became something more. It was a difficult and short-lived relationship. Both of them were relieved when they agreed to go back to being just friends. Eric moved on to a woman he met at the vet clinic after she brought in a puppy for shots – it was the kind of romantic beginning that should have worked but was equally as short-lived.

And then Kenneth came back.

He had been there, enrolled in her class, and he was waiting for her to come over – just like old times. When he called her, all of the joy she had felt was sincere. At first, she'd been too happy to care that two years had passed, that he had refused all of her attempts at communication, but now, in the silence of her own home, memories tugged at the back of her mind, overturning old feelings of hurt...

He hadn't spoken to her in years; hadn't told her he'd returned, enrolled at the college, moved into Albert's. He had her phone number all this time, and how many of her texts had he ignored?

The girl who turned and walked back to the door was not the naïve one who had waited for him. Her heart was not secretly pining anymore; she would not lose sleep over him. She would go to see him, because she still cared about him, but whether or not she would forgive him for cutting her out of his life, she didn't know yet. There was an anger that needed to be dealt with first, and it was justified and sharp.

She left the house, locked up, and headed out into the forest. It was a dark night, but the moon was bright and clear. His house wasn't far; she hated a secret part of herself for discovering that her feet still knew the way, that most of the markers along the path – the oak that had fallen over and rotted halfway through its trunk, the familiar skunk den – were still there, decomposing at the rate of the earth's steady pace.

She shoved her hands into the pockets of her jean skirt, a war raging in her heart. *He didn't even sound... Guilty? Upset?*

But when had Kenneth *ever* owned up to his feelings?

Her anger grew corroded by pity, and she recalled now how relieved he had sounded on the phone when she picked up. She remembered a summer when she was sixteen; her mother had whispered, "Jacqueline, I think that boy's depressed..." and it had sounded just like when her mother told her that her father had cancer.

Kenneth had probably been terrified of calling her. He probably had his reasons for never reaching out to her. She'd seen a darkness in his eyes over the years, one that grew and sometimes confined him to Albert's house, that made him stare listlessly at the wall for hours and hours...

Jacqueline, turn around, a voice in her head said. She looked up, trying to glimpse the moon through the trees, and shook the thought away. No. She wouldn't ignore Kenneth, even after his long silence.

Jacqueline – turn around. Please, the voice said again. She shivered; why did the night seem unusually cold? The August heat was finally beginning to melt away into cooler evenings. Her foot caught in an upturned root; she stumbled forward, then caught herself. Her heart leapt with a sudden rush, and she laughed inwardly at the prickly feeling creeping up her spine.

She found the path again – it had been worn down from years of her racing back and forth to his uncle's house. She hadn't seen Albert in town at all lately, although she rarely ever had, after all. He only made it down when he could catch rides. He would probably be sleeping, and anyways, Albert never minded when she visited late, if he was sober enough to care –

Jacqueline, turn around!

She stopped abruptly. The voice in her head was getting louder.

And it didn't belong to her.

"Who are you?" She asked the empty air; her voice shook. "What do you want?"

A throaty growl began behind her, shattering the emptiness of the night.

Run, Jacqueline! The voice cried out again. *GO!*

She took off without so much as a scream, tearing through the underbrush, away from the path.

Jacqueline turned, risking one glance behind her.

A huge animal was running, lithe and maroon. It snapped its jaws at her ankles and suddenly fell back, darting off to the side – it was chasing her, leading her in a certain direction, coming in close to terrorize her with its gleaming fangs and darting away before she could get a clear view of it.

Low-hanging pine branches tore at her as she fled deeper into the forest. Her breath came in short, quick gasps. Jacqueline's hair whipped behind her as she fought to control her panic, urging her legs to move, faster, *faster –!*

Deep into the darkness, she continued to run.

The trees thinned as she exploded into a clearing, her chest burning. The forest was still; no sound followed behind her. And yet...

I'm not alone, she thought, her senses awake.

She couldn't see anyone, but she could feel something tighten inside her. Inwardly, she recoiled and winced, watching as the tiny hairs along her arm prickled and jumped up into gooseflesh. She wrapped her arms around herself and took a tentative step forward, summoning her courage. She had to keep going – she had to escape the forest and find her way back to Kenneth, to home and safety.

She took three more steps forward, then noticed him.

The shadowy form of a young man was standing at the far edge of the clearing. She sucked in her breath and froze, terror striking her still.

"Kenneth?" She whispered. Had he come to meet her?

The figure stepped forward, raising his arms up, palms flat in a disarming posture.

"Hello?" He called, his voice equally uncertain.

Jacqueline swallowed. *Not him,* she thought.

Something inside of her twisted with a swift, lacerating pain; she nearly cried out, but the feeling was gone as quickly as it came. He stepped forward at the sound of her truncated gasp; his features were just visible in the darkness, gray and blurry.

But his eyes...his eyes were intense. Even in the darkness she could see the striking, almost fake blue, brighter than anything she'd seen before.

He smiled at her, lowering his hands, and drew closer. He wore a pair of clean, pressed trousers and a button-down shirt that hung lightly off his frame. A hand passed bashfully through dark brown hair.

"Did you see it, too?"

"See it?"

He nodded and closed the distance between them, moving with a silent sureness under which no leaf or twig snapped.

"There was an animal," he said. "I was out driving and hit it. I pulled off and thought I'd come take a look, see if I could find it...and now I think I'm lost. Not very smart of me." He laughed, then stopped suddenly. "I'm sorry, I must have scared you – my name's Jake."

She didn't offer her name.

"Are you lost too?" He turned back toward the trees, ignoring her pointed silence and indicating for her to follow him. "I can lead you back to the road, if that helps. I know I came this way..."

The road seemed like a safer bet. "Thanks." She followed tentatively, glancing behind her, and wished she had had the good sense to bring pepper spray.

"What's your name?"

She considered lying, then yielded to the truth. "Jacqueline."

He glanced over his shoulder. "Nice to meet you. Awkward circumstances, but nice all the same." There was something penetrating and firm about his stare, something that made her heart hitch a bit. It was if his eyes were holding her soul in their gaze, turning it over and inspecting it carefully. She shivered again, and he looked away.

"You said you saw the animal – near the road?"

He nodded.

"It looked just like that one that was in the paper – did you see it?" He asked.

He turned back to her again. His eyes seemed to almost glow in the night with that eerie blue. *It's flat,* she realized. *The color is all the same...they're contacts.* That had to be what was unsettling her. "No," she admitted. "What happened?"

"A girl was mauled to death. Someone took a picture of a strange animal up on the Parkway, and some officials think it's what got her, since the prints don't match anything they've ever seen before."

"That's terrible..."

"The odd thing was, the paper reported that she was mauled to death *in her car*. From *behind.* It's a strange world, isn't it?"

He sounded faintly amused. Jacqueline swallowed, her fists

curling. This wasn't the kind of conversation she'd have with someone in a dark forest in order to put someone at ease. She didn't have a weapon, but if something happened, she was prepared to fight: she had teeth and nails and not enough fear for her own good.

Be brave, Jacqueline, the voice from earlier whispered. *You must be brave now.*

Jacqueline tried to ignore the ice in her veins. She walked a little straighter. "I think I saw a wolf..."

"A wolf? In *North Carolina*?" Jake came to a halt, pausing. They were halfway through the clearing now. He looked up at the dark clouds making their way across the sky. "I don't think so."

She felt that chilling feeling again, as if something was crawling all over her skin, touching her with cold, probing fingers. She tried to shake it off, but the feeling remained.

He hadn't resumed walking.

She hoped she hid the tremor in her voice. "Are you from around here?"

"Actually, no. I'm from near the Blue Ridge Parkway. Just visiting at the moment."

"Oh."

"And you?" He asked. "Are you from around here?"

"All my life," she said. "I was just walking to a friend's house."

"Not a good night for a walk." He pointed up at the sky. "Too dark, I think." It would be, in another few moments; the clouds were drifting toward the moon, already encroaching through most of its light.

"I don't mind it."

"Your friend lives close by, then?"

"Just up a ways. Once we hit the road, I can just follow it to his place. He's expecting me," she added, jutting her chin out, *which means that if you pull something and I don't show up, he'll call the cops, and they'll search for me.*

"I could just give you a ride."

She glared at him as he turned to face her, squaring herself up.

The eerie feeling had never left, even as the strange numbness tightened its hold around her heart. If he was going to make a move, she would be ready for him. Her arms bunched with tension, prepared to fight.

He looked at the girl in front of him, his eyes going wide at her wildcat appearance, her muscles taunt and prepared to strike, and gave a short, embarrassed laugh. "I'm so sorry," he said; he took three quick steps back, giving her space. "I just realized how pushy I sound. Random guy in the woods asks you to get into his car – I'm really doing a great job tonight." He let out another rush of nervous laughter. "Look, I'm so, so sorry – I wasn't trying to make you uncomfortable, and you obviously don't have to come with me. I feel like an idiot right now."

He looked at her with such abashed sheepishness that for the first time, her wariness subsided somewhat. "I was getting a bit worried there, yea."

"I don't blame you. Sorry again. But if you change your mind..."

She was about to say *no thanks* again when suddenly, overwhelmingly, all the bitter hurt she felt toward Kenneth rose to the surface, accompanied by a fiercely shocking pain in her mind. It was as if someone had found a secret chamber in her heart and thrown the door wide open, and suddenly she felt foolish and angry all at once. She was out here, in the middle of the night, walking through the woods and being chased by – by a wolf, she was certain – for a boy who hadn't even had the decency to call her once in *two years*. Not weeks or months: *two years,* her heart cried out, furious. He had made a fool of her. And she was going to go over there now, knock on his door, just like old times – for what? She tried to grasp at the pity she had felt earlier, tried to reclaim the thought process, but it was gone, buried under this bile that was being lifted to the surface. At the corner of her eyes, tears stung.

Oh God, it hurts. It hurts so much... Every feeling she'd fought against, every bitter thought she'd pushed away had sprung up and swallowed her.

But there was another pain, as well, one that felt like cold knives, slipping into her rib cage...

And the young man just stood there, staring at her.

Jacqueline had rarely cried in her life; she had been all stoicism and smiles in the face of her father's illness, but this...this was a battle for control. Her fists clenched, her body shaking with the effort to contain her sadness.

It was grief, she realized; it had felt like he was dead, that Kenneth had been gone from her, and the silence that stretched between them was the agony of the unbreachable void. She had respected him at first by not calling, not being the first to reach out, until she tried and tried and got nothing in return; this...this *goneness*, this total desertion, and then this reemergence, was too much.

If he had cared about her, why had he made her suffer?

It was like when her father had died, and all that answered her pleas was silence.

Tears threatened to spill, but Jacqueline bit her lip, throwing her head back. She could hear her mom's voice in her mind. *Men, women, everyone – we all cry over the people we love. It's not a weakness to cry over the people we care about.*

*The people we love...*was that how she still felt about him?

Jake stepped closer to her; *god, he must think I've lost it,* she thought.

But he stared at her with perfect understanding, as though he knew exactly what she was feeling, if not the *why*, and didn't speak. Slowly, he reached toward her fists, drawing her hands close to his chest. There was less than a foot between them now; he towered over her as he reached forward, one hand reaching up and slipping through the long strands of her hair, pulling it over her shoulder, letting it glide over his knuckles.

And all the while, his gaze remained unbroken.

She felt hypnotized, looking into his eyes. Something almost gentle was touching her heart, and her thoughts were far away now. She was close enough to feel the heat of his body.

Before she could stop him, his hands suddenly traveled up her arms, pulling her close, his chin resting on top of her head. She froze as one hand moved to the back of her head, the fingers curling through her hair. "You're so sad," he said simply, with the air of someone appraising the bouquet of a wine. "Is it your friend, the one you were going to see?" And then, thoughtfully, whispering close to her, "And angry, too. *Resentful.*"

His hand moved expertly, slipping down to trace the lines of her neck, trailing down the bones of her clavicle where her chest heaved in trembling breaths. Every nerve in her body had ignited with terror, but her legs were traitors: they would not run.

His open palm rested against her cheek, caressing her face while his thumb slipped down across her lips.

Everything was *wrong*. She knew she was in danger, but worse... she felt as if, through his touch alone, some secret part of her was being stolen by a thief.

It left a hollow, empty feeling in its wake, worse than even the sadness from before.

"...Your eyes are beautiful," he said, tilting her head back. "It's like they were made just for me."

He leaned in and kissed the tip of her earlobe.

She wanted to shove him away, to rake her nails down across his face and scream, but her body remained frozen with paralyzing fear. Before she could gather her courage, he leaned down and kissed along the nape of her neck. She felt his lips, soft and warm, pause a fraction away from her own.

It felt like the jaws of an animal had closed around the fear in her heart with a force strong enough to wrench a gasp from her lungs. She tried to scream just as Jake crushed his lips against hers.

One fist closed in her hair, gripping her in place, his other arm moving down to the hem of her skirt. She unfroze at once, fighting against him, but his strength was as overwhelming as it was unexpected. Warm fingers, soft and unstoppable, slipped under and brushed against cold skin, but something worse was gripping her in some invisible place, somewhere close to her heart, closing in on some secret part of herself and trying to tear it out of her core. It felt like razors were slicing at her very mind, and at last a scream tore out of her throat, desperate and pained.

Fight, Jacqueline! The not-her-voice shouted.

"What was that?" Jake reared back, his voice ragged. He looked up suddenly, confused.

Rage moved in her then; maybe she didn't have the strength or the size to win the battle, but she would put up a damn good fight.

Kenneth appeared in her thoughts again, but this time, there was no anger or sadness. Yes, he had caused her pain; he would have to live with that as much as she would, but if he was worthy of her, *he would*.

Because she loved him.

At last, Jacqueline came unglued from her fear, and with a wild cry, she shoved hard at the arms still holding her in their vice grip.

Jake suddenly stiffened, his arm twitching.

"Let go," she whispered. *Kenneth.* She had to get to him, had to get out of the woods...

Dark eyes glared down at her, furious.

Warmth was spreading through her – it was if everything that had been stolen was returned by a gentle hand that was detangling her from whatever had her heart in its grip.

"Let me *go*," she repeated, her voice strong, but his hand tightened further until she cried out in pain.

He wasn't looking at her. His eyes were darting all around, searching for something. "Come out," he growled. His voice was nearly inhuman in its fury. "Whatever you are – *come out!* This one's *mine!*"

"Who are you talking to?! *Let go of me!*"

"*What are you!?*"

The clouds finished their trek across the sky, and suddenly the moonlight washed them in a faint, gray light. Jacqueline looked up at the boy now, his face contorted with rage and confusion, and saw that his hair, which she had thought a dark brown, was in fact a deep *maroon*.

Blood, she thought.

She recoiled, his teeth shining in an inhuman snarl.

"Come out!" He screamed at nothing.

With all the power she had, she wrenched herself to the right, her mouth clamping down on his forearm, and *bit.*

Blood, bitter and unnatural, burst in her mouth. She gagged as Jake wrenched away, cursing.

She turned and spat the blood from her mouth onto the grass and watched, horrified, as it withered and died under the moon.

Jacqueline did not need a voice in her head (hers, or anyone else's) to tell her what to do.

She ran.

Behind her, the boy continued to scream.

SEVEN

"Jacqueline!"

He'd been shouting her name for ten minutes now, his voice growing hoarse, when an answering shout found him in the dark.

"Kenneth!"

"Jacqueline!" He waved the flashlight, trying to lead her with the light. He could see something moving toward him, something making its way through the underbrush –

She threw her arms around him, and Kenneth's mind didn't have time to stop him with his usual doubt or fear: he pulled her in close, crushing her to his chest.

"What are you doing out here?"

"I was worried about you. Something – something happened, back at my house, and I was afraid..."

She was equally as breathless, her eyes darting in every direction. She clutched his elbows, and through her grip he could feel her whole frame shaking. "There's someone out there," she whispered. "He assaulted me, and then he started screaming at – at nothing. We need to get to the road, we need to get out of here – I need to call the

police, maybe they can catch him, and there's a wolf or something
–"

Kenneth felt his breath catch. "What color was the wolf?"

Something in his tone froze all her movement. Her eyes traveled
up to his face, searching.

He could feel every drumbeat of his heart slamming against his
rib cage. "...Was it maroon?"

She nodded, a short, jerky assent. "Run," she whispered. "My
house is closer – follow me. *Now!*"

It was a strange reunion; by the time they flung themselves
through Jacqueline's front door, they were winded and rattled, each
trying to hide their fear from the other as they flew through the
house, checking all the locks.

"I don't know how they got in," Kenneth was muttering to
himself as he checked her front door for the third time. "I must have
left it unlocked, because it was open when they left...Jacqueline, is
your mom home? We need to warn her not to go outside."

"She moved away," Jacqueline said, and suddenly a new tension
that hadn't had time to creep around them in the forest crawled out
of nowhere and made itself comfortable between them. "...She
moved to Georgia last summer."

"Oh."

Kenneth finally paused long enough to look around at the
familiar living room – it was like nothing had ever changed. A large
stone fireplace filled half of the den, with dream catchers dangling in
the corners. In front of the fireplace, a large, circular rug with the
Cherokee national flag embroidered on it lay on the bare wooden
floor, two couches bordering the open area.

He didn't know what to say. He wanted to ask why she hadn't
moved as well, if they had gotten into a fight, but his mouth was dry.
The adrenaline in his blood was leaking away, and an intense fatigue
was moving in its wake. He sat down heavily on the couch and
sighed.

Jacqueline took a seat on the couch across from him; he looked up through heavy eyes and watched as she brought one hand up and ran it through a wing of hair, letting the strands fall away. It was something he had seen her do a hundred times before; his chest tightened, and it was suddenly hard to breathe. He wondered what it would be like to have the courage to stand up, sit down next to her, and take her hand.

She'd probably hit him, and he would deserve it.

"I need to call the police," she whispered. "I want them to find that bastard." She was staring out into the blackness beyond the window near the front door. She shivered again, her arms coming up to wrap around her bony elbows. "What did you mean about people 'getting in'? What happened?"

He stood up on shaking legs and walked over to her couch; she looked up, surprised, and suddenly light snapped back into her eyes as he sat down next to her. "You first. Tell me what you saw. Tell me what happened."

Jacqueline looked at him for beat, long enough to decide whether or not to trust him with the truth, and told him everything.

Kenneth listened, his pulse speeding up again until finally it was almost impossible to breathe.

"He's probably still out there. I can give the police a good description." Jacqueline's fingers curled into tight fists. "At the end, it was like...like he was yelling at someone, someone only he could hear." She sat up straighter suddenly, as though a thought had just occurred to her. "Or maybe not – maybe I heard it, too."

Kenneth's mind was running in a different direction. "...You saw the beast, and then you saw *him*? You didn't see them at the same time?" When she shook her head, puzzled, he forced himself to take a steadying breath. "I think I met the same person. He broke into my house just before he attacked you. That's why I was in the forest; I knew you were coming, and I was...afraid."

She was on her feet in an instant, grabbing for her phone. "The police –"

"I know, just – hold on. Oh fuck," he groaned, his head sinking into his hands. "Oh fuck, I think I might be going crazy."

A reassuring hand pressed between his shoulder blades. "Kenneth, what's going on?"

"...I want to tell you about what happened," he muttered to the floor, "but I'm afraid you'll think I'm having a breakdown or something."

"I won't," she promised. "What *happened?*"

Kenneth sat up and decided not to give himself time to think. It all spilled out of him: the photos on the Parkway, the paper, the police interview, the implication that the animals were connected to the dead girl left in her car on the side of the road.

And then this was the part where he had to put his head down again and just get the story out without looking at her face. In a jumbled rush of frantic words, he told her of the break-in: two people, one of whom *looked just like him.*

And the other who had eyes and hair like blood.

They were people, right up until they *weren't.* They had been standing there, and then it was as though they had simply winked out of existence, replaced by – by...

"I don't know what," he mumbled. "Not wolves. But they were the same color as their hair: black and maroon. I...I don't know what to think. They told me to stop publishing the photographs, and then they ran out of my house, and I think you ran into the maroon one."

He finally risked a glance at her, fully expecting her to look at him with utter disbelief...but Jacqueline was thoughtful, her mind working, brow drawn with concentration. "I want to ask you a few questions, just to make sure I understand."

"Okay."

"Do you believe the same animal you saw on the Parkway was the same animal that killed that girl? The one you say they reported on in the paper?"

"...I don't know."

"Do you believe the animal you took a photo of was the same animal that attacked you at Albert's tonight?"

"Yes."

"And there were two tonight, but you only saw one the first time. Do you believe they were the same *type* of animal?" He nodded. "And at multiple points in the attack, the animals disappeared and then there were *people* there instead?"

"...Yes." His cheeks burned admitting it, but he felt certain of what he saw.

"And one of them looked just like you."

"Better than me." He felt foolish. He studied the fibers in the rug to avoid her eyes. "A better *version* of me. Taller, for one. Stronger." A detail returned. "And he was hurt – there was something wrong with his leg."

"And at no point you saw the animals and the people at the same time? It was always one or the other?"

"Right."

"Do you believe that the animals *were* the people? That they were somehow changing back and forth?"

He cringed. "When you put it that way... It sounds ridiculous."

"Is it what you *believe* you saw?"

He ran his hands through his hair and stared firmly down at the rug. "I don't know what I believe."

"But you said you believe the black animal you saw at Albert's is the same you saw on the Parkway."

"So?"

"So logically, it must have followed you."

That was a horrifying thought. "...I guess."

"Then that's one hell of a smart animal."

"It could follow my scent, I guess."

"In a car? All the way from the Parkway?" She shook her head. "You said that during the attack, they were doing something to you and it hurt." She paused, chewing at her lip. "What did it feel like?"

"It felt like..." A word sprang up and he bit down on it,

embarrassed, and searched for something else. "It felt horrible. Like a hand was trying to rip something out of me. It was burning and cold all at once."

"Like something was touching your soul?"

Their eyes met. "I'm not sure I believe in souls, but...yea. That's a good way to describe it."

"And you think it was mainly the maroon one that was attacking you? And he had...*maroon* hair? Specifically? You're sure?" He nodded. "And you said you saw the shadows *move?*"

"Right."

"Is there any chance you ingested something by accident, something that might have made you see or hear things –"

He snorted. "This happened less than two hours ago. If I had, it would still be in my system and I'd be high right now. *No.*"

"Well, maybe we're both on drugs and just don't know it, because I think I met the same person in the woods, and I think *you* think I did, as well...and if I'm hearing you correctly, you're saying that person *turned into an animal.*"

It was Kenneth who broke the silence first; he tried to laugh, but it fractured into something that sounded almost like a panicked sob. "If I tell the police all this, they're going to think I'm insane. I – I can't talk to the police."

Jacqueline sat back down and picked up her cell again, turning it over in her hands. "We could call Eric," she suggested; she was equally troubled, her voice a low, uncertain whisper. "He could talk some sense into us, find a way to explain...this. Tell us what to do. What to say."

Kenneth shifted his weight uncomfortably. Eric didn't know he was back. "It's late..."

"He'll be up. He always is."

"Right, but..."

"...You haven't talked to him yet, have you?" Kenneth didn't reply, and Jacqueline stood abruptly, turning away from him. "I should have figured as much."

He felt shame claw its way up his throat. "I'm sorry about not calling," he whispered.

"Or texting?" Her words slashed at him, but she hadn't so much as raised her voice. There was a quiet indifference that cut so much deeper than anger. "Did you delete my texts after you read them, or did you let them just pile up on your phone?"

Kenneth sunk his head back into his hands; he wanted to throw up, to lock himself in the bathroom and curl up in the tub. Self-loathing wouldn't even allow him to look at her in order to apologize. "I never deleted them. I read them over and over again, on the days when I couldn't do anything else. I...I should have called you a long time ago. I'm sorry."

He looked up and saw that Jacqueline was smiling at him, but it was small, and it was sad.

"I wish you had," she allowed. She looked down at the phone. "But you're back now, and...and you did call. So there's that. Now it's my turn," she said brusquely, changing the subject. "Who am I calling: the police, or Eric?"

Kenneth squeezed his eyes shut, and chose.

He heard her on the phone as she talked in hushed, fervent whispers. When she was done, she came back and announced that Eric would be over within fifteen minutes. There was a new silence for them to fill; he decided to try and make small talk, distract himself from the stress that was pummeling the inside of his skull.

"What's Eric up to these days?"

"He's working as a vet tech, actually." His surprise must have registered. She nodded and pushed her hair behind her ears. "I know, he's not exactly an animal lover, but you know Eric. He's all logic and reason. He had money set aside from his parents' will for community college, so he chose 'the shortest program with the maximum yield.'" Her impression of him was spot-on: flat, vaguely superior. "So he lived for free with his aunt and worked full time while completing his program, pocketing all that money, and now he works as a vet tech and saves every penny he makes. You know what he really wants to do? He ever tell you?"

Kenneth shook his head; he appreciated her willingness to fill the silence rather than torture themselves with the wait.

"He's saving all that money so he can become an *investor*. A *venture capitalist*. The first time he told me, I laughed. I'm sorry I did, but it just seemed...so like him. What a dream, huh?"

"I guess...we all want different things out of life. That's fair, right?"

"The only thing Eric wants is to be rich."

Kenneth watched her fiddle with the ends of her hair. A strange shift in her tone caught him unawares, and before he could stop himself, he asked, "...Were you and Eric ever...?"

Her reply was merely a stare at him; he didn't need to finish the sentence, and she didn't need to respond. He could see the answer. He tried to hide whatever it was he was feeling (envy? Surprise, sadness?), but some of it must have showed. Jacqueline gave a grimace of confirmation. "It was *very* brief. A couple of weeks at the most. I love Eric as a friend, but he's...who he is. We couldn't work out if we tried."

"Did you try?"

"*No*. We were both happier as friends. We both moved on."

The brief conversation had taken a turn that Kenneth couldn't come back from. Neither of them spoke again until a knock at the door made them start. Woodenly, he rose, braced himself, and opened the door.

Eric Gallagher stared back at him with pale gray eyes underneath neatly combed red hair and nodded as if he'd just seen him yesterday, and it was not unusual at all to be summoned in the middle of the night by an ex-girlfriend and an ex-best friend who hadn't deigned to speak to him in years. "Kenneth."

"...It's been a while."

"Uh-huh." Eric pushed past him into the living room. Jacqueline moved forward and gave him a one-armed hug. A pang of jealousy hit him as Eric sat down, his face the same mask that Kenneth remembered. 'Calm' wasn't quite the right word to describe Eric; when he first met him as a kid, he thought Eric was a creepy loner who didn't speak and leered at everyone. He didn't *glare,* but he *stared.* Everyone knew his parents were dead and that he was poor and lived with a sick aunt; even Kenneth, who visited once a year, had heard it.

He was an oddball, and Kenneth, who was two parts insecurity and one part anxiety, found someone who existed like a black hole, someone capable of pulling all that negativity toward himself and making it disappear without so much as a smile, like he was the center of a void. Whatever interior life he had – if he had it – had always been well hidden. He was two years older and had known Jacqueline for a long time through some family connection, which was how they met more than a decade ago.

And despite the distance, the time, the silence, Kenneth had come to regard Eric as his best friend.

He was pretty sure Eric would have regarded him as his *only* friend, if not for Jacqueline.

"I'll get us drinks." Jacqueline disappeared into the kitchen, then left through the hallway to go to the garage.

Eric watched her go. "You know," he said, in the same, expressionless voice he'd always had, "She's leaving us in case you feel awkward and want to say something."

"Yea..."

Eric looked him full in the face, unbothered. "You don't have to say anything to me."

"Are you mad?"

"No. It's not that. I just don't think people owe each other explanations, is all. You live your life." And then, as an afterthought, "It's good to see you, though."

Kenneth burst out in laughter that hovered on the edge of true hysteria, and the ghost of a half-smile appeared on Eric's face.

A door shut. Jacqueline came in cradling three sodas in her arms and placed them on the coffee table.

"So, what's going on?"

She cleared her throat, sat down, and spread her hands flat on her legs. No one reached for a drink. "Kenneth and I both had something happen tonight. I'm going to let him go first, since I think he has more pieces of the puzzle that will help this make sense. I just want you to listen to everything we have to say and just...keep an open mind. Don't interrupt. And then tell us what you think we should do. I think we need to call the police, but the situation is... complicated. Okay?"

Eric blinked. Kenneth knew that was his cue and began to speak, surprising himself; it suddenly felt like old times again, with the three of them here. Even the night didn't seem so scary anymore, and the words came easy, though some sounded ludicrous even to his ears. When he finished, Jacqueline picked up the narrative, and when they were both through, they waited.

Eric regarded them before speaking. "Are you done?"

They nodded.

His eyes narrowed. "You both sound like fucking lunatics."

Jacqueline sighed. "You'll never change, will you?"

He shrugged. "You asked for my honest opinion. I don't know why you need it. *People* cannot change into animals. *Animals* cannot track a person *in a car* to their home address. *Shadows* do not move. Once you rule out the impossible, you have start thinking clearly about the situation. For instance, if the people broke into your home to scare the shit out of you, *why?* Why not just kill you?"

"I think the maroon one was going to, at one point. The other one...he stopped him."

"You mean the one who looks just like you?" Eric's tone was full of mockery. "It's not impossible for two people to look like each other."

"It was more than that." He was adamant. "He looked *exactly* like me, just...a better version."

"You said that. 'A better version' isn't *exact*."

Kenneth felt his throat closing against the effort to convey the horror of what he'd seen. "It was like looking into a nightmare. Like looking at a perfect version of myself that I'd never be."

Eric seemed almost embarrassed by Kenneth's display of emotion. He moved on. "So why didn't the maroon one kill you?"

"...I don't know."

"*Think*, Kenneth: what did they tell you to do? They didn't kill you because they need you to revoke permission to publish the photographs. That means they're worried about the police investigation, and they're not stupid enough to kill you because that would draw more attention to themselves. They still run the risk of you going to the police with the info, but they're probably banking on you fearing for your life, since they know where you live and threatened to kill you. Have you considered carbon monoxide?"

"*What*?"

"Carbon monoxide can make people hallucinate. So you weren't on drugs, but maybe they found a way to release gas into your home. Make you think you're seeing things."

"I'm seeing *people* change into *animals?*"

"No, but you might think you see *shadows moving* if you were under the influence of something and they were using light. Flash-lights, maybe."

Kenneth tried to hide his frustration. "They didn't have any flashlights."

"That you noticed," Eric countered. "I think it's likely that two men have trained some animals to attack people and are having a fun, sadistic time doing it, and they don't want you ruining the sport. If they're threatening you over the photographs, it's likely they're responsible for that girl's death."

"Then why don't the prints match anything that Fish and Wildlife has on file?"

"Either because they're manipulating the physical evidence that they can't help leaving behind, or because they found some unusual dogs in a pound somewhere that have odd proportions. Greyhounds mixed with wolves – who knows. It's *possible,* unlike the insane, cryptozoological bullshit you're implying."

"But the color –"

"People bring dogs into the clinic all the time with their fur dyed. It would make the animal more difficult to identify in case there were witnesses."

Kenneth glanced over at Jacqueline. She had wrung her hands in her lap and looked down at the floor, shaking her head. She didn't buy it.

But as for himself...he felt relieved. The way Eric put it, it all made sense. How could he have ever thought...? He swallowed, burning with embarrassment.

"Eric, it sounds so *right* when you put it that way," Jacqueline said quietly, but she continued to shake her head. "But I just don't think it's true."

Eric turned to him. "And what do *you* think?"

Two sets of eyes stared at him, waiting. He felt his palms grow slick with sweat and wiped them absently on his knees. "I know what I think I saw, but...I think Eric's probably right. It makes sense."

Jacqueline's eyes widened, then narrowed; she didn't bother to disguise the hurt and anger in her tone, her words clipped. "Okay. If that's what you think."

Eric continued. "I would report what happened at Albert's to the police. You can't let these people intimidate you, especially if they're responsible for at least one murder that you know of *and* they know where you live. That makes them a credible threat. Plus, you said that one of them was hurt. The police will want to know – he most likely got injured attacking someone. They might be able to revisit the scene and recanvas for his blood, or put out a bulletin asking if anyone knows of anyone with an unexplained injury. They can notify the hospitals to be on the look-out for anyone matching his description with an injury in their leg."

Jacqueline nodded in agreement, but although she found Eric's advice sensible, she was clearly annoyed. "I'm also going to report what happened in the woods. My description will match Kenneth's and support his story."

Kenneth said nothing; he knew Eric's advice was sound, but he still wasn't sure if he was going to speak to the police. Fear remained his conqueror, paralyzing him with indecision.

"And what was Albert doing the whole time, anyways?" Eric asked. "Was he passed out upstairs?"

Kenneth swallowed. "It's not Albert's place anymore. It's mine. He...he died."

Jacqueline sucked in her breath. Eric stared, then gave a slow nod.

"I'm sorry to hear that. I liked him."

Kenneth managed a wan smile. That was high praise from a man like Eric.

Eric's cell began to ring; he excused himself and went into the kitchen. In the silence, they heard something like surprise in Eric's voice, but that seemed almost as extraordinary as people who could turn into animals; Eric wasn't the type to be surprised by much. He dropped his voice, and it was a few more minutes before he returned, his expression troubled. "Seems like I'm having a busy night. That was...a friend of mine." Jacqueline shot Kenneth a knowing look. "She needs me to come help her with something." He turned to address Kenneth. "Call me if you need me for anything else. My number hasn't changed."

Kenneth walked with him to the front door; Eric paused in the doorway, the night nearly swallowing him. "...Keep all the doors locked. Call the police *now*; don't wait until tomorrow. If they're still out there, they might be able to apprehend them." His gaze slid over Kenneth's shoulder to where Jacqueline still sat in the living room, her back to them, and his voice dropped. There was a shift in his demeanor, a sharpening. "How nice it is for the two of you to have each other again," he said.

It was an impassive, cool remark, but Kenneth looked up sharply, wounded; was he imagining it, or was there an underhanded barb concealed within his words?

After he left, Jacqueline made the call, then set the coffee maker to brew. "We're going to be up for a while," she said, passing him a cup. Dispatch had said that officers were on their way and would be there shortly. "I'm sure the police will have lots of questions, and we need to decide how much we're going to tell them...about what we *think* we saw," she said, her voice thick with judgement.

Kenneth wasn't sure what he thought he saw...and he was fairly certain he wasn't going to talk to the police now, no matter what Eric said. They had threatened his life; they had already killed one person.

He didn't have Jacqueline's courage or Eric's good sense.

Kenneth only had fear, and a snaking darkness inside him that whispered to him that there was nothing he could do.

Jacqueline tucked her legs under herself on the couch. "As for me...there's one thing I can't shake. It's worrying me."

Kenneth looked down at his reflection in the coffee; misery stared back at him.

"What is it?"

"If the maroon one ran into the woods...then where did the black one go?"

But the night gave them no answers.

EIGHT

Kuro woke up to the sweet, familiar scent of musty hay and dirt. Something heavy stomped close by, snorting in agitation. He rolled over and pressed his ears against the ground, hoping it would *shut up*, but a distressed neigh shattered through the quiet of the early evening darkness.

His eyes flew open. He was in a barn.

He was in *the* barn.

He groaned and rolled over. *Why did I come here?* He thought. Weak moonlight filtered through the gaps in the wooden slats. He couldn't have been here long, but his sense of time had grown disjointed in a floating, hazy way. Dimly he recalled nudging the door open, slipping inside, the soft embrace of hay as he sank into the stall, the tang of his own blood still haunting the air...

He forced himself to sit up, momentarily surprised by the realization that he had woken as a human, the hay scratchy against his bare palms. He passed a trembling hand through his hair, his body leaden. *Why did I come here?* He asked himself again, but fever had robbed him of lucidity. He must have been in the grip of delirium; his fever had crested to a fiery high-water mark until the heat had transformed to chilling cold, and though he still burned and there was a slight quavering in his fingertips, the wave was retracting now. He was weak, sluggish...and starving, and that singular need had driven him back to this place.

The old mare in the stall across from him continued to shy and snort. She gave a half rear, her nostrils flaring, eyes rolling back in her head.

He closed his eyes and nestled down into the warmth of the hay.

The sound of tires crunching over gravel suddenly arrested his attention. He heard the car stop, the engine turn off; a door slammed.

Footsteps then. A front door opening, closing.

The girl.

You know what you have to do. He shifted his form, his claws extending and retracting, and the horse backed up to the very edge of her stall, swinging her head, her ears pinned back. *You can't go on like this.*

I can't...

You've killed things before. You've killed fish, raccoons, birds, even deer. You had to – you were hungry or attacked. Now you're both.

He stood, avoiding placing any weight on his injured leg. The mare neighed and reared again, her lips drawing back over crooked yellow teeth. Kuro slipped past her and paused at the door of the barn. He knew if he thought too much about what he had to do, he wouldn't have the courage to do it. He needed to be quick, then find his way back to the forest; he wasn't sure how long he'd been gone, but Jaden would return for him eventually. He would have medicine, Kuro told himself, and that would stop the burning in his leg, and the girl would be dead, and he would be able to feed again, and the photos would stop, the story would go away, and everything....everything would be alright.

And it all started now, with a torn throat.

He nudged his snout through the door and crept out of the barn, sparing a glance at the moon; it hadn't climbed much higher in the sky. Good: he hadn't been here long. He had plenty of time.

He slunk to the house, bracing himself for what was to come. If he could do it quickly, without giving himself time to think, if he could just push past the anxiety that was clawing up his spine and buzzing in his veins, it would be best.

You'll need to hide the body, afterwards, he told himself. *Or someone will find it, see the claws marks...everything Jaden wants will happen, and it'll be your fault.*

The thought of touching a corpse turned his stomach over. His mouth filled with saliva, and dimly he realized he was going to be sick. He fought the nausea, steeling himself, and won.

She had left her front door open, and behind it, the screen. From where he crouched in the darkness, he could see directly into a small kitchen; she had brought in a bag of groceries that now sat on a circular table just a foot from the door, and guessing by the way she turned, keys still in hand, she intended to come out and get the rest. He watched her for only a few seconds, his belly pressed down to the ground.

This was his chance. Already she had turned back to the front door.

He knew the moment she spotted him in the darkness. There was a startled gasp; Caroline dropped her car keys and lunged for a knife in the cutting block on the counter just as Kuro made it to screen door. He shifted forms, human hands throwing it open as she turned to face him, ready to defend herself. He ignored the bolting pain in his leg and moved faster than she anticipated, throwing his weight against her as he shoved her backwards against the counter. Her arm shot up, the knife flashing to attack him, but he was prepared for her: he grabbed her by the wrist, pressing against her more tightly, and forcibly slammed her hand against the wood.

She cried out but kept her hold on the knife; he caught her other, flailing arm, the nails aimed at his eyes, and yanked it down to her side. He used his full weight to pin her body, his legs between hers, and tightened his grip on her right wrist, crushing the soft tendon. There was a choking, surprised gasp, and then the knife clattered to the floor.

Kuro at last looked down at her expression; her terror had flowed out of her, wrapping all around him. He drank it deeply, like a man dying of thirst stumbling upon on a spring in the forest. To taste again, to *feed* again; he let his head tilt back as he breathed in deep satisfaction.

When he looked back down, she was staring at him, waiting and frozen... He just had to move quick, and her throat would open and blood would cover them both...

His thoughts must have been visible in his eyes; she cried out again and tried to wrench away, screaming. He held her tighter, caging her with his body so that his hips ground against hers, willing himself to do it, *do it now –!*

This close, her heat radiated against him; he could feel her pulse skittering beneath the delicate skin, feel her chest rising against him in short, frightened gasps. Her hair brushed against the underside of his jaw; he drew a ragged breath, breathing in her scent: lavender, the sharp spike of adrenaline and fear.

Her soul was intoxicating, overwhelming him. He looked down at her and swallowed; he could picture what she would look like dead on the ground, limp and unmoving, but he couldn't see himself walking out the door, away from her body, and living on as though it didn't matter to him. Jaden could do it: he could snap up a fish as easily as he could kill a person.

I can't do this, he thought. Her struggles increased; fear had sharpened her resolution to fight, and in his weakened state, it was taking more strength than he possessed to restrain her like this.

I have to, his mind argued back. *You HAVE to!*

I can't.

His grip loosened just a fraction.

Caroline yanked her leg up and kneed him hard in the bullet wound.

He released her at once and staggered back into the breakfast table, stars exploding in front of his eyes. A wooden napkin holder shaped like a mallard duck clattered to the ground.

She ducked and snatched up the knife she had dropped, brandishing it at him. He had sunk down onto his good leg, overcome by pain. Fresh blood flowed between his fingers as he pressed down onto the wound.

"Demon." She hissed the word through clattering teeth.

He reached out to the table for support, hauling himself up. She kept the knife held out directly in front of her, the widest possible distance between the two of them.

He managed to stand on shaking legs and hold up his hands, the bloody palms flat up. The pain in his leg nearly robbed him of speech, but he knew he had to try, even if nausea was drumming into his temple now. "I don't want to hurt you," he said.

Her chest heaved as she struggled to gain composure. "I don't believe you," she whispered.

He wasn't sure how to reply. He didn't need to reach out to feel her soul; it was pulsating, filling the entire space between them, always there whether he liked it or not, and her terror was huge, and growing. Fear, panic, and mistrust overflowed from her. He fed upon it, and the strength allowed him to speak a little easier. For the first time in nearly a day, the pain from his leg receded just a little; he could have wept in relief.

"I know. But I'm not going to hurt you. I... just need to talk to you."

"I don't believe you," she repeated. The knife hung in the air between them, six inches of accusing cold steel waiting to bury itself in his gut.

His mind raced, fighting against the pleasurable haze that was descending on him from drinking so much of her fear in. *I can't kill her, I can't do it...*and he hadn't planned for this contingency. He had no idea what to say, or what he hoped to accomplish beyond getting her soul to...to do what, exactly? *Let me go,* he thought. He needed her to release him somehow, and killing her was not an option.

At least, not an option he could choose.

So then he would have to dislodge her soul's grip on him somehow, and that would require her trust, or at the very least, her help. If he left without accomplishing that, he would only be back to where he started: starving in the woods, and then, either working up the courage to return to her and kill her without hesitation, or else submitting himself to his own death.

"How can I make you believe me?"

She didn't speak. Kuro noticed that the tip of the knife was trembling in the air in front of her as adrenaline unsteadied her arm. Her hair had fallen forward in a tumbling mess.

The knife jerked to the right. "Go that way. Into the living room. Slowly. And keep facing me."

He did as she said, scooting along the wall slowly a few steps until he came to the entrance of her living room, where the tile ended and the carpet began. In the small space, an armchair and an old couch each sat against one wall, a tall curio cabinet wedged into a corner. An old, vintage television perched on a low table, facing them.

"Back up."

He did, carefully, keeping his hands still high and open. She had yet to put the knife down.

Her purse had fallen from the table during the scuffle. She kicked it over, and still keeping the knife brandished toward him, she reached down slowly with her free hand, fumbling through the contents. First, her hand found a small canister of something with a wrist loop. She looked at it, glanced at him, then flicked off the lid, setting it close to her foot. Her hands groped again in the purse until they emerged, holding a pair of handcuffs.

She straightened back up. "Turn around."

Kuro felt his blood freeze at the prospect of being handcuffed again. "I won't hurt you," he tried, but she shook her head in fast anger.

"You attacked me," she repeated. "I don't trust you to not do it again. *Turn around*, or..." She reached down and grabbed up the small canister, pointing it at him. "I'm going to pepper spray you."

He didn't know what pepper spray was, but her tone suggested it was going to be painful. Well, he'd become an expert in misery; he'd endure whatever form this new suffering entailed. Mutely, he shook his head once more in protest.

Her eyes narrowed. Her grip on the knife tightened, and when she raised it again, the blade no longer quavered. "*No?* Fine. If you don't turn around, *I'll stab you*. I might not kill you – I don't know – but I *will* stab you."

He could feel the utter conviction of her words in her soul. She'd already shot him, and he had just attacked her in her own home; he paled, understanding the position he'd put himself in.

Kuro swallowed and did a passable job of hiding his own fear when he spoke. "If I turn around, will you promise to let me go after we speak?"

"...Yes."

His stomach turned over; he could feel the lie in addition to hearing it in her voice, but what choice did he have? *If you lunge at her now, you could still do it. You could kill her. Just clamp your jaws around her throat, sink your claws into her shoulders, tear down. She might get one good thrust in with the knife, but you'll survive that. You can't trust her; she can't trust you. Just end this in the quickest way possible...or you're going to starve. You're going to die.*

He swallowed again, blinking rapidly, trying to outthink her.

But her resolve was absolute. He felt underneath her own terror a firm center of self-preservation and courage, and he discovered with a maddening, sudden jolt, that he was every bit as afraid of her as she was of him. No, that was wrong: his skin prickled at the realization that *he* was far more afraid than *her*.

"I'll turn around." He was surprised to hear how distant his own voice sounded, the way it shook ever so slightly. "But only if you put the knife down."

"I'm not putting it down."

He eyed it anxiously. "Then just...just don't touch me with it. At all."

"I won't attack you if you cooperate." They both remained standing, rigidly fixed, waiting for the other to move.

Kuro's voice grew tight with apprehension. "I won't hurt you, but...there are things about me you don't understand. I can't touch that knife – and it can't touch me. It – it *can* touch me, obviously, but – it would... hurt."

The edge of the knife hovered a fraction lower. "What do you mean?"

His skin crawled. Everything in him revolted against divulging information, but on the other hand, the thought of the blade slipping and grazing his skin was too much to bear. "I – that is, we – can't touch human weapons."

"What happens if it touches you?"

He cringed away from her gaze. "It'll hurt me. That's all I want to say. Please just put it down. I just need to talk to you..." He was openly begging; her expression flashed with momentary surprise before narrowing with distrust again.

"Turn. *Around.*"

He did as he was told, staring out the little window into what appeared to be a garden on the side of the house, the details lost in the night's shadows. Trembling hands suddenly grabbed his wrists and pulled them backwards, and cold metal cut into the side of his skin as the cuffs pinned his arms behind his back. He felt his heart slam against his rib cage in terror; he tried to calm himself, to take one, two deep breaths, but his head buzzed with anxiety.

She stepped away, and Kuro turned to face her once more, his eyes searching for the knife.

It was on the floor, back where the carpet met the tile.

He let out a sigh of relief and allowed himself to sink down, his back leaning against the armchair. He stretched his bad leg out in front of him, groaning as the weight came off it.

She moved cautiously, her eyes never leaving him, as she sat down on the other side of the room. The space was so small that even opposite one another, only a foot separated them. He leaned back and closed his eyes, feeling her soul all around him; the terror had abated into watchful apprehension, and in its wake was confusion, alarm...but more than that, curiosity. Mistrust remained rooted, a lighthouse in an ocean of her anxiety.

"...Why did you come back?"

He opened his eyes and stared at her. He was surprised to see the effect it had; she jumped slightly.

"This will be....hard to explain."

"You're going to have to try."

He shifted his weight, twisting his wrists behind him; the cuffs were horribly uncomfortable, biting into him, and every time he felt their pressure, panic swelled. He looked up at the ceiling, trying to collect his thoughts.

"I need you to let go of me." The words tumbled out before he could give them sense or meaning.

Her brow furrowed. "I'm not touching you."

He shook his head, frustrated. "No, it's not like that...it's...I'm not good with words, and..." Her gaze had remained on him, steadfast, and oh god, it made his skin crawl. He could feel the bullet in him all over again. "And...you're making me nervous."

She gaped, incredulous. "*I'm* making *you* nervous?"

Kuro looked away, his face burning. 'Nervous' wasn't quite the right word; *scared* was apt, but he could never admit that out loud. He could barely admit it to himself. "You know how you need to eat to survive? And drink?"

A nod.

"I have to, as well. But there's something else I have to – have to feed on. It's not like eating or drinking, but it feels the same way."

He could see her mind working, processing everything as rapidly as her rational mind allowed her to grasp the situation, to make new sense of the impossible, challenging even her confidence and faith, but Kuro had no choice. He pushed on, cringing as he spoke.

"It's...it's your soul. It won't let go of me."

She stared at him for a long time without speaking. He risked a glance at her and discovered that she was staring in total disbelief. Kuro turned crimson and tried again. "I can feel people's souls – I feed off them. It doesn't *hurt* you anymore than taking a drink from the river would hurt the river, or an ocean. Maybe 'feeding' isn't the best way to describe it, since if you eat something, it's gone...but I don't take anything from you. It's just, anything you're feeling, I can feel – and some of it, I...consume. And I have to, or I'll starve."

She leaned forward, her hair falling over her shoulder. "Can you feel my soul right now?"

He nodded.

"How? I don't see anything...or feel anything."

He'd never had to put this into words for anyone before. "When I do it, it feels like my arms reach out, but I don't actually move. It's like some invisible part of me reaches forward and...and touches your soul." His face grew hot again; he fought the urge to throw up. "It's a lot like a garden; there're all the things you're currently feeling and experiencing on top, and they're the most visible, easily graspable... but you have all kinds of things inside of you, deeper down: your foundations...your roots. I can't see any of your memories or know your thoughts – just the feelings, and if I touch them deeply enough, I..." *I can make them grow,* he was going to say. *I can lift them up, amplify them.* Instead, he let the sentence trail off, unfinished.

She was shocked, he could tell, but she was handling it well; after all, she believed in demons with enough unquestioning certainty to *shoot him on sight.* Her mind wasn't moving from a state of disbelief to belief: it was simply updating something she already had faith in.

Somehow, that scared him even more.

"And you can feel *anyone's* soul?"

"I *could,*" he corrected. "That night, when you shot me...I felt your soul. I reached out to it, and fed from it, but...it did something that I don't understand. It reached out to *me*. It *touched* me." He shuddered at the memory of the feeling. "Human souls don't *do that*. You're...I think you're holding on to me."

Caroline stared at him in open amazement. "And you're... 'feeding' off of my soul... right now?"

He nodded, ill. "It's filling up everything, like it's all around me... I don't even have to reach to feel it. I don't understand what's happening." He hoped he didn't sound as terrified as he felt.

"What am I feeling?"

"Afraid, mostly." He closed his eyes and leaned into it, letting it wash over him, her fear helping to ameliorate his own. "You don't trust me. You probably think I'm lying. You're curious. At the center, you're resolved to stand your ground – you were really going to stab me, I think," he added. "I felt...conviction." He wasn't sure why he was telling her this much, but it came forth far more easily than he had expected. She was there, eager to listen and hear him; he couldn't remember Jaden ever listening to him this intently.

"You could probably guess all that, though." She folded her arms over her chest and leaned back, scrutinizing him. "What if I change how I'm feeling?"

"If you're asking me to prove I'm telling the truth, it would have to be a drastic change, wouldn't it?"

"Let me think of something," she said.

He watched her, waiting. Her eyes swept over him, and between them, the tension grew. Finally, her gaze settled on the wooden mallard napkin holder that had fallen in the kitchen when he crashed into the table. She stared at it for a long time, her eyes lingering on its details: the chipped paint, the upturn of the tail.

A surge of love and longing hit him with such astonishing force that he gasped and pitched sideways, curling in upon himself. It felt like knives had slipped through his ribs and pierced right into his lungs. He tried to shove her soul away, but its grip remained firm.

"*S-stop*," he begged. "Whatever it is, *please* stop..." An overwhelming urge to scream stole upon him; he convulsed with the effort to fight it back and control himself.

Hands suddenly pressed themselves against his forehead, pushing away damp bangs. He realized he was shaking with humiliation. A sudden rush of concern stabbed down at him, a sword into his gut this time; he choked again, bereft of air, and pushed away from her. Bile rose in the back of his throat.

"Not that," he groaned. He kicked away feebly, staring up at the ceiling. "Don't feel that way – I don't want your pity, or concern. It *hurts*." *Hurt* was an understatement; it felt like acid had been pumped into his veins, burning him right through to the nerves. He wanted to crawl out of his skin to escape the torture.

Caroline sat back, her hands limp in her lap; she struggled to reel in her emotion; as she wrestled it down, the burning feeling receded. "What happened?"

He swallowed. His tongue felt thick in his mouth. He kept his eyes tightly shut as he struggled to push away from something he couldn't see as the soul continued to suffocate him. "I can consume some things...not others. Other things are like *poison*. Love," he groaned. "Whoever made the napkin holder, you love them...powerfully. Please think of anything else – think about how much you hate me," he pleaded. That would burn, too, but nothing like this internal flaying.

She bit her lip, her gaze glancing back down toward her empty hands. "I don't hate you."

He sighed. "It would be easier for me if you did. I can't *not* feel your soul – it's all around me. I've gone from dying of thirst to – to *drowning*. Please, just let me *go*. I'll never come back. You'll never see me again." He could hear the desperate plea in his own words, a prisoner begging for his own liberation.

She shook her head. "I don't know how to let you go. To me... nothing feels any different."

"Try anything. Try to make yourself feel differently, or...or shove me away. Try *anything*." He still lay on his side, blinking rapidly; all the colors in the room had melted together, like watercolors.

She looked at the unshed tears in his eyes and nodded. Around him, he felt her soul collectively shiver, like a living thing shaking off a gentle frost. It lingered before him like the heavy scent of perfume, and despite its poison, he couldn't control the way he drank from it now, tasting the edges of it to feed on the pockets of feelings where he could. It snaked around him, winding between him, touching the edges of his consciousness as it shifted its hues, rapidly shuddering through fluctuating emotions as it forced itself upon him: love, hate, envy, fear, pride, uncertainty, greed, rage, joy – it all came and went, a chameleon of feeling, tantalizing him, touching him, filling him until he rolled over completely and arched into it, desperate to be free of it and willing to lay himself down, abject and wholly a slave to it, if only it would give him those exquisite hues of sadness and fear again, if only it would *let him go* –

"How about now?"

Her voice sounded as though it had come to him from the end of a long hallway. He opened his eyes like a man coming out of a deep, troubled sleep.

It was still all around him, still holding onto him, flowing into him. He could neither shut himself to the pain, nor deny himself its pleasure. This wasn't like feeding from a person.

This was something new entirely, and it had him at its mercy.

NINE

Helplessly, he shook his head.

"I'm sorry, Kuro." It unsettled him, how naturally she said his name. She looked down at him. "I tried to imagine myself curling into a small ball, or reeling in a fish...I tried to think of everything and just hold it in as tight as possible, but it didn't feel all that different from how I feel now. Did you feel anything change?"

Once more, he shook his head in mute wretchedness.

"...How's your leg?"

He looked over at her and stared. "My *leg*?" His eyes rolled upward; he wanted to laugh, but he lacked the energy. "My leg is the least of my problems."

"...Can I see?"

"I can't refuse, can I?" He gave a hard twist of his arms, wincing as the metal bit into his wrists.

She brushed the hair from her face with a fake casualness. Her eyes looked away from his stare. "Hold on." She stood up, walked to the purse, rummaged in the spilled contents, and pulled up a small key, then returned and knelt beside him.

"Roll onto your side."

He obeyed, feeling the pressure release as the lock sprung open. His hands came apart just as she moved back, waiting to see what he would do.

He lay there, sighing. An island of cautiousness had surfaced in her sea of misgiving, and on the island grew a seed of trust – tempered by a veritable forest of apprehension.

"...Now may I look at your leg?"

He lay on his back and carefully stretched it out toward her, watching her movements. Caroline leaned over him gingerly, touching the edges of his pants.

"Kuro...this looks infected." Cool fingers pressed into the flesh; her eyes widened as she sucked in a breath. "Why did you take the gauze off?" She tried to lift the frayed fabric, but it was stiff with the mixture of dry and fresh blood. She examined his face now, her expression shifting into one of alarm as she studied him more closely. "You don't look well, either...your skin is hot. How far has this redness gone up your leg? If the infection is spreading..." The way the words lingered hinted at dark consequences to come. She tried to lift the torn edge of the pant near the wound, but the dried blood had crusted securely against the edge, and he flinched.

"Sorry. I can't get a good look."

He opened his mouth to speak, closed it, then tried again, his mind dizzy with fear but desperate for help. "I...I could show you what I look like, and then you'll be able to look at the wound. That would be easier."

She straightened up, her eyes wide again. She pulled her hands back instinctively. "You mean – what you really look like?"

He nodded, sick with anxiety. He knew he shouldn't do this, but... "Just promise not to hurt me."

"Hurt *you*?" He felt the flare of indignation, but he glanced back at the knife on the ground.

"If you become scared. Just don't panic. I won't move – and I won't hurt you," he said. "I...I need help," he finished. His voice came out weak, terrified even. "Medicine. I don't know. *Please.*"

Pity moved in her soul again; it would have robbed him of breath if not for the guilt that followed past, growing in its wake.

She lowered her eyes and nodded.

Kuro found it hard to look at her anymore. He shivered, and with a sense of letting go of something, he shifted, closing his eyes.

He heard a quiet, stifled gasp.

For a long while, Caroline didn't move. He was right; her immediate reaction was fear, and an overwhelming need to protect herself...but he remained still, as still as he could, his body stretched along the carpet of her living room.

He felt two things at once; first, the giving way of terror into awe, followed by the soft, tentative touch of her hands on his back leg. He hadn't realized he was holding his breath; he exhaled at her touch, and the rise and fall of his chest drove her away, but only for a moment. Her hands reached forward again, the fingers sliding between his fur. Cautiously, he extended his back leg a little more, stretching it out toward her. Gentle, probing hands felt around the edges of the wound, pressing. He let out a wheeze of pain, controlling himself just enough to prevent all but the twitch of his tail.

"If I wrapped it in fresh gauze, would the bandage stay on, when you...when you change?"

I don't know.

"Oh!" She nearly fell backward, catching herself. "Your voice... was it in my head?"

If someone else was here, they would be able to hear it, too.

"Oh...I see..." She stood up. He felt her footsteps walk past him as she told him to wait. Within a minute she was back, kneeling closer, lifting up the leg and pulling it forward over her lap. Nervousness had blossomed and taken root, and she spoke to him as she cleaned the wound with a cold, cooling gel-like substance.

"It's infected, Kuro; this is just a first-aid ointment. It's not going to do much, but it's better than nothing. You definitely need to see a doctor, I think. You need this flushed, you need stitches, and antibiotics, and you need to keep off it –"

I can't go to a doctor. I don't know what would happen...

Her soul was thrown into sudden turmoil; guilt and shame buffeted him, calming him even as she spoke more quickly, her breathing shortened. "I have a friend, a good friend, actually, who works at the vet clinic. He's taking care of Feral – you really gave him a few good scratches, you know. I mean, I don't blame you, and he's okay, he just needed some stitches on one wound on his back. It's nothing compared to...to this. When you dug into your leg with your fingers, you...you tore yourself up a lot. I might be able to get him to come over and help, even if this is a little...unconventional." Shaking hands pushed a fresh wad of gauze deep into his thigh, then wound it tight, over and over with a stretching bandage that she secured with metal clips.

"Feral bit you pretty good," she whispered. Her hands passed over his leg, feeling the marks and punctures her dog had left beneath his fur. Kuro shuddered under her touch, feeling the gentle weight of her palm pressing down. Entranced, her fingers slid up through his fur, gliding over the silky expanse; without thinking, he rolled onto his back, his paws hovering above his chest.

She touched them gently, pressing her fingers against the soft pads, slipping her thumb over the silver claws. Her fear had abated now, lost in a sea of amazement; it tingled in a slowly burning way, half-pleasure, half-pain. His liquid black eyes opened and stared at her; she was oblivious to his gaze as her hands moved, sliding up his front legs toward his throat, feeling the soft ruff that gathered there. She caught him staring at her and moved to pull away, her face flushing.

In an instant, he had changed back. Her left hand remained flat on his human chest, her fingers splayed, the rumpled surface of his shirt now where his fur had been.

He clasped her right hand in his own grip, arresting its withdrawal.

"Please," he said, his voice thick. He shivered. He didn't know what he was asking for; he wanted her soul to let go of him; he wanted her to help him save his leg.

He wanted to feel her hands pass over his body – his *human* body – again.

No one had ever touched him like that, or seen him as he was for that matter; no one had looked at him in awe and wonder before, and the feeling had clouded his senses and left him dazed, prone under her hands. The hot pain in his leg felt distant now. *It's the fever,* he thought suddenly, his mind confused, swimming.

She blushed, but she didn't pull her hand away. "You...you're beautiful." She looked away, unable to meet his stare. "What *are* you?"

"*Kitsune.*" He let her hand go and let his arm fall to the ground. He shifted forms, and once more, the tremendous fox lay before her. There was no transition, no growing and retracting, merely the blink of an eye, and one form was exchanged for another. He rolled over so that he lay on the ground, the tip of his nose pointed toward the doorway, his long tail flowing out behind him. From the kitchen, the mallard duck stared at him with one eye. *A demon fox.*

"A demon fox who feeds on human souls," she repeated, her voice slow, marveling. She let out a long breath. He closed his eyes in secret enjoyment as she absently passed her hand down his back, feeling her fingers move through the fur. Her hand lifted and came back, starting at the scruff of his neck and moving down toward the base of his tail, like one would pat a dog, lost in her own thoughts. "Can I ask you a question, Kuro?"

He nodded. The movement was enough to startle her hand away; he fell still again, and it returned.

"...That was you in the paper, wasn't it? That picture they published?"

He let out a long hiss. Her fingers gripped his fur, startled, and he stopped. *Yes. That was me.*

"What happened?"

I was just curious about the person, is all. I didn't realize he had a camera. I was stupid and careless.

"Were you going to attack him?"

His jowls drew back; silver fangs glimmered as he bit down on his bitterness. *No.* He drew the word out in one long, frustrated growl.

"...Are you planning to?"

Concern entered her soul; he hated it and wanted it to go away. *No,* he said again, restraining the menace from his voice. *Why – do you know him?*

"No, but if I were you, I'd be upset about it, so it's a reasonable question. Did you know they published a second photo of you?"

Yes, I saw it. They think I killed that girl.

She opened her mouth; a question started, but stopped, hanging in the air. He could feel her forcing herself to go on. "...Did you?"

I already told you: no.

"You could have been lying."

If I told you 'no' again, I could be lying now, too.

"I know. That's why detectives ask the same questions, over and over again; lies can be difficult to keep track of. Sometimes the truth slips out. Do you know who – or what – killed that girl?"

He froze absolutely still. He understood what she was doing. Her soul was pulsing around him, burning him, *seeping* into him. His tail moved once, slowly to the right, and then again, carefully to the left.

No, he lied.

She let out a long breath of relief. He felt, more than anything else, a curious sense from her that she *wanted* to believe him.

"So the tracks near her car – those weren't yours?"

He had hoped lying got easier the more he did it, but it was equally as difficult to whisper a second, convincing *no.*

"I suppose it wouldn't make sense to kill something you could keep feeding on, would it?"

No...I suppose it wouldn't.

"Then why did you attack me?"

His ears swiveled around. He turned to face her, the dark pools of his eyes drinking in her expression of amazement. *I thought I would kill you, to get your soul to let go of me. But I...I couldn't.*

Her hand stopped its movements. The waves of pleasure ceased. "But I can't get my soul to let go of you. So...now what?"

The edge of fear had returned. Kuro turned away from her and let his head fall back onto the carpet in a forlorn sigh. *I don't know. I told you, I'm not going to hurt you.* As good, as satisfying as her fear was, as much as it strengthened him...it annoyed him, too. He didn't like the way her eyes darted back to check the location of the knife, the way she started at his slightest movement, and he wasn't sure why. He had far more to fear from her than she from him. *I could make you a promise,* he said rashly, with a note of anger. *I could promise that I won't attack you.*

"How could I believe you?"

Demons can't break promises.

"Or touch human weapons?"

Yes.

"How do I know that's the truth, that you're not just making it up?"

Hm. He huffed, annoyed. *I'm not making it up.*

"You're asking me to just believe you."

His tail swished, annoyed. *Yes. I'm asking you to just believe me.*

"How about this: what if I touch you with the knife and see what happens? If you're telling the truth about that, I'll assume you're telling the truth about not being able to break a promise."

His reaction was immediate. He shifted to a human and scrambled back against the wall as fast as he could, pressing hard against it. The pain in his leg from the sudden movement was excruciating.

"*No.*"

"Okay." She put her hands back in her lap, studying him. It

dawned on him what he must look like to her: a frightened animal, pressed into a corner, ready to spring and yet too terrified to run. "I'm sorry I suggested it. Will you...promise me, then?"

He glared, and the words came out in an almost inhuman growl. "I promise I won't attack you."

"What happens if you break your promise?"

He drew his leg toward him, gritting down on the pain; the bleeding had begun again. Already he could see the first shadow of blood swelling beneath the fresh gauze. "It depends on the nature of the promise. Nothing good will happen to me – that's really all you need to know." The adrenaline left him. He relaxed a fraction. Her fear had receded, and with it, a rush of excitement and wonder had moved in. It made him feel nauseous. "I think it's fair if I get to ask you a question, now. Why did you shoot me?"

Caroline was too absorbed in her own thoughts to answer him. He noticed she was pointing at his leg. The bandage hadn't changed, and the diameter of his leg being different, it now hung lose over his thigh. "Your clothes...they just...appear? Where do they go when you change? I was touching *you*. If I put the bandage on you as a human, would it disappear when you turned back into a – a *kitsune?* Are the clothes even real? Are they..." Her eyes widened, horrified. "Are the clothes *your skin?*"

"The clothes are just clothes," he muttered. "They just –" *What was the word Jaden used?* "If I have something on me for a while, it'll sort of 'click' with me. *Resonate*, I think," he continued. It was coming back to him now. "So if I get some new clothes and keep them on me for a while and give them time to resonate, when I change, they just...assimilate." She was staring at him again in that openly amazed way that left him feeling much too exposed. "So they disappear, but nothing ever really...disappears. I still carry them with me. If I had something that was too strong to assimilate – if it had too much of someone else's imprint, like the way a person's scent lingers – it wouldn't disappear. With the bandages, they're just too new. I would need to leave them on for a while."

Caroline frowned. "But even then, say you *did* leave them on as a human for a while, when you changed back to yourself, the bandages would disappear. They would assimilate...so effectively, you'd have no bandage on."

"...Probably. But this is also *myself*," he corrected. "It's just...a different way I can look." She was still staring at the bullet wound. He put one palm over it, self-conscious. "You didn't answer my question. Why did you shoot me?"

"Oh." She looked up at him, hesitating. Her eyes reminded him so much of a doe: soft, liquid, with a gentleness that belied the fact that she had shot him, then threatened him with a knife. She blinked and looked away, her voice suddenly hoarse; sorrow and regret welled up in her soul, flowing into him like cool, spring rain. He let out a breath of grateful air, relishing it.

"...My brother came back. He's not here often, but he visits when he can. All his life he's been...different. Things have troubled him. I don't want to talk about it. Anyways, he came back suddenly, and he was so upset... He was pleading with me to come with him. He lives in South Carolina right now. I told him no. He said there were 'things' in the woods. He was frightened out of his mind."

She was nervous; her words sped up. "He grabbed me, shook me, shouted at me, pointed at the woods, and said demons were behind the trees, that I had to go. But he's said these kinds of things before. We've – my parents, that is – sent him to get help when he was younger. He takes medication. I told him if he was so scared, he could stay with me and protect the place. You would have thought I slapped him." She looked down at her hands, ashamed. "I shouldn't have said that. This place holds nothing but bad memories for him. It's not healthy for him to be here. He said he couldn't, and he asked me to promise him that I wouldn't go outside without a gun, and he gave me his. I guess, like you, I couldn't bring myself to break that promise. Then he left. And there I was, up on the roof – I go up there to think, and... I saw you. From a distance, you looked almost like a wolf, but I knew that wasn't right. We don't have wolves here –

and definitely not solid black ones. You looked huge, but your legs, your tail...everything about you was unlike anything I'd ever seen before. I couldn't make sense of that at the time. It's like when adrenaline hits you, and there's no time to think. There's just the immediate reaction. It felt like everything was upside down and only the impossible made sense, because where the animal had been – where *you* were – there was suddenly *a person,* and in that moment...I believed everything he ever said. I went on autopilot. I picked up the gun...and I didn't stop to think. And I shot you." Her voice grew quiet. "And I'm sorry."

"...So your brother was right, in the end." She looked up, confused. "About there being demons in the forest."

She managed a weak smile. "Well, there's one, at least. Is there more of you?"

Another chance to lie, to hone his skills at deception. "No."

"Mm." She stood up and began to walk to the kitchen. "Listen, I want you to make me another promise."

He snorted. "No."

She ignored him. "Promise me you won't leave until my friend looks at your leg. I know he'll come over if I ask, and he can help you; he can do stitches, give you medication. I just need to call him and –"

"*No.*"

She turned, puzzled. "Kuro, you're badly hurt. It's clearly infected, and you can't keep a bandage on; you need stitches. You *mutilated* the wound, and I can see you have a fever from here. You need –"

"No. One human knowing about me is one too many."

"*Human?*" She recovered, then plowed on. "He doesn't have to know what you are. All he'll see is a person, and he can give you all the help you need. I'll make up a plausible reason why you can't go to a hospital."

"*No.*"

"Why not?"

Her frustration nipped at him. He wished he could push her soul away. "I told you, my leg is the least of my problems. It'll heal. I need to figure out how to get your soul to let go of me."

She turned to face him, her shoulders set for an argument. Strangely, she was upset. "You'll die from that infection long before starving becomes a problem."

They glared at one another. Kuro felt an idea form in her before she even felt it herself; a new rush of adrenaline had caught her, galvanizing her soul. She stooped suddenly and picked up the knife in the doorway.

"What are you doing?"

"I'm threatening you." He could feel that she was nervous, but determined. "And you promised you wouldn't attack me, so you'll just need to sit down now."

Kuro recoiled against the wall, his mind racing.

He had to get out of here.

Caroline kept one eye on him and picked up the phone, dialing, but his vision had narrowed to just the knife. He didn't even hear the conversation; his mind worked, assessing the situation, seeking some escape. The only door into the home was in the kitchen. It was maybe six, seven strides to the kitchen from the living room, if that, then another six or seven steps to the door. He would be moving fast, running: twelve steps, then.

I don't think she'll stab me. Her soul was still everywhere, and a radical shift had occurred in its movements in the last half hour. He didn't understand why, or how, or even precisely *when,* but just as certainly as he knew earlier that she *would* have stabbed him, he knew now that she *wouldn't.*

But then again, she wouldn't need to. His skin crawled at the thought of the blade touching him even slightly. And what if she lunged at him, and he pushed her aside? *I would be defending myself – would that count as attacking?* He tried to think like Jaden, reaching for cold logic to comfort him. *An attack is offensive. Defending myself ISN'T attacking. But if I lunge first, is that still defending?*

He didn't have the intellect to puzzle it out. His muscles

bunched as he prepared himself. *So this is what it comes down to: which one will be less painful, breaking the promise, or touching the knife?* He'd never broken either taboo before; even the contemplation of the transgression was enough for his instincts to kick into jolting alarm, flooding him with cold dread.

The knife, he decided. He would have to be like Jaden, after all: Jaden wouldn't be afraid of a little pain.

Caroline hung up the phone. "He says he can be here in an hour, after he goes home to get some supplies. He's at a friend's place." She turned to him, her arm still outstretched, and watched as he drew to his full height, tensing.

Kuro stepped forward.

Caroline's eyes flashed. "Kuro, I'm warning you – just sit down."

Another step. "You won't stab me."

Her free hand reached out, gripping the back of a kitchen chair. "According to you, I won't have to."

A third step, a fourth. "I'm going to leave now." He wanted to get as far as he could without running, catch her by surprise.

"That won't solve anything!" The knife rose higher. "It won't solve your problem, and it doesn't change that you'll have to come back or – or that you could die if you don't get help!"

Two more steps brought him to the tile. To his surprise, she stepped back in succession, backing up to the kitchen sink. He felt stronger; she was suddenly terribly frightened, but he couldn't understand why. He wasn't trying to threaten her, though he walked with steady sureness, hands down at his sides, and yet her eyes were almost wild, her lips pressed together, and her free left hand was reaching next to her, in the drawer closest to the sink –

She pulled out the handgun and pointed it at his chest.

He froze, the wind knocked out of him in shock as terror slammed a cage down upon his mind.

"Kuro." She drew a shuddering breath. Carefully, she placed the knife down on the counter and brought the gun up, holding it with both hands. "You're going to sit here. You're going to get medical help. You're going to stay."

He took one stumbling step backward, the caught himself. "So you're going to just point that gun at me for an hour?"

She advanced to the carpet; he flinched with every step. "If that's what I have to do."

"And then when your friend gets here? What will he think? What will you *say*?"

Her gaze was unwavering. "I have an hour to figure that out."

Panic electrified him now; his gaze careened wildly around the room and landed on the kitchen chair.

It was a gamble, but if he could shift and run past her, he could upend the chair and trip her up. It could give him the extra second he would need to shift to a human, open the front door, and run into the night. If she was unwilling to stab him, she surely wouldn't shoot him again, and the reach of the gun was far shorter. He could get past her.

He had to.

He flung himself forward, shifting at the same time. He moved under her arms to the right, whipping his tail under him as she turned, crying out his name. Too late; his tail caught the chair and sent it crashing to the ground, and she stepped forward, her knees colliding with it. From the corner of his eye, he saw her fall.

The door! He reached forward with a human hand, gripping the doorknob, yanking it open.

The warm comfort of a humid night and the sweet scent of late summer pines greeted him with its open arms, promising freedom.

And then something struck him in the back, and white, explosive pain knocked him out cold.

TEN

K uro was certain he must have screamed at least once, because his throat felt as though the inside had been raked by thorns when he awoke. He was lying on his back on the kitchen tile, and hands kept pushing his hair away and saying something – *my name?* – but everything was too bright and too loud and *spinning...*

The initial pain had cracked through him like a blow to the skull, but behind it stretched lingering, burning fire in his body. He groaned, his hand groping for something to steady him. Hard wood met his efforts. He pulled on the table leg, hauling himself to his side, and vomited on the floor.

Caroline's voice cut through the fog. "Oh my god, I'm so sorry..."

He wanted to ask her if she had shot him again, but it was too difficult to speak, and fear was choking him with dizziness even as the colors continued to spin around him. Was this to be his life, then? Tortured relentlessly by this *human...*?

He tried to stand, a bolt of lightning shooting through his leg, and crumpled to the floor, defeated at last.

She kept saying something over and over, but the sound couldn't quite reach him. Everything in him – the fight, the energy, even the panic – was gone, his vision narrowed just to the tile in front of him now as he stared at the floor. Dimly he became aware that something was happening to him, some animal *thing* that he could no longer fight against.

Shock. He was going into shock.

His body began to relax, but his heart continued to race. He squinted at the watercolors of her face, trying to understand what she was saying, and found the effort too taxing. And his head...the disorienting whirling wouldn't stop. He leaned over and wretched again, a weak stream of clear fluid.

"Kuro, you're going to be okay, you're okay..." She didn't sound like she believed it.

A hand reached out to touch him. He gasped and jerked away, bumping against the table.

"*Why?*" Why did she keep doing this to him? He didn't want to hurt anymore; he wanted to be in his forest, safe and whole, the sweet scent of moss cradling him at last. The blood in his ears was roaring.

"I didn't want you to go, you need *help*, but I...I didn't understand..."

He doubled over; a surge of fire seemed to rise again in his stomach and spread up toward his head. He cried out, arms wrapping around himself as he pressed his head against the cool kitchen tile.

She was there again, arms on either side of him, helping him to stand. He managed three fumbling steps into the living room before sinking down onto the floor, gasping.

He'd cut the leg off, he decided. He'd never run again, but at least the pain would be gone.

It was a few minutes before she returned. The blood in his ears was moving slower now, a steady whooshing that left him feeling hollow, and his pulse had grown erratic. He fought the urge to heave, his legs drawing close to him.

He lay on his side, gasping. Something cool touched his forehead. He opened his eyes to see her lifting his bangs, felt the momentary shock of a wet washcloth placed against his skin.

"Focus on this."

He convulsed a final time and fell still. She moved closer, lifted his head, and held him so that he was pillowed in her lap. Hesitatingly, she reached down and began to stroke his hair.

"I threw the gun at you. It hit you in the back. I didn't know what else to do." Her voice was barely audible. "I didn't want you to leave."

His words were slurred. "...I feel...like I've been shot...and burned..."

Her hand stopped moving. "...I'm sorry. The gun wasn't even loaded."

He groaned. That only made him feel worse. Another surge of fire moved through his veins.

"You're still shaking...you'll be alright..."

Kuro closed his eyes. Slowly, things began to still: the sound in his ears, his heartbeat, even the air seemed to settle into a hot calm. Caroline had resumed stroking his hair; he focused on the movement of her fingertips as they drifted to the back of his neck and then lifted, returning to his bangs. All but the pain in his leg began to fade away, but his energy was spent.

"You're burning up," she whispered. "...Kuro?"

He moved his head against her thigh, comforted by her heat, and opened his eyes into a squint.

"I want you to know, I promise I won't do that again. You can get up, right now, and leave if that's what you want."

It was an effort just to speak. "I couldn't get up and walk out of here if I wanted to." He was so tired now. He didn't even have the energy to push her away. What he really wanted to say was, *a human's promise is worthless,* but instead he turned his face away, shivering as she stroked his arm in long, cooling passes that raised the hairs on his skin.

Fifty minutes crawled by in hushed silence until a knock came at the door. Caroline started, put his head gently down on the floor, and left him to go answer it. The smell of pines drifted inward, this time accompanied by night-blooming jasmine.

Voices, footsteps, and then a young man paused at the entrance to the living room. Kuro had never been good with ages, but he would have guessed he was in his mid-twenties. He had red hair – the normal, human hue closer to orange – above gray eyes so pale that they could have been considered colorless. His face was smooth and drawn, with an expression of someone who had never laughed easily or smiled often. He wore a brown jacket over denim pants, and in his hands he carried a small but bulging leather bag.

He came to an abrupt halt, the blood draining from his face, his eyes going huge. Kuro stared back at him and felt his own heart freeze.

The man choked out a single, indistinguishable word.

They looked at one another for an unnatural length of silence, neither able to look away.

Caroline joined him in the doorway. "Eric, this is...this is my friend. He's – are you alright?"

Eric was not alright; his mouth had fallen open. He crossed the threshold into the living room in a jerky motion, as though he were a puppet whose strings had become tangled. He swallowed, but a tremor had begun in the tip of his right index finger. One swift glance passed over Kuro, lingering on the bloody wound in his right thigh, and the tremor progressed up to his wrist.

Eric drew a sharp breath and snapped his jaw closed with a force that Kuro heard from where he lay. He watched as Eric slowly flattened his palm against his thigh; it was an act of pure, dominant will, the trembling conquered. His features smoothed out into flat, calm assurance...*almost*. Kuro thought he saw a twitch at the corner of his right eye, one small, broken bit of gadgetry in the clockwork of his brain.

Eric recovered himself, but the awkwardness of the moment

lingered. Something had flashed in his eyes, but whatever it was, it dove down into some hidden cavern in his soul and remained unacknowledged. "I'm fine," he said. His voice was impassive, uninterested; he was entirely unruffled now, as if nothing had disturbed him whatsoever. He walked fully into the room, all smooth polish, and knelt beside Kuro. "I was just thinking your friend looks a lot like someone I know."

Caroline nodded and joined him.

"My name is Eric. You are...?"

Kuro used the last of his strength to push himself up so that his back leaned against the couch. He stared at Eric. An uneasy feeling was growing in him; he was almost certain there had been a flash of recognition in Eric's stare...

"Kohl."

"Kohl. *Kohl*," he repeated, as though testing its weight. "Nice to meet you. I don't know if Caroline explained this to you, but I'm not a doctor or a nurse. I'm a vet technician." He spoke in a dry, matter-of-fact tone. "This means that I cannot give you the best medical care, or even technically legal medical care. I'm assuming that you have reasons to avoid the hospital beyond not having medical insurance. Is that correct?"

Caroline wrung her hands. Kuro nodded.

"It would be best not to tell me those reasons so that I can maintain plausible deniability. What do you need help with?"

"He's been shot in the leg," Caroline said. Kuro wasn't imagining it; he was certain he saw a flickering in Eric's expression, that twitch again that he clamped down on, but only for a moment. He wished he could feel the man's soul, see where that expression led to. Eric looked down at Kuro's leg as Caroline continued. "We already removed the bullet."

Eric gave no indication of surprise. He merely stared for a long time at the wound in Kuro's leg, silent. Kuro wondered what it would be like to feel his soul – he theorized it would either run very,

very deep, or else be too shallow to feel much of anything at all. There would be no in-between with someone like him.

"When was he shot?"

"A few nights ago."

Eric looked up from the wound to study Kuro's face; Kuro tried not to jolt, but his skin crawled. "Have you been here since that incident?"

He had no desire to speak to this man, but if it would potentially save his leg.... "No."

Caroline was quick to jump in. "He was shot in the woods, and I was the closest home for help. I did what I could, but he left before I could stop him."

Eric hadn't turned to look at Caroline. He continued to scrutinize Kuro, his stare unblinking, focused. "Where did you go?"

This time, Kuro did not reply.

Instinct told him not to trust this man.

Caroline answered for him; he could feel her anxiety climbing. "He tried to get back to the road and head home, but he was in bad shape. He got lost and came here for help."

Eric continued to ignore her. "You look like you're not doing so great. I would have thought you were shot a few hours ago, at most. You look like a dog that's been in shock."

At last, he turned away; Kuro let out a quiet rush of air, flexing his fists.

Eric set his bag down and pulled out a small medical kit, drawing on a pair of gloves.

"Please remove your pants."

It was a struggle; the fabric had dried into the crusted blood, and removing them meant ripping the scab (which in sections was as hard as a black beetle's shell) forcibly off his skin. He yanked and felt the stinging, tearing sensation, grinding his teeth with his ineffectual struggle. If he could stand, it would be easier, but the fabric fought to lift away from his flesh.

"Never mind – hold still." Eric opened the kit and brought out a pair of scissors. "Moving like that may open the wound up further. I'll just cut them off."

He worked from the bottom hem at his ankle up to his waist, shearing through the fabric. Even split open, it was difficult to peel the top flap off his thigh, but Eric had no regard for his pain; with a sudden, almost vicious tug, he yanked the fabric away from the wound, and fresh blood began to trickle once more.

Eric paused for a thoughtful second at the sight of his blood in the dim light. "Dark," he whispered. "Must be deep."

Kuro swallowed a hiss and held himself still, focusing on the prospect of running on two legs once again. He could put up with a little more pain and far more humiliation if it meant keeping the limb.

Eric glanced at the other leg. "I might as well cut the whole thing off at this point." He worked efficiently until Kuro was left in his shirt and underwear. He drew his good leg to him, and Eric turned back to study the wound in his outstretched thigh.

Caroline helped Eric to shove towels under his leg. Eric then pulled out cotton balls and a cleaning solution, rubbing slowly and painstakingly at the area around the wound, exposing its ragged edges. When he came to the center itself, he studied it, prodding interestedly around the edge with his index finger. The skin was puffed and enflamed, a yellow liquid oozing from the edges.

Kuro drew in his breath.

"With the blood cleaned up, it's easy to see that it's infected." Kuro watched as he withdrew a series of pipettes from the bag. He reached into the box and pulled out a small metal instrument that ended with a curved edge. Kuro clenched his fists in anticipation of some fresh new agony, but when the cool metal touched the edge of the wound, no bolt of fiery pain struck him down. Whatever it was, it wasn't a weapon.

With one hand, Eric squeezed the pipette's content into the wound, and with the other, the metal instrument pressed down or pulled the flesh open as needed, flushing it out. Kuro broke into a cold sweat, teeth clenched, as pain raked at his mind, threatening to drive him from himself.

Eric's gaze remained fixed on the leg as he worked. "Caroline, what did you use to remove the bullet?"

"I had tweezers in my first aid box."

"Going by the damage to the tissue, I would have thought you used a fork."

"He tried to dig it out with his fingers first."

Eric paused at that for a moment, his eyes flicking up to Kuro's face with new appraisal, then resumed. When he was flushing the wound, Kuro could see the damage to his leg in earnest now. The wound was a little over an inch and a half in diameter, the site of the bullet entrance enlarged from his clawing at it.

Eric leaned closer and studied it. "See how this section here is inflamed? That's the infection. Here, though – you see these bright, white edges? It's trying to heal...I think your prognosis is good, with antibiotics. Do you feel a numbness?" He pressed against the right side of the wound; it took everything in him to hold still, to not yank away from this man's touch. "You're going to have permanent nerve damage."

Eric turned back to the box and began to set up his equipment. "Let's get you stitched up," he said. He explained the process in an uninterested way, lifting up the needle holders and the needle as he did so. Kuro nodded sickly and watched as Eric worked with the two instruments. He gasped involuntarily as the first struck through him, and despite his efforts, he flinched back against the couch.

Caroline was at his side in the next moment. She kneeled beside him and grasped one of his clenched fists, pulling it into her lap, and held him steady.

Eric stilled himself for only a fraction to look at their hands, but it was long enough for Kuro to see a momentary flash of jealous anger in that cold glance.

From then on, Eric worked quickly, without consideration or pause. When he was done, Kuro stared down at his leg, where nine dark stitches had sewn the center of the wound together. "Those will dissolve on their own, beginning in about two weeks," Eric said. "I'm going to give you some antibiotics to take in the meantime. If the site begins to swell further or pus anymore, the infection has spread. There'll be no avoiding the hospital then. If it spreads, it'll most likely be blood poisoning, and I won't be able to help you. The best thing to do is to keep off of your leg for the next few days and monitor the rate of its healing. If it looks okay, it probably is. If it doesn't," he added, speaking only to Caroline now, "Don't call me."

"Eric, thank you so much..." Caroline helped him pack up. Kuro wondered briefly how they knew each other. They walked into the kitchen, and just around the corner from his view, they stopped, whispers rising into a hushed argument.

Kuro strained to listen. Something about missing medical equipment, jeopardizing his career, and something about *him*. There was a silence, a low, pleading murmuring, then a sigh, and suddenly Eric came back around the corner and re-approached him. This time, he didn't kneel. He placed his bag on the couch next to Kuro's head and reached inside. Kuro heard the sound of glass tinkling.

He glanced over his shoulder. Eric had pushed a hypodermic needle into a small vial and was drawing the liquid into it.

"...What is that?"

"One last thing." He sounded almost amiable, but icy fear suddenly washed over Kuro. "Caroline has asked me to give you something for the pain. And to help you relax."

His spine was prickling now. He tried to rise, but a hand clamped down on his shoulder and shoved him down roughly, holding on.

Eric looked down at him. There was something steely and cold in his eyes. Too late, Kuro's instinct kicked in, and he realized why he had felt a current of alarm from the moment the man walked through the door: Eric's eyes were the eyes of a predator.

Looking at him was like looking into the stare of a wolf.

Eric's voice was subdued. "Ketamine hydrochloride. The highest dose we give cats is around 30 milligrams. I've heard they give 40 milligrams to apes. But my understanding is that people are given much higher dosages. I wouldn't know; I'm not a doctor." He pulled out the syringe and unceremoniously stuck the needle into Kuro's arm before he could move away. Kuro winced and recoiled, but Eric maintained his grip on him, his fingers digging into the soft flesh, and when he spoke, his voice was knife-sharp in its callousness. "Let me know how you're feeling in the morning."

Eric replaced the syringe in his box, snapped the lid shut, and turned back to Caroline, who had appeared in the doorway to check on them. "He's not going anywhere."

Kuro watched as he walked away. Eric paused and glanced back at him one final time, but already, his image was growing blurry and dark. He saw a final, convulsive twitch above his eyebrow; Eric looked like a man who had arrived at a terrible destination in his thoughts, a place where truth was brutalized by denial, fear...and other, darker things.

"You really do like someone I know," he whispered.

And then everything was gone.

Kenneth woke with a start, his body sprawled on the living room floor, the blanket kicked away.

"Morning," Jacqueline called from the kitchen. "Come get a cup of coffee." She leaned around the edge of the counter, worry in every line of her body. "You're going to need it..."

He shuffled in and found a newspaper waiting in its clear plastic sleeve.

There was no need to remove it from the wrapper: *Attack leaves second victim dead,* read the front-page headline in bold, unfeeling letters. Despite the heavy sensation weighing down on him, his heart leapt at the sight of the picture: it was a dark photograph of the police searching in the woods with Mathew's name printed in all-capital, bold letters beneath the shot. He studied the lighting carefully; it was nighttime...but there was the barest hint of gray in the sky beyond. It had happened shortly before dawn, then – the paper had probably had to stop the presses to get the story in.

If it bleeds, it leads, his very first professor had told him.

Then the attack had happened after they had each escaped their separate encounters, after they had called the police, after they had decided what to tell them...and what to hold back.

In the end, Jacqueline was the only one who gave a report. Kenneth couldn't bring himself to do it: the moving shadows, the animals, the threat...he had sat for too long thinking of what to say while he waited for law enforcement to arrive, knowing he should prepare his statement, and cowardice won over and conquered.

They'd think he was crazy.

Jacqueline had tried to get him to change his mind, at one point even threatening to tell the police herself...but she saw Kenneth's expression, saw the darkness encroaching upon him, and finally let the matter drop. She wasn't happy about his change of heart, but she saw the way his shoulders sagged, his body slumping into the couch, unwilling to face this, and knew that arguing with him would be a losing battle. Jacqueline's statement would be enough: when the police arrived shortly after midnight, he sat beside her as she explained her encounter in the forest, including the animal she saw. That would give them something to go on, Kenneth hoped.

Now Jacqueline sat down next to him in the living room and handed him a plate; shimmering syrup lazed off the edge of two slices of French toast, trailing away into a pool of melted butter.

His stomach turned over.

"I don't think I can eat..." He tried to refuse it, but she pushed it back insistently.

"*Try.*"

"Jacqueline." He put it down and pointed at the picture; she had pulled the paper out of the packaging as though it were contaminated, then tossed it down on the coffee table. "...Is this my fault?"

Jacqueline made a sound and then looked out the window.

Sunlight had broken through and filled the air with a new sense of security and purpose. The night seemed far away now, and with it, all its hidden terrors.

"You're not at fault for that murder," she whispered. "You didn't kill that person."

"I didn't tell the police what I saw," he whispered. "They said they'd kill me if I didn't do what they wanted. Maybe this was a warning..."

And if so, that meant someone had died because of his inaction... because of his fear. Eric had told him to call the police, and Kenneth had instead allowed himself to slip into terrorized silence.

And now someone was dead.

He picked up the plate and managed two numb mouthfuls of breakfast before his stomach refused anymore. His cell was in pocket; he took it out and found he had two missed calls, both unknown numbers, and two voicemails. *Probably the Times. I should call them...*

"Go back to believing in the impossible with me."

He looked up sharply. Jacqueline's expression was stern. "If we don't listen to Eric and we start by *not* ruling out the impossible, then those things...those things aren't *animals*. When it was chasing me in the forest...I felt something strange happening. I felt like something had grabbed my heart and yanked it. You felt it, too, at Albert's...at your place. Gas or drugs or whatever Eric theorizes didn't make you feel that way. And then when I met the boy..." She paused. "...I had the same feeling. It felt like I was being pulled apart."

He didn't want to believe in the impossible; the impossible didn't make him feel sane, and although Kenneth suspected something was wrong with him, he was hoping it wasn't that. "...What is it you think they are?"

There was a word on her lips; he could see the way she was cringing away from it, searching for something, anything other than the answer that had come to her mind.

"Whatever it is you're thinking, Jacqueline...just say it."

She took a long breath. "Maybe...maybe they're shapeshifters."

He was about to protest when she cut him off. "Maybe you would call them 'demons,' if that's an easier idea for you to consider. That's not the same thing as a shapeshifter, but if it helps you wrap your head around the idea..."

It didn't. Kenneth set his cell phone down and shook his head. "*Demons?* Do we need to exorcise my house now?"

Hurt flashed in her eyes. "There's no need to be sarcastic."

But once they had thrown light onto the impossible, Kenneth realized it was also the improbable, the ridiculous. Speaking the word aloud threw him into his full rational faculties, and he shook his head. Eric was right. Jacqueline had always had flights of fancy; this was no different. This was serious: two people were dead, and Kenneth feared for his life.

He wasn't going to entertain these ridiculous notions.

"No. I thought I was seeing something there that wasn't. I think...I think people are training those animals to kill, and they broke into my home to scare me, just like Eric said. I think people's lives are at stake; they killed another victim to send a message. They're *people,* Jacqueline, not...whatever you think they are. *Dangerous* people."

But Jacqueline's expression hadn't changed. She shook her head in adamant insistence. "That doesn't explain how the shadows moved."

"I only *thought* I saw shadows moving. Lights could have...could have flashed by, and I was stressed...and maybe they did use some sort of drug in the air, how would I know?"

A gulf grew between them, unbridgeable. Kenneth could feel Jacqueline receding from him with every new protest that left his mouth. "Jacqueline," he tried, a soft plea in his voice, "you don't really think...?"

"You're trying to rationalize the situation," she said. Her words were quick, heated.

"I was probably just–"

"–Hallucinating, I know," she said. "You know, some things never change. You and Eric have always been like this. Neither of you have ever believed me with this kind of stuff in the past."

He was equally as frustrated now; the headline kept dragging his gaze down, taunting him with a death that should have been his own. He wanted to throw up the few bites of breakfast he'd swallowed. "That's because none of it is *real*. *This* is *real*. When you say 'shapeshifter' or 'demon' out loud, can't you hear how ridiculous it sounds? We need to call the police again –"

"Kenneth." Her eyes were fierce and clear. "Before I was chased, I heard a voice. It kept telling me to turn back, and then when it was too late, it told me to run. It was like something was trying to protect me from that boy – that...that *thing*. I know what I felt. I know what I saw. And then, when he...when I thought he was going to hurt me, I felt warm all of a sudden, like something was protecting me, and he began to scream at something – or someone. He knew *something* was there, and I was able to get away. That doesn't add up with men who've trained big dogs to attack people," she finished, her eyes blazing with defiance. "That was something else entirely. It spoke to me; *it was real*. That *thing* could hear it, too; it's why he let me go. That's what he was yelling at. I *know* what I experienced, even if I don't understand it; why are you trying to convince yourself otherwise?"

Kenneth sighed. He couldn't bring himself to believe what she wanted him to, and he only shook his head.

His phone began to ring; Jacqueline was waiting with an angry glare for him to say something, but he picked it up instead.

"Kenneth?" Mathew's voice came over the line, hurried. "You want to explain why we've got a copy of an incident report with *your name* mentioned in it? Didn't anyone ever tell you *don't be the news?*"

"I –"

"Can't wait to hear the explanation; expect a call from Meihui soon, or better yet, want to meet her in person? We've got a dead body on our hands."

"What?" Kenneth stood up at once and nearly dropped the phone; Jacqueline had settled into a frown and was staring out the window again. He noticed that she was looking out into the woods, scanning them with narrowed intensity, as if daring anything to emerge. "What are you talking about?"

Mathew began to speak rapidly. "It just came over the scanner – I've been awake all night, haven't slept yet after we broke the center-piece story and got everything in, and now this shit is happening, hot on its heels. Can you pick up some coffee for me? Black, no sugar. Biggest size they've got, and I don't care where you get it from."

"The centerpiece story? The second victim?" Kenneth's mind was reeling with the effort to keep up.

"They found the second body last night – or rather, this morning, if we're being accurate – and the slash marks were identical to the girl from earlier. I tried calling. Anyways, a camper just found a *third* body – killed the same way, but with *human* tracks in the dirt. No animal prints in sight. Only difference is that the camper was male. According to the scanner, more police are on their way as we speak, so if you get my coffee and leave *now*, I'll let you in on this."

Kenneth had turned white. "Why?"

"You brought it in first – I feel for you, kid. Been there, been scooped, and Lisa hasn't seen the incident report yet, which is lucky for you, because I'm pretty sure that as soon as she does, that'll preclude you from any further involvement in the story. Sorry, conflict of interest and all. This is me throwing you a bone before the gate slams shut."

"But – but he's *dead*?"

"Listen, you want stuff for your portfolio?" Mathew's tone was crisp. "I've got news for you – it's tough to get a job in the newspaper industry anymore. They could have a rotating crop of six interns a semester do an entire staff's job for free. You want to make money at this someday? Good, then get moving. No one is in the office yet after the late-night pull. Everyone else has off until 9 a.m., so this is your one and only opportunity. Don't you want to sell your cheap, penniless labor for the chance at an unpaid internship?"

Kenneth heard him snort just before he hung up.

Mathew sounded almost flippant about *another dead body.*

All Kenneth could think about was that another person had died because of him.

He made it to the kitchen sink before throwing up his coffee and French toast.

Jacqueline followed, swift on his heels, and pressed a hand into his lower back as he heaved into the sink.

"Jacqueline, I'm sorry – I have to go." He gulped water from the faucet with shaking hands. "There's..." He didn't want to say it or upset her. He winced. "They...they found a third body."

Jacqueline's hand fell away with a short, stifled gasp. "Is that where you plan on going? To where that body is? *Kenneth!*"

"I've got to go. I've got to talk to the police, I've got to tell them what happened...I should have said something last night...about the people, and the dogs..."

"The dogs. I see." She didn't argue. She looked like a person who had opened up too much of their heart and let their sincerity pour out into the world, only to have it tossed back at them, and she had grown silent.

He wanted to hug her so desperately that the desire nearly robbed him of sense. He took a step forward, but she shook her head.

"I'll give you a ride home." She didn't glance back at him as she grabbed her car keys. They walked outside without talking, climbed into her car, and sped over to his cabin.

There was so much he wanted to say to her before the word 'goodbye,' but the disappointment in the set of her frown kept him silent in his own driveway. Her grip remained firm on the steering wheel, her eyes straight ahead.

"After you talk to the police, go see Eric, if you get a chance. He acts more stoic than he is, and I know he'd like to see you." And then, more quietly, her voice heavy with dismissal, "And then you can tell him how right he is about the *people,* and their *dogs.*"

He watched as she backed out and drove away; he didn't have time to sit and face his own guilt and shame, to second guess his sanity. He had to go inside, grab his camera – and find a place to get coffee.

He had a crime scene to get to.

ELEVEN

D emons didn't dream. Kuro was no exception (except for the one, always the same images, always repeating), but in the fog of the drug, a memory Kuro had been trying to push away lifted up out of the shadows of his mind. It was strange, like watching *himself*, distorted in the recall, yet vivid as the moment he lived through it.

He lay prone and helpless, watching in his mind as two *kitsune* peered curiously from the shadows of the trees on the Blue Ridge Parkway as a boy he would shortly learn was named Kenneth McMahon drove away, their eyes reflecting the light of the newly risen sun behind him.

I don't want to remember this, Kuro told himself. *I don't want to watch her die again.*

But he would.

Jaden had called to him, annoyed. *Well?*

Kuro slouched across the road and lunged upward, his claws

digging into the earth for support as he hauled himself back up the incline.

It was him, he said. *I'm certain of it.*

Jaden wasn't impressed. *He came here once – it's not surprising he came here again.*

But it's been years!

The *kitsune* rolled his eyes. *They live for quite a while, you know. Did he do anything?*

No, he just crouched there...he was taking photos.

He was doing what? Jaden suddenly sat up, maroon ears swiveling. *He took a photo? Of what – you? Or the mountains?*

The mountains. Kuro hung his head, his tail lowering. *Me. Both, maybe. He was photographing the mountains, but then he heard me, and he...turned around.*

Did you hear it click? Did the camera make a sound when he turned and faced you?

He hesitated. *...I think so.*

Are you saying it's possible he photographed you?

Kuro's tail drooped, sweeping along the ground. *...Yes.*

Jaden let out a harsh, inarticulate bark as he leapt down, prowling toward the road. He froze and looked back over his haunches, his ears flat against his skull as he hissed. *Come on.*

Kuro followed obediently. *I only said it was possible – it's not likely. He moved too fast, and if he got anything, it's probably out of focus or...*

In the dirt, a small collection of notebooks and papers were being tugged away by the wind. Jaden brought one paw down upon a page and sniffed it, his claws stabbing through the center. *According to this...he's been in Asheville.*

Kuro sat on his haunches, distressed. The tip of Jaden's tail was quivering, which only happened when he was working hard at controlling himself. Cold anger burned in Jaden's eyes as he scanned the paper.

The letterhead of the Asheville-Buncombe Technical

Community College had a name scrawled above the syllabus for a photography class; *Kenneth McMahon*. It was dated a few days ago.

But that's so far away – Kuro began, but stopped; Jaden's tail had gone still.

That was a bad sign.

He'll be on the road to Asheville. We could catch him. Jaden snarled as he removed his claw from the paper, rounding on Kuro.

We don't have to – there's no point! Even in the worst-case scenario, that he took a photo and it was clear, no one would believe him! They'd think it was a prank!

Or not. A long, angry growl emanated from Jaden's throat. *Is that something you want to risk? If others see it, they might come to this place.*

That's unlikely. There's no way he took a photograph –

We wouldn't be able to stay here. Is that what you want?

Kuro pressed his tail down further, his head sinking below his shoulders. He looked out at his forest, smelt the river on the breeze, and shrunk into himself. *No.* Jaden's sudden wrath had caught him unawares; he was pummeled by it, and yet Kuro felt more confused than anxious. Jaden was usually more in control of himself than this. It was almost like watching an actor enthusiastically assume a new role, so suddenly had this change come upon him.

Then we need to leave now and track him. We don't have any time to lose. If we act fast, follow him, and ensure that there's no photograph, we could be back here within days.

Kuro slumped. *I'm sorry.*

The fur on the back of Jaden's scruff settled; his muscles relaxed, the claws retracting. He lowered his snout, his dark eyes peering levelly at Kuro, who remained looking down at the ground. *I warned you not to do it.*

He had...right after he had pointed the boy out to Kuro, nudging him with his snout.

I know. I'm sorry.

Jaden softened and turned, his tail trailing behind him. *...Sulking* *won't help. We don't have time to lose. And anyways...I enjoyed Asheville the last time we were there. Perhaps I'll enjoy it again.* He sighed. *Come along, Kuro.*

There was no arguing with Jaden; they began to walk.

For the first hour, they skirted along the border of the asphalt as *kitsune*, then climbed up onto the gravel along the road and switched to their human forms.

It was all Kuro could do to keep his mouth shut as they walked, biting back down bitter thoughts as he replayed what had happened and how it had been his fault. Maybe that was his problem – he didn't have as much to think about as Jaden, so he thought about the same things, over and over, and each memory was as clear as the experience itself...

And that was how he knew he had met the boy, Kenneth McMahon, before, years ago when he was younger. Seeing him again held no particular significance; after all, it wasn't as though the boy had ever seen *him* all those years ago, but something had drawn him toward him, that feeling of a longing to know if it was indeed the same boy. *Curiosity,* is what it had been; it was such a foreign sensation that Kuro had hardly recognized its pull.

And now Kuro's feet hurt terribly, and with every couple of steps he took on the road, he let Jaden know.

"You should have *listened to me*," Jaden snapped. He was beginning to grow annoyed again; the two of them had been walking as humans for the past two hours along the winding roadside of the Parkway. They'd stolen clothes some time ago, but shoes were harder to find: they had to fit just right. Human bodies weren't made for long walks on their bare feet, and if they were going to try to catch a ride, they needed to look like people – not animals.

Finally, in a fit of exasperation, Kuro sat down squarely on the side of the road.

"I'm done," he said. And that was that.

"You're *done?*" Jaden demanded. "What do you mean, you're *done?*"

"I'm done walking," he sighed, closing his eyes. "This is a waste of time and energy. I don't think he got a picture of me. We're just going to leave the mountains for nothing. You *want* to leave the mountains," he added, switching tactics. In a dim way, he felt as though he had hit upon something here; Jaden had brought up the possibility of living permanently amongst people before. It was harder and harder to get him to leave and come 'home.'

To his surprise, Jaden smirked down at him, then squatted beside him.

"Kuro." Jaden nudged him in the ribs.

Kuro grunted and opened his eyes, frowning.

"Put your thumb up," Jaden ordered. "Get us a ride."

"Why don't *you* do it? You're the one insisting we go."

Jaden spoke in a measured, amused tone. "Kuro, look at my eyes. We've been over this before. No human is going to want to give *me* a ride."

Kuro sighed and thrust his hand out into the air, one thumb up as the sound of a car engine rounded the curve of the road, ignoring them. Jaden had a point, after all; unlike a fox, *kitsune* were a single, uniform color, and as humans, that was reflected in their hair and eyes.

And Jaden had eyes the color of blood.

It was another thirty minutes before a second car approached, slower than the first.

Kuro unconsciously reached out with his senses, his eyes glinting in the sun, shining with unnatural charm. The car came to a stop a little ways ahead, clouds of dust drifting away from the tires as its engine rumbled in the gravel.

They scrambled up from the side of the road and approached the passenger doors, smiling in at the driver; she was a young girl with strawberry blonde hair and big, blue eyes. Brown freckles peppered her face.

"Could you give us a ride?" He asked. He did his best to smile in a disarming, friendly way, but the attempt was poor. Perhaps it was his natural temperament or his lack of wit, but nothing about Kuro came off as immediately 'friendly.' *Grouchy,* a human girl had once described him, speaking to Jaden – *what's up with your grouchy friend,* she had said. Kuro did his best to smile. He could feel everything the girl was experiencing; she was exhilarated, for one; this was probably the first time she had picked up hitchhikers, and she was attracted to him in a way that was wrapped up with a sense of curiosity and brazenness. When he smiled, her soul did a tumbling movement like a pirouette, and she blushed.

"Sure thing," she said. "What are you boys doing up here?" She flashed the friendly, bright smile of someone who lived in a town with no strangers.

"We were camping," Kuro said. He could come up with a lie when he needed to, but he wasn't good at it, and even the plausible lie didn't sound believable.

A strain of caution flowed into her soul. The girl tilted her head with a healthy dose of skepticism. "Where's your stuff?"

Kuro rested his elbows on the open window and shrugged. "A bear came and just...scared the life out of us. We ran and left everything behind. We're trying to get back to town, get fresh supplies. We'd like to get to Asheville."

It was his worst attempt at lying yet. Out of the corner of his eye, he saw Jaden reach up to hide his face in his palm, shaking his head in disbelief.

But remarkably, the girl's soul was reassured: people liked explanations, and there was something paradoxically more believable about a ridiculous lie than a plausible one. "Wow!" She gasped. "I haven't heard any reports of black bears lately. Asheville's pretty far from here, though. You sure you don't want to just go to a ranger station?"

"Asheville." He put everything into the smile he gave her, feeling like a horrible fraud from head to toe.

There was another moment of hesitation...and then it passed. "Alright then, but it's gonna be awhile. I'm heading that way, lucky for you. Go ahead, get in." The automatic lock clicked, and Kuro opened the door, Jaden slipping into the back seat quietly, behind the driver, where he couldn't be seen as easily. He caught sight of the rearview mirror and ducked low, out of view.

Kuro felt a wave of uncertainty pass through the girl at the sight of Jaden; his unique traits were unavoidable to stare at, and Kuro knew how much it bothered him when people stared. It was cruel, in its own way; Kuro believed, though he had never dared to voice it, that Jaden secretly wished he *was* human – it was too bad he would never quite fit in, at least not in the way he wanted, and a perverse streak of spite held him back from the obvious solution of just dying his hair. Kuro had black hair and eyes so dark that they could startle people if he stood in bright sunlight, which made it difficult to discern his pupil – but almost always, he looked like he belonged.

Kuro watched as Jaden bristled involuntarily as he felt the girl's stare in the rearview mirror.

There was no hiding his eyes. He held her gaze for one fraught second...and then a smile spread, and Jaden put on a refined, easy-going person-mask that could make anyone feel reassured, if they were willing to look past his eyes. He smiled in the mirror at the girl, and she flushed in response.

"What are you guys' names?" She asked, pulling back onto the road.

Kuro was caught off-guard. He had never come up with a human name he liked. He fumbled for a suitable response. "Well..." Kuro cleared his throat. "*He's* hungry...and *I'm* starved."

"He's a terrible joker, is what he is," Jaden cut in, smooth as always, but Kuro caught his look in the rearview mirror: it seemed to say, *really, Kuro?* "I'm Jack. This is...Kohl." Jaden suddenly grinned, a little too toothily, delighted. In the passenger seat, Kuro's mood soured. He didn't particularly care for the name.

"I'm Brittany," she said. "Brittany Alice. Do y'all live in Asheville?" The *y'all* sounded forced, as if she was trying to sound more Southern than she actually was. It was cute, in a way.

"Yes," Jaden answered from the back.

"Oh really? So do I! Well, I mean, I sort of live near there – on the outskirts a bit, where it's smaller. Where do y'all live?" There was that *y'all* again – definitely fake, Kuro thought. She probably moved here when she was young enough to be marked as an outsider from her lack of dialect; young enough to want to belong, but too old to pick it up naturally.

Jaden flicked his eyes toward Kuro; they knew each other's glances and the secret language between them. Jaden's look now said *get her to stop asking questions.*

Kuro yawned and stretched wide, one hand resting behind the girl's seat. The car jerked forward as her foot twitched automatically on the gas pedal, her heart racing.

"We just moved here," Kuro answered lamely, his hand remaining behind her head. He tried to sound casual, but he was uncomfortable; years ago he had become aware that people found him attractive, and though occasionally he saw a beautiful woman who stirred a feeling deep within him, a hot, coiled, nameless sensation in his gut, he had never acted on any desire. The thought of...intimacy...left him feeling nervous, not excited; he fled from it. He felt guilty now, too; her soul shivered with fluttering anxiety, and it discomfited him to be the cause of that feeling. He knew exactly what a young woman might fear, what a man of his size and strength could do to her; he almost wanted to warn her "Don't ever pick up anyone again," or reassure her "I'm not going to touch you," but he remained silent, his fingertips resting on the cushion behind her head. He wanted to pull his arm away, but Jaden had locked gazes with him in the rearview mirror, his expression stern and wordlessly commanding.

He tried to focus on other things beside the effect he was having on the girl.

He leaned back in the chair and remembered how comfortable human life could be. Jaden was always trying to persuade him of how much better it would be to live as a human; he wanted to move to a city, settle down permanently around people...Kuro shook the thought away, dismayed at the idea. He tried to close his eyes; a familiar feeling of nausea crept up in him. They'd hitch-hiked before, and the fact of the matter was, it took only a few minutes for him to start to feel motion sick. Nausea began to climb up his spine, settling into his skull. Saliva filled his mouth; he concentrated on not throwing up.

Brittany remained somewhere between a state of excited curiosity and nerves from their presence, but neither of them spoke again.

When the first five minutes of awkward silence passed, it became unnecessary to try to make conversation anymore, and the three of them remained quiet as they drove to Asheville.

"Pull over," Jaden said suddenly. They'd been in the car for more than two hours; Kuro's head was spinning, and he was certain that the moment he stepped out of that passenger door, he was going to throw up everything in him. He had squeezed his eyes shut and felt worse; now, the sight of the city greeted them as they came around a mountain bend, sloping down toward rolling pasture.

Brittany pulled the car off the road near a soft, grassy acre of fenced-in land. She smiled shyly.

"You sure you want to get out here?" She asked. The fake accent was gone.

Kuro didn't say anything; he was nauseated beyond speech. He glanced back for guidance from Jaden, but Jaden's face was blank. He couldn't read his thoughts. A flash of worry went through Brittany's eyes as she glanced in the rearview mirror toward the stranger behind her.

Jaden reached forward from the back and touched her cheek lightly with his fingertips, his left hand coiling in her hair. She was afraid now; her fear welled up inside of the *kitsune* like a great fountain of bubbling champagne, dizzying and intoxicating, a sharp eruption of terror.

Kuro opened his mouth to say something, but he never learned exactly what words were going to come out, because in the next instant, Jaden shifted back to his *kitsune* form in an imperceptible blink, slashing open her throat with his claws, his other arm reaching around to her abdomen, shredding it. Her arms pulled backwards as if to try and fend him off, and then fell lifeless as her intestines spilled out.

Kuro had barely enough time to recoil before blood spurted over the upholstery.

"*Jaden!*" He whirled and grabbed the first thing he could – the tail, curling up over the center console. Jaden batted him away with his right front leg, and the claws sliced three thin runnels of blood in his chest. Kuro grunted as he wrenched backward and hit the glove compartment door, popping it open and spilling its contents. He pulled himself up onto the seat, shaking.

The girl's blood began to soak into the flannel upholstery, her eyes glassy and wide-eyed, lifeless now. Kuro's nausea and headache had been replaced by cold, numbed horror.

Jaden sat back sullenly, fully human. He glared at Kuro in disapproval.

Kuro was in no mood to entertain his anger.

"Why did you do that!?" Brittany's sudden fear had strengthened him, if only for that one moment, but all he could feel was revulsion; she had just *helped* them. "*Why!?*"

Jaden growled at him, his face and arms smeared with blood. He licked his canine, human teeth now, defiant and silent. He was used to Jaden's mood swings, but he didn't know if he could become used to... *this*. The slain girl lay with an expressionless face, blank in death, but he started, surprised.

One of her eyes had changed color.

One bright blue eye had turned a murky brown, a tiny film with a blue dot resting on her cheek. Jaden leaned forward, equally curious, and stared at it.

"I think..." Kuro plucked it up carefully, using his index finger and thumb as forceps as he lifted it from her cheek, his stomach turning over as the stench in the car intensified. "I think she had this... *on* her eye," he said. The idea revolted him. He desperately wanted to get away from the body, get out of the car, to throw up –

An idea seemed to strike Jaden suddenly; he leaned over the center console and plucked the disc from his hands.

"Get that."

"What?"

Jaden had pointed down at the floor; Kuro found it hard to follow the instructions – everything seemed so surreal, as though time had somehow turned itself inside out. Kuro turned in slow motion to look down at the floor, his hands digging in between the papers and maps that had fallen out of the glove compartment until he found what Jaden wanted.

A small case had tumbled out; inside, two, unused blue contact lenses remained clipped to the interior. A small vial of liquid was inside the case beside them.

By the time Jaden managed to get the lenses on, half blinded and blinking, almost twenty minutes had melted away, and all the while Kuro's gaze shuttered between the dead girl and his friend. The smell was growing overpowering.

Why had he done it?

Ask him.

I can't ask him. And that was the truth: he couldn't ask Jaden why he had killed the girl; Jaden had already ignored his question once. It was possible Jaden didn't even know. It was more likely that if he *did* ask again, Jaden would stare at him, unspeaking, and refuse to answer.

Are you afraid *to ask?*

No.

Then ask!

"Jaden," he began, trying to sound as uninterested as possible while Jaden leaned forward, squinting into the mirror as he struggled with the lenses. "The girl – not that I care – but why...why did you...?"

"Kill her?"

Jaden settled back, a smile of deep satisfaction playing across his features. He shoved the case and the vial of tear drops into his pants pocket. His eyes blinked rapidly, glistening.

Kuro stared. Jaden's smile didn't reach his two new, blue eyes.

"What will happen when I change back?" Jaden wondered. "Do you suppose they'll keep with us like the clothes?"

Kuro thought, which was not something he did often, eager to seize the momentary distraction. "Your clothes stayed on...so I guess those will, too, if you wear them long enough." Jaden didn't reply at once; he sat for another minute, staring into his blue eyes. He seemed to be deep in thought.

"You're right," he concluded. "I'll need to take these back off, carry the case in my jaws for now..." He sighed and began to remove the lenses from his eyes.

"Jaden," Kuro tried again, trying to grab at the thread of something that had deserted him. The smell of coagulated blood and the stink of dead flesh and souring organs was choking him, stoking a panic in his chest that threatened to overwhelm him. "The girl...why..."

"What about her, Kuro?"

Jaden stared at him sternly; his smile was gone. His look was a command, and Kuro shrunk under his withering glare and did what Jaden demanded: he looked away, and obeyed. Kuro swallowed and looked pointedly out the window, over the girl's dead body, and noticed how perfectly Jaden's new eyes matched the color of the sky.

"What do we do now, I mean?" He asked. Jaden looked out the window at the green acreage; the sound of a car caused them to glance up in alarm.

"We run," Jaden said. They slipped out of the car, pressing themselves under the steel traffic barrier.

This way.

Kuro had made to go into the grass, but Jaden indicated they were to run to the left, where the ground was muddy. His tone was final, and Kuro did not question his command, even if it left his paws dirtied...and left tracks behind.

Two sleek animals took off racing through the pasture as a vehicle slowed to a stop near the parked car.

There was blood on the driver-side window.

TWELVE

I t felt like his thigh muscle was convulsing – the *good* one, that hadn't had a bullet in it.

Kuro rolled over onto to his side and groaned, fighting against the sudden urge to vomit. His mouth filled with saliva automatically as he came out of a cotton daze. He tried to stand and crumpled, limbs weak.

He could hear running water coming from somewhere in the house. *A bathroom*, he thought stupidly. A sudden, intense longing for water seized him. Looking up, he could see a water dish on the floor next to the refrigerator, a foot after the tile began outside the living room. Digging his elbows into the carpet, he crawled along the floor, desperate.

It smelled of dog. For one moment, he had a clear picture of himself: crawling, drooling, one shaking hand frantically trying to scoop water from a dog's dish into his mouth, failing and splashing it down his face.

This, he thought, *is hell. There is nothing lower than this.*

The water stopped; then, footsteps.

"*Kuro!* What are you doing?!"

She was next to him before he could look up, helping him into a sitting position, wiping the water and saliva away from his face with a towel. It was strange to feel her hands on him, pressing into his shoulder as she braced him. He could smell fresh lavender. He tried to speak and battled one last wave of nausea as he tried to pull out of her grasp; the concern in her soul nipped at him with a pricking sensation, like – *like the needle...*

She didn't allow him to pull away. He was surprised to discover how strong she was; one hand pulled his arm over her shoulders, and the other came around his lower back, hoisting his weight onto her. "Come on," she huffed, pulling him to his feet, "let's get you something to eat."

Her hair brushed against his throat; he had only ever been this close to one other person before, and it had felt wholly different; there had been no tight ball of fear and fire in his chest like there was now in Caroline's embrace.

Cold air replaced her presence as she helped him to sit. She took two careful paces back, watching him warily.

When she at last broke the silence and asked if he wanted anything, he managed a weak 'no,' then dug his palms into his eyes, supporting his head. The last of the dizziness was subsiding. She moved around the kitchen, and within minutes, smells began to coax him out of his misery: something greasy, warm...savory.

"I know you said you didn't want anything, but you need to eat. Your body needs calories to help it heal. At least...I assume it does." She pushed a plate toward him. Two sunny-side-up eggs sat next to the strips of bacon; the egg whites were curled brown from frying in the bacon fat, and next to them, a plump link of sausage waited, a sheen of hot grease glazing its skin.

She placed a tall cup of water next to the plate and stood there, waiting. *Guilt* occupied the space in her soul, not that he had to feel it to tell: her whole posture was one of penitence and worry as she shifted her weight, wringing her hands.

He looked down at the plate of food, then back at her. She sat across from him and waited, expectantly.

He didn't know what to do. He was sitting across from a human who had shot and captured him, and who had now made him breakfast.

His stomach roiled with unease, and again he pictured the needle sinking into his arm. He remembered the man – Eric – his eyes narrow, *cold*. He didn't touch the food. "What did your friend do to me? I feel like I've been drugged."

"You were." She pulled her hair back into a pony-tail and grimaced; her soul was bucking with anxiety now, and he had the sense that she had done the motion just to have something to do with her hands. "I asked him to give you a sedative so you would rest. I was thinking he'd give you something like a stronger version of Benadryl. I had no idea he was going to give you ketamine until he did it. You were out cold – I doubt you heard me screaming at him...and that's not an exaggeration. I let him have it. I'm – I'm so sorry. About everything. I should give him a call and let him know you're up –"

"No." She paused at the firmness in his voice. "I don't like him."

She sat back a little straighter with alarm, and he felt the tiniest ribbon of regret unfurl in her soul. "Eric is...a tough person to like. I can understand that. But I'll give him this: he helped you."

He shook his head again, insistent. "Don't ever talk to him about me. If he asks, just say I was fine, and I left."

"You *can* leave, you know." Her words were quiet, ashamed. He blanched as the feeling struck him. "I won't try to stop you again. Although, I wish you'd eat something. And also, here." She stood and returned with a small bottle of flat, white pills. "It's an antibiotic. Take this for the next four days, every six hours. *Don't* forget. If you forget, it could make it worse for you. It might upset your stomach some."

He didn't touch the pill bottle, either. If he was wise, he knew that he ought to stand up from the table, abandon the food, and limp with his tail between his legs back into the woods, where Jaden would be waiting.

Jaden.

Caroline startled as he jolted suddenly, his heart slamming in his chest. Bright morning sunlight was coming through the windows; he'd been gone for at least twelve hours. Jaden had left and said he would be coming back for him, with medicine...but then, Kuro wasn't there.

He looked at the door as though he expected the demon to walk through at that very moment.

For once, his mind was quicker than his actions: he remained unmoving, two realizations striking him simultaneously:

The first was that, once Jaden returned for him, once he noticed Kuro was gone, he could have easily found him. He could have followed his scent or, even more apparent, the probable trail of blood he left behind. So if he had come back, he had ultimately not cared enough to find Kuro and help him.

The second was somehow even worse: Jaden had not come to find him because he had simply not come back. He had left Kuro to his fever and infection, and finding himself either angry or distracted or utterly unmoved by his friend's suffering, had simply not bothered to return.

In either scenario, he had been left to suffer, like a discarded toy that a child could come back to anytime they wanted. Jaden was not going to walk through that door; if he had any interest in where Kuro was, he would have come for him *hours* ago.

And now he was here, sitting across from a human who was waiting for him to eat breakfast, to take his medicine. He had come back to her, threatened her, and yet...she had helped him.

He didn't move or blink, searching her feelings for some reason for...*this.*

Breakfast. Medicine.

A queasy feeling entered his gut; she was ashamed of herself and what she'd done, she was worried about him, and...she was longing for something. He pushed past the nausea and found it, the foundation of *need:* desire, *want.*

He shied away from it, unaccountably frightened, and for some inexplicable reason thought again of the soft heat of her lips against his. He struggled against a sudden, intense desire to push back from the kitchen table and flee. "What do you *want* from me?"

"What makes you think I want something?" She blinked suddenly, her eyes wide. "Are you feeling my soul right now?"

He nodded, and despite himself, he retracted as far from it as he could, like curling into a fetal position in his mind, and succeeded in eliminating all but the faintest trace of it. "...I stopped. I'm not touching it right now."

"I'm surprised. I thought that I would know...but I didn't feel anything."

Leave, now, his mind whispered.

Instead, he found himself talking.

"Under certain conditions, you might know...depending on what I did, and how I did it."

Her soul danced with curiosity, a graceful movement that twisted in upon itself, like a ribbon undulating in the air. "Can you do it in a way that I would feel?"

He frowned, and despite himself, picked up the fork and stabbed at the sausage. He hadn't planned to eat any of her food, but the grease was congealing... He bit into it; the skin snapped, flooding his mouth with the juices. It was ecstasy.

She laughed in relief.

It was a beautiful sound.

"Sorry, it's just – you looked a little like a fox there, for a moment. But...you didn't answer my question."

He moved on to the eggs and bacon, speaking between mouthfuls. He hadn't realized how ravenous he really was until he began to devour the food. "You wouldn't want me to. It would hurt."

"Physically?"

He pressed a strip of bacon down into the yoke, mopping it off the plate, and didn't meet her gaze. "There are other ways to hurt."

"...I see."

When he was finished, she took his plate and washed it in the sink, then turned, staring at him again.

The *feeling* returned, but it carried no answer, no explanation.

He'd try again, then; he nearly squirmed with discomfort under her scrutiny. "What do you *want*?" He couldn't stifle the note of fear. He could feel her arms around him again, pulling him up from the floor, the heat of her body pressing through his clothes...did she want *him*? That was all he knew of desire, from what Jaden had told him, and the few things he had seen – things he tried to forget. He was no scholar when it came to the hues of human desires and could not understand the nature of this nameless feeling that begged him for a foreign *something*. He didn't want to be touched; he didn't want to feel her hands on his burning skin again, didn't want her gaze upon him –

She tugged at the end of her loose ponytail and lowered her eyes to the floor.

"It'll sound stupid if I say it."

His voice was tight with strain in his effort at projecting an ease he didn't feel. "It can't sound any more stupid than 'I fed a demon breakfast.' Just *say* it."

Her gaze was clear and pained as her soul stirred. A cold knife slipped into him, cutting him from within. "Forgiveness."

Kuro recoiled from the emotion even as relief washed over him. "*Stop* that," he rasped. "That feeling...it's going to make me sick. I'll throw up everything I just ate."

She tried to laugh, but it was false. He wasn't ready to think about forgiveness, or anything, really. His mind was reeling. He thought if he changed the topic, her soul might shift away to something he could actually consume.

"Where did you meet that guy?"

"Eric?" When he nodded, she continued. "He works at the vet office closest to our precinct. We got in four pups for our K-9 units, and I handled all of the scheduling as far as check-ups, vaccinations, that kind of thing. They worked with us to send a vet tech over to our office and do all the check-ups at once. It was easier on the handlers rather than scheduling everything individually, and the dogs were all from the same litter, so they were on the same schedule. We just got to....to talking and got to know one another, is all."

"So you're friends?"

"We were." She brushed a loose wisp away from her face, and her eyes moved away from him. Something came unsettled in her soul, a bubble of unhappiness escaping and floating to the surface. Kuro let it flow into him, feeling the tension drain at last from his shoulders. He hadn't even realized he'd been hunched into himself this whole time. "Why do you ask?"

Kuro shuddered. "I don't like his eyes."

She shrugged. "You don't have to like his eyes. How do you like his stitches?"

He stretched his leg out and scrutinized Eric's handiwork. The stitches had held, and the inflammation had notably decreased. There was still a light redness, but the shiny, puffy quality was gone. "...It's alright."

"That's what I thought. Wait here..." Kuro watched as she walked down the small strip of hallway; he could see there were three doors: a bathroom door on the right, immediately next to the refrigerator, and then after a few more feet, two bedroom doors facing one another. The entire home was probably seven hundred square feet, if that. She went into the room on the left, and the sounds of a closet and dresser opening leaked out. When she reemerged, she was carrying a clean set of clothes.

"These belonged to my brother. I don't know if they'll fit you – you're taller than he is – but it'll do for now."

He looked at the clothes, a sudden feeling creeping along the back of his neck. Was this a goodbye, a get-out-of-my-house?

You should go, he told himself again.

He remained seated.

Caroline seemed to sense his thoughts.

"You don't have to go now, if you don't want." Her words came out in a tumble. "I just thought you'd like something clean, you know. Something – something to wear." She made an ineffectual gesture, and he looked down, puzzled. He was in a pair of boxers and a white T-shirt that was all but shredded from the dog attack, bloodied and soiled with dirt.

He looked up, and their gaze locked; a red flush spread across his face.

Her feelings were crowding in on him again. The house suddenly felt too small. He stood up on shaking legs, his knuckles white on the back of the kitchen chair as he braced himself for support.

"I want to go outside," he said, his voice hoarse. He needed fresh air, fast. "I feel...trapped."

She held the door open for him. He stumbled into the sunlight and hit the ground on four paws, gasping and stretching into the fresh morning light.

The door shut behind him. She hadn't followed him.

He stepped tentatively forward, exhaling. The wound was the same size regardless of form, and the sutures held tight. It still ached, but the feeling of spreading fire had subsided. And she was right, too; breakfast had made him feel better.

He pressed his nose into the ground and smelt the ripe scent of upturned dirt. He followed it absently, lost in his thoughts. *She wants me to forgive her for...for what? Shooting me?* He shook his head, pressing his ears flat back. *Why?*

He thought about the way her eyes had looked. They had been shining with unshed tears, if only for that moment.

If I had hurt someone...would I want them to forgive me? It depended on the situation, he decided; did the person deserve it? *Even if they deserved it...would I regret it?*

Does SHE regret it?

He knew she did. He could feel it...but he couldn't understand it.

He came around the back of the house and paused, his eyes scanning the small expanse before him. A three-acre hobby farm lay in front of him, neatly laid out in productive rows of vegetables, flowers, and fruits. He crept into it, curious; the world burst into a riot of scents, ripe and fresh, still speckled with dew.

Tomatoes stood, their stalks draped over the cages, the heavy fruit ripening on pale vines. Their scent was strong, stinging. He moved on to a row of cucumber racks not far off, the spongy, broad leaves spread wide. He sniffed at the hanging vegetables and pale yellow flowers. He nudged one with his nose, and the cucumber fell to the soil. He started and moved off sheepishly, skirting down the rows of Brussel stalks, the thick, waxy leaves of the tops brushing against his fur.

Her garden was small but industrious. Strawberry plants stretched along the ground, a few final berries ripening in the last of August's heat. The season was over for them, and the plants looked tired and sagging, her blueberry bushes spent. Egg plants dangled from their stalks like rich jewels, and a large pepper patch boasted an assortment of a dozen varieties: bell pepper, habanero, jalapeño...too many to count. He walked along the rows of herbs and breathed deeply: lavender, fragrant and dying in the August sun. Basil, thriving. Rosemary, tall and woody, thyme, and –

Sage. He snuffed, moving away. Awful smell, that.

Chamomile and mint were planted a ways off, isolated in their own pots. The chamomile looked charming and fluffy; the mint had exploded, determined to break out of its prison and make it into the ground. A pair of discarded scissors sat next to its pot, ready to cut back on its dreams. Kale grew, leafy and huge, and nearby, he could smell rows of onions, the green stalks pungent in the air but beginning to brown and droop over – harvest would come soon.

And everywhere, flowers.

He knew that the ones that stood as tall as corn were sunflowers; their centers were as large as black plates, and bees hovered, landing and crawling over the surface. There were vines of jasmine planted near the entrance to the garden, but the whole space was filled with plants whose names he didn't know. Small yellow flowers with orange centers that grew all in a big bush – what were they? And there was another flower, thick with tight petals like mini pom-poms, that she had planted in so many colors that he tried to count the varieties and lost track. Another one, tall and thin, looked like small, violet shooting stars on thin green stalks...

"Columbine."

He whirled around, head lowered and ears back, tense. She stood at the entrance to the garden, leaning on a rake. She was wearing a dirty T-shirt under a pair of familiar overalls, gardening gloves on her hands. Her hair was still tied back, but it waved loosely in the wind, all the way down at her hips like a horse's tail. Her harvest basket was at the ready, and a broad, ridiculously floppy hat shielded her from the sun. "That one is called a columbine."

He walked gingerly up toward the pom-pom flowers, nudging one with his nose. *What's this one?*

"Dahlia."

There're so many colors...

"I've got about three dozen varieties planted, and that's nothing. There're *thousands* of types."

You've got quite a farm.

"And only half of it's in use – I could do more, but it's a lot of work, and I care for the whole thing myself." She beamed. "This is mainly the vegetable section, but I've never been able to resist planting flowers where I've got the space for it. I call this the 'salad' department: see the tomatoes and cucumbers? The pepper patch is where the lettuce used to be, but that's a spring crop. Would be nice if they had the decency to be ready at the same time of year, but no. Then the berries, and the herb and tea section, and in the back if you looked over there, you'll see I've got a few fruit trees next to the bees."

The bees?

"See those three boxes? Those are hives. Besides getting fresh honey, I need the bees to help pollinate the plants. Over to the left, in the back, I've got my toolshed, and see in the right corner?" She pointed to the back, where a small green house stood, about fifteen feet long. "It's not much, but that's where I start the seeds for planting."

She pointed off to the left now; her soul was happy, but he felt the current of anxiety that was spurring her to hold him with her words. "I've got a strip over there I've been thinking of using for either wheat or corn. Right now the whole thing is covered in crimson clover, just to help replace the nitrates. It looked *beautiful* in the spring, but nothing doing now. I figured I've got some time to decide what to do with it. Behind that are my squashes and a few other fall harvests – they've got a long way to go. I should be bringing in a lot of peppers this week." She walked over to the bell peppers and snapped a squat green one off.

Do you eat it all yourself?

"I make baskets and give them to the officers every once in a while. If I get a big crop all at once, I make a donation to the food bank. It's the process I enjoy; I couldn't even begin to eat half of the product."

Why is the center just grass?

She smiled. "You noticed that?" She put the pepper in the basket at her feet and laid the rake aside. He followed behind her along the dirt path to a circular patch of grass, empty of other growth, in the middle of the garden. She sat down and looked at him, her face bright in the morning light. Kuro drew closer and shifted his form. He sat down a few feet away from her, his injured leg carefully stretched before him.

"This is *my* spot," she said. "I like to come here and feel surrounded by it all. I like to have a picnic, or take a nap. In the fall I come out here with this big wool blanket I have and drink apple cider. You ever do anything like that?"

He thought she was joking, but her curiosity was sincere. "No."

"What do you do, in the fall?"

He tried to push away the surreal thought that he was having a conversation with a human about what he – a demon fox – did in the fall. He did not altogether succeed. "I don't blend in well, so I move deeper into the mountains, further away from people. I try to stay warm."

"Right..." Her eyes moved down to his leg. He felt suddenly self-conscious, exposed. He shifted back to his *kitsune* form and lay in the sun, sighing.

"How do you decide which one you want to be?"

Which one?

"Human or...fox. Is it based on your mood?"

I don't know. I've never really thought about that before.

"What do you prefer?"

This.

"It's still hard for me to process. It happens so fast – I blink, and you're a human. I blink again...and you're not."

"I'm never a human." He lifted his chin at the insult.

She laughed. "See what I mean? I didn't even see you change."

There was that sound again; the smallest of a shy smile tugged at the corner of his mouth, but he clamped down on it. She took her hat off and shook her head; he was aware that he was not the only one who found this experience unmooring.

"You know what I can't get over the most? You're not what I imagined a demon would look like. *Be* like."

He felt the ghost of the smile he had conquered melt away entirely. "What am I supposed to look like?"

"Ugly. With horns and bat wings and fangs –"

"I have fangs," he interrupted, defensive. "And claws. Sharp ones."

"But you're so beautiful," she protested. She laughed suddenly, blushing. "I mean, as a fox," she tried to amend, but Kuro only frowned. "I'll bet you look beautiful when you run."

"Maybe I look this way in order to lure you to trust me. You're *prey*," he added, the word twisting in his mouth. That was something Jaden had suggested once. He could understand that he was better looking than the average human because it was a fact that confronted him whenever he looked at people. Jaden had once read a book that he had tried to share with Kuro that, Jaden was certain, applied as much to them as any other animal. He'd been nearly bursting with excitement in his effort to impress upon him some theory of survival, that their physical attractiveness was essential to their ability to lure in humans and feed from them, to get their attention and trust. There was probably something to that; hadn't he just seen Kenneth, the boy whose form he had modeled his on? He was no copy of Kenneth. He was something much, *much* better, broad-shouldered and sculpted.

Caroline's smile fell away into something sad. "Perhaps the devil cloaks his demons in beauty to lure souls to their damnation."

He couldn't stop a sudden bark of laughter. "Ridiculous."

Two pink spots appeared in her cheeks. "Why?"

"I know all about your 'devil' and stuff like that." Well, truth be told, he didn't know *much,* but he'd picked up on a few things here or there, and it was all absurd. "I don't believe in any of it."

He expected her to be offended, but to his surprise, a half-smile, bittersweet, graced her lips. "...I don't much either, anymore. My parents, on the other hand..." A rich, deep wave of sadness rolled outward from her soul; he sucked in his breath and let it fill him, savoring it, the warmth spreading through his spine and filling his limbs with a sudden boneless liquidity that left him nearly stupefied: this was old, and *deep.* There was hurt there, and so much more... "They were...militant."

Kuro swallowed and tried to clear his thoughts; he could have given himself over entirely to that sadness. Whatever the pain was, Caroline was practiced at repressing it: it sunk back down as quick as it had come. He struggled for the thread of the conversation, returning to the present. She was still speaking. "Why did you run away when I prayed, the night that I shot you? I thought maybe... the power of prayer..."

"It was the way it made your soul feel. It had nothing to do with the words. I don't even remember what you said."

"I said the 'Hail Mary' prayer."

His response was a blank stare.

"Forget it. What *do* you believe?"

No one had ever asked him that, and he'd never given it much thought. He reached up and passed his hand along his neck, turning away. "I don't know much about what we are...or where we come from, or why." He had been abandoned at birth without understanding or guidance; everything he had learned he had acquired through time, trial, and error, spare the few things that dark instinct had made him acutely aware of beyond words or thought, like taboos he couldn't break...or his true name.

"For what it's worth... I don't think you're evil. Not anymore."

"Great. Thanks."

Her voice grew quiet, and the laughter in her soul disappeared. "Meeting you... has changed my life. I have so much to think about now...it makes me see the world differently."

He tried to hide the edge of bitterness in his words. "It certainly changed *my* life."

It was as though he had struck her; her soul *cringed* and withdrew as she winced, a hot spike of guilt lancing through him. He swallowed, his tongue suddenly thick in his mouth.

"What are you going to do about my soul? Is it still holding on to you?"

"I won't know until I try to feed off of someone else, but...I think it probably still is, given the way it's just – around. And I couldn't feel Eric's soul." He waved his hand in his face, like trying to shew away a fly. "I have to keep pulling *away* from it, rather than reach out to feel it. It doesn't leave me alone."

"And it's not doing you a whole lot of good, is it? If I was depressed, or angry...that would help you, wouldn't it? I'm sorry that I don't feel that way."

"Stop being so sorry about everything," he whispered. A flicker of sadness had appeared in her soul, and even though he instinctually went for it with a great hunger, it brought him no satisfaction. He felt suddenly guilty himself; her eyes were shining again in the sunlight, and she was looking at him, her mouth a small 'o' of surprise –

"Your eyes are so *dark*."

He looked quickly away, heat creeping up his neck. He tried to pull back from her soul, shoving it from him again. It kept flowing around him, settling on his shoulders. "They're black. It's only a little strange in direct sunlight; otherwise, it just looks like I have dark eyes."

"I see."

In their silence, the bees roared into life, moving from one section to the next as the sun climbed, evaporating the last of the dew. Kuro watched their movements and wished his own life was so simple: pollinate, produce honey. Fly. Die.

Her soul crept upon him again, moving up his forearms, *poking* at him. It slipped around him like warm water, like arms around his waist, fingertips at his lower back –

Kuro let out an unsteady rush of air. "I forgive you."

"What?"

The words surprised even himself. He cringed and rested his head on his knee, drawing his good leg close, wrapping his arms around it as he stared sullenly at the cucumbers. A millipede had begun to crawl over the one he had knocked down. "I *said*, I forgive you." Maybe he did, but his anger made his words unconvincing. "You were frightened and stupid. You shouldn't have shot me, but you did. And if it makes you *stop that feeling*, I forgive you."

A shadow fell on him. Before he could react, she had knelt beside him and embraced him. He went rigid, unmoving beneath the feeling of her sudden weight and warmth. "I'm sorry," she whispered again; he felt the words close to his neck and found it was impossible to breathe, let alone think.

A wave of relief from her soul crashed over him, and he allowed himself to be swept away in its dizzy spell, like a man surrendering to a sickness in his skin. She pulled back and he turned, staring at her in cautious wonder.

"Thank you, Kuro."

He gave a stiff nod; her relief had edified into a gentled happiness; it stung him from within, a peppery burning that left his skin crawling. He didn't fight against it, and even though it hurt, he was unable to halt a tentative, small smile in return.

She saw it, and her happiness flowered at once into joyful gratitude.

Kuro leaned over and promptly vomited in the grass.

When he was through, she sat next to him, rubbing his back between his shoulder blades. The rhythmic movement and pressure of the steady circles, the feeling of her hand pressed against the tight muscle, left him unsteady. His breathing grew shallow. "It's okay," she said. "I've got an extra toothbrush you can use. I didn't realize my breakfast was that bad."

He had to get away from that touch; it left his head feeling muddled and clouded in a haze not unlike the drugged state he'd woken to, and his heart hammered painfully in his chest, afraid without understanding why.

He shifted next to her, and her hands passed down his sleek back, fingers between his fur. She jumped a little, startled, and withdrew her hand to his intense relief. *It was your feelings, not the sausage.*

"Oh."

Her emotion began to waver, changing. The happiness petered away in little spurts until it was gone, and a growing feeling of concern grew in its place, tempered by a healthy core of trepidation. It was a gradual transformation, but as it grew more pronounced, he swiveled his head to look at her, liquid eyes blinking in the light. The feelings renewed him, flowed into him like a cooling balm...but her eyes were downcast, and a crease appeared on her forehead.

He decided he didn't like that look.

What are you thinking about?

"Something I read this morning. I was thinking if I thought about it, it might change how I feel right now, and that would be good for you."

...You don't have to do that.

"Won't you starve, otherwise?"

It'll take awhile...

The emotion continued. He sat up next to her, wrapping his tail around himself and yawned, his jaws stretching wide. Her eyes went huge, but the small bud of trust in her soul reassured her, smoothing away her alarm. *What are you thinking of?*

Caroline reached over and grabbed her hat, pulling it down onto her head. With her head lowered, the brim hid her expression.

"I was thinking that I was glad you were here last night. It means you didn't kill the others...and when I realized that, I thought, you were telling the truth: you didn't kill that girl, either."

In an instant he was a human. Without thinking, he reached out and grabbed her hands, squeezing. Surprised, she looked up into his panic-stricken face.

"*What others?*"

"There was another death; it looks similar to the first one. It was in today's paper. I checked the Web site, and they've got a second story up now, too, about a third victim – I'm sure we'll see it in print tomorrow. I'm going to have a hell of a week..." She gently pulled her hands out of his grasp; he'd been clutching them. He pulled his own back hastily, his face drained of color. "The first was a girl – she died the same way as the other one. Same wounds...but the other was a young man, a camper. His death was...different." She would say no more, but a strong wave of panic hit him.

So this was what Jaden had been doing when he left Kuro to his fever. He had indeed never returned with medicine for him; he had found other avenues to entertain himself.

"Caroline, you've got to take me to the city. *Now.*"

She was startled out of her thoughts. "That's the first time you've ever said my name..."

He didn't hear her; he had struggled up to his feet and was moving swiftly to the house, leg be damned. By the time she caught up with him, he had dragged on the pants she'd left on the kitchen table, wincing as the fabric caught on the stitches. She opened the door just as he stripped off his bloodied shirt; she blushed and turned her head to stare out at the truck until he was done changing.

"Kuro, your medicine."

He grabbed it and shoved it into his pocket. She had been right; the pants were too short and tight for him, but even if he looked foolish, he was at least dressed.

He turned and faced her in the doorway. She looked back, her soul calm and unafraid, but there was an artificial quality in it. He found himself again looking into the appraising eyes of a woman who had picked up a gun and shot a demon, and her voice was steady when she spoke.

"Kuro. Do you know who killed those people?"

A knot formed in his throat. She gave him so many opportunities to practice his lies. "No."

"Their families deserve justice. If you know –"

"I don't know," he said, too forcefully.

"Then why are you in such a rush to go?"

"Because –" His mind raced for something halfway believable. "Because people might think it's me, because of that photograph. I need to get out of here. *Please.*"

She said nothing and picked up the car keys, then held the door open for him as he staggered out into the yard.

Her truck smelled of cracked leather and dog.

"Where to?"

He didn't know. He couldn't give her Kenneth's address – that would be too suspicious. But Kenneth didn't live too far from the community college. There had been a park next to the college, where he had waited for Jaden, and it was across a highway. What was the name of the highway?

"Kuro?"

"I'm thinking. Give me a moment."

Jaden would have no reason to go back there...but eventually, *surely,* he would return to where Kuro had been last night. They were used to separating when they wanted and finding each other again; he would start there, at the obvious location, still close to Kenneth's home, then go to the city if he had to. He'd have to risk it. He recalled the name of a street sign.

"You know Chunns Cove Road?"

She didn't hide her surprise. "Do you know where you are right now?"

His stomach sank. "No."

"I live on Covewood. Off of Chunns Cove Road. I can drive you back to the turn off and take you further up the road if you want...Is there a specific place you're looking for?"

"I just want to get into the trees."

Her mouth opened as though to protest, but she stayed her thought and nodded. The car backed out, and soon they were heading down the lane until it turned back up, the forest on either side of them. Fences bordered by the final, fading wildflowers of summer moved past, then a pond –

A vague memory; a smell of water in the night, a cool drink when fever was burning...

"Stop here."

She pulled off. He popped the door open even before she came to a complete stop.

"Kuro!"

He cringed; her soul was tugging at him, clinging to his ankles and wrists even as it lifted from his shoulders; it was like being manacled. He glanced back at her. He could feel that she was confused, wondering so many things, bursting with words – but like a gardener, she held it all in check, and with a controlled, sad smile, said, "Be careful, wherever you're going."

"...Thank you." He slammed the door, and without looking back, walked off into the trees. As soon as he was sure she couldn't see him anymore, he paused behind a trunk, listening. The engine started up, the tires moved on the gravel, and she was gone.

The emptiness left behind by her soul was immense.

THIRTEEN

I f he shifted and moved as a *kitsune,* he'd have to take the clothes off first and carry them in his jaws; it would be cumbersome. That was out. He wasn't sure he'd move all that much faster, either.

Don't panic, he told himself. *You'll find him. He'll come back here eventually.*

He moved quietly behind homes, through the back acres of small hobby farms and modest estates. Every ten minutes, he'd call out Jaden's name, listening. He closed his eyes and searched for the other demon's presence, the *holy dark* moving inside him, searching...

Two hours passed before he felt it. His head snapped around, the feeling at once familiar and present. Without hesitation, he threw back his head and yelled.

"JADEN!"

The feeling grew closer.

"Jaden!"

"Kuro!"

He spun around. Jaden jogged over to him, his eyes huge with relief. "You're walking! And you're not bleeding."

"I got stitches."

Jaden paused, his brow drawing down in mild surprise. "...Stitches?"

Kuro swallowed. He had rehearsed the lie over and over in his head over the last two hours, and he tested it now, as convincingly as he could manage; Caroline had given him enough chances to hone this new skill. "I broke into a clinic and got stitches."

Jaden tilted his head slightly, peering at him with interest. "You mean, you got someone to give you stitches?"

"...I did it myself."

"*How?*"

"There was a computer. I looked online."

He didn't think Jaden was going to believe him, but suddenly he laughed and clapped him on the back. Perhaps he was still too relieved by his marked improvement to question him much. "That's... Kuro, I'm actually *impressed*. I wouldn't have thought you had it in you! But those pants...planning for a day at the lake? They look ridiculous. They're too short. And the shirt is too tight."

"You've got on new clothes, too." He was dressed smartly in a pair of creased khaki pants and a white collared dress shirt. He was approaching what he really wanted to say now, coming at it from a cautious angle.

He laughed appreciatively. "Mine got a little bit dirty. I needed a change."

That was exactly what Kuro had assumed.

"Jaden." Kuro looked at him hard, and Jaden's smile fell away. He felt his own heart race as he took a deep breath, steadying himself for this. "*What have you done?*"

Recognition flashed in Jaden's eyes.

He blinked slowly, then smirked. It was all the answer Kuro needed.

His body moved without him realizing it. He lunged forward and grabbed Jaden by the collar of his shirt, shaking him in fury.

Jaden let him, not fighting back, and Kuro screamed at him, demanding an explanation.

"*Why? Why!?*"

"Let go of me, Kuro." He spoke like a parent exasperated by a child's tantrum.

Kuro released him, suddenly exhausted. He slumped back against a tree and stared at his friend. Jaden carefully pulled on the shirt cuff, adjusting it on his frame, then stared at the crumpled spot where Kuro had gripped it with sweaty hands.

"I need to iron this, now..."

"Jaden, *why?* You promised –"

"I promised not to kill Kenneth McMahon," he snapped. His answer was explosive, and behind him, the phantom of a maroon, ephemeral tail whipped in fury. "I didn't break any promise to you."

"You promised not to kill him because it would just give the police more reason to investigate. Everything I wanted to avoid... you've brought down on us."

Jaden got control of himself. His rage subsided, but his annoyance was still present. "Don't be stupid. It was the specific link to McMahon that was the issue. The officials have no match for our prints, no match for our DNA – we have no human prints in their database, they have *nothing*. We could be ghosts, for all it matters. They will *never* catch us."

Kuro was brought up short; this was an entirely different strain of logic than what Jaden had said earlier, when he had been impressing upon Kuro the need for them to flee, to go somewhere far bigger than here. The sudden shift in tactics left him feeling like he was again two steps behind, outclassed in a game he hadn't even known he was playing.

"But they'll investigate." Kuro felt a familiar buzzing in his head as he fought off the need to be sick. "They won't give up. Those people have *families*. Those families will demand justice."

"*Justice?*" His eyes narrowed, and the word came out of him like an oath. "Where did you hear a thing like *that*?"

"And the slash marks, the pattern from your claws –"

Jaden scoffed. "I thought about that, with the man. The girl couldn't be helped, but I did a better job with the evidence on the other one."

Kuro looked up, sickened. He hadn't even thought to ask Caroline for any of the details that had been in the news. "What do you mean? Jaden, *what did you do?*"

Jaden looked into his eyes; a dark strain glimmered there. He came closer and put a comforting hand on his shoulder, and Kuro fought the impulse to draw away. "Nothing, I just made sure to stage it in a way to...give them pause. I even left human footprints this time. That should keep them busy."

Kuro shook his head again. "You said...we've got to leave...we've got to get out of here now..."

You can't leave, he thought. *You can't feel anyone other than Caroline. You leave here, you starve. It'll be slow and painful...who knows how long it will take?*

"Don't look so panicked." Jaden gripped both his shoulders, hard, and forced Kuro to meet his gaze. He was smiling.

Kuro hated it when he smiled.

"You're wrong. We don't have to leave. I know you don't even *want* to leave...and we don't have to. *We're not going anywhere.*"

"You killed those people –"

Jaden's grip tightened further, clenching; there was a flash of madness in his expression. Kuro winced, and suddenly Jaden released him. "Don't worry."

"I *am* worried. You have to stop, you can't –"

"I'll stop. I was just conducting an experiment, increasing my sample size, if you will. I learned what I needed to know." He turned to him. "I want you to listen to me. We're going to stay here in Asheville for a while."

"What?" He felt whiplashed by this sudden change.

Jaden pressed on, excitement in his words. "I want to tell you about something that happened last night, after I left you.

Something *incredible.* Will you stop your protesting and *listen?* You asked me why I killed those people – here it is."

Kuro shut up and slid down to the forest floor. He let his head fall backwards against a tree trunk and exhaled, waiting.

Jaden proceeded to tell him a bizarre story of how, when he had left Kuro, he hadn't wandered particularly far into the woods until he came across a girl, a small, unremarkable thing. He chased her for a bit as a *kitsune,* moving her toward where he wanted her to go until they came to a clearing, thinking that he would feed on her for a bit... perhaps have a bit of fun.

Kuro felt his stomach turn over, his hands suddenly clammy. His voice emerged as a hoarse whisper. "Did you hurt her?"

"I didn't lay a hand on her."

Kuro didn't believe him. His heart twisted; why was Jaden lying to him again?

And how often had he lied to him before?

How often had Kuro been willing to accept his lies?

He continued; he had tried to feed on the girl when *something –* something warm, and shining somehow without light or substance – *shoved him away from her*. He could feel it all around him, pushing him away from the girl, and before he knew what was happening, she had run from him, leaving him in the woods for a moment with the *thing.*

"And it spoke to me." Jaden was pacing as he told the story, his hands gesturing wildly. Kuro had never seen him so animated. "It said, *'leave this place.'* And then it disappeared."

He continued, recounting how he had wandered off into the night as though electrified. He had always assumed other *kitsune* or demons existed, even though they'd never come across others: it simply had to be the case, given their very existence. This thing was like him, supernatural: powerful, unseen. It didn't even have a physical form, or at least, not one that he could discern. He'd read about different types of demons, but everything seemed as unreal to him as *kitsune* must seem to humans: how could he know if anything else was indeed real at all?

"But the thing is, Kuro...I don't think it was a demon. I felt it with the *holy dark*. It was like...something inside of me *knew* this was different." Kuro could tell he'd been building to this moment. Jaden turned to face him, his fists bunched at his sides, and his eyes were shining. "What did it mean – *'leave this place'*? The clearing? The city? The state? It *stopped* me. And I was left wondering if it would stop me again."

He closed his eyes against this, horrified. "Is that why you killed those people? To try and draw out – whatever it was?"

"Yes. But it didn't work. I wondered, is this thing protecting this area? These people? The girl I killed close by, not far off the high-way...but nothing happened. *Nothing appeared.* The man I found a little further out, camping. Still, nothing. I don't think it cares about *this place.* It certainly didn't care about those people. I think it was only concerned about *one thing.*"

Kuro reached up and held his head in his hands, sighing down at the leaves, overcome by weariness. "And what is that, Jaden?"

"That girl."

He looked up quickly. "What girl?"

"The girl I told you I met," he said, impatient. "Kuro, are you *listening* to me?"

"Sorry. Yes."

"I think it was specifically protecting *that girl.*"

"Why?"

"The first question is not 'why.' The first question is *what. What* is it?"

"You tell me," he said, his shoulders sagging. "You seem to have a theory."

"Kuro." Jaden could hardly hide the excited tremble in his voice. "I think it's an *angel.*"

Kuro looked up at him. Jaden was expectant, waiting. He scowled. "Are you telling me you murdered two people because you think an *angel* was protecting some *girl?* Have you completely lost your *mind?*" An angry knot had formed in his throat.

Jaden turned from him. "You didn't feel it. It was *powerful.*" His voice grew quiet. "It felt like touching fire, like meeting our own kind...but stronger. It spoke to me, and *I knew.* I felt frightened of it, for a moment. Hearing it, feeling it, made me think of something I'd read once – 'Here is a deity stronger than I; who, coming, shall rule over me.'" Jaden shuddered, his teeth clenched.

Kuro's fists balled with the desire to hit him. "What the hell are you talking about?"

His lips pulled into a sneer. "Read a book sometime, Kuro. You might be shocked to discover you can learn things."

He ignored the barb. "It might not even be an angel. It could be some other form of demon –"

Jaden was gazing off through the trees. "Fundamentally, is there a difference?"

"Between us and some other type of demon? I have no idea, we've never met –"

"I meant between us and an angel."

Kuro shook his head. He could never follow Jaden when he got like this. He struggled to his feet and wiped the dirt and leaves off his pants. "Jaden, this has to stop."

"I agree. I've already worked it all out, what my next steps are. I came back to discuss it with you, and....here." He reached into his pocket and tossed him a bottle of acetaminophen.

Kuro caught it and stared down at it, unmoved. His body felt too heavy. "What about the police?"

Jaden turned and dismissively waved away his concern. "The police don't matter. I've already worked out how to resolve that. And you'll be happy to know that I agree with you now; there's no need to kill anyone else. It's not working; it's just wasted effort." Kuro wanted to snap at him that he had fundamentally misunderstood why the killings had to stop, but he kept his mouth shut; at least no one else would die.

Maybe. If Jaden could be believed.

He had turned back and was studying Kuro's face, his eyes narrowed.

"I think sometimes you look at me and see...what is it you see, Kuro?" He sounded almost disappointed. His voice had gone soft. They stared at one another, and when Kuro didn't reply, Jaden continued in his previous tone. "As I was saying, there's nothing to be gained by killing. It doesn't work to dislodge souls, and it didn't work to draw out the angel.

"As for the police, you're right: they *will* keep investigating. It's a big story that's stirred things up. That's fine. They won't find us; we don't need to leave...and I have no intention of leaving any time soon. Regardless, should things escalate... I have a plan, something very tidy." He reached into his pocket and withdrew the flat contact case that he had taken from Brittany, giving it a rattle.

"I don't know if you read the news story, but there was an update. Besides the animal tracks, they found unknown human prints in Brittany Alice's car." Jaden grinned and tapped the contact case.

"I don't understand."

Jaden laughed and slipped it back into his pocket. "Of course you don't. That's alright. There's no rush. Just know this – eventually, I'm going to need your help with something."

Kuro looked up sharply. "I'm not going to hurt anyone."

"You won't need to. And stop looking at me like that," he said, his temper flaring. "You're looking at me like I'm some sort of monster. You're no different than me, Kuro – get over it."

Kuro dragged his gaze away. "So what happens now?"

"I want to find that girl. All I've got is a first name, but that's a start; she was on foot, which means she lives close by. I need to do some research, need to think...Another idea occurred to me last night, and I've been turning it over..."

"Another idea about what?"

"Souls. And how to eat one. I finally understand what I need, what I've lacked..."

"What's that, Jaden?" He risked glancing back to see Jaden smiling again, a calculated, cold grin.

"*Time.*"

Kuro stilled.

"There's one last thing I wanted to tell you. It's really...something special." Jaden chuckled. "There was a moment when I was with the girl when the moon came out from the clouds. The light was weak, but it was enough. She saw the color of my hair. Her face... I remember that more clearly than anything else. That stuck with me."

"...It's always bothered you, how they look at you."

He refused to acknowledge what Kuro said. "And then, you know, I told you what I got up to in the night. But in the morning, I found a small pond, a ways away from where I had killed the camper, and I looked down in the water. I kept staring, and staring...and *then.*" His lips pulled back in a ferocious grin. Kuro watched as he passed a hand through his hair.

Starting at the top of his head and spreading toward the end of his long bangs, like paint silently poured from a can, flowed the color *brown.*

Kuro gawked. Jaden burst out laughing, pleased at his expression. "I finally have my trick, Kuro...my own ability. I'll admit, it took me a long time, but I've finally got it. It's just my hair for now, but I can feel it in my bones: eventually I'll be able to change my eye color, too. And what *then?* Imagine ten, twenty years from now – who knows what I'll be able to do?" Jaden laughed again, delighted. "Who knows what *you'll* be able to do, either? Isn't it amazing?"

"...Yes."

Jaden crossed his hands over his chest and gestured with his head back the way he had come. "I don't want to have to drag you around – you get all mopey. I don't want you to feel like you have to keep an eye on me, either. I told you: I'm not going to kill anyone else. I've got things I need to do...thoughts to pursue."

Kuro tried not to hide his relief, though he didn't like the idea of Jaden going off alone again. "I need some time on my own, too...I need to rest." He indicated his leg, and Jaden nodded.

"I think that would be good for you. Let's make a plan to meet back here every three days and check in. Here," he said suddenly. He walked over to the soft trunk of an aspen and shifted halfway to his true form, slashing four rivets into it. "I do want to take steps to establishing ourselves, though. If we can *look* like humans, I don't see why we can't *live* like ones. Cell phones, for instance. But that requires paperwork, and – well, like I said," he paused, reeling himself in with satisfying assurance. "Everything takes *time.*"

Kuro was relieved to see him go, but before Jaden went, he paused and looked back at him, his voice almost gentle now. "I'm glad you're doing better. Stay off that leg. *Rest.* I'll see you soon."

Kuro nodded and sat back down in the forest, watching him go. He wanted to believe him, wanted to believe with his whole heart that he would not wake up tomorrow to another headline about another dead human.

He tried to think about what Jaden had said to him: he didn't understand what the demon's goal was; he had been talking about eating a soul again, but also, he wanted to provoke the angel? And then what? He wasn't sure; he couldn't see whatever Jaden was planning, but he was certain of one thing: that girl Jaden had met was in danger.

And so what? What was he supposed to *do*? *Stop him? How?* Push him to make another promise? He wouldn't do it.

...I can't help her, he decided at last. He closed his eyes against the shame of it. No, it wasn't that he *couldn't;* he just...wouldn't. He wasn't strong enough to oppose his friend.

He never had been.

He remained seated for a long time, so still and quiet that even the birdsong eventually returned.

Mercifully, it was louder than his thoughts.

FOURTEEN

Mathew and Kenneth stared at the scene in front of them. Neither reached for a camera; each heard sirens in the distance, closing in fast. If they were to take any photos, now was the time.

But when Mathew's hand moved, it did so to come up to his face, very slowly, and cover his mouth. He let out a long wheeze that might have been a sigh or a gasp, and said nothing.

Kenneth took a tentative step forward, then another. He stopped.

He could smell the blood more than he could see it; the earth had soaked up so much of it, but the stains were still distinct, a big puddle where the camper's torso lay. The morning light was strong, glinting off wet, shining things hanging from the branches.

Viscera.

Intestines dangled, draped repeatedly over the branches in careful, gleaming loops. For a dumb moment Kenneth stared at them, not understanding what he was seeing. Grayish-purple tubes hung like garland on the trees, and beneath them lay steaming hunks of lumpy, discolored things – damp things that sagged with shapes he remembered once from a Biology text book a long, long time ago.

He turned away, his gorge rising. In the ferns to his right, an arm – too far away from its body – had been discarded, the fingers curled. The torso was limbless, a sack with distinct slash marks splashed broadly across the chest; somewhere in all this greenery lay three other discarded parts, and the head...

Mathew was staring at it, unmoving. His hand still covered his mouth.

It lay about twenty feet from Mathew's sneakers. It was clearly a head, but lumpy, shattered. It had been torn or gnawed off, the neck shredded with thick, hanging skin, the esophageal tube still trailing behind it. The lower jaw had been ripped off and bashed against a nearby tree repeatedly, smashed until all the teeth had been knocked out. The pulverized remains of the jawbone had been tossed a few feet away.

Someone had taken the bottom teeth and neatly lined them up next to the head. Bits of bloodless gums still clung to the roots of some of the larger ones. A very clear, partial human footprint was next to the teeth, as if the killer had balanced halfway on one foot while placing them; squatting, perhaps, leaning over his work.

Kenneth became aware of a roaring in his head. The sound of flies buzzing filled his ears until he thought it would explode. He turned away, took two steps back to Mathew, and promptly fell to his knees, heaving.

Two officers immediately grabbed Mathew and began to shout something at him. Kenneth could hear their words but make no sense of them. Someone yanked him to his feet and shoved him along, and both of them found themselves pressed against a police car. A press badge kept the handcuffs off, but an officer was assigned to them, and in a gruff, angry voice that sounded as though it came from underwater, they were told not to move. Time dilated, then retracted; police tape sprung up, and officers multiplied like gnats. The two officers who had grabbed them swarmed into two dozen.

Next to him, Mathew cleared his throat. "I wasn't expecting that," he said in a weak voice.

Kenneth strained to hear him over the sound of the police radios. He didn't try to hide his judgement. "You were expecting a dead body."

"I wasn't expecting *that*. We'd never published that. Not in a million goddamn years."

"Was it the intestines? Was that the 'line' where you thought, 'This won't make the front page'? Or was it the *teeth?* What *would* you have published?" Kenneth turned on him, his stomach empty, his head spinning. "What will you publish *now?*"

Mathew straightened. His jaw tightened, and with an air of restrained professionalism, he raised his camera, steadied the lens, and took three photos of the police tape and the uniformed officers.

"There. That's what we'll publish."

The officer stationed with them snapped his head around. "Hey – give me your goddamn camera!"

Kenneth turned away to let Mathew argue his rights. He glanced inside the cruiser and saw the glow from the interior laptop.

There were pictures on the screen.

At one point, the young woman lying among the fallen leaves and mosses had been beautiful. Her body now cast shadows at awkward angles in the flash, her eyes glassy and open in shock. Her skin had turned a waxy, whitish color from the lack of blood, and the leaves beneath her were visibly soggy with her life.

Her throat had been slashed open, along with her chest. Something had gored her, shredding apart her flesh in what looked like a mauling. Her organs protruded from her lower abdomen like the exploding stuffing of a doll. A furious, fast slaughter...all rage and destruction.

He turned away. There was nothing left in him to throw up. An animal had attacked that girl, but *this*...it was so distinctly *human*. Intestines draped over branches, the spacing neat and uniform. The limbs, thrown...and the *teeth*. All laid out in a row, a task suited for human fingers, with a footprint nearby...

His mouth went dry. "I need to speak with an officer."

Neither Mathew nor the officer heard him. Mathew was arguing loudly that this was *public property*, that he had a right to take photographs where he pleased, that he was *the press*, and the officer was furiously threatening to book him for tampering with a crime scene, obstructing justice, trespassing, and resisting arrest if he didn't turn over his camera.

Mathew stood his ground. "Am I under arrest? I haven't been read my rights. If I'm under arrest, I want a lawyer, and my first call is going to be to my editor."

The officer unleashed a string of obscenities. Kenneth stepped forward and raised his voice as loudly as he could and repeated himself. "I need to speak with an officer."

The officer paused and looked at him. His own voice sounded remote and a little pitched when he spoke again. "I think I may have information about the person who did this."

"*What* did you say?"

He didn't give himself time to think, let alone breathe. "I was attacked in my home by two persons who had with them animals like the one I photographed. I'm the one who took the photo of the animal that was published in the *Times*, the one that might have killed that girl. Brittany Alice. It was the same animal that came to my house." He was rattling, he knew; the officer stared at him in stupefied confusion, not following anything he was saying.

Mathew gaped. The officer hooked his thumbs through his belt, weighing his options. He saw something – perhaps Kenneth's fear or sincerity – and forgot all about Mathew's camera. He spoke into the radio clipped to his front pocket, barked at Mathew to remain where he was, and then gripped Kenneth by the elbow, steering him away.

He spoke, but the words seemed to come from someone else. He found himself unusually calm and lucid. Could he give a description of the attacker? Attackers, he corrected: *plural*, and yes, he could:

they were both probably the same height, tall – if he had to guess, he'd say anywhere between six foot two and six foot four. They were both lean, muscular, with runner's physiques. One of them had dark maroon hair and matching eyes. The officer asked him to repeat that. He annunciated his words clearly, adamantly.

"And the other?"

Kenneth hesitated. He thought of human teeth all neatly lined up in a row. "He looks a lot like me."

A pause, a narrowing of the eyes. "What do you mean by that?"

He tried to describe the version of himself that he had seen – the same black hair, similar dark eyes. The officer seemed especially interested in knowing that the individual appeared to be wounded. They spoke for about thirty minutes, with Kenneth answering the same questions over and over again.

The sound of barking suddenly rose over the officer's radios; a K-9 patrol car had pulled up with two other police units, and the handlers had let the dogs out of the back of the cars.

The officer finished by getting his contact info. He assured Kenneth he'd be in touch soon and then turned swiftly, walking in the opposite direction toward the K-9 units.

Kenneth looked around, scanning the growing crowd. Mathew was over by the clearing, his head bent low near another officer who appeared to be speaking in a hushed, hurried manner. Mathew took no notes; he only nodded, his mouth pulled down in a grim frown.

Kenneth made his way over to him. Mathew shook hands with the officer, but the man looked angry. There was sweat above his mustache.

"Mathew, you pull this shit one more time and I'll haul you in for tampering with a crime scene and hold you as a suspect, so help me, I will."

"I know Luce, I know."

"If I see a single picture –"

"You want the memory card as a parting gift? We didn't photograph anything besides tape. Even I've got standards."

The officer jerked his head at Kenneth. "Then stop dragging interns into your bullshit."

"Him? He's not an intern, just a stringer."

"You pay either of those?"

"Hell no. See you at the bar? I need a fucking drink after this."

"See you at the bar."

The officer turned, waving them away.

Five minutes later they were back in Mathew's truck, cruising back up in the mountains.

"Kenneth – what the hell was that?"

"What do you mean?"

"What the *hell* did you say to the police? Did I hear you correctly, that you think you have information on whoever is committing these murders?"

Who, not what, he noted. "So the police think it's a person then? They don't think it's an animal anymore?"

"That guy I was talking with, Max Luce, is an old friend of mine...he lets me in on things, strictly off the record. Yea, they think it's a person. He said the detectives were at the crime scene for less than five minutes before they changed the whole investigative direction of the case. I can tell you right now we're not going to print much information, though, other than an update on the Web about this one."

"Why not?"

"Something like this, the press needs to be lock-step with law enforcement on what gets released. J-101, kid – aren't you at least that far along? We're going to go tight-lipped on this because fucking wackadoos who are bored out of their minds like to call the police and pretend to confess to bullshit they'd never do and don't have the imagination to dream up. They get the details from the paper and they run with it, wasting the detectives' time. The point is, eventually, a good way to validate if someone is the guy police are after is if they have information that only the killer would know, stuff that was never released to the public. You know, like the bottom half of a set of teeth, all lined up in a little row, or intestines strung up like Christmas trimming. Jesus *Christ,* I'm never going to get that image out of my head. There's probably a lot of evidence forensics can dig up from this crime scene, too, so the police have a lot to go on."

Kenneth reminded himself to breathe. "That's good then."

"In the broad picture, sure. If you know what's good for you, you won't mention any details to anyone. You don't know how it could spread, and it could impede the investigation, and if it got traced back to you, no lawyer will come near you with a ten-foot pole, and then I'd be taking *your* picture for the paper."

Kenneth slumped in the passenger seat and watched the trees blur in the sunrise. "What else did your friend tell you?"

"The victim was identified as a man named Oliver Floyd, age twenty-three. His wallet was found close to his head, the placement clearly intentional. Obviously they'll get the Wildlife officers and animal control down there to weigh in, but Luce said that by glancing at Floyd's torso, it looked like it had the same slash marks as Brittany Alice and a woman killed earlier in the morning, Tonya Rios, age twenty-six."

"Are all the victims in their twenties?"

"So far. Luce thinks that might indicate the killer's own age, or otherwise indicate crimes of opportunity: young adults are more likely to be out late at night. Anyways, Alice and Rios' deaths look almost identical, except that Rios was attacked from the front...and she's missing something. Luce wouldn't say what, just said 'something was taken' from the scene. We're not printing that detail, either. Poor guy has been up since three a.m. dealing with this shit, just getting shuffled from one crime scene to the other – like me. I thought I'd be able to at least catch an hour of sleep....so much for that. And that man's body... You saw it."

Kenneth shuddered. He never wanted to think of it again.

"There's no sign that any weapon was used. You ready to hear this next bit?"

Kenneth nodded, sick.

"Luce said it looks like the limbs were *chewed* and *torn* off. The damage looks just like what the K-9 units do when you get on the wrong side of a bag of cocaine. The animal had trouble with the head, since the throat –"

"I saw it," he reminded him. He closed his eyes.

"Most importantly, there was a partial footprint in the dirt. It looks like the person put all their weight on their front right foot. Sometimes they can get a lot of information from a footprint. The indent into the earth can tell you weight, and combined with the length can sometimes offer an approximate height, and if they can identify tread, they can put out a bulletin to local stores that might have sold the brand. They don't have that information yet, but Luce said this is a partial, and since the murderer was balancing on one foot, the amount of pressure he put on it can't tell them too much as far as the weight goes. It's like the bastard left it just to say 'I was here.'"

"How do you know all this?"

Mathew gave a wry laugh. "I used to work for the precinct, believe it or not. I specialized as a crime scene photographer before I changed career paths. The key to being a good crime scene photographer comes down to three things: speed, light, and angles. You've got to be in and out – and trust me, you want to be in and out as quick as you can. You've got to understand where the light is and how it changes the scene; a blurry photo could mean a case goes unsolved. Detectives may end up working a case for years, and your photos will be the only window they have left to actually *see* what happened. Plus, you've got to understand angles and proportions and capture the way it would look to enter that space without exaggerating or reducing any details. I'll tell you all about it, some-time. It's not a bad career path. If I'd stuck with it, I'd be down in the dirt, photographing that man's shattered jaw instead of giving advice to a stringer. Anyways, Luce said the cops are whispering that some murderous fuck has trained a hybrid wolf-dog to attack people."

"That's basically what I told the police...but it was two people, not one. They attacked me at my home last night and warned me not to publish anymore photos."

"Holy *shit*." Mathew turned to gawk at him. "And you didn't *tell* anyone?"

Kenneth winced and tried to shrink into himself. "They threatened my life, and...they'd already killed that girl, and one of them attacked my friend in the woods. She spoke with the police last night."

Mathew at last looked away to return his eyes to the road, jerking the steering wheel, hard. The car skidded. "The incident report. I wanted to ask you about that. I'm going to need another cup of coffee. Fuck." He cranked down the window for fresh air. "You get a good look at them?"

"Yea." Kenneth repeated what he'd told the officer, but this time, he didn't mention that one of them looked like him. He remembered the officer's dubious reaction.

"Well, damn. I'll have to talk to Bernard, but that sounds like a follow-up story to me, timeline and all. We'll have to see what the police say. They may not want that released, either. They're all-hands-on-deck now that the narrative has shifted to the attacks being carried out by a *person*. They don't want to use the words 'serial killer' just yet, because then the whole thing will really go sideways. They don't want people to panic. Are the police going to meet you at your home?"

"I don't think so. The officer didn't say anything about doing that."

"What do you mean, he didn't say anything about that? If they broke into your home last night, there might be prints. Forensics could come in and look for hair samples, cross check it against anything found at the other crime scenes. If they attacked you, there might be blood, especially if one of them was already hurt. I bet one of their dogs attacked them."

"Could be... I punched one of them...I'll look and see if there's any blood."

"Did he mention arranging any type of protection for you? If they know where you live…"

"No, he didn't say anything about that. He just took my statement."

"What in the *hell*?" Mathew shook his head. "That can't be right. I know all the guys here – they've got their shit together on this. They'd be over at your place looking for evidence right now – that's a third crime scene…actually, yours is the *first* crime scene, if I'm following the timeline correctly. Wait – hold on. Oh Christ, who did you talk to?"

"The police…? The same guy who stopped us."

"Did you get the officer's name?"

"…No."

Mathew groaned. "Kenneth, it's a good thing you're a photographer, because you'd make a terrible journalist. I'm willing to bet you talked to a Madison County police officer. I wish I looked at the guy's cruiser. I just kept thinking about that head…"

"Madison County?"

"Asheville is in *Buncombe* county. Madison got involved due to Brittany Alice's death – she was killed right at the Madison county border. Jesus, haven't you ever read about all the serial killers that *don't* get caught? It's because they do it along county and state lines – none of these jurisdictions have any obligation to share their information with the other. They might show up at a crime scene if a hot tip comes in, but even cops with good intentions can hoard evidence with the hope of breaking a case. *Madison* isn't going to send anyone to your home in *Buncombe* county. I'll bet they don't want to tip off the police here, or else they want to look into your story before making a move."

"But why wouldn't they share that info? Don't they all want the killer caught?"

"You looked at a dismembered and mutilated body today, and you're still this naïve. That's kind of amazing. Don't lose that, kid.

Listen, as soon as I drop you off at home, get right in your car, get down to the police station, and give someone your statement."

"I already gave it to the officer –"

"Then prepare to give it *again,* and whatever you do, make sure it's the *exact* same statement. You don't want any discrepancies when the counties get around to playing nice with one another, and they *will*, eventually – this is going to be big."

"Would it matter?"

Mathew suddenly grew quiet. He cleared his throat and shot him a serious, level glance. "...It might."

"Why?"

"You got photos of that animal before it was news. You brought them in right at the time of the first killing. You're claiming now you were attacked in your own home, a few hours before these two murders."

"So?"

Another sidelong glance. "So that's a great alibi if police were to investigate and discover matching animal fibers in your house."

Kenneth's heart stopped. "Mathew, what are you saying?"

His voice was measured and stern. "Another hallmark of serial killers: they love to insert themselves into the investigation, such as by showing up at the crime scene and offering assistance. It gives them a sense of control. Don't look at me like that; you're making me feel like I kicked a puppy. I'm just telling you what the police might think, and as time passes and as families grieve, they grow angry. When they grow angry when there're no new leads, they grow vocal. They start criticizing. And the police start getting desperate for suspects or breaks – and they don't like coincidence."

His voice came out strangled. "You don't think *I* –"

"Of course not. But I *do* think you better get your ass down to the precinct and get your story on record, but consider getting a lawyer first."

The sun was working its way into the sky when they arrived back at the *Times* office. Kenneth said nothing as he walked over to his car, his mind lost in his thoughts.

"Kenneth!" Mathew slammed his car door shut. "Listen to what I told you – go over to the station right now, okay? It's not safe to go back to your house until you've talked to them."

He nodded, ashen.

"I'll call you. Stay safe!"

Kenneth gave a half-hearted wave as Mathew disappeared inside the office. He yanked the door of the truck open and dragged himself inside. Everything was too heavy now; all he wanted to do was go to sleep, but what Mathew had said weighed heavily on him. He needed to get to the police station...

He checked his cell phone. A notification of a new voicemail blinked at him. He put the phone to his ear and listened to the dry, flat voice of Eric asking him to call him back.

He didn't have time for that right now. He'd ignored Eric's calls for two years; surely Eric could wait a little longer. Kenneth tossed the phone down into the center console holder and put the car into drive.

Jacqueline had never been a great reader. She was a little embarrassed by that fact and hoped that college would effect some change in her, but she never seemed to find the patience to sit down and move her way, page by page, through a book. She had inherited a restlessness from her father: she was kinesthetic through-and-through, and though she had no hobbies into which she channeled her energy, she had two feet that constantly wanted to move, even when there was nowhere to go.

Today, her feet led her down the stone and brick path toward the Pack Memorial Library. It was practically empty at mid-day, the hushed atmosphere silencing even her footfalls. A few searches at one of the computer terminals took her over to the seclusion of the non-fiction section.

She had done a little searching on the Internet, read a few things that felt like promising leads, but had been overwhelmed by the sheer amount of information out there. Studying Kenneth's photographs hadn't helped; every time she tried to describe it in a new search, the Internet unhelpfully suggested search results for 'werewolf.' She didn't think it looked too much like a wolf – well, a *maned* wolf, maybe, what with its long legs. It reminded her of *something,* but not that, not at all...and then, when she squinted, when she studied the angular hint of its blurred snout, the grace in its long legs, a spark of recognition sent her down a new path of exploration. She read for more than an hour online before checking her local library for resources; she wanted something she could hold in her hands, to steady them.

She stepped in between the shelves and took a deep breath. It wasn't musty or old, but there was a smell – crisp, papery – that drew her in. So many books, so many inviting leather bindings, crinkled paper jackets, laminated covers... She straightened her skirt, tugged at her hairband, and began to scan the books, her heart beating wildly. The solitude was so quiet.

It didn't matter that Eric thought she was crazy. It didn't matter that he had convinced Kenneth to believe in the rational and logical, rather than the *actual.*

It didn't matter if she was alone.

Her finger ran over the spine of *The Encyclopedia of Demons in World Religions and Cultures.* She found *The Demon Dictionary* next, but she cringed at its declaration of *Know Your Enemy! DEFEAT HIM.* She put it back on the shelf. She plucked two more books on Christian demonology (she wasn't a Christian herself, but that seemed like a familiar place to start), another compendium of demonology, and a final scan for the volume she was really after: Frank Hamel's *Human Animals...*

Not there. She squatted, checked below, then stretched her calves to check above. There was a conspicuous book-sized shape where it should have been. She hadn't been able to find that one online in any open-source forums, either. She'd start with her modest stack, she supposed.

Jacqueline turned to go and gasped, dropping the books.

He moved quick and sure, clamping a hand down over her mouth as he shoved her against the bookstack, caging her with his body. His other arm grabbed both her wrists as she lashed out at him, yanking them above her head with a strength so absolute that there was no struggling against it. She gathered her breath to try and scream through his fingers, and he leaned down, his lips brushing against her earlobe, and whispered, "If you scream, I *promise* you, I will kill you before the sound even leaves your throat. Do you understand me?"

Jacqueline heard the irrefutable certainty of his words; he had said them almost amicably, but there had been an underscoring of violence that left her assured of her death if she made a sound. Instead, she exhaled slowly, the scream evaporating.

"Smart girl," he whispered. He looked down at her and grinned, his eyes the same flat, unnatural blue that she remembered. "Are you going to bite me again? Say *no.*"

Cool air rushed her face as he lifted his hand from her mouth, but the other still pinned her arms in an unyielding, painful grip. "*No*," she whispered.

"*Good* girl," he amended, his grin wide now. He brushed the hair from her face; she flinched back, but his fingers skated over the skin of her cheek with a tenderness that was both more shocking than a blow and somehow more cruel. He pressed his weight against her a little more tightly, his right knee moving between her thighs.

Jacqueline made a sound, a choked, quiet gasp of fear and rage, and the demon squeezed her wrists sharply, twisting. She bit down on her lip to keep from screaming; she was losing all the circulation in her fingers.

Any moment, she hoped, someone would come up here, someone would turn a corner and see them, *help her* –

Their eyes met and held each other. A trickle of cold began at the top of her spine and then moved down, but with it came a flowing warmth. It settled around her, pooling in her ankles, traveling back up through her stomach and into her throat. The demon tilted his head, curious; she glared up at him, studying his features: his maroon hair had been replaced with a flat, uninteresting brown.

"Hope and defiance." She could feel his chest move against her when he spoke, the vibration of his words travel through the fabric to her skin. "You're a spiteful, determined little thing, aren't you?"

Jacqueline gnashed her teeth and tried to wrench out of his grasp; he held on all the more tightly, staring down at her with amused curiosity, then leaned down, and again his breath tickled her ear. In the teasing voice of a lover, he said, "If you try to get away from me one more time, I won't kill you, but I will hurt you *very badly*."

Jacqueline fell still.

"What a practical young woman you are," he smirked, observing her now. He began to stroke her cheek absently, smiling. "And your eyes...there's something about your eyes..."

She felt another strange tingling make its way down her spine, as though a roach had crawled upon her and left a trail of ice in its wake. She gasped and bit down on her tongue, hard enough to draw blood; the cold intensified in her veins with unnatural ferocity, so that she was twisting again without realizing what she was doing –

The warm feeling came again, flowing down from the top of her head, and Jacqueline held herself still, her heart pounding loudly in her ears.

"You're *haunted*," he said suddenly, grinning with new appreciation. "Someone betrayed you...and it's *haunting* you. There's a door open in your soul – and it leads to darkness. You can feel me touching you, can't you?"

She didn't know what to say; he saw the confusion in her eyes, and his grin smoothed at the edges into a slow smile. "Not like *this,*" he whispered, and his hand left her face, running down her torso now, his fingers pressing against the curve of her waist, the thumb hooking over her hip bone, pressing in with a possessiveness that made her want to scream. "I mean, *here.*"

The feeling that came upon her was one of violation and *wrongness,* of knives cutting into the sinews of her heart, fingers pushing in against the secrets of her mind, cold and fear and agony all at once. She went rigid, not sure if she could swallow the scream a third time, but before it could claw its way out, the warmth began again and spread with a heat more intense than comforting.

He hissed; the pain inside of her lifted with the totality of a light being switched off, and all that remained was the fading warmth, already departing.

He stared down at her with a new, wondering appraisal: the humor, the sureness had melted away into the mask of a man carefully concealing his next move. "So it's attached to *just* you," he said at last. "What makes *you* so special?"

She didn't know what he was talking about. Jacqueline focused on her breathing and glared up at him, silent.

"I was disappointed when you ran off," he said; the mask had shifted again, now adopting a casual tone. "I thought I'd follow you; I hate to have unfinished business, and I thought you and I were having such a nice conversation. But, we weren't alone, were we?"

She knew what he was talking about now; the warmth, the voice...

His lips ghosted against hers; she recoiled backward, but there was nowhere to go. He chuckled. "And I don't think we're alone now, either."

No, no they weren't. She had felt him do *something* to her...and every time, a steady warmth had removed his touch, forcing him away.

Her eyes blazed up at him, and though she remained silent,

Jacqueline bared her teeth. He blinked in mild surprise, then laughed quietly as though she were a child, ignoring her silent threat.

Jacqueline wanted to tear his throat out.

"Read anything interesting in the news lately? Any bodies turn up in the woods? *Speak*," he said suddenly, as though her silence annoyed him; she knew what he was referring to. She felt the balance of her life in the answer.

"...It was you."

"Maybe," he allowed, amused.

"What do you want from me?"

Something changed in his expression; it rippled from the edge of his brows downward until a light seemed to dim in his eyes, the cruel curve of his lips falling away into a frown. An emptiness looked down at her; his gaze was lost and searching as he stared down into her eyes, as though he was seeking something in the very bottom of her soul.

All at once he released her wrists. His hands dropped to her arms, his palms flat, gliding over her skin, up over the slope of her shoulders, up through her hair, his fingertips tracing her neck, lifting her chin to stare up at him. His touch had gentled again in that horrible way that left her terrified; she could feel his hidden, brutal strength tensed in his body, could feel the heat burning through him —

He leaned down, and for a moment, she thought he was going to kiss her, but no; he was only looking more deeply, down, down into her core...and the crawling feeling had returned, intensifying, and the warmth that stopped it before was struggling to rise. Something fell away inside her, and the feeling of a sharpened blade slipping through her ribs made her gasp. Whatever invisible power he possessed had found its way inside her, and it was moving...it was like that night, in the forest, and something that *hurt* inside her soul was being touched by a hand that meant her harm.

"I'm not afraid of you," she whispered. "I know you attacked my friend. I know there are *two of you*. And I know what you are. What do you *want*?"

His answer was a slow, dangerous blink. "Your friend?"

Jacqueline sucked in a breath; she shouldn't have said anything.

His eyes narrowed. "If you know what I am, then you know there's nothing you can do," he said. "Here we are, in broad daylight, in a public place – where can you go that I can't follow? I know where you live. I could come for you in the night. I could slip inside your home, in your bed, and Jacqueline..." His lips found hers then, tilting her head back as he crushed himself against her, his tongue pressing against the inside of her mouth, sliding against her with bold, claiming strokes; he overpowered her with his size and strength even as she tried to pull away, and at last he broke from her, his eyes terrible. "*I could make you scream.*"

"I'll kill you," she snarled. "I'll find a way –"

He snorted. "I'm sure. Do you intend to go to the police?"

"I've already told them about last night –"

"How did they react when you told them about the man who turned into an animal?" He saw the change in her expression and laughed. "No, you didn't tell them that. You know better. And if you know what I am, then you know that I can do whatever I want. I'm not concerned about *police*," he added, contemptuously. "Feel free to call them again when I leave."

Her heart sped up. He chuckled at the spark of hope in her eyes and brushed her cheek again with the back of his knuckles. "You didn't think I was going to murder you here in the library, did you? Why would I ruin perfectly good books like that?"

For the third time, Jacqueline ground out, "*What. Do you want?*"

"You," he finally answered, simply. "I want *all of you*...and I don't know why," he added, but the light tone was belied by a sudden, angry darkness in his words. "It's...unnatural, this...*desire.*"

Fury and fear roused her to boldness. "What do you intend to do? How many more people are you going to kill before you come for me?"

"I don't know," he answered, truthfully. "Probably none; I'm not one to waste effort; I was just conducting a small investigation, trying something out. And I think, between you and me, that you're going to take a lot of effort. I just hope I have it in me to succeed, before..."

"Before what?" She rasped.

His right hand had slid up her chest, but there was nothing sexual in the movement as it passed her breasts, closing around her throat. His breathing increased suddenly, hitching; she felt his grip squeeze infinitesimally, as though he were holding himself back, and the light of real, maddening desire flashed in his eyes.

"Before I kill you," he whispered. His hand sprang open, and he pulled his arm away, fast.

"Then do it now," she challenged; her body shook with the force of her words, but her voice remained hardly above a whisper.

"No." He stepped back suddenly, releasing her. Jacqueline nearly fell forward, but caught herself. "No, it's not your life I want. I'm after something much bigger...and not just *you.*"

"Leave Kenneth alone," she said suddenly, her fists bunching as though to strike him, this man who could kill her with a single, swift movement.

His brow arched. "*Kenneth?* Ah; your friend. It didn't take him long to open his mouth, did it?" He snorted. "No, Jacqueline, I didn't mean *Kenneth.* I can assure you, he's safe from me." He even rolled his eyes, then, but stopped. "I meant *this.*"

The cold, stabbing feeling returned to her chest with the sudden impact of a sword; she staggered, but the warmth was ready for it and shoved it away again, burning.

"Curious, that," he said. "I'm going to drag whatever *that* is out into the open for a nice, long chat, and then I'm going to consume you...*all of you.* But not today," he finished, pleasantly.

She reached for the bookstack, steadying herself. "Why?" Her voice was strained with feeling. "Why tell me what you intend to do to me? I'll be prepared – I'll be ready, I'll –"

He laughed at her. "That's the *point.* You and I are going to see a lot of each other...or rather, I'm going to see a lot of *you.* Run, if you want...but I don't think you will." He flashed her a grin, his teeth much too sharp. "Tell anyone you like – no one will believe you. I know Kenneth won't," he added; he had said Kenneth's name with a pointed derision. "I felt his soul: he's a coward, and he lives in denial. I could feel him fighting against believing what he was seeing even as he stared me full in the face. No one will help you – *that's* why I followed you, and why I'm telling you this now, Jacqueline." He lowered his voice, smiling, and it was worse than all his jeers. "I want you to know *all of this,* and *despair.*"

The voice that had spoken to her in her mind under the moonlight returned, a whisper in the back of her thoughts that only she could hear.

Run, Jacqueline.

But she didn't need to – he was already turning away. "I'll see you around some time...Jacqueline." He smiled again, and then he turned and left her, standing alone.

She forgot all about the books she'd come to get.

FIFTEEN

The beginning of autumn was still a few weeks away, but already it had kissed the tops of the trees, where a speckled yellow had begun to curl and spread. Pale white cloud cover hung over the world in a heavy, slumping dreariness. The summer heat had finally broken, and the coming fall warned of cold days ahead, but for now, the world was in a state of fitful transition.

For three days Kuro had moved about the woods, eager to press his nose deep into the moist earth and breathe in the scent of freedom, but something had changed. A new sense of listlessness had invaded him, the feeling that he wasn't doing what he wanted to do, that he wasn't where he wanted to be. He told himself it was because the woods were small compared to the vastness of the mountains, but he knew it was a lie. On the second day, he had laid down in the grass and watched a spider build a web for hours. It used to be the kind of thing that could entertain him: he liked the way the silk caught the light of the sun, enjoyed its careful, graceful movements.

It had bored him.

He had never been bored before. *Jaden* constantly complained about boredom, but he had never felt it touch his heart: how could it? The world was filled with so much discovery: holes in trees that held secret dens, rocks that grew heated in the sun, perfect for pressing against to feel their warmth, mice and rabbits to hunt and eat. The world had been perfect.

Now it was empty.

The same emptiness was inside him, growing, his hunger intense and expanding to the point where he thought about it unceasingly. Once, he had crept down toward the main road and tried to feel a group of bicyclists that went by, but it was as though he were trapped under a glass cloche – he could see the world, but it was cut off from him. He was imprisoned inside an invisible cage, and slowly, he was starving.

At least his leg was healing; the angry redness had at last been driven away by the medication, and two days of consistent rest had enabled the stitches to hold the wound together, and the flesh had begun to knit. He could walk slowly, carefully, though he was aware of a slight numbness in his thigh.

On the third day, he waited as a human for Jaden to return, idly splitting apart fallen pine needles, braiding them and snapping them in agitation. Jaden appeared mid-afternoon, waving and calling to him, a shopping bag in his hands. Kuro stood, dusted the pine needles off himself, and felt a momentary relief from the monotony of his days. Jaden looked down at his pants and crinkled his nose in disgust.

"I knew you'd still be wearing those ridiculous pants. Here – take these." He passed him the bag. Kuro scowled and stripped off his shirt, grabbing the new one out. He undid his pants and gingerly tugged them down over the bullet wound.

"Hold on, let me look at it." Kuro sighed and stood still. Jaden knelt and pressed his fingers against the wound, examining the edges. "...You did a remarkably good job stitching this. It looks so...professional."

Kuro stared down at his gaze unflinchingly, in no mood to have his lie challenged.

Jaden looked at him a beat longer, then returned his attention to the wound. "It's healing. The infection is gone." He glanced up at him again, his voice softened. "Does it hurt?"

"Not like it did before." Kuro carefully stepped through his new pants, buttoning them. "Now it just aches, mostly."

"How does it feel when you walk? You seem to have a slight limp."

"For now. I'll be fine." Kuro examined him, sensing that something else was on Jaden's mind. There was a distracted quality to his words. "...What is it?" His heart leapt suddenly – had Jaden done something else? Kuro had intentionally kept to the forest, unwilling to learn of fresh horrors from any more newspapers. He sat down, bracing himself for the worst.

Jaden turned from him, walked five quick paces away, then rapidly turned back.

Jaden had always reminded him a bit of a cougar with the way he was almost supernaturally still. He'd only met a cougar once, but it had left an impression upon him. Its eyes had looked at him with a yellow menace, every muscle in its body taunt, like an arrow prepared to fly. It saw something in him, something that moved, and turned away at last, disappearing on silent feet.

He had never seen one since. He found out later that cougars hadn't been spotted in that area for more than seventy years, but that hadn't surprised him. The animal came with the shadows and disappeared into darkness. Who would spot a living ghost?

But now Jaden was pacing with an excited energy Kuro couldn't remember him ever possessing; something had come loose in his mind, rattling away the confinement of his tight control, and soon, he began to speak, his words halting, fevered – something about a girl, a feeling...an angel? *Not this again...*Cold dread washed over him; what did he expect? He'd left Jaden to his own devices after he'd killed two more people, then confessed to a brief infatuation with some girl. Guilt robbed him of breath; he knew what would happen to her. *You knew, and you let it happen.*

"Did you kill her?" The words were barely a whisper, his eyes fixed on the forest floor.

"What?" Jaden came to an abrupt halt, annoyed. "Kuro, are you even listening to me?"

"Yes. Of course." He wasn't. He was still thinking of the yellow eyes of a predator, but Jaden's words at last sunk in.

"That girl – she's..." He rounded on him, his hands open in the air, grasping for something – an idea, a notion perhaps – that he just couldn't put into words. "You should see her. She's small," he said quickly, dismissively, as though that displeased him, "*tiny*, with dark hair. It's heavy...thick."

Something had even robbed him of eloquence. Kuro stared at him, not bothering to hide his curiosity now. He cared less about what the girl looked like and more about the enraptured energy with which Jaden described her; he had never expressed this kind of intense interest in anyone before. His eyes were distant and bright, as though he could see her now in his mind.

"And her eyes...Kuro, you should see them." He sucked in a long, slow breath, savoring his next words. "She's *haunted*."

The description had the effect of a waiter telling a customer that their food had been dropped on the floor, then casually stepped on by muddied feet. Kuro drew back with disgust.

"I know, I know," Jaden said. "But you can see it in her eyes. The light, the way it shifts..."

Kuro blanched again. No one wanted to eat spoiled meat; a haunted soul was the same thing. They had met haunted people before: their souls had one foot on the earth, and the other...well, some other, darker place. It felt like a door was thrown open in their souls, a door in which, on the other side, a black void stretched, its maw gaping and sucking and pulling.

...Just like the darkness inside him, Kuro now realized; it was just like the *holy dark* within him, starving now.

To feed on a haunted person, no matter how inviting, was to touch that sucking void. Everything was bitter, soured. Although they had only come across a few haunted individuals, the impression they left behind was strong, like a sip of household cleaner.

Something, at some point, opened up that door inside people... and where it led to, instinct told him to never, ever go. Every person was different. Some doors had a thousand locks and couldn't budge, Kuro figured; for others, a weak keyhole, easily sprung...and things could creep in from the other side of that dark door: perceptions, for instance. Haunted people could feel them touching their souls.

A thought suddenly occurred to him. Hadn't Caroline said something about her brother always saying strange things? He'd felt her sorrow then, and something even below that – regret, longing.

He had been the one who had told her that there were demons in the woods. How had her brother known that? They had just arrived; she had said her brother had made these claims his whole life, that his parents had assumed he was mentally ill. So had Caroline.

What if he wasn't? *Demons in the woods,* Kuro thought again. That was the kind of thing a haunted person might say...

She might want to know that, he thought, and an idea began to form in his mind, dangerous and tempting. *She might be interested to know...*

His chest tightened with a hot, nervous twang, as though a chord inside of him had been struck.

The idea rooted itself, and the twisting, unsettled listlessness suddenly lifted, replaced by a purpose. *You can't go back there,* he thought, pushing it away quickly, already knowing he would. *You have to go back there,* another part of him argued back. *You're starving.*

This would be a suitable excuse; he could share this with her, feed from her soul, sustain himself a little longer while his leg healed, while he tried to give thought to how to free himself from her soul's grasp. Three days of quiet thinking had yielded no answers.

And worse, his thoughts often went down roads he didn't want to travel, paths that were starting to grow well-worn in his mind: the feeling of hands pushing back his hair, an arm around his waist, her gathering strength lifting him up. The scent of lavender.

He tried to focus again. His voice was oddly tight when he spoke.

"What do you want to do with a haunted girl? You're not going to feed off her, are you?" He was unable to keep a note of revulsion from his voice.

Jaden had begun pacing again. "That's the thing – I *can't*. Every time I tried to touch her soul, no matter how carefully, that *thing* stopped me. And it's *hot*, Kuro...it feels like fire. I don't think it likes me." His eyes flashed dangerously, and he grinned a wide, toothy smile. "But I broke past it...it was hard, but I did it. I could feel her soul. She could tell when I was touching it."

"Haunted people always can. Did that...that thing speak to you again?" Kuro couldn't bring himself to say 'angel.' He didn't want to believe it was possible.

"No. But it was there, actively trying to keep me from touching her soul."

It dawned on him that Jaden wasn't referring to the night he met the girl in the woods. "Wait – did you see her *again?*"

Jaden ground his teeth and whirled around. "I *knew* you weren't listening."

"I am now." He straightened up, his back against the tree. "Jaden – just leave her alone. What do you *want* with her?"

"I want her soul." He bit the words out, his arms bunching suddenly with tense need. "I don't understand it. There's – there's a *roaring* in my head." He stopped, licked his lips, his eyes too bright, and shook himself suddenly, clearing his thoughts. "I don't even *want* to want her, and I *do*. I want to consume her soul...but I need to get rid of that thing that's protecting her, first. I want to *see* it. I want to *speak* to it."

Kuro stared at him in slack-jawed shock. He couldn't imagine consuming an entire human soul (privately, he didn't think it was possible, despite Jaden's continual, deadly efforts), and second, the thought of consuming a *haunted* one in its entirety was enough to make his stomach flip.

There was also the problem of the *thing*...the 'angel,' as Jaden seemed convinced of. Whatever it was had put itself in opposition to Jaden: he ought to have the good sense not to antagonize it. Nothing good would come from fighting against an unknown opponent.

Jaden took an unsteady breath, one hand pressing against the base of a tree for support. Kuro could see that his hand was trembling. He had never seen that before, either. He felt alarmed by the sight of it. "I keep thinking about her eyes. And...I think I've met her somewhere before."

"Here? We've been in Asheville before. It's been a few years, but –"

"No." He shook his head emphatically. "It's not that. I can't place it. It's not even a memory, just...a feeling. And I keep thinking about other things, as well." He grinned suddenly, and for a moment, the ghost of a fox seemed to creep into his face. His teeth looked too sharp.

"What things?"

He laughed and sat down beside him, covering one eye with a shaking hand. "You really want to know?"

"I asked, didn't I?"

"Oh, don't get so offended, Kuro." He laughed again, then stretched out his hands, the palms up and open. He was mastering himself again, his voice growing quiet. "There's this spot on a woman's body, right above her hip bone. It's *soft*. I keep thinking of pulling that girl on top of me and putting my hands on her hips, and pressing both thumbs into those exact spots on either side of her waist, pulling her forward and down–"

Kuro made a harsh sound and looked sharply away.

"You're so modest, Kuro," he snickered. "You have such a polite sense of decorum. You would finally relax a little if you learned how to enjoy yourself."

Kuro eyed him with scorn. Deep down, Kuro didn't actually

think Jaden was attracted to the people that he...coupled with? Assaulted? He wasn't sure how to describe it and had only witnessed him in his overtures a few times. Even now, he didn't think Jaden's words were particularly tinged with lust: there was desire, yes, but it was a desire to exert his dominance...not sate some animal need. Kuro's thoughts were formless in this regard, nothing he had even put into words in his own mind or could quite understand...it was just a feeling that he gleaned once from watching Jaden stroke the wrist of a woman who had handed him a coffee. She blushed to the root of her hair at the soft touch, and Jaden had looked at her with a yearning, open desire that left her breathless...and his expression had disappeared the moment she turned away, flustered. He had not truly desired the girl; he only desired to manipulate her, to see what he could make her do, and feel.

No; he was tempted to think that ultimately, Jaden felt nothing, not even enjoyment...except that this girl he was fixed on now had clearly provoked a response unlike anything he had ever witnessed in his friend before.

When he didn't speak, Jaden said, "Forget it. Put your hand out."

Kuro grimaced and did as he was told without asking why. Jaden leaned backwards, and with much twitching and pulling, managed to remove the blue contacts. He set them down in Kuro's hands, then reached into his pocket for a small vial of clear liquid. Kuro stared down at the contacts in his hand and felt his skin crawl. The whole thing struck him as distasteful.

"I have to tell you, I fucking *hate* those things," Jaden hissed, the drops hitting his eyes. He blinked rapidly, and one spilled onto his cheek. His eyes were red and puffy, and with the liquid leaking out of the corners, it was the strangest he'd ever seen him: it looked like he'd been crying. Jaden had never shed a tear in his life.

Kuro would have almost promised he was incapable of it.

"How long have you had those in?"

"Three days." Jaden took them back and placed them in the

protective case, then slipped it into his pocket. "It took them that long to assimilate. My eyes have been *burning* waiting for that."

"Still can't change your eye color?"

"It took me ten years to change my *hair* color, Kuro. Give me a few more days to manage the next step."

Kuro pushed the dirt idly with the heel of his shoe. "And the girl – you're really going to...try and consume her soul?" There was so much more he wanted to say, but all he could manage was that single, stupid question.

"We've never met another demon, and we've certainly never met an angel. I want to drag whatever it is out into the open and see it with my own eyes. I have *questions* – about our existence, our kind. I want *answers*."

"And then what?"

"I don't know." Jaden smirked at Kuro's expression. "You always look at me like I have all the answers, like I can solve every problem. Half the time that feels very gratifying, and the other half...frustrating. I feel like this is an exciting opportunity to learn more about ourselves, about *everything*."

"What if it attacks you? You don't know if this thing is dangerous or not." What if he came back here, three days later, and Jaden was gone, dead somewhere? His voice rose in panic. "What if this thing *kills* you? How would I ever know?"

"Kuro...have you forgotten my promise to you?"

For a moment, with Jaden's steady gaze on him, he thought he was referring to his promise not to kill Kenneth...and then he remembered another promise, from their youth, and he nodded solemnly. "No," he whispered, reassured.

He reached over and clasped his shoulder. "Then don't worry: I won't let this thing kill me. It seems to just be protecting the girl."

Kuro couldn't look at him when he asked his next question. "Do you intend to kill her?"

"No." Jaden pulled away and flexed his hands. "If I kill her, her soul will disappear, like all the rest. Killing doesn't work. I have a different plan in mind. Something a little more...patient. I'll kill her eventually, I think," he amended, thoughtfully, in the tone of someone wavering on whether or not they would order dessert. He looked down at his palms, considering, his voice heavy with a sincerity that left Kuro shocked. "I don't know if I could stop myself from doing it, even if I didn't want to."

Kuro grabbed him by one shoulder, turning him to face him. Jaden blinked at him in surprise.

"*Don't*. No more death, Jaden."

"Kuro – *get your hands off me*." He never raised his voice, but Kuro pulled away, surprised at the sudden flash of malice that came and went. "It's touching, your sudden...compassion. Annoying, but touching all the same. Rest easy for now: if I kill her, it won't be tomorrow, or the next day. Remember when I told you that I needed something I hadn't had before? *Time.* I think I figured out why I haven't been able to eat a whole soul yet. *Teeth*, Kuro."

He was lost. Jaden grew exasperated and spoke slowly, as if to a child. "If I tried to pull a tooth out of your jaw, root and all, right now, I wouldn't be able to do it. It's stuck in there, firmly, and I could yank and tug and put all my strength into it, but realistically, it's not going to happen. *Trust me*," he suddenly laughed, and Kuro saw something dark gleam in his smirk, "It's *hard* to pull healthy teeth out of a gum line. They're very...secure. Embedded."

Kuro stared, confused as Jaden continued. "But if it's *loose*...if the tooth is already *loose*, you can keep wiggling it. You can nudge it, and the give gets greater until, with just a little tug...it's out. All this time I've been trying to pull out healthy, intact souls. It's impossible. But a *haunted* soul, one that's already got one foot in the doorway, one that succumbs to futility, to struggle, to fear and despair...that one might simply *give up*, and *yield*."

Kuro shuddered. He wanted to tell him *leave her alone*, or *don't do this*, but instead, his traitorous heart asked, quietly, "...How much time do you need?"

How long could he stay here in Asheville?

"I'm not sure," he said slowly, thinking. "A while. I want her to know that I'm watching her; I want her to be terrorized every day knowing of my very existence, that I could take her at any moment I choose. I want her to experience long stretches of *nothing* so that my very absence fills her mind with nightmares of me. I want to wait," he finished, his breathing suddenly labored.

Their eyes met. His had gone empty in the center, where something unknowable now burned. Jaden looked at him with an intensity he had never known, and in a low, certain voice, said, "I want her more than everything I've ever wanted. I don't know why, Kuro...but I feel like she's *mine*."

Kuro's stomach felt sick. He didn't know what the consequences were for eating an entire soul, for the human *or* Jaden, but certainly, Jaden wouldn't let her live. He shuddered at the look in Jaden's eyes and realized he had been brought to a crossroads: speak, and stop him.

Do nothing, and stay here in Asheville, return to a farm with a garden and a girl...

Kuro swallowed the lump in his throat, his decision made: he couldn't stand in Jaden's way on this. The girl's fate would be her own.

You're a coward, he thought.

Then I'll be a coward, he answered himself. There was death in Jaden's hard, vacant stare now, and Kuro knew it was a death he couldn't stop.

"One more thing, Kuro. I might need your help."

His heart froze. Kuro looked up; Jaden was studying him with a level, unblinking stare. He had never asked...this...of him before. There was an unspoken understanding between them: Kuro would not question him, nor oppose him...but he would also not participate in his...activities.

The air stilled in his lungs. "What do you mean."

"I think," Jaden said, slowly, "That you know what I mean."

"*Why?* What could I possibly do –"

"She knows Kenneth."

His jaw slammed shut with force enough to stun him. It took all his effort to unglue it enough to ground out the word, "*So?*" Jaden had promised not to kill the boy; he didn't see how he figured into...*this,* this abhorrent terrorizing of some poor girl.

"He told her that we attacked him in his home; he must put a lot of trust in that girl, to tell her that. The night we met, she was walking to 'a friend's' house. I would assume it was his, based on where I encountered her."

"*So?*" He repeated, his breathing quickening.

Jaden's look was remorseless. "You look like him."

Kuro had often felt lesser than Jaden, dwarfed by his intellect, but now he felt grateful for his lack of imagination, because instead of leaping to whatever Jaden was insinuating, his thoughts instead tumbled into nothing: he saw no connection, could dream no dark plans, grasp at no threads of understanding. Jaden stared at him, waiting, and when comprehension didn't immediately dawn, he at last said, "How awful it would be for her, to meet someone like *you.* How much it could hurt."

He became aware at last that his lungs were burning. He could see the edges of the terrible vision now, coming into view: the acute horror of being attacked by someone who looked so much like someone you cared about.

"...No." He swallowed, repeated the word again, firmer this time. "Whatever it is you're thinking: *no.*"

"What do *you* think I'm thinking, Kuro?"

"I don't know," he said, honest; he could hear the weariness in his own voice as he spoke. "And I don't need to know. I won't do it, or be a part of it. I'm not going to hurt this girl, or help you hurt her. I won't...I won't stop you," he whispered, ashamed. "But whatever you're asking of me, the answer is *no.*" He wouldn't be persuaded or compelled to do this; there was nothing Jaden could do to make him hurt this girl, nothing to threaten him with into obedience.

He could feel Jaden's eyes pinning him. He looked up and found the scrutiny unswerving, narrowed. "...Kuro," he said, slowly now as he pointedly changed the subject, "are you keeping something from me?"

The shift in topic momentarily startled him out of his thoughts. He drew back in genuine surprise. "No."

No, it didn't become easier, the more he lied...but at least the lies came quicker.

"Alright, Kuro." Jaden stood with easy grace, stretching, his voice suddenly light. "I'm heading out. Are you alright out here? I assume you'd rather stay in the woods..."

"I'm fine," he said, too quickly. "What will you do now?" He forced himself to sound interested, but his blood was still rushing in his temple.

"I'll head back to the city. I don't know her last name yet, but I have an idea of how to find out. Library cards," he said. "She went to a library to check out books, and Jacqueline isn't a common first name – that's her name, by the way," he said. "I'll see what information I can find...see if I can find *her*."

"Don't be reckless," Kuro warned. "Don't draw attention to yourself."

Jaden waved over his shoulder, already walking away. "Says the *kitsune* who got *shot*. See you in three days."

He had barely disappeared before Kuro scrambled to his feet and took off, gingerly limping on his bad leg, eager to get away from this place. His pulse quickened.

His own interests were elsewhere.

SIXTEEN

Kuro watched her from the edge of the forest, his body pressed low, hidden among the shadows.

The mare trotted in the pasture between the barn and her home, kicking up clouds of dust. Caroline stood in the center of the pasture, the horse moving around her in a brisk circle. The last of August had stretched on dry and hot, and the horse's gray flank had been stained a dirty brown. Caroline clicked her tongue and the horse slowed, approaching her. It tossed its head back as she moved forward to catch it, bringing its muzzle down close to her face. The mare nibbled at her shirt. Her laughter was carried to him by the breeze.

She led the horse over to the spigot and began to hose her down; the mare pawed at the resulting mud and tossed her mane, splashing a fleeting rainbow into the air. Caroline gave up on the bath and began to dry and brush her, stooping in the mud to inspect the front hooves. No sooner had she turned away to get a pick, the mare lay down in the mud and rolled on her back. Caroline turned and shouted, laughed, and pushed the horse back to her feet. Another bath, another drying, and this time, a swift return to the barn.

Her hair was slightly damp, her shirt muddy as she emerged, boots slick with dirt and water. She made her way past the house and strode to the garden. Kuro's ears pricked up; she was just close enough now to be able to feel her soul. He reached out tentatively, cautious, and drew in his breath.

She was feeling the simplistic happiness of a day ending, the quiet comfort that comes with routine, of having a home to care for, a place to love. It was better than starving, but it was like drinking sea water. He gagged and reluctantly sipped from it.

But more than hungry, he was curious; what would it be like, to feel *that*? He tried to think – when had *he* ever felt this feeling? There must have been a time, a single moment, that he had been simply, uncomplicatedly, happy.

Caroline stooped and picked up a large bucket, then grabbed a pair of shears from the ground, approaching her sunflowers. There was still about three weeks of summer left, but the season had spent itself early, and the heat had finally broke. An early fall was creeping in; the nights were cooling, and all around him and in her garden, the plants were wilting and accepting their end. The sunflowers slumped in the final days of their bloom, the stalks bent double, their faces staring down at the ground. Caroline reached up and examined the broad, spongy leaves, running her fingers over them. He shivered suddenly at the memory of the way her hands had felt running over his body, and his heart suddenly lurched forward.

She didn't have to stand on her toes. She was as tall as he was, and she reached up with strong arms tanned from the summer and began to clip the stalks, carefully placing them down in the bucket. Finished, she walked among her plants; she was so *serious,* like a general inspecting new recruits for any signs that needed immediate correcting. She tied back two tomato vines, her eyes narrowed at the green fruit, displeased by their insubordinate delay in ripening. The cucumbers had found great favor, and she clipped down a dozen, stacking them in a long basket. He watched her squat in the dirt, gently turning an eggplant in her hands, examining it, and then, with a satisfied nod, yank it from the stem.

She gave everything attention. He felt around the edges of her soul and winced; no, not attention – *love.* It was a simple love, one note, but it was joyful and sincere, and the world around her reacted to it, sprang up to her touch with greenery and blossoms. The sight of her dahlias, still blooming strong, made her smile. She touched the soft petals and beamed, and when she gathered a bunch of fresh basil and breathed in its scent, the edges of her eyes crinkled with delight.

A sudden feeling moved in him, a thought: how would she feel if she saw *him?*

Frightened, he thought. *The demon returns.*

He crept forward, the very first fallen leaves brushing under his belly. He stood at the edge of the forest, and with his head lowered to the ground, his tail long and elegant behind him, he emerged, the sunset bright on his back.

She looked up and gasped.

The feeling of joy nearly knocked him over. Her happiness sharpened and struck out at him, and he sucked in his breath, wincing. When he stepped forward again, leaves crunched under a pair of human legs, and he looked up, dizzy, to find her *running* toward him.

She came up short at the edge of the forest. "Kuro!"

"Hi."

She gestured for him to come over. He couldn't quite bring himself to meet her eyes. Everywhere, her joy was crackling in the air around him like fireworks, shimmering. He swallowed and looked up, meeting her gaze. She was beaming.

"I was hoping you'd come back."

He wasn't sure how to respond. His instinct was to blurt out 'why,' but his nerves kept him from speaking. He cleared his throat and gestured at her house. "Is your dog back?"

A flush spread across the bridge of her nose. "I actually boarded him for a week...just in case."

"In case of what?"

"...In case you came back."

He looked down at the ground again. In a month, it would be damp and sodden, the debris of a dying world lining its floor. For now, the dust had settled in the final light of a fine day. Caroline gestured over to the garden. "Would you mind helping me bring some stuff in? I've got something exciting to share with you."

He followed behind her, wondering what he was doing. He kept trying to bat away her soul, but it practically *thrummed* with delight, and the insistence of it made him dizzy and irritable. He was angry at himself and he didn't know why. That *feeling* that was bothering him – what was it? It had to have a name, an explanation; he thought about the way her hands felt on him, and the way she smiled, and it flared up again. His face drew down into a scowl.

"Here." She passed him two of the buckets of sunflowers, and head down, he followed her out of the garden and into the house. He set the buckets down and watched as she moved over to the sink, filling them up.

"Go ahead and have a seat; I'll be done in just a second."

He sat, watching her. Her loose curls had dried, and they hung and danced down her back as she moved. A scent hung heavy in the hot kitchen, something savory and crisping...

The oven was on. He peered through the door and saw something vaguely oval cooking in a pan. She turned and caught him staring.

"Roast chicken. Easiest thing in the world to make. Put it in a pan and come back in an hour. I like mine with salt and mustard, personally." She caught herself and stopped. "...Are you hungry?"

He nodded. She glanced at the oven, then back to him.

"...Is that why you came back?"

Kuro snorted. "I didn't come back for a roast chicken."

"...I meant, for my soul."

"*Oh.*" Her eyes were large, saucer-like, earnest and concerned. That *feeling* was like the residual effect of plunging his hand into stinging nettle. He hated it. He looked away, glancing down the empty hallway. If he were to tell the truth, he'd have to admit that he was *starving*. He kept snapping and sipping at bits of her soul in an effort to scrape together some sort of satisfaction, but all he could manage were painful morsels of what tasted like poisoned, bitter food. To a starving man, even poisonous food was appealing, and hunger drove him to desperation, even as it burned him.

But that wasn't why he had come back.

"No...that's not it. I didn't come back for that."

Her face brightened as she joined him at the kitchen table. "So then you can feel other people now? You'll be okay?"

She looked so hopeful. For a moment, he considered lying to her. He was shocked at the realization that he didn't *want* to take her hope away when he told her the truth. It stunned him so much that he sat in silence, staring back at her expectant face, unable to understand himself. *Why?* He thought, *why would I not want that?*

"...No. I can still only feel you."

"Oh." And there it was: her smile fell away, and for a moment, a cooling, pleasurable rush of disappointment surged upon him. He closed his eyes and drank from it as deeply as he could manage in the few seconds that it flowed, and then it receded, the tide going out. He opened his eyes to find her sighing.

"That must be very hard."

"...It is."

"But then, why did you come back here?"

He stalled, unsure of what to say. "Why did *you* think I'd come back here?"

"I didn't think you would. I just – hoped."

That didn't make sense either. He scrutinized her, trying to understand what was going on in her soul. She had found the ends of one of her curls and was plucking at it absently. She cleared her throat and told him to wait a moment, and rushed into the living room. In a moment she was seated in front of him again, two books in her hands, her voice clear and rapid.

"This is what I wanted to show you. I wanted to learn more about *kitsune* so I looked online, but there's so much...it's hard to make sense of it all. I decided to start with something smaller and give myself a jumping off point, so I got these two books from the library." She slid them over to him. One was called *Human Animals,* and the other, *Kitsune.* "I've been reading them in the evenings, and it's fascinating! I wonder how much of it's *right*? But I've been learning a lot, and if you came back, I wanted to ask you questions and see if you could tell me if some of the things were true or not."

He slid them back to her. The *Kitsune* book looked distantly familiar. A long time ago, Jaden had read it in a library and told him about it, but Kuro hadn't been interested. Her face fell again. "Aren't you curious?"

"It's not that, it's just..." The memory came back to him, sharp and painful: Jaden behind the glass of a quiet study room, staring down at a book, his eyes wide and unblinking. He looked calm, a student in deep concentration...but his hands had been in his hair, holding his head up, the elbows on the table, and Kuro remembered clearly how his forearms had been shaking.

When Kuro spoke, the words didn't belong to him. They were something Jaden had once said. "It's just, from the moment you're born, you have a whole culture waiting for you, and every moment of your life, you begin to learn more and more about it. You learn about the whole history of your people, your race, your species. You have art and technology. You have people to guide you through everything – your changes, your births and deaths. We don't have anything. We're abandoned at birth and then...we just have to find our way. Or if there is more...if there are others...or answers...we've never found them, yet."

Well, *he* hadn't. He thought of Jaden and the angel he thought he had discovered, and shivered.

"'We?'"

"...*Kitsune.*"

He didn't need to meet her gaze; he could feel the sympathy flowing from her. "How have you managed to learn about yourself?"

"Some things we just *know* – instinct, I guess. I *knew* I was a *kitsune;* it wasn't a word I needed to learn. I knew I couldn't touch weapons or break promises, and later, after –" The words came to a tumbling halt.

"After?"

After the *holy dark* first moved in him, waking, nothing was ever the same. Needful, hungry and yearning, he was *awake*, and *it* was alive in him, and it was hungry. He shut his mouth and felt a sudden need for air. He didn't want to share that experience with her.

At least, not yet. "Nothing."

She stood up and moved to the oven, slipping on a pair of mitts. "Kuro," she said, without turning to face him. The aroma of crisp chicken filled the kitchen as she set the pan down on top of the stove. "I understand if there are things you don't want to tell me. I won't press you. But, if you ever want to share...I'll listen."

There it was, the feeling again; it would be good for someone to listen. She turned and he looked away as quickly as he could, feigning a sudden interest in the tile. She brought the pan over, his body leaning forward, unguardedly ravenous.

"It's too hot to eat at the moment, but would you like to share this meal with me?"

He nodded. She set down plates and filled cups with water, and then he cringed, watching as she lifted the same kitchen knife she had threatened him with. She carved the chicken and served him a breast, thigh, and leg, and without waiting for her to serve herself, he tore into it, making short work of the meat, his hands burning as he tore through the skin to reveal the unctuous fat underneath.

"When's the last time you ate?"

He ripped the last strip of meat from the leg bone and thought. "Yesterday?"

"You don't sound so sure."

She served him the remaining meat, and when he was done, she gave him four slices of bread. He soaked them in the juices and melted fat in the bottom of the pan, savoring the drippings.

"I've been busy at work." She spoke as he ate; he could tell that the silence made her uncomfortable. "The police think a man has trained a wolf to attack people. That poor man..."

He swallowed the bread. "What happened?"

"I'm not supposed to talk about it. I spent all day yesterday labeling evidence bags. I took two personal days so I didn't handle a lot of the paperwork myself, but I saw the photos..." She paused, shoving the memory forcibly away. "I've got to get caught up at work this week. The last I heard, the police investigated another crime scene they think might be related."

Kuro sat up straighter. "Another crime?" Jaden hadn't mentioned anything. He grew tense, waiting.

"From earlier, prior to the murders; no one was hurt. Something about a robbery, I think, or a break-in. I was out and heard about it second-hand. I put on a uniform when I go to work, but it's just show – I just file the paperwork," she said, and laughed, but it was half-hearted. He relaxed; they hadn't robbed anyone, so it must had been something unrelated to the murders. A fleeting thought (*could it be Kenneth?*) came and went; no, he was certain the boy wouldn't press them further and report them to the police....

But the thought remained, needling at him.

"It's usually pretty boring and quiet being a secretary, even if it's a police secretary, but this has really got everything off-balance. Like you," she added, and smiled. "You've got me off-balance. That's why I've been reading about you." She pointed to the books. He pushed the plate away, contented and a little curious despite himself.

"And what did you learn?"

"*Kitsune* are 'demon foxes,' but it's a poor translation, I think... there really isn't an equivalent here, in our culture, of 'demons.' I think 'spirit' might be a bit better."

"'Our' culture?"

She explained her sense of Eastern and Western cultures. Kuro listened to her, more focused on the movements of her lips than the words that came out of them. Culture, time, and place were concepts almost too large for him to grasp. The Pisgah forest seemed huge; to imagine an entire state, a country, a continent, an entire *world* stretching backwards for thousands and thousands of years was a hard thing to wrap his mind around. Christianity, she told him, was largely dominant in the West, and the sense of 'spirits' – otherworldly creatures that inhabited the world with them, or partially, on some separate 'plane' (he didn't know what that meant) – was largely absent.

"The native peoples had beliefs like that, and there are still other things that people believe – ghosts, for instance, but *you* don't fit neatly into that category. By the way – are ghosts real?"

He rolled his eyes. He couldn't say for *sure,* but he doubted it. Jaden had said that when souls departed in death it was as if in one moment they were there, and the next, like an extinguished candle, they were simply gone.

"Anyways, your kind seem to have begun in the East – China, Japan, Korea – but there are stories from all over the world. What I'm trying to say is, you...you're not *evil*. At least, I don't think you are. I hope not," she added, and Kuro could see she was trying to keep a hold of herself. When she got nervous, she was like a horse out of the gate, her words plunging ahead. "You're a demon, but it's not like what I thought. And there's so much more! I've only just started, and I've been jumping around, skimming, but – did you know that there're two kinds of *kitsune?*"

He tried to think back. He couldn't remember if Jaden had mentioned that or not. He shook his head.

She pulled the book over and opened to a dog-eared page. "There's *myobu,* who are 'good,' in a relative sense. I don't want to bore you, but I read a few stories about certain ones. They...well, they're usually, um...lighter in color. White. They're usually guardians of some sort." When he remained silent and listening, she pressed on. "And there's *nogitsune,* their opposites: mischievous tricksters, often causing trouble and chaos. They're usually black."

He snorted. "So I'm a *nogitsune?*"

"I don't know – are you?"

He thought about it. He didn't know.

"And did you know that nearly all of the stories are about *female* foxes? You look surprised."

"I've never met a vixen." He thought about it: a female *kitsune* would have to be *beautiful*. He held back a grin.

"And many of them have multiple tails. You only have the one."

"You sound disappointed."

"I'm just pointing it out! Oh, and did you know how long you can live for?"

At the rate things were going, Kuro figured he had a week or two until he starved to death. "Is it going to depress me?"

She laughed. "It says you'll live for a thousand years! That's *incredible*. How old are you now?"

He'd never done so much thinking before. He tried to remember the first time he saw Kenneth; the boy had been...twelve? Thirteen? And he was what, twenty now? Possibly twenty-one. And Kuro had been in the woods for about ten years before that, but it was hard to know for certain...

"I think I'm twenty...twenty-two? I don't know."

She laughed. "You're practically a *baby* for your kind! That can't be right. Have you always looked like this, or did you age like a normal person?"

"I'm just making myself look like this. It's...flexible."

She stared, opened her mouth to speak, then stopped to compose herself. "Can you make yourself look younger?"

"Or older. But...I can't really imagine past a certain age, so it would be hard for me to push it. I could do younger pretty easily, if you want."

She shook her head. "Can I see what you look like older?"

"I can try." He crossed his arms over his chest, searching inside of himself. This wouldn't be like shifting easily back and forth; this would require concentration, effort...this form, *this* age, came natural to him – he supposed it was because it was a match for how he felt. But, she wanted older; the best he could picture was a thirty-five year old. He could see himself with a strong, solid frame, jaw set, and with a feeling of stretching, he shifted.

The book fell away from her fingertips, its spine open on the table.

"How do I look?"

"Older," she managed. He could feel her soul around him, fluttering nervously like a bird trapped in a house. He switched back in an instant; it felt like letting a rubber band go, snapping back to a place of comfort. She let out her breath.

"You didn't like that," he said.

"How did you know? Oh. Right."

"Why not?"

"Somehow, that was far more unsettling than watching you shift from this to your *kitsune* form. It sort of...reminded me of my own mortality, I guess. Don't do that one again."

He gave a short bark of laughter. "I won't."

A sharp pain of happiness caught him right in his solar plexus just as she smiled. "I've never heard you laugh before. Not like that, anyways."

He decided to evade her comment. "Any more questions?"

"We're going to come back to that *nogitsune* thing once I do some more reading," she warned, her voice playful, "but yes, I've got a few more. Can you do any illusions?"

"Oh, sure."

"*Really?*"

There was something pleasing about all of the attention. He nodded, shy but undeniably thrilled. "Yes, but not a variety. Each *kitsune* gets their own trick, a special illusion or ability only they can do."

"What's yours?"

He lifted his eyes to her face, and everywhere, her soul trembled with excitement. He felt suddenly bashful. "I need some more light... and some darkness. Do you have any candles?"

"Candles?"

"They would work pretty well."

She stacked the dinner plates in the sink. Outside, the sun had settled into a murky dusk, and Caroline returned from the back bedroom with three candles and a lighter. He followed her into the living room and watched as she set them down on the curio, the floor, and tv, the flames dancing.

"Don't start a fire," she said; her tone aimed for casual ease and fell short, underscored by her nervousness. Kuro sat down on the floor, his own nerves pricking; she had sat close to him, their knees practically touching.

"I can show you this, but I don't have a lot of strength right now...so I'll need to feed from your soul a little bit." He meant it as an explanation, but it came out sounding like an apology. "What I mean is, it might hurt – you might feel it. I don't think you will, you *shouldn't*, you haven't before, I don't think, but just – in case..." Did he always sound this stupid?

"Oh." Caroline pulled her hair over her shoulder, thoughtful, but decided. "Okay."

He closed his eyes and felt the edges of her soul. She was still nervous; he unraveled the threads of her anxiety and used it to pierce a little deeper, searching. The further he pressed in, the more she would feel it, especially if he began to dig up the painful, hidden things the mind fought so stridently to repress. Everyone had wellsprings of pain; some were just hidden better than others.

But inside of her, there was little subterfuge. He found a sadness and touched it, gripping it, letting it fill him. *Finally;* he was so, so hungry... He opened his eyes to see that she had shivered, but the feeling had gone otherwise unnoticed.

"Now – watch."

The candles flickered around them, the shadows dancing on the walls. He knew the moment that the gasp escaped her lips that she saw it: the movement changed. The shadows began to twist away from their sources, crawling up the walls in a hideous, jerking movement. Her nervousness twisted into fear, and he felt himself come alive. Her fear filled his belly with a hot heat, the hair on the back of his neck rising with a pleasurable tingling; for the first time in days, the gnawing hunger was being fed: his breathing evened out, his eyelids heavy.

But then he turned, watching, and he could see the shadows through her eyes: they were swarming, overflowing into a hideous thing of legs and eyes and fangs. Her eyes were widening, and she was shuddering now –

He grit his teeth, and with a great effort, smoothed them out. The monster dissolved, and concentrating, he moved them again, this time with as much grace as he could muster. They flowed like water, dripping down until they formed trees. A branching forest made of shadow spread across her living room wall, and in the forest a herd of deer walked on legs of velvet darkness. Their antlers rose with the arcing of their necks, ears swiveling, and suddenly they leapt away, disappearing deep into the woods.

The trees collectively trembled and wove themselves together until they formed the scales of a large snake. Caroline gasped as it uncoiled and moved across the living room wall, stretching its body across the ceiling. Her hand shot out and gripped his arm. The touch bolted through him, and the snake suddenly turned, opening its mouth, a tongue flickering.

Her grip tightened. He laughed, the illusion dissolving. It scales lifted away in the form of black moths, their wings gently returning the shadows to their homes where they belonged, where they resumed their dance behind the candles.

"So... that's what I can do."

She looked at him in awe. "Kuro – that's *amazing*." He could feel her astonishment, her wonder; it delighted him. He felt suddenly like a shy child, eager for praise.

"Do you want to see what else I can do?"

"You can do *more?*"

"Moving shadows is unique to me, but I can show you something all *kitsune* can do. I'm not very good at it," he added quickly, embarrassed. "Since I've had my trick for so long, I never bothered to really get good at this, but...well, here."

He held out his free arm, his fingertips stretching upward, palm open. A glowing orb of blue flame appeared, faint and flickering, hovering in the air above his hand.

"Fox fire," he said. "Don't worry – it doesn't burn like regular fire...but don't touch it."

She didn't speak. The blue flame danced in her eyes, and slowly, her grip on his arm relaxed. His skin was cold when her fingertips left it, and mesmerized, she reached for the flame.

Before he could stop her, her fingertips brushed it.

"Caroline!"

She cried out and yanked her hand backwards. In an instant, the blue flame was gone, and her hand was in his. He was gripping it too tightly, but he didn't want to let go.

The brief flash of pain in her soul would have been delicious to feed on.

He shoved it away, disgusted with himself. "I told you not to touch it!"

She offered a sheepish smile. "I have a bad habit of not doing what I'm told, same as my brother. We just don't listen." She looked down at their hands, still clasped. "...You said it wouldn't burn."

He could feel her hurt; she thought he had deceived her. Kuro squeezed her hand more tightly. "I said it doesn't burn like *fire*," he corrected. "It doesn't burn anything physical, like fire does. Look." He lifted her hand up for her to see. The skin on her fingertips was smooth, unharmed. He felt relief – his own – as her sense of betrayal eroded away into curiosity. "It burns other things... things you can't see."

"Like what?"

His whisper was quiet and ashamed. "Your soul."

"Oh." She looked away. "It was beautiful, though."

Her hand was still in his. He looked down at it, then back at her. His throat felt too tight, and that feeling was back, the one with no name that had come to occupy so many of his thoughts.

"Kuro – what is it?"

When he didn't immediately speak, she reached out and touched the side of his face. He didn't mean to, but he leaned his cheek into her touch, his eyes shut. "I keep seeing this expression on your face, like you're angry with me. I'm sorry. For everything. I know I already apologized, but –"

He let go of her hand and reached up, his hand passing through her hair, cupping her face. She stopped mid-sentence, her voice hitching. Nervousness flared up again, but in the fog of his own feelings, he couldn't tell who it belonged to. He was drowning, he was on fire, he was being buried alive – it felt like every torture combined, this feeling in his spine that made him pass his hands up through her hair, pulling it toward him. He had never thought very deeply about himself before, and now, faced with an interior life he didn't understand, with emotions he had never known, it was easier to walk away from it, not think about it too much.

Easy, and yet impossible.

SEVENTEEN

Her hair was softer than he had expected. He let his palm curl around it, twining his fingers through the waves, and a sudden need to bury his face in it inflamed him. His hand moved down to her shoulder, feeling the firm groove of her body, the curve of her muscles, and without thinking, he pushed her onto her back in one fluid, sudden movement. He supported himself above her, amazed by this woman who stared up at him now in shock; he wanted to study her the way she had looked at him, to know and understand her...

To kiss her again, to feel the soft brush of her lips. He leaned down, breathing in the scent of her hair, his cheek brushing against hers.

But Caroline had frozen still, her body rigid. With a start, he became aware that all around him, a feeling of intense anxiety had spread, electrifying the air, and that it was swiftly crystalizing into fear. He moved his head to look into her eyes and saw that she was caught between a panicked feeling of wanting to run and a terror that froze her in place. He had brought his forearms down on either side of her, and Kuro was suddenly, acutely aware of what he was doing.

He sat up fast, mortified; Caroline also rolled and pushed away quickly. His face was burning. He had been feeling something new and powerful, and he had expected to see it mirrored in her eyes. He was disgusted with himself, angry that he had acted without thinking, and frustrated that she would look at him like *that*, like he was something to be afraid of.

Like he was Jaden.

You ARE something to be afraid of, he realized. His jaw clenched. *Imagine what she looks at when she sees you. Imagine what she thought when you pushed her down like that.*

He tried to see himself through her eyes, and the portrait nauseated him. He was as tall as her, but powerfully built with unforgiving strength: he could crush bone or break an arm if he needed to. She surely knew that a good, solid blow to the head would knock her unconscious in one swing, not that he would need to: he had the strength to fully restrain her, even if she fought him. And he was handsome, with dark eyes she couldn't see into, that hid unknowable thoughts. But beyond all that...he was inhuman, a thing that could change in an instant to an animal with claws and fangs, a thing that could hiss at her and twist shadows on her walls, a monster that could cut open her skin, slice through muscle and fat, and end her life.

That was what she saw when she looked at him.

He felt a soft touch on his shoulder, but he didn't move. He continued to stare at the floor, concentrating on slowing his breathing. He didn't know why, but his blood was rushing in his head.

"Are you okay?"

He bit out a response, his anger at himself breaking free. "Are *you*?"

"What do you mean?"

He risked a glance. Her hand was still on his shoulder. "...You looked at me like you expected me to hurt you." He drew an unsteady breath. "And...I wouldn't have. But I shouldn't have done that. I'm – I'm sorry."

Her hand withdrew, and the coldness returned. "I was just surprised, is all."

"No. You weren't 'surprised.' I can feel *exactly* how you feel." He drew his legs up toward himself and passed his fingers through his hair, holding his head. He felt the anger drain out of him. "I'm sorry. You don't have to...have to *defend* how you feel. I would feel the same way if it were me. I didn't mean anything by it – I just wanted to look at you..."

"Kuro." She moved in front of him. Her hands laced through his, pulling them down and toward her. He looked up, and she smiled. She held his hands gently, and he felt a wave of tenderness that brushed him, like nails being driven into his bones.

A channel of empathy opened up between them. He felt it grow and fought the urge to pull away from her, frightened suddenly. Empathy was rare and fleeting and sneaking, a creeping thing that opened paths between people, and it stole upon him now, its cold coils twining around his heart. Kuro looked up into her eyes, his heart beating wildly, and saw that she was still smiling. A warmth moved from her to him, and it burned.

He swallowed, and like a man facing the firing squad, tentatively turned to face it.

It flowed into him with fiery abandon, and even though he wanted to squeeze his eyes shut, to cry, to run from the pain, he forced himself to smile back at her, to let it come into him. It *hurt,* but her hands felt so good in his, and if he pulled away, he was sure he would lose that feeling.

"I think we're both frightened of each other," she whispered. "And that's okay. Let's not apologize for how we feel?"

He nodded.

"...Let's start today over. Tell me why you came back here."

Right. He'd had a perfectly good excuse. "...I came back to tell you about your brother. I was thinking about him."

"You were?" Shock flared. "*Why?*"

Kuro watched the candle flickering, his thoughts lost in its movement for a moment. "I was thinking about how you said he was always saying odd things, or seeing things. You were...upset, when you told me."

"And you remembered that?" She was incredulous. He couldn't understand why she was so surprised. She pulled away from him, and the feeling, the path of openness, was gone. He felt even more empty than before, even as the pain receded.

"Why wouldn't I?"

Her hands twisted in her lap. "It's just – your world is so much bigger than mine. There're so many other things to think about."

"My world is *bigger* than yours?"

"My world is very small, Kuro." She smiled again, but he felt an edge of sadness, a twinge of longing. "I have a small job, which I enjoy, even if it's hard some days. I have a horse, a dog I care for, a garden I plant and harvest from...I have bills to pay. I never went to college. It's all very...small. But *you* – the whole world is open to you. You don't have anything like that."

He stared back at her, and when he spoke, his voice cracked with a hurt he hadn't known he harbored.

"I have *nothing*."

A silence came between them. Caroline winced and joined him in staring at the candlelight.

"I didn't mean –"

"Forget I said it," he said. "It's not important. I was talking about...what is his name?"

"Christopher."

"I was thinking that he might be... *haunted*."

"Haunted?" Her head was resting on her forearms, her knees propped up against her chest. "By a ghost?" She shook her head. "No, don't be ridiculous." Her cheeks colored, and he felt a sheepishness creep across her soul. "I can't believe I just said that to *you*, of all people."

I'm not a person, he thought, but he was swift enough to catch the words before he said them aloud. "Not by a ghost," he said. "A person who's haunted isn't haunted by a creature or something like that...it's more..." He struggled to finds the words and came up short. Caroline sat up, interested, and urged him to continue.

She was eager, and something almost desperate was bubbling in her soul, anxious and quick. She was fighting against it. He looked at her and couldn't stand the thought of disappointing her, and the realization of it – *that he didn't want to disappoint her* – stunned him anew.

"Kuro?"

He recovered and moved past his own feelings, speaking. He tried to explain the feeling of feeding on a haunted person, that feeling of standing on the edge of a sink hole and staring down, fearing that you might fall in at any moment; the sensation of eating spoiled meat, of maggots crawling out of green-tinged flesh; of emptiness, of bitter draughts, of flies drinking the sweat on the surface of your skin. His words came out ineloquent, stilted. He started and stopped so often that he realized he was rambling as he tried to articulate his meaning.

It was the feeling of coming back to your home in the middle of the afternoon and seeing your front door thrown wide open, not knowing who was inside, not knowing what was gone, the violation of an invasion.

"How does it happen? When does it start?"

He wasn't entirely sure, but he'd come across enough haunted people to form an opinion at least. "I think something happens – something different, something unique to the person. I suppose it could start any time after that 'something' occurs."

"Something like what?"

He shrugged. "Something powerful enough to...to open up a door, is how I would describe it. Something that throws open a door in their soul."

"What's on the other side of the door?"

The Dark. He knew it from instinct, from the roiling of the *holy dark* inside him...but he didn't know what that meant and feared to put it into words. He only shook his head, bewildered.

"Can they close it – this...door?"

"I have no idea."

Caroline's voice was thoughtful. "But what *is* it? What's haunting them?"

"It's themselves," he said. "They're haunted by themselves."

He expected her to be relieved: here he was, presenting her with a possible explanation for the behavior of someone she cared about, but her soul wasn't responding how he had thought it would. Wouldn't she be happy to think that there was a possibility that her brother hadn't been imagining things? His brow knit. He looked her up and down, trying to see an explanation in the slump of her shoulders, the way her eyelids drooped...

"So he might not have been crazy," Kuro concluded. "He could be haunted, and maybe that's why he heard or saw things." His words sounded harsh in the silence.

Caroline flinched. "Don't call him 'crazy.' You don't know him. He has a mental illness – and...he hates that word. *I* hate that word."

"That's what I'm saying." Her soul was starting to move, but it was pitching with the early signs of a storm; whatever was coming was building, strong and raging. "You said he used to say strange things, that he told you demons were in the woods. I'm trying to tell you that he might not have been imagining things after all."

Her voice came out in a hushed whisper. "Don't say that."

"He might have been telling you the truth."

"*Don't say that!*"

He felt as though he'd been struck. She looked up at him, her eyes filled with tears, her mouth twisted in anger. Her soul rose up around him, lashing at itself. Pain, more pain than he had ever felt, broke through the surface. He blinked rapidly to try and focus, but it was dulling his senses, filling him and intoxicating him, and she was crying –

He fought against the temptation of it, refusing the meal, this *feast*. She was trying to rub away tears from her face, knuckles frantically scrubbing at her cheeks, but it wouldn't work.

"Why would you tell me that?" Her voice broke on a sob.

He lifted himself on his knees, reaching for her. She knocked his hands away, furious at him, at herself. The rage exploded in the pain, striking toward everything before turning back upon itself in self-loathing.

"Caroline, stop this," he pleaded. Her feelings were everywhere around him, bursting from some locked corner of her heart. The *holy dark* moved in him and responded to her; he felt helpless, unable to resist, and tasted of it. It was sweet and filling and lovely. He closed his eyes, took a deep breath, and opened them again to see her, her body wracked with the effort of controlling her tears.

"Why would you tell me that?" She repeated, her voice rising.

"I thought..." He breathed again, trying to keep her soul away, but he was weak and wanting. "I thought it would make you happy."

Her eyes widened. "*Happy?*" She stood up on shaking legs, her breath catching now. The sobs were coming, and they would not stop. "You thought that would make me *happy?*" She laughed, and it was the harshest, worst sound he had ever heard. "Why would *you* want to make me *happy?* Isn't *this* what you want?" She spread her hands open, her body shaking, tears streaking down her face, joining under her chin, and gasped with all the pain of her heart. It was about to shatter, and she was fighting against it.

She was on the edge of breaking down. If he wanted, he could have reached out and made it crumble.

"This isn't what I want," he whispered.

"*This* is why you came back –"

"No, you're wrong –"

"You're starving, and this is how you get what you want. Well, you can have it." She pressed a fist to her mouth to stop herself from crying out with the pain of a memory, and with a muffled sound of anger, rushed out of the room. He heard her bedroom door slam and lock.

But her soul still filled the small home, and the turmoil held him, arrested, in its grasp. He sat in the living room, surrounded by it, and felt like a man below the pounding force of a waterfall. The waves of her emotion crashed into him and beat him down, and his heart was fighting against his own will – something inside him was opening its jaws, hungry and desperate, and this was everything it wanted: pain, rage, and a terrible, heartbreaking sadness that hated even itself.

He knelt, gripping his hair as he arched his back, pressing his forehead into the floor, fighting it. Feeding on it would make it worse. He concentrated, groaning, eyes squeezed shut, and felt the edges of the maelstrom, searching for a way in. Something this powerful had roots that went deep into the heart. He touched the outer threads of the pain and followed it into the labyrinth, struggling against the threat of losing himself to her sadness. It was everywhere around him, a cloud of such oppressive weight that it choked his other senses. He tasted just enough to give him strength and wrenched himself away, tracing the patterns into her soul.

A feeling like this, something that had been oppressed for so long, grew deep beneath the surface in a place of great pain. He remembered back to the night he met her: there was love, fierce and burning, somewhere at the center of all of this. He would find it.

There, in the heart of her sorrow, the twin snakes of regret and shame lay entwined, breeding self-loathing. He found it and tugged at it, and a hot spear of anger came at him. He gritted his teeth and pressed further in. Whatever had happened, whatever she had done and was thinking about, she hated herself for it.

But underneath that hatred of herself, there stemmed a foundation of something else, and he could *feel* it, buried there...He tried to coax it out gently, brushing the edges of it, but it burned him. He sucked in his breath and tried again, but it was small and weak, and the sadness around it was like a hurricane, tearing Caroline apart.

Kuro took a deep, gasping breath, and plunged in. It felt like leaping into boiling water. He opened his heart to the love in her and fed from it, closing his jaws around it and drinking from it. If he fed from it, he could intensify it, make the soul aware of it, *lift it up* –

He fell on his side and curled in upon himself in agony, biting down on his tongue to keep from screaming, but he held his grip. He pulled at the feeling, amplifying it, and painstakingly, like drawing a thrashing sailfish to the surface of the water, it materialized and grew visible. The hurricane slowed, the winds ceasing, and the feeling emerged like an island of stability in the turmoil of her grief.

And there her heart came to rest. The storm had passed.

He swallowed and tasted blood in his mouth. It took a force of will to unclench his arms from his hair. He staggered out into the night on his injured leg, the feeling of knives in his gut. After he had stumbled thirty minutes in the dark he collapsed completely and heaved until he was dizzy from the lack of air, and still he felt gripped by the pain of the love he had devoured, *lifted* in her soul. He wasn't meant to feed from that; it had poisoned him, but there was no expelling it.

He could only endure.

He stumbled onward, deeper into the night, back toward the woods. He wouldn't see her again, he decided, falling down next to the pond. He was so used to feeding off of other's feelings that he had never given much thought to his own, and he had felt strange tonight, acted impulsively, and he had scared her...and everything he had done made no sense, he thought, drawing his legs up toward his chest. It made no sense to share things with her, secrets; to not want to upset her; to fight to take away her sorrow.

It made no sense to kill himself this way.

Kuro drifted off into a fitful sleep, his eyes filled with the slow motions of a duck upon the dark water, and dreamt of nothing.

The cattails had begun to explode.

He woke up and sneezed; a puff of white fluff had fallen onto his face and scratched him. He patted it away, rubbing his eyes, then stopped.

He was still in his human form.

He went to stand, but his legs gave out from under him, and giving up, he remained stretched in the weeds, watching the brown tubers slowly unzip, the seeds carried away by the breeze.

He closed his eyes, and when they reopened, the sun had moved on in the sky, and a voice was calling from somewhere down near the road. Probably the owner of one of the nearby pastures. He didn't bother to move; unless they came stomping up through the underbrush, he could remain hidden, quiet. The only thing he was worried about were water moccasins, but the ducks didn't seem concerned.

The voice shouted again, louder as it drew near. He closed his eyes and tried to sleep, but a sudden thrashing disturbed him. Someone was scaling up the hill now, coming up from the road. He propped himself up on his elbows, ready to shift his form and slink away.

"*Kuro!*"

The shock of hearing his name froze him in place. He opened his mouth to sputter something, but nothing came out. In the next instant, Caroline was visible on the other side of the pond, wearing a pair of overalls over a floral-collared shirt. Her hair was free and wild around her, and she was searching, frantic. Her voice was raw from continuous yelling.

"*Kuro!*"

"Caroline?"

She turned, searching, eyes wild. He tried to sit up and struggled, but rose high enough for her to see him. The moment her eyes found him, she took off bounding around the pond, her long legs splashing in the muck.

The muddy, sweaty girl fell on her feet next to him, and before he could speak, she had thrown her arms around him.

He was about to reach up to wrap his arms around her when she pulled away.

"I've been searching since dawn. It's almost two o'clock...I was so worried."

"You've been... searching for me?"

"Yes." She took a deep, gulping breath; her voice was hoarse from shouting. "I started at the bottom of the road I dropped you off at the other day, and I've just been working my way up. I've been going into the woods, climbing over property – one guy caught me and thought I was trying to break into his shed. I've never run so fast in my life." She laughed suddenly, joyful and nearly manic, and the feeling bubbled out of her and tickled him. "I was starting to lose hope. But I found you."

"...Why were you searching for me?"

He looked into her eyes, trying to understand why she was looking at *him* with surprise. "Because you left."

"...You were angry with me."

She sat down in the reeds and drew her legs forward. The ducks beat their wings against the water, and with an angry rustle, flew away.

"...I was angry with myself. Not you. I didn't mean what I said."

Kuro turned away from her and watched as the pond's surface grew still again. Caroline hesitated, then spoke. "I felt like everything inside of me was shattering...and then I didn't feel that way anymore. All of sudden, I just felt so...calm, and I remembered – other things. It happened so suddenly, like a valve shutting off." He started with shock; she had put her hand down on top of his, her fingers lacing down through his own, and he faced her again, nervous. "That was you, wasn't it?"

He didn't know what to say, and so he only nodded.

"What did you do?"

"...I looked for something in your soul, something...better. I just brought it to the surface. That's all."

"That must have hurt you."

She had no idea. After he had emptied his stomach, he had continued to wretch bile tinted pink with blood. He didn't even have the strength to stand now, but she didn't need to know that. His response was to shrug.

"I feel like I owe you an explanation. And an apology."

Kuro shook his head. "You don't owe me anything."

"No, I...I want to explain it to you, my reaction...but not now. Later. It still hurts too much to think about. But please – can I at least say that I'm sorry? Because I am, Kuro." Her grip tightened, just a little bit. "Ever since I've met you, I keep thinking about...everything, really. Everything I thought I understood is different now. Everything about people, this place, this world...even myself. It's all changed. I don't know what I believe anymore."

"...I'm sorry, too."

"Don't apologize." Her fingers curled around his, and she lifted his hand up, staring into his eyes. "It's all changing, but...this is good." The wind caught her hair, pulling it toward her face. Without thinking, he reached up and pushed it away, then drew his hand back, waiting to see how she would react.

She smiled at him again, and he felt kindness radiate from her. "You can come back any time," she said. "You don't need an excuse. You could even come back now, if you want." Her smile turned suddenly shy, and she shrugged, gesturing back toward the road. "My truck isn't too far, but...if you don't want to..."

"Can I have a chicken?"

"What?"

"Can you make another chicken?"

Her laughter sparkled. She nodded, and after helping him to his feet, led him out of the woods.

EIGHTEEN

C aroline was gone when he woke up in the morning, a note left on the kitchen table: *Gone to work. Will be home by 6.*

Home. He thought about the Blue Ridge Parkway and imagined what it would be like as autumn came on. He and Jaden would be moving deeper into the mountains, racing against the fall by seeking out high, solitary ground, a warm place to pass the coming winter...

But for now, the sun was shining, warm and crisp, while Kuro lazed out in the garden, watching its steady arc across the sky. Winter was unimaginable at the moment, and even though the trees hinted at the coming change September would bring, here, under the noonday sun, even the approach of autumn seemed like a dream.

His mind wandered, and in the silence, fresh worries competed with the whine of the cicadas. Caroline had mentioned a report about a break-in...he had tried to push it away earlier, but the thought returned to him again, persistent: what if it *was* Kenneth? He had been fast to dismiss the possibility; surely they had scared him too badly for him to risk going to the police. No one would believe him. He couldn't be that stupid.

...But what if he was?

Not stupid, his mind corrected. *Brave.*

If it had been him, oh well; perhaps it was as Jaden said: the police wouldn't find them, and more importantly, Jaden had promised not to kill the boy. He was safe.

Safe from death, he thought. *There are other, painful things.*

Kuro was rapidly discovering that the more one thought, the more thoughts came. He scratched behind his ears and stretched his body out in the grass, breathing in the garden around him, wishing he had a distraction. He didn't know what a police secretary did. Paperwork, she had said. It would only be a matter of time before she saw a report, and if it *was* Kenneth, he might have said what he saw... about *two* people, or *two* animals...

He shook the thought away, but another snuck in: the girl...*Jacqueline.* What was Jaden doing right now?

He tried not to care; whatever he was doing, it was keeping him busy, leaving Kuro's days free.

He was surprised to find himself anticipating Caroline's return as the sun began its downward slant. He tried to understand the feeling inside him: it wasn't quite excitement, certainly wasn't happiness...if anything, it felt like anxiety. His heart beat too fast, the blood rushed too loudly in his ears. He rolled onto his back in consternation and gave himself a good jolt of pain from his leg.

He heard the truck before he saw it, clamoring up into the driveway. Dust floated around her as she got out. Her police uniform surprised him; he'd never seen her look so clean.

"Kuro!" She waved at him from the front yard. He slunk out of the garden and came around the front, his body pressed low. She was carrying a grocery bag. He switched forms and held the door open for her, silent.

"I've just got to do some chores, then I'll make dinner."

He nodded. He had waited all day and now found he had nothing to say. A certain embarrassment came over him, a creeping, uncomfortable uncertainty...a feeling that he didn't belong.

But if Caroline saw that he was uncomfortable, she worked to dispel his unease, filling the awkward silence with easy chatter as she moved about. She came back from her room, having changed into a pair of dirty jean shorts and an oversized T-shirt, hair flowing freely down her back. He followed her outside and switched back to his *kitsune* form.

She moved about her business easily, and when she caught him looking at her, she smiled. He watched as she led the horse out of the stable, releasing her to the pasture. The mare snorted at him.

Caroline patted her flank. "Her name's Molly."

Molly doesn't like me.

"Well, maybe she'll get used to you. Not so sure about Feral, though, and I'm bringing him home tomorrow."

He trailed like a shadow behind her.

A half hour later, as sunset drew on, he followed her into the garden, silent and fascinated, studying her habits. She was all business, speaking only by way of explaining herself here and there. She didn't care about dirt on her bare knees; she sunk her full weight down into the ground, weeding around her strawberry patch. He followed at her heels, watching as she examined a blueberry bush. Her brow furrowed, leaves dappled with white spots between her fingers. "That's not a good sign," she said, and he could feel her make a mental note to follow-up.

The golden hour emerged, the sun sinking to the tree level. Its light was warm and rich, and her body glowed with the sweat of her efforts. She had picked up a hoe and was digging in the garden, furious.

"These damn blackberries!" She cursed. "I don't know how they keep creeping in here. If you don't dig out the root, they keep coming back!"

He wasn't sure when it had happened, but he noticed that he had changed back to a human at some point while she dug, his back pressed against a fence post, his arms crossed over his chest as he watched her. She brought her arms up high with the swing of the hoe, and the muscles on her forearms were toned, taut. Swing; *thud*. She huffed a little with each movement, and the sweat made her hair cling to her temples. The sound of her breathing – labored, panting – elicited a sudden heat to rise steadily up his neck. She wiped her forehead and smudged dirt across the skin, and Kuro felt nearly dizzy at the sight of her mussed hair.

"*Oh!*" She sprung backwards then stopped, laughing at herself. He was upright at once, moving forward as though summoned, but she held out a hand to stop him, pointing.

A foot from her, coiled in the brambles, a large gopher snake twisted. She hadn't struck it, merely wakened it from its slumber. It unwound itself and began to move slowly, sliding on its belly out of the bush, its yellow stripe gleaming.

She leaned on her hoe and smiled at it, watching as it slithered over to the tomato vines and lost itself in their midst.

"You're not afraid of snakes?"

She shrugged. "He startled me, is all. I'm glad I didn't hit him – I would have felt terrible. And no, I'm not afraid of snakes. That little guy is a big help, actually. You should have seen me a few years ago, battling the moles." Her eyes rolled back in exasperation. "They were unstoppable. Then one day, a snake showed up. Then another, and another. There's actually a bed of them out behind the bee hives, and I'll admit, I don't make a habit of bothering them, but they're harmless. They eat the moles and the damn mice. Everything has to eat, right?" Her smile faltered. "Even you."

"Even me."

"...How are you doing?"

The answer was the same: he was starving again. It was growing worse every day, and in his effort to distract himself from the gnawing emptiness, he had tasted a little of her calm and pride in the garden. It hadn't come close to filling him and had left him feeling twisted in knots.

She looked worried. He did his best to feign nonchalance and shrugged. "Fine. Hoping you got a chicken."

She grinned. "I did, but just the thighs and legs. Figured I'd fry it up."

An hour later she had put the mare away and cleaned herself up. Kuro watched as she cut the chicken and rolled it in flour and seasonings. She lowered it into a pot of frying oil, the flour bubbling and fizzing as it sunk into the golden fat.

He sat at the kitchen table and searched his mind for the most human thing he could possibly say to fill the silence and felt like an idiot as soon as the words left his mouth. "How was work?"

She guffawed and responded with the blandest answer she could think of. "Work was work." She dried her hands on a dishtowel and fished for the pieces of chicken in the pot with a fry strainer; they had turned a golden brown, and he watched them glistening and drying as they sat on a plate of paper towels. Another batch was lowered in, the oil darker now. "In all seriousness, it was busy. Lots of calls today, working on different things, trying to keep everyone up to date. I'm way behind on paperwork and files, but there's three of us, so I'm mainly taking calls at the moment. The murder cases are taking up a lot of the detectives' time, but that doesn't mean other people aren't finding ways to hurt each other." She sighed, fished the remaining pieces out of the pot, and set the plate down in front of him.

He ate with relish, crunching through the crust of skin. She watched and nibbled, but her curiosity won against her hunger. "Do you eat a lot of human food, or do you mostly hunt?"

"Depends." He bit into the thigh and licked at the juices on his fingers. A memory came to him, and he stopped, cautious. He wanted to share something, but it felt...odd, sharing a part of himself.

She sensed his hesitation. "What is it?"

He put the chicken down and sipped a glass of water she had set out for him. "Once, in the wintertime, I wanted a hot chocolate. It was all I could think about. I was hours from any city, deep in the mountains, and it had snowed...it took me five days to get out of the mountains and get to Gatlinburg just to get one. I don't think anything in my whole life ever tasted so good."

She laughed. His face flushed.

"I'm so sorry – I didn't mean to offend you! It's just...that's really sweet. You don't look like someone who likes hot chocolate. It's very...incongruous."

He picked the chicken back up and smiled despite himself. There was a part of the memory he hadn't shared: Jaden. They had been in a shallow cave, and Kuro had been pitiful, melodramatic even in retrospect. He had only to ask Jaden once if they could leave, and Jaden had given a great, long sigh...and stood up, leading the way. He had complained for five days about the freezing cold, the miserable snow...but he had never suggested they turn around, never for a second denied him, and he'd even bought him the drink himself, even if he did roll his eyes while ordering it. And then Kuro had wanted another, and another, and another, and then he had been violently ill from the whipped cream and drunk, because neither had realized the hot chocolate had Peppermint Schnapps in it.

It was a good memory; the glow of friendship warmed him from within. Jaden had taken care of him that night, looking utterly harassed about the entire incident...and had never held it against him.

"What are you thinking about?"

"Nothing," he said, too fast, and finished his dinner.

The evening settled around them with a quiet peacefulness. Caroline cleaned up and brought a pillow out to the living room, setting it on the couch.

"I noticed last night you slept as a human," she said. She wasn't meeting his eyes for some reason. "Or at least, you were human this morning when I left. You looked like one, I mean."

He nodded. She draped a blanket over the couch.

"I usually just watch television or read in the evenings. I don't want to bother you with a million questions, so...I'll probably just head to bed."

He nodded once more, a little slower this time; something was bothering her, something brought on by the night. She apologized, explained she had a long day, and left him, walking down the hallway. In another minute, he heard the shower turn on.

He could feel her soul, left behind in the going of it. Something was unsettled. He tasted it, hoping it was something palatable, and felt a twinge of guilt; anything he could eat would be painful for her to bare: the more he fed from it, the more it would grow. He sighed and sat down on the couch, studying the room. It was an odd thing, to be human, he thought: it was so much work. Someone had to buy this couch, invent these materials; so much industry, so much civilization had gone into the creation of this small home, and still she toiled herself, a tiny fragment of her society, straining to carve her mark into it with an even smaller garden in a smaller corner of the world. Who would bother with so much effort?

The memory of her arms raised high returned to him; he recalled the way the sweat on her skin glowed in the final hour of sunset, golden and radiant. He remembered the sound of her laughter, the curve of her bicep as it flexed, straining.

The shower stopped. The sudden lack of sound snapped him out of his thoughts, and he was surprised to again find his heart at a gallop. That feeling of listlessness returned. Surely it was more comfortable to sit here on a couch and wait for dawn than to lay in the woods...especially because he had kept waking up as a human, over and over again. It turned out the forest floor was uncomfortable for a human spine, and the cold seeped into his bones without fur to keep him warm. He listened as she left the bathroom and went to her room, the door shutting. The smell of fresh soap floated out to him, and he sighed.

If I was Jaden, what I would be doing right now?

Kitsune were cathemeral, and it was hardly nine in the evening.

Somewhere, he thought, maroon eyes were probably watching a girl named Jacqueline.

He needed to distract himself from that thought.

Kuro slipped quietly off the couch and made his way to the kitchen, where the book *Kitsune* lay on the table. He flipped through the pages, curious. In one illustration, a god named Inari walked with two invisible white foxes at his ankles. He found that curious; he couldn't turn into an *actual* fox, but the illustration was clear. Was that something only certain *kitsune* could do? In another, a beautiful woman, her breasts bare, draped her hair over a bucket, cleaning it. He read on; in Japan, he learned, the *kitsune* was adroit at changing herself into a beautiful young woman, seductive and irresistible.

He raised an eyebrow. Where exactly were these seductive vixen?

The female *kitsune,* he read, would seduce the man and exhaust him of his energies, and then, quite quickly, the man would die. He snorted; that was at least one thing the author got wrong: a soul was inexhaustible, like the ocean: feeding on it couldn't kill it. It was continuously generative, expanding.

He turned the page. A fox stroked its tail, and fire ignited. On the other hand, he thought, you *could* burn a soul, and once burned, that bit of the soul was destroyed...do it for long enough, that would probably kill. They didn't know if a human needed a soul to live, but Kuro was almost certain that the answer was yes.

There were so many stories; a fox appeared to a man as his wife; a fox maiden cried over the faithlessness of a samurai. Always, always, the foxes were finding themselves on a collision course with humans.

In that, he could sympathize.

He'd been reading for more than an hour when he became aware of a change. It crept upon him at the edges of his senses, but his mind, starving, reached for it, leaping at the chance to feed. A quiet sadness was seeping down the hallway and pooling around him. He leaned into it and drank deeply, then yanked himself away, revolted by his own action.

Caroline. He could hear her...was she speaking? She was. She wasn't loud, but the house was so silent and still, he could hear her soft murmuring.

He stood and walked down the hallway, quiet. He felt suddenly intrusive, but he knocked on her door all the same.

Her voice abruptly stopped. There was no sound for a minute, and then the door opened.

She stood in the doorway of her room wearing a nightshirt and a pair of flannel pajama pants. Her long hair had been braided and hung over her shoulder.

He stood there and found himself unable to meet her eyes. "I just – I heard you. I felt something. I wanted to make sure you were okay."

Her smile was sad and slow. She nodded and gestured for him to enter.

Her room held a bed, and next to it, a nightstand with a lamp. A dresser sat snug against the wall behind the door, and beside it stood an extra chair that would have gone with the kitchen table. He sat in the chair, watching her as she sat down on the edge of the bed, facing him. The room was so small that their knees practically touched. He noticed she held something in her hand.

She held it up, and it dangled like a necklace.

"It's a rosary." She stretched it out, the light from the lamp catching the black beads. "Onyx. Each set of ten beads is a decade. There's usually five, but I think we must have had an especially bad ancestor: this one is almost double the length at nine. It's been in our family for generations." She clutched it in her hands, her eyes cast down upon it. "For every bead, you pray a 'Hail Mary,' then an 'Our Father' – that's the Lord's prayer. I used to do this every night when I was young. It made me feel like I was speaking directly to god."

She took a deep, steadying breath. "But I stopped over the years... and then I stopped going to church after my parents died. Lots of things chipped away at my faith, I guess. They say to build your faith upon a rock, but I suppose mine was built on sand. It shifted over time. I still believed, but only because I didn't think very deeply about anything. I've been doing a lot of thinking lately, though."

The sadness moved again, touching him. Kuro watched as she moved the beads through her fingers, rolling the smooth stones over her thumb. "And I keep thinking about Christopher, more than anything. Someday, I'll tell you what happened to him...and what I did. How he still loves me, how he came back here to tell me there were demons in the woods. I believed him, and you appeared. So...I've been praying, for old time's sake. It's just meditation for me now. The sound, the rhythm...I get lost in it, and that helps. It's the same prayer I said when I thought you were going to attack me."

Her cheeks colored suddenly, and she looked away. "...You remember what you did, when I was praying?"

"...I kissed you."

Her face was burning now, and her eyes seemed to have found a fascinating spot on her dresser. "Why did you do that?"

"It seemed like the best way to get you to stop praying. It was pulling your soul away from me, so I wanted to stop it."

A hint of a smirk played at the edge of her lips. "You do that often?"

He shook his head. "Never." He swallowed and tried to hide his embarrassment. "That was the first time I ever did that. I was desperate."

"...That was your first time kissing someone?"

He nodded. She looked at him and smiled. "Kuro," she said, and her voice was warm and kind, "I don't know what I'm going to do with you."

He looked away. Her kindness clung to him and made him dizzy. "Start with forgiving yourself."

"What?"

"I can feel your soul..." He felt like a sailor trapped in the hull of a sinking ship, and all around him, the ocean of her feelings was coming up, dragging him down, pressing in on him, pulling him under to suffocate. "That sadness will eat away at your whole life if you don't forgive yourself for whatever it is you're thinking about. I know. I've met souls that felt like moth-eaten blankets, filled with holes where they had torn into themselves..."

She shook her head. "...I can't. I can't change what I said, or what

I did. I can't change how I let our parents treat him." She offered no further details, but the sudden pain in her soul was bright and acute.

He closed his eyes. He could picture a girl in a car, her eyes wide, surprised; he could smell her blood, see it splashed on the car window.

He spoke slowly, more to himself than to her. "That's true...but that's the point. You can't change anything. There's no way to go back. The only thing you can do is try to forgive yourself for what you did...what you didn't do. *That's* the point. It's not about change. You can't change the past. It's about...moving forward. It's about what you do *now*."

Something altered in her feelings, a shift, but it was hard to see its edges and know its nature, like pinpointing the exact moment that blue transformed to green in a rainbow. He opened his eyes to see her staring at him and he realized, as he felt that sharp pain, that he had reached her.

Without thinking, he stood up and reached forward, taking her hands. "You've got to believe in that," he said, the words rushing out. He could still see that dead girl, the contact fallen on her cheek. "You've got to water that feeling, nurture it – you've got to tend to it, like something in your garden. You've got to let it grow, or it will die. Everything in you will fight to kill it, and you'll think about how you could have been better, or done better...and that's *true,*" he admitted, "but you've got to ignore it. If you don't...this sorrow will drown you. It's almost drowning *me*," he said, and shook his head in an attempt to rid it from himself. "So try. Pray if that helps. Just try to forgive yourself."

He didn't know where his words had come from, but he meant them, and if she believed him, maybe that would help give her peace.

Caroline suddenly stood, and kissed him.

He froze. She pressed her lips against his; they were warm, soft, and her skin smelled of fresh soap. Something in him relaxed a fraction, and his lips parted. She felt his tentative invitation and kissed him again, deeply, and without thinking he brought his hands up, fingers reaching to caress the soft curve of her face. He leaned in and returned the kiss, his tongue slipping over the velvet inside of her cheek, the nerves in his body igniting with heat. Her response was a small sound in the back of her throat as his tongue slid over hers, his hands winding up through her hair, tugging at her braid.

Kuro moved with sudden, intense desire, pushing her down onto the bed so that he loomed over her, standing, his legs caught between hers. Heat climbed up his body and dulled his mind to everything except for the feeling of her hand reaching up, slipping under his shirt, touching his bare skin. Her fingertips traced down the hard edges of his abdomen, slipping down the groove of his muscles, resting at last on his hip. No one had ever touched him like this, no one had ever ignited this kind of fire in his core. He pulled back only for a wrenching gasp of air, then buried his face again at the column of her throat, his own arm ghosting up her body, his palm cupping the edge of her breast. He had no idea how to touch a woman, what would be considered too eager or clumsy or harsh, and the sensation – so, so soft, giving away under the barest pressure of his thumb as it slipped over the crest, feeling her hardening beneath the fabric – was almost more than he could handle. Worse: he had no idea how to allow *himself* to be touched, to open himself to this new experience.

She reached up and grasped his hand, pulling it away; he was going to apologize, but the words caught in his throat.

She had pulled his arm down instead, pressing his hand flat against the strong expanse of muscle of her inner thigh.

He suddenly hated the clothes that were blocking him from touching her skin. He was trapped between a desire to wrench them down and off and freeze from the sheer shock of this. He did neither; instead, he moved his hand up, slowly, until his thumb came to the soft joining of hip and groin. His heart was in his throat; here was her waistband, where his fingers could so easily slip under the elastic, slide down, and seek the tight warmth of her body. He had never imagined such a thing, never felt the hot inner walls of a woman, and had no idea what he was supposed to do; now, at the precipice of this invitation, he found his own need stiffening even as his nerves threatened to overwhelm him with anxiety.

His mind was a hot haze of confused need, desire, and fear; he made an inarticulate sound between a plea and a gasp, and Caroline's soul responded to him, guiding him just as her fingers curled against his hip, pulling his thigh down and closer –

He drew his knee up to prop himself onto to the bed, to press their bodies fully together, and the rosary slipped to the floor. The sound shattered the silence, and Kuro jolted, pulling away at once, their breathing uneven.

He stood there, his heart slamming against his rib cage. A thousand different thoughts were suddenly very loud in his head, and her soul was thrumming against him, clouding his mind with its own emotions. He wanted her, badly...but this was terrifying and new. Fear conquered lust; he wanted to run from it.

She saw the look on his face and said, "I'm sorry." Caroline stood up in a hurry, collecting the rosary from the ground. "I'm so sorry. I don't know what I was thinking...I shouldn't have done that."

He turned away from her, hiding his face. He was struggling with himself now, torn between a burning desire that threatened to conquer him, and a familiar one that urged him to run, *run now*, because this was a dangerous path to go down.

He fought against himself and slowed his breathing, but his pulse still raced.

I don't know what I'm doing, he thought; his arms were shaking.

"Kuro...are you angry at me?"

"I'm not angry." His voice was hoarse. He moved to the doorway, his back to her. "I'm sorry..."

"What are you sorry for?"

He didn't know. He just was.

"I'm going to go lie down. Just...think about what I said." He left without saying good night, and a minute later, he heard the bedroom door close.

Kuro didn't get much sleep that night.

NINETEEN

In the morning, neither one of them talked about what had happened between them. This time, Kuro was awake when Caroline emerged from the bathroom, ready for work. He leaned in the doorway of the living room, watching her in the kitchen. She made him eggs and coffee, and he studied her movements as she lumped two tablespoons of sugar into the mug and slid it toward him.

"I've got to pick up Feral on my way home today," she said at length. He nodded. Her soul was in turmoil around him, kicking like a young thing penned up in a too-small space.

She stood in the front doorway and paused. "Kuro," she started. He looked up, and their eyes held one another. Whatever she had to say came to a faltering stop, and she gave an awkward, pained smile. "See you later."

He spent the day pacing gingerly in the garden. She was right; there *was* a bed of garter snakes back behind the beehives, and they didn't like him snuffling around, disturbing them, but even the snakes were no distraction from his thoughts. He kept thinking of the way her hair smelt, the feeling of her lips, the hard muscle of her thigh...

And he cursed. He whirled around and found himself on human legs, fists clenched, angry at absolutely everything and not knowing why. Caroline had let Molly out into the pasture before she left, and the mare looked up at him, shaking her head in derision.

Why would she kiss me? He walked past the tomatoes, tail swinging. *Why would she do that?* He was over by the berries now, striding on human legs. His right leg didn't feel too badly today; he could almost put his weight on it. *What does she think about me?*

And worse, another thought: *what did he think of her?*

He came to a halt in the middle of the garden and faced it. What *did* he think of her?

He thought he liked the way she smelled. He liked her laugh, the way it was so clear and bright, like a river in spring, when the early sun melted the snows and the water gushed down in great torrents.

He liked the way she was always smudged with dirt and didn't care, the way she picked millipedes out from under her strawberries and tossed them away, not the least bit squeamish about all those legs.

He liked the soft brown of her eyes, and the way she smiled.

He fell onto his knees and clutched at his head. His mind was spinning. He could think of all the reasons why he would want to kiss her, and it all came down to the simple answer of *because I wanted to.* Was that why she did it, then? Because *she* wanted to? He thought again of how she must see him: an animal, a demon, something dangerous...but that's not what her eyes had said. That's not how her soul had felt.

He realized he was scared to death. He felt like he was standing on the edge of a cliff and looking down, deep into a void that was ready to swallow him, and the emptiness inside him was driving him distracted. The *holy dark* moved in him and he felt sick, desperate and hungry. He was starving, and all he could think about was what it would feel like to trace the outline of her shoulders, to feel her skin under his palms, yielding to his touch.

He stood up and walked back to her house, searching for a pad and paper. He didn't think he could face her when she got home tonight, and besides, he was supposed to meet Jaden tomorrow. He would leave now, he thought. He needed time...and distance. Especially distance.

What to say? She'd want an explanation for his absence, but he didn't know how to put everything inside him into words. In the end, he settled on a perfunctory scribble of *Gone for now,* with no signature, and left it on her kitchen table.

Molly lifted her head again as he slipped outside, slinking down the driveway like a dog with its tail between his legs. She whinnied at him as if to say *good riddance!,* and Kuro flattened his ears backwards and took off running. He tested a shy leap over her rotted fence, landed with only a little pain, and disappeared into the woods.

Jaden found Kuro near the duck pond on Cove Road the next day. He was seated as a human, his head rested on his arms on top of his knees, and he was staring into the waters, lost in thought. Judging by his stillness, Kuro had been like that for some time. He'd never seen him quite so moody before.

He called to him from a distance but got no response. As he drew closer, he studied Kuro's eyes: they were sunken. His hair was dull, his skin sallow. He looked like a man in the grip of a bad illness.

"Kuro."

Kuro blinked and looked up, dazed.

"What's wrong with you?"

"Nothing."

Jaden scoffed and demanded to see his leg. Kuro shifted and showed him the wound. He pressed aside Kuro's fur and examined the few remaining stitches, the skin: it was healing nicely. That was a relief.

Kuro shifted back and sat, staring out at the water...*he's brooding about something,* he thought. He hadn't thought Kuro had the capacity to *brood* on anything. Brooding required an awful lot of thought, which would have been a novelty for the black *kitsune*.

"What's going on? You look ill."

"Did you know there're different types of *kitsune?*"

The question took him off guard. Jaden took a seat next to him in the grass, hoping to avoid any stains on his new pants. They were expensive; humans toiled their whole lives for money, but they were restricted by laws, morals, and legalities. He felt certain that with a little ingenuity, he could make a very, very comfortable life for himself in very short order...but for now, resources were scarce.

"Yes, of course – I told you that, years ago. Remember?"

Kuro nodded. Jaden had looked up information on *kitsune* after he had taught himself to read and write, his mind apt and quick at learning. There was so much out there, so many stories, so many gnarled webs of partial truths that it had ultimately proven to be an aborted journey of self-discovery. It would take living and meeting other *kitsune* and demons to verify what he had read, but so far, they only had one another.

And they were young; they would grow older, and more power-ful. Jaden had faith they would find others – and with them, answers.

He was already on a promising track, after all. It would only be a matter of time.

"...I remember. I just don't remember being very interested then..."

"You never were." Jaden had always been frustrated by Kuro's lack of curiosity, but in many ways, his simplicity was convenient – endearing, even. His wants were basic, his needs easily met. "Why are you thinking about this now?"

"...I just am."

Jaden studied him, searching his face. Something was troubling him. He didn't like seeing Kuro disturbed like this.

A suspicious, uneasy feeling stirred in his chest.

He tried to sound easy, slightly uninterested. "What are you thinking about?"

Black eyes turned to him, and there was something scared and hesitant in their depths. "...Are we good?"

"*Good?*"

"Do you think we're the good kind?"

He fought back a sudden urge to laugh; what a stupid, childish question. He sounded like a lost infant, and when he looked up at Jaden, he looked miserable, sickly. Real alarm went off in his head now, and Jaden reached out and gently placed his knuckles against his forehead, searching for a fever.

But there was no flush. Kuro blinked at him, and Jaden pulled away.

"Do you think we're *myobu*...or *nogitsune*?"

Kuro didn't listen to things he didn't care about; there was no way he would remember those details from years ago. Jaden's memory was sharp and clear: he had tried to talk to him, and Kuro, completely uninterested, had said that none of it mattered since they didn't know if any of it was true anyways, and then had asked when they could go eat. And now here he was, troubled, throwing out these words that Jaden had spoken to him more than a decade ago, looking like he was ready to keel over any second.

Something was wrong.

"I don't know, Kuro." He was trying to be reassuring; Kuro was simplistic and usually easily mollified....but he was staring at him, a desperate pleading in his eyes. He knew the answer was no: they weren't *myobu*, but Kuro looked like he was on the edge of shattering. He'd never seen him so fragile...or weak.

He didn't know how to fix this distress, but he wanted to.

"What's gotten into you? Why are you thinking about these things?"

"...No reason."

And he was *lying* to him, too. That was new – well, not *that* new. Kuro had lied artlessly about how he'd gotten the stitches in his leg, but Jaden had dismissed it, willing to let him have a secret or two of his own.

Jaden turned from him now and stared out into the pond. Three ducks paddled slowly in a trailing circle, their beaks dipping into the water and coming back up, shaking their heads. He decided to change the subject and distract him.

"...I've been watching the girl," Jaden said. Kuro looked up, half interested. Jaden tried to grin brightly, to lift him out of his thoughts. "I got her last name from her library account, and I watch her from a distance. Her life isn't interesting – coffee, class, chores. I love her defiance: she knows I'm watching, and she changes almost nothing about her life; no hiding behind barricaded doors for that one. I follow her, when she leaves...but when I reach out to try and feed from her, that *thing* still pushes me away, and – Kuro, are you listening?"

"I'm listening."

"She lives close to our mutual friend." Kuro stared at him blankly. "*Kenneth*," he reminded.

"Oh... him."

Jaden stared at him in wonder. He looked so troubled, and his voice was low when he spoke. "We should leave him alone, Jaden. He did what we asked – there hasn't been any more pictures."

Jaden didn't care if there was or wasn't. He had seen how Kuro suffered and connected Kuro's wound to the boy in a series of cause-and-effect rationale that left him eager for retribution. It didn't matter that Jaden himself had set these events in motion, that he had seen Kenneth's camera and seized an opportunity. He would have never gone through with any of it if he had known it would have resulted in Kuro's harm, let alone near death. When they had reunited after Kuro was shot, Jaden had felt as though the foundation of his world had been shattered: there had been a single, terrifying moment where he feared for Kuro's life, and following that moment, there had been *rage:* if he could find that hunter, he would have torn the man limb from limb, a slow, agonizing death...

But there was no chance of finding that man, and instead, Jaden blamed the boy: in a strictly sequential sense, his photo had led to Kuro's wound, and that was intolerable to him.

Kuro was stubborn, idiotic, and sullen – and he was *his,* to protect and guide.

He was ready to permanently get rid of Kenneth as soon as they were prepared to leave Asheville for good, whether it be a week or a month or six from now.

As soon as he had eaten the girl's soul, he would take care of Kenneth quickly and efficiently. He had promised Kuro he wouldn't kill him, and he didn't need to: the world offered a number of solutions, and Jaden had already taken steps toward a conclusion he favored.

"I haven't given him any more thought...so don't worry about it," he said. Kuro only nodded. "I'm thinking more about Jacqueline, and Kuro...I'd really like your help." He had an idea in his mind, a plan to help move things along –

"No." The answer was immediate and firm; Jaden had finally succeeded in breaking him free of his troubled thoughts, but the result displeased him. He didn't like being told *no,* especially in that tone.

Jaden's eyes narrowed. "I haven't even told you what I want to do."

"It doesn't matter what you want to do – I *know what you do,"* he snarled suddenly, surprising them both. "Do you want me to go over there and scare her, move the shadows in her home so she runs out into the night, into your arms?"

"Into *your* arms," Jaden corrected, his voice low, insistent. "I need you to hold her still –"

"I'm not laying a hand on her," he snapped. "I don't want to see this girl, I don't want to touch her, *forget it.* There's nothing you can say or do that would make me hurt that girl, Jaden. *Don't ask me again.*"

For half a second, Kuro's true name was on his tongue; he was so close to saying it, just to punish him and remind him of his power over him...but no. A muscle jumped in his jaw as he swallowed the impulse; he wouldn't do that to him, unless he absolutely had to. He had never used his name against him to compel him to do something he didn't want to do, but then again, he'd never *needed* to...he understood that Kuro was too soft for his own good, that he would need to be protected and directed by the guidance of a strong hand, a keener mind than his own. He indulged Kuro as much as he could and encouraged him to look away from the things that Kuro was not ready yet to see in himself, but this...this new *defiance* was an unprecedented change.

Jaden held back and merely stared, displeased.

"How very altruistic of you."

"I'm not stopping you," Kuro whispered. He had lowered his head again, and he spoke the words as if passing judgement on himself. "But I won't help you."

He decided a change in subject matter was needed. "What did you do for the last three days?"

"...I was here. I ate, slept."

Another lie. Jaden nodded as though he believed him and stood. He put a comforting hand on Kuro's shoulder, squeezing. "I'm going to head back to the city. Why don't you come with me? You look like you need to take your mind off your thoughts."

Jaden watched as Kuro considered it for a moment, but something held him back, and he shook his head 'no.'

"I'd rather just stay here."

"...Of course. See you in another few days?"

Kuro nodded, his head sinking lower in his arms. "See you then."

Jaden turned, and as he walked away, his eyes narrowed. He needed to fix this. He wanted to go back to the city and follow

Jacqueline, and he would...but he didn't need to rush. There was time. Oh, there was plenty of time.

And it was clear from the way that Kuro slumped, staring blankly out at the pond, that someone else needed his full, undivided attention.

TWENTY

"Do you know how to shoot a gun?"

"*Jesus Christ*, Eric!"

Kenneth dropped the gun onto the coffee table as though it had burned his hand. Across from him, Eric only raised a single eyebrow, whether in judgement or surprise, Kenneth didn't know.

Eric's house was small and mostly bare. The walls had a few old, framed giclées of countryside landscapes, leftover decorations of his aunt's. Eric hadn't cared enough to take them down or replace them with anything more his style. Probably because he didn't have a style.

But he did have a gun.

"Why do you even have a gun?"

"I live alone. *You* should have a gun."

"Why are you giving me a gun?"

Eric gave him a hard, penetrating look. "Why did you come back here?"

The question caught him by surprise, but that was Eric's specialty; everything about him tended to catch people off guard.

Feelings, questions, comments all bounced off him. Kenneth had often thought that there was something missing inside of Eric, some spark of humanity that most people seemed to have...whatever created light in people's eyes, Eric didn't possess it. He was an impenetrable rock.

But he was also his friend. He'd never been able to square that contradiction.

Kenneth had wanted to come over sooner, but he'd spent the previous day watching the Buncombe police comb through his kitchen and living room till late in the afternoon. He'd followed (most) of Mathew's advice, and even though it had been uncomfortable, he told the police officers the same story he'd already told once...almost.

He'd decided not to mention his resemblance to one of the intruders who had broken into his home.

Buncombe reacted and sent investigators over to search through his house, and though they wouldn't tell him what they found, Kenneth had seen them pull up a few long black hairs and place them in a clear bag. After that, he'd been asked to sit outside. He hadn't even been allowed back into his house until sundown, and exhausted, he had found sleep difficult.

He kept picturing a row of teeth in the grass.

He kept waking up, checking to see if the shadows were moving.

Here now, he felt foolish about their earlier conversation. He kept telling himself he didn't need to be too embarrassed about getting swept up in the theory that two *demons* had attacked him and murdered those people – lots of people believed in a lot of stupid things, he reasoned.

Faced with the crime scene, everything made more sense. Demons were not real: the blood and viscera that lay behind the yellow rows of tape *was,* and it was terrifying. It dispelled every thought of anything not firmly grounded in reality.

Kenneth hadn't heard anything new from Mathew over at the *Times.* He assumed Wallace and Cantrell had decided to temporarily sit on the report that the killers might have broken into his home, at the behest of law enforcement, and he'd seen no mention of Jacqueline's incident report, either. The news articles that had been released in subsequent days were short, empty: no new leads. Police "have evidence, are investigating all avenues." The quotes from the officers promised action and reported no results.

And while Jacqueline wasn't exactly ignoring him, he could feel a new distance between them, even as they sat next to each other in class.

There were new circles under her eyes. She looked tired, but she wouldn't talk about it, hurrying out of class without pausing to say goodbye, and he didn't have the courage to call her again, and so at last he had called Eric back and gone over to his house.

"Kenneth."

Eric was waiting on an answer. Why had he come back here? It was simple, really. "Because Albert died," he finally settled on.

But Eric didn't buy it. "You know, your problem is that you've always been depressed."

Kenneth huddled into himself. "Don't say that. I'm not depressed."

"You've never wanted to admit it."

"I'm *not*."

"Fine. You came back here because of *Jacqueline*. Can you at least admit that?"

He winced away from the words, afraid of facing the truth and the inevitable rejection.

Something flickered in Eric's eyes, and he shifted his weight, leaned back into the couch. "Kenneth, we've known each other for a long time...all three of us. She cares about you." Kenneth shook his head – that didn't seem possible, but Eric's tone was firm. "She spent a lot of time moving between wanting to let you go and holding on to the memory of you. Her dad's death didn't help any."

Kenneth sighed and felt his throat tighten. Albert. Jacqueline's dad. Eric's aunt. The words came out in a frightened whisper. "There's so much death here."

"It'll get us all in the end," Eric shrugged. "Have you talked to her since the incident?"

"Not really..." After he'd left that morning, a hurried exchange of terse words here or there in class didn't count.

"Don't worry – she'll get over it. In the meantime, you need to protect yourself." He set a magazine clip down on the table. "This is a CZ 75 SP01, 9-millimeter. The magazine holds eighteen rounds. Have you shot a gun before?"

Kenneth pushed himself farther into the couch. "Is this a joke?"

Eric persisted, placid. "It's got a manual safety. It's steel, so it's heavier than the usual handgun, but that means it's got less of a recoil and steady aim. Technically, any person getting a gun by gift or purchase needs a pistol purchase permit...but there's no firearm registry and no permit needed to carry it, so you don't have to worry about filing the paperwork if you don't want to. You'd get a slap-on-the-wrist misdemeanor. They'd never be able to track the gun back to me as long as you kept your mouth shut. Welcome back to North Carolina," he dead-panned.

Kenneth stared back, flabbergasted. "What do you want me to do with this?"

"Pick it up."

He felt the rubber grip in his hands, the weight of the gun. Eric came over and showed him how to put the magazine in, then removed it again and flipped the safety. "Get used to holding it. I'll be right back."

Eric fixed himself a drink in the kitchen before he returned. Kenneth was used to his extended, thoughtful silences and waited patiently, the gun still heavy in his hands.

"On the night that you and Jacqueline were each assaulted, a friend of mine called me over to her place. She's got a little farm up in the northeast part of the city."

Kenneth gave him a surprised look. "I heard you on the phone, but I didn't think you had those type of friends who gave you those type of calls."

"Would you be surprised if I said I do?"

Kenneth laughed uncomfortably. "I wouldn't believe you."

Another wan smile. "You'd be right...we dated, briefly. It didn't work out. But I thought..." Kenneth watched him, amazed; he had never known Eric to stumble over his words or be embarrassed, but he cleared his throat suddenly, and the ghost of whatever feeling he was hiding was again tucked away, and he continued as though whatever thought had interrupted him had never come. "I know this girl from the police station. She's one of the secretaries." He explained how he'd met her while vaccinating the K-9 units, and soon they had started 'talking.'

"'Talking.'"

"Sure."

"I didn't think you really... 'talked' to anyone, either."

Eric seemed to consider this. Kenneth felt a hot flush; he wished he hadn't said that out loud, but Eric gave a slow, thoughtful nod. "I have a lot of acquaintances," he said at length, "but you're right. I think you both might be my only real friends, but she...I liked her a lot." Something in his face was tightly controlled, and he spoke with too much forced detachment, a clinical approach to an emotional problem. "But I have trouble connecting with people, and that got in the way. Of us, I mean."

"I'm sorry I brought it up."

"Don't be. It's better to face the truth." He took a deep breath, and Kenneth noticed that he appeared slightly uncomfortable by what he had to say. "I went over to her place because she said there was someone there who needed help, who couldn't go to a hospital. She was asking me to break the law, to risk my career...but she sounded panicked. When I got there..." He trailed off. Kenneth waited. His palms had that piercing feeling again, like knives being thrust through them, and his sweat was clammy on the rubber grip of the gun.

"...When I got there, I thought I was looking at *you.*"

"*What?*"

Eric took a sip of his drink. "There was a guy in her living room. He looked just like you, until I really looked at him." Kenneth's skin crawled as Eric fixed his eyes on him and delivered a familiar description. "*Taller.* Better looking, broad-shouldered, muscular. *Strong.* His eyes were darker. He looked at me with this expression that I've seen before at the vet...a woman once caught a diseased fox and brought it in for help. I don't know what she thought *we* could do." He shrugged. "It pressed itself against the back of the cage. I remember the look in its eyes. It was deciding between attacking me and killing itself. It would have gnawed its own body apart just to fit through the bars. This guy looked at me just like that, like a trapped animal, like he was deciding whether or not to kill himself or me." Eric's eyes dimmed with the memory. "I think he could have killed me with his hands, if he wanted."

Kenneth's mouth had gone dry; his thoughts were going in too many directions. "What did you do with the fox?"

"The fox?" He blinked, surprised. "I euthanized it."

Kenneth swallowed, nodded. "What was wrong with the guy?"

Eric didn't look away, and with a calm, matter-of-fact tone replied, "He'd been shot in the leg."

The gun slipped from Kenneth's hands and fell to the floor. Eric knelt, picked it up, put the safety back on as though Kenneth hadn't just done something considerably dangerous, and continued. "My friend said he'd been shot in a hunting accident and got lost, that he couldn't go to a hospital because he didn't have insurance. She's not a good liar. She was lying." Another sip, the clink of ice in the quiet living room, the quiet thud as he placed the gun on the table. "He said his name was 'Kohl.' Besides the bullet wound, he was covered in scratches and bites. Funny thing is, I've been caring for her dog for a few days now at the vet. She brought him in because he'd gotten into a scrape with something, then had us board him. I was surprised at the time – it's a nice dog. I've never even heard it growl, let alone attack something."

Kenneth didn't stop to think; he reached forward and grabbed the gun off the table with trembling hands. "Eric. You remember what I told you, about the people in my house. One of them had a hurt leg. One of them looked just like me."

"Don't." Eric set his drink down, his glare suddenly hard. "I'm not Jacqueline. I don't leap like that. It *might* be the same person."

"You can't be serious."

"The world is filled with a lot of coincidences."

"Then why do you want me to have this gun?"

"...Just in case."

Kenneth picked up the magazine and slipped it into his pocket. "Did you tell the police?"

"No."

"He could have killed those people, Eric. In the paper, did you read about it?"

"Yea, I read about it. It's possible...but they were murdered early Saturday morning. I saw him around the same time, probably before those people were killed, based on what I read in the news, and I can assure you...he didn't go anywhere. I left you a voicemail on Sunday."

"And you didn't go to the police?"

Eric's voice was hard, each word punctuated with years of icy bitterness. "You didn't call me back."

"Shit, Eric!" Kenneth stood up, took two steps and then rounded on him, shouting. "Why didn't you call the police? Jacqueline talked to them that night, and I made a statement to them on Sunday – they know about the break-in at my house. They now think it's a *person* doing the killings, or two people. One of them has to be him! What's your friend's name? If she's hiding him, keeping him at her place, you've got to tell them. She works at the police station, for Christ's sake! What if she's helping them evade arrest? They've got to go over there and investigate."

Eric's voice was uncompromising in its demand. "Kenneth, *sit down*."

Kenneth hesitated, then returned. Eric slid his drink over to him and motioned for him to drink it. He picked up the glass and finished it in one shot. The whiskey burned on the way down.

"I thought about going to the police."

"Why didn't you?"

"You *didn't* call me *back*," he repeated, his voice very near to anger now. "How was I to know that you made a statement to the police about the two guys who came to your home? I told you to go to them, but I didn't know for sure that you had until just this moment – because frankly, I didn't think you would. You couldn't even call your friends for *years*; did I think for a minute you'd actually *call the police?* No." Kenneth cringed under the sting of his words; Eric was unsparing now, his lips curling back in annoyance. "You haven't even told me what you said. Did you tell the police you saw 'moving shadows'? I hope not. That's a great way to get involuntarily committed for a psych eval, and Kenneth, *you don't want that,* and *you know why*. Did you tell them that one of them *looked like you*? I didn't want to endanger *you*, Kenneth. Did you think about what would happen if I gave them a description of someone who *looks like you*?"

Kenneth was scrambling to keep up. "You think if you tell the police, the killers will know? If your friend is working with them, hiding them or telling them about the investigation..."

Eric cocked his head and looked at him as though he were stupid. "No, she wouldn't do that. I don't think she's in any way connected. She was lying about what happened to the guy, but I don't think she's involved. She's guileless, and..." The strain came back to his face. "And if she's mixed up with them without knowing who she's dealing with, I didn't want to get her into trouble. More importantly, I'd have to tell the police why *I* was there and what *I* was doing. I stole medical supplies and illegally treated a person without a medical license. That's worth about three years of my life in prison, more if it turns out that guy is a murderer and I was aiding and abetting him, even unknowingly. You think I want that?"

"Eric, people have *died* –"

"I haven't – I'm still here." His words came out with the forceful slam of a guillotine, devoid of all sympathy. "Sorry I'm not so eager to admit to a couple of misdemeanors. And more importantly, if that guy – 'Kohl' – is one of them, then it's not just the killers you need to worry about."

"What are you talking about?" Mathew's words suddenly flashed in his thoughts. His heart began to beat too fast again. "You mean the police?"

"...You look alike. Like twins."

Kenneth felt the world tip sideways.

Eric continued to speak slowly, rationally. "You need to be safe and have something to protect yourself with. And I don't care if you think it's selfish – I don't want to risk going to jail."

"And you don't want to endanger her. Your friend. She could *already* be in danger. He could be coercing her –"

Eric bit down hard, his jaw clenched. Whatever he thought about that, he didn't say. "I don't want to endanger *myself*. Promise me you'll keep that gun on you."

Kenneth looked down at it and sighed, the fight escaping him. He felt utterly spent and hopeless.

Eric cleared his throat. "I know you want me to make a statement. My concern is this: if he's over at her place, maybe they'll arrest him, but based on what you told me, the other one seemed far more dangerous...and he wasn't there. No sign of him, no mention of him. I'm worried that if they catch one, it might galvanize the other to react. They've come after you once. They might come after you again. On the other hand, they might do that, anyways, and catching one of them might draw the other out into the open. And if they don't catch him, they have another eyewitness account of someone who looks exactly like you."

"*Almost* like me," Kenneth corrected.

"*Enough* like you that a jury might overlook discrepancies that could be chalked up to poor lighting if the police decided to charge you."

Charge *him*? "I haven't done anything wrong," Kenneth protested, but he couldn't hide the sick trembling in his voice. He sounded so pathetic even to his own ears. "There's no reason they would charge me, no evidence..."

But he thought again about what Mathew had said, about coincidence and desperation, grieving families and drawn-out investigations, and he thought about those little plastic bags with the dark hair inside them, carried out from inside *his* house.

How he had been the one who took the photographs of the animals.

And how, he now realized, he had been driving the same road as Brittany Alice the morning she was killed.

People had gone to prison for less.

Eric studied his face. "It's dawning on you now, isn't it? You're in this. Maybe the police can protect you; or maybe..."

Kenneth nodded. He felt sick.

"Considering everything now, do you want me to make a statement?"

All he could do was shake his head *no*.

"Go home. Check for anything missing. You don't know how long those guys were in your house – maybe an hour, maybe a minute. If they took anything, that could be a big problem for you... especially if it turns up at a future crime scene."

Kenneth fought the urge to throw the whiskey back up. "Eric, the police already came by and turned the kitchen and living room inside out. If those guys took anything, I wouldn't know. I hadn't even thought about that possibility..."

"Time to start thinking about it."

When Kenneth didn't reply, Eric got up and went back to the kitchen. This time, he fixed them both drinks, three fingers of whiskey deep, and the two of them sipped in long, steady, companionable quiet.

And all the while, Kenneth stared down at the table, where the gun lay waiting, and wondered what he would do with it when he at last picked it back up.

TWENTY-ONE

"*Oh!* Kuro!" The rake clattered to the ground. "You scared me!"

Kuro lay prone in the grass in the garden. He could hear and feel her steps as she drew near, and suddenly the warmth of the sun was cut off as she blanketed him with her shadow.

He opened his eyes to look up at her, but he didn't need to. She occupied so much of his thoughts that he could catalogue her now, and with her standing before him, the image made flesh, it only solidified the picture he had created in his mind.

She put her hands on her hips and stared down, her feet near his head. "How long have you been out here?"

"A couple of hours."

"Why didn't you come to the door?"

"Your dog's back."

A knowing look dawned. "So *that's* why Feral's been acting strange all morning...he's been pacing for hours down the hallway."

"He probably knows I'm out here."

"Kuro, where did you go? You left so suddenly..."

He sat up in the grass and didn't answer. Beyond her farm, past

the rotten, slanting fence, stood the forest, and in it waited the darkness. That was the world he had once belonged to, but something
had changed. His world, once so full of rich sounds and scents, felt
empty now, and this patch of grass in the middle of a small garden in
the corner of an even smaller farm kept calling him back.

It reminded him of something from what felt like a lifetime ago,
one of the few things that had stuck in his memory: Jaden had once
shown him the picture of a tapestry, and in it, a creature called a
unicorn sat hemmed in a tiny, circular fence. There was a collar
around its neck, and from the collar, a chain extended to a tree, and
the animal was bleeding, wounded.

He felt like that creature now, caught somewhere between
fantasy and reality, wounded and chained to this plot of grass.

Not the grass, he corrected himself. He turned and stared up at
Caroline, and her eyes widened at his expression. *It's not the grass I'm
chained to.*

"Kuro – what's wrong?" She knelt beside him and yanked her
gardening gloves off. She reached up, drawing his face to look at her,
and he felt the heat from her fingertips trace upwards along his cheek,
pushing his bangs away.

"What do you think of me?"

He reached out fully to touch and know her soul, opening
himself up to it as much as he dared – and he dared it all. He
wanted to know, to *really* know. It rushed in upon him with the
force of releasing a dam, spilling into him, good and bad and all.
He braced himself against it, orienting himself, watching as her
eyes grew clouded, searching for an answer. She drew her hand
away.

"I'm not sure."

That was a lie. He could feel a whole current of feelings, strong
and formed, within her. He looked at her, his expression drawn, and
she looked away. "I don't know if I can put it into words..."

"*Try.*"

She grappled with herself. He closed his eyes and searched her soul for an answer and realized he was searching for something in particular, something he hoped was there.

"I think you're my friend." She let out a rush of breath. "I think you've changed my life. I don't know if I'm right, but...I think I've changed your life, maybe. A little."

"A lot." His voice was pitched.

A mirror of pain flared inside her, a channel of empathy and regret. "It doesn't sound like I've changed it for the better, though."

He didn't answer.

"I've been thinking a lot about how you moved the shadows." She reached out tentatively and touched the edge of his thigh. He opened his eyes and looked at her; something was moving inside her, and it was powerful and it *hurt* so badly, but he drank deeply from this feeling that was burning and targeted directly at him. "And I know this is a stupid thing to say to someone who shouldn't exist, a *demon*, but...it's impossible to move shadows. Shadows don't exist. They're just the absence of light."

"So?"

"So what I mean is, what I've been thinking..." She wasn't looking at him now, and he could tell from the way the tip of her fingertips trembled that her heart was beating rapidly, and anxiety was welling up inside of her...but it was different, almost pleasant, tingling. "What I've been thinking is, you're not moving shadows, Kuro. Maybe it feels that way to you, but that's not how shadows work. You must be moving the light. And something that can do that...something that can move *light* like that...can't be bad. And so I guess what I'm trying to say, is that I think you're..." She faltered, unable to finish the thought, but her soul spoke in its own language to him.

He leaned forward and kissed her without any sense of hesitation. She was startled for a moment, but then her lips parted and received him. He moved and pushed her backwards, and she sank below him onto the soft grass. This was not like before, sudden and jarring; he moved tentatively, searchingly. Kuro leaned over, pressing his face into her hair: it smelled of sunshine and dying sunflowers, of soil and earth and *her*. His arms came up, reaching to pull through it, to push it away as he kissed her again, deeply, and moved to her forehead, her ears, her neck. She made some sort of sound he had never heard before when he kissed the hollow of her throat, and his heart nearly leapt out of his chest.

His hand was shaking and needful as he unhooked the right button on the top of her overalls, pushing the strap aside. He was holding himself on top of her very carefully, and somehow, their legs had become intertwined. He let his hands drift over her body and felt the groove of her back, the tone of her thighs through the jeans, and when he saw her eyes staring at him, the liquid eyes of a doe, yearning and answering him, he let his shaking hands touch her breasts, grazing them through the fabric of her shirt.

His breathing had gone ragged, and her soul was filling him entirely with this feeling of *want* and *need* for *him*, because she possessed this feeling he had felt in her once before, shining and intoxicating and more painful than anything he had ever known, a feeling forbidden to him that he was not supposed to feed from, and he reached out to touch it, because it was just for *him* –

And just as he moved to kiss her, to tug at the other strap of her overalls, to give himself entirely over to her, something sharp exploded in his head, and he passed out.

––––––––––––

It must have been a few hours later when he woke up, close to noon. The sun was directly above him. A towel had been put under his head, and an umbrella had been propped up to cover his face.

He groaned and rolled over, pushing the umbrella aside, his skull throbbing.

"Kuro – are you okay?"

A bolt of terror hit him; her fear was acute, and it filled him, numbing away the headache, strengthening him...but it left a strange, bitter aftertaste he hadn't known before. What should have been immediately satisfying felt...burnt, almost.

He remembered what felt like only a second ago and felt a hot flood of warmth in his body.

She was kneeling in front of him, shaking him. Her fear was ebbing away, but only just barely.

"Kuro, are you okay?" She repeated. Her cheeks looked red and shiny, like she had scrubbed them. With a start, he realized she'd been crying. "Are you alright? Please tell me you're okay."

"...I'm fine." He shook his head to try and clear his mind, but her soul was completely focused on him. "...I'm sorry I scared you. I didn't mean to, I..." He didn't know what to say, how to defend himself.

To his shock, she buried her face against his chest. He brought his arms up hesitantly, hugging her.

"I think you had a seizure." She pushed herself back, but he held onto her hands, and he could feel the panic she was fighting against. "I don't know what happened, but all of a sudden, when you – when we were...your eyes just sort of rolled back, and you fell down and started to convulse. You didn't wake up, and I was worried I was going to have to take you to a hospital. I tried to move you, but you were too heavy."

It had been her emotions, he realized; he had let something inside him too poisonous for him to consume, and it had skewered him in one stroke of all-encompassing pain, driving him far from consciousness. He let his thumbs slide over her hands, his head spinning. She was frightened, but not because she was afraid of him – she was afraid *for* him. With a great effort, he tried to draw completely away from her soul. She saw the effort he was expending in his strained expression, and her eyes only widened more.

He pulled his hands away, his arms shaking. "It was your soul."

"My *soul? I* did that to you?"

"You..." His voice felt too thick, his mind hazy. He found the words she had been searching for earlier, words she had tried to communicate without saying but that her soul had told him, and terrified that they were a lie, he nevertheless spoke them out loud with slow, growing wonder. "You care for me."

Caroline stared at him in amazement. He didn't think she'd realized it until he said it, but now that he had, it dawned on her, lifting to the surface inside of herself. Her mouth was slightly ajar; she closed it and nodded, quietly.

"Yea," she whispered. "I do."

He looked away. He knew the answer to the question she was about to ask before it was spoken. Her soul had already asked it of him.

"...Do you care about me, too?"

He nodded. Yes, that was what had been growing inside of him all this time, where his thoughts had been leading him to. The realization seemed to shift the very earth beneath him.

"And that feeling...it hurt you pretty badly?"

Another nod. And then he spoke, his words directed at the trees. They stood in the distance, calling to him, welcoming him back. He didn't move.

"I think I'm dying."

Caroline gasped. Kuro cringed and spoke again, his words pained. "I can't feed on anyone except you, and even when you feel something I can feed on...I hate it. I don't want you to feel that way. *I* don't want to make you feel that way. And right now," he said, anger and bitterness creeping into his voice as he turned back to her, "you're *sad*. But you're sad because of this situation, and that sadness is because you *care* about me. I can't even feed on that – it's like drinking bleach. It's *worse* because it's directed *at* me. And I've never..." His voice broke. He clenched his fists in defeat, "...I've never felt anything like that. And I want to," he finished. "But it hurts. It hurts and I can't keep away from it."

He leaned his head backwards, eyes closing, and let it flow into him until he drew a rasping breath and pulled away at last, unable to take anymore.

He heard a sound next to him and turned to look. Caroline's eyes had filled with tears, and she was fighting against them, blinking. Dirty knuckles rubbed into her left eye as she took a steadying breath, her chest heaving.

"Okay." She stood up suddenly; he felt a great shift in her soul, as though all its energies were redirecting themselves somewhere else. He stared at her, perplexed. "Okay. I get it. We've got to fix this. We haven't really tried since that first time, but when I've got a problem out *there*," she said, stabbing an accusing finger at her garden, "I don't just say 'well, I guess that plant is going to die now.' I *figure it out*. And it takes work. Pruning, raking, weeding, a lot of hauling actual shit by the wheelbarrow, but I *get it done*. We're going to take the same approach, because you're right – I care about you, Kuro," she said, and he was startled by her intensity, the way she now clenched her fists. The tears she hadn't let spill were already gone, and a blazing determination had formed inside her. He grabbed hold of it, afraid to hope: it was like a rock, unshakeable. "And if you care about me – if you truly do – you won't put this all on me. You'll help me fix this so you don't starve. Will you do this?"

She reached out, her hand open. He nodded, and with her full strength, she drew him to his feet. On a sudden impulse, she reached up and tussled his hair, then grabbed him by the hand, yanking him toward her barn.

"Then let's get started."

"Okay, you were in here when it happened."

Caroline pointed to the back stall, across from the mare's. She had cleaned up the blood at some point and disposed of the hay. It held no answer for Kuro, but he obliged her and walked to the spot where he had once cowered, terrified for his life.

"And what happened? What were you feeling, when my soul touched you?"

Kuro thought back to that morning. He remembered her fear like a man recalling a favorite dish eaten long ago; it had been exquisite, consuming all his senses. He felt guilty remembering just how good it had been, lifting him up and dulling the pain from where he'd been shot. He glanced at her waiting face and felt a stab of hot shame; he wouldn't tell her about that.

"You were afraid," he said, and then, "very afraid. I was planning on killing you."

He held his breath as he waited for her to react to the words, to look at him in revulsion and distrust...but nothing changed. She nodded.

"But you didn't," she said matter-of-factly, and her tone indicated that she considered the business concluded. He let out his breath.

"No. I knew...I knew it was wrong. But I was feeding from you, and then you started to pray – the 'Hail Mary' one – and your fear went away. You grew calm. It felt like all the air rushed out of me..." He settled on an image, trying to explain the feeling. "I felt like a bay at low tide. Everything was sucked away suddenly, and I was desperate – I wanted you to stop, I wanted your fear again, so I kissed you to get you to shut up. And that's when your soul reached out to me."

"How did it feel?"

He visibly shuddered at the memory, but it was hard to put into words. Very few humans could actually feel it when he fed from them, unless they were haunted, or if he and Jaden had crowded in on the soul too quickly.

Or if Jaden had lashed at it with particular intensity.

"Not good."

"That's the best you've got?" Caroline hoisted herself up onto to the banister. "'Not good?'"

He looked back into the stall and could almost see himself, kneeling, bleeding, reaching for her, hungry and desperate. "I felt... exposed," he conceded.

"Have you ever been shot before?" When he shook his head, she continued, her legs dangling. "You were in a lot of pain. I was threatening you. You were frightened. Maybe all that combined to open up something inside you, like an invisible wall, and that allowed my soul to touch yours when you were feeding on me. To – I don't know, maybe sneak inside."

"...I don't know if demons *have* souls."

Her legs stopped moving. "Everything has a soul, Kuro. Even you."

The thought hadn't occurred to him, and he wasn't sure he believed it. After all, he couldn't feel Jaden's soul...so he assumed *kitsune* didn't have them. He never realized what a big assumption it was before.

"So let's assume there was a barrier of some sort that kept yours from mine. I'm a human, you're a *kitsune* – a lot of things are different about us." She laughed at the simplicity of her argument. "I know that's an understatement, but follow my reasoning: our souls are probably different, too. The problem is that mine is holding on to yours."

Kuro considered this; it was *possible*. When he thought of her soul as holding on to him, he never considered that the 'him' in the equation could be his *own* soul. The thought was still so foreign that he found it nearly unbelievable, but he followed her enthusiasm, allowing himself to feel the quiet thrill of hope. She had sprung off the banister and was heading out of the barn, and he trailed behind her, out into the sunshine.

He drew in a deep breath of the afternoon wind. Molly whinnied in her pasture, insulting him. He thought of the *holy dark* inside of him, moving and starving, and wondered if that played some role now in her inability to let him go. He hadn't told her about it and wouldn't. Some things – many things, now that he thought about it – were better kept to himself.

She whirled in the dirt, and a cloud of dust rose at her ankles. "Here's what I want you to do. I want you to open yourself up completely, as much as you can. Drop all your barriers – let your guard down. Maybe I didn't let go, or maybe something got trapped inside you. If it did, this might be a way to let it out again."

He shook his head. He didn't like the idea of exposing himself like that.

Her leg kicked out and showered him with a spray of dirt. "Don't look at me like you're frightened of yourself!" She commanded. "Kuro, find your spine! We're trying different things here. You don't even have to look at me," she said, her voice softening. "Look up at the sky, if that helps."

He took a deep breath and rolled his shoulders back, staring up into the sky. The clouds were the kind of thin, wispy things that looked like the whispered brush strokes of a paintbrush, too delicate to block the sun. The world was bright and clear, and a turkey buzzard circled high in slow, lazy loops, its partner following in a counter-clockwise direction. They were scanning for death, and finding none, had resigned themselves to float on the last hot winds of September.

He closed his eyes to the sunshine and tried to let every barrier within him down, to relax, but the moment he felt his hands release at his sides, Caroline's soul rushed in on upon him. It flooded him in its entirety, filled with warmth and care and concern, hope and *optimism*, and before he realized what had happened, she was standing over him, her hair brushing against his face, shaking his shoulders.

He must have passed out again.

Optimism, he thought, sickly. *That's a new one.*

She helped him sit up in the dirt, dazed.

"Was it me?"

"Yea." He held his head, pressing against a forming headache. He gave a wry laugh. "I think it was all the positivity that did it. You really thought that would work."

She still held on to his shoulders, steadying him. "What did it feel like?"

"Like a flooded valley. Everything rushed in on me at once. Most of the time, I have to work to keep your soul away from me. Like this," he said, and half-heartedly thrust her away with one hand, keeping her at arm's reach. She bit her bottom lip. "If I had to describe it...it's like a fly. It keeps moving around me, bothering me. I keep shoving it away, but it just keeps coming back. I'd kick it if I could."

"And yet, to me, it looks like you're just sitting there."

"It's sort of like existing on two different planes, I guess," he said. She waited for him to say more, but he couldn't. It was an idea Jaden had expressed once, and like so many things, he hadn't listened hard enough. He wished he had, now.

"Okay, well, that could have gone better." She helped him stand. He staggered for a moment and fell forward into her arms; she caught him, and they looked up into one another's face for a moment before pulling apart.

They were getting good at ignoring something they needed to talk about, Kuro thought.

"Are you willing to try again? If it hurts, I don't want to keep going..."

"It's better than the alternative."

"The alternative?"

"Dying."

"Right." She shoved her hands in her pockets and faced him again. "Look back up at the sky. Or look at me, or Molly. Whatever is easiest. Try again."

He sighed, tilted his head back, and let her soul smother him.

They continued well on into the night, and every time, he grew weaker and more stunned, like an animal that kept senselessly charging into an electrified fence. Eventually sunset had come and he retreated to the far edge of the forest, watching from a distance as she brought Feral outside on a leash and led him, snarling and barking, to the barn. Feral could smell him outside, and the dog unleashed a volley of furious barking as soon as he entered the stalls. Kuro shivered at the sound; he would never hurt Caroline, but he wouldn't mind taking a swat or two at that dog.

She had locked the barn and invited Kuro back into the house. He'd managed to eat a few bites of a pot roast, but in the end, he was too dazed from his repeated attempts to open up himself as much as possible in an effort to get her to let him go. It didn't work.

"I actually think this is making it worse," he groaned. He was lying on the couch, a pillow under his head. Caroline draped a quilt over him, and he rolled over on his side, pressing his face into the cushions. His head felt rent in two, and he was concentrating very hard on not throwing up, but his stomach kept clenching with pain. The only good thing was that her optimism had faded, and with it, her sense of hope had numbed a bit, diluted by dread and a burgeoning sense of dismay. He tried to feed on that to lift himself up from this state of misery, but again, the strange burnt, bitter aftertaste left him recoiling after only a few moments.

He didn't tell her about that, though. He didn't understand it.

Saturday dawned. "Things aren't quite as eventful as last week," she said, "so I'm staying home today." She slipped him a drink at the breakfast table.

He sipped and looked up, surprised.

Hot chocolate.

Her face lit up with a warm, mischievous grin at the look on his face. "You're not the only one with a good memory. I figured you'd need your strength today," she said.

He nodded and drank.

"Okay, this time, *I'm* going to try and focus on *my* soul. You sit there," she said later, pointing to the circular patch of bluegrass in the garden, "and I'll be here. I want you to touch my soul, but I'm going to try and see if I can retract it."

"We tried that already, before."

"We tried it *once*," she corrected. "It's worth trying again."

And they tried, over and over. She sat, her legs crossed, the wind carrying her hair behind her, and Kuro forgot half of the time to even feel for her soul. He was content to just stare at her and study her, to learn her curves by observation. He noticed new things, like that she had a single freckle on the bridge of her left ear, that her eyelashes looked like fine ink strokes, and that when she concentrated, she pursed her lips out, and they looked full and inviting.

She once opened her eyes and caught him staring, and they both knew what he was thinking, and they both ignored it.

But try as she might, she could exert no power over her soul: it moved within and without her, as was true of all humans. She could concentrate on herself and sit in quiet reflection, but the byproducts – the feelings – were mostly beyond her control unless she had a drastic change in mood.

When he pictured the *holy dark*, he could feel it moving within him, and when he touched her soul, he imagined that two arms that moved independently of him – black, shadowy things, long and spindly that ended in claws – reached out and tried to gather all her soul up, but it moved in and out of its fingers, tumbling free, like unwoven strands of silk. The tapestry could not be contained. It could only spread.

An eye opened. "Anything?" A bumblebee landed tiredly on her hair. She lifted a finger up and helped it out, setting it on the ground. Kuro watched it waddle through the grass.

"Nothing."

Two days passed in this tortured way, with effort expanded and wasted. He preferred it when she tried to retract her soul than when he tried to open his up. More than once he had collapsed to the ground, dazed and unconscious, only to wake up with a bruise and a headache.

When Monday came, she announced that she had taken off work, but he slumped.

"I actually need to head out for a bit," he said. "I'll be back in a few hours, hopefully."

She laughed. "You have a hair appointment you're late to?"

"What?"

"Never mind." She poured herself a second cup of coffee. "Feral will be happy to come back inside the house. See you soon."

And she leaned over, reached for his hand, and squeezed the soft flesh between his thumb and palm. He thought about that feeling as he headed out into the woods, climbing back up toward the duck pond, and the more he thought about it, the more other thoughts crept in, like the way her skin felt and tasted...

He grew anxious as he waited, but the sun continued to climb. He paced for an hour before flopping down into the reeds, disturbing a goose that he hadn't noticed. It flew at him in a rage, and he ran off, tail between his legs. Another hour passed; he circled through the nearby woods, sniffing, searching for Jaden's presence and scent, but felt and found nothing.

I should wait, he thought. It was nearly noon. Four hours had passed and he hadn't yet turned up. His temper flared. Who knew when Jaden would get there? Hours could pass – it could be sunset before he decided to appear. The thought of Caroline, home and waiting for him, a day wasted, spurred him to impatient frustration.

Maybe he should just leave, he thought; he'd head out, then come back around sunset just to see if he'd been there or not. They were demons; they left some sense of their presence behind, an imprint. Jaden would be able to tell, so even if they hadn't met up with one another, he'd know he had waited for him and would come back in another three days.

Kuro padded off through the forest, controlling himself from breaking into a run. His leg was still sore but healing, and he knew better than to push it. Better to save his energy.

He slipped out of the edge of the forest and saw her rotted fence in the distance, the barn coming into view. He approached and sniffed at the dirt, creeping toward the front door. A familiar feeling began to prickle at him, out of place and unexpected. From inside the house, Feral was barking viciously, growling and tearing at the screen. He backed away, hissing, and shifted to a human. If she was inside, he wasn't going in there.

He'd wait in the garden.

Maybe, he thought, she'd be out there waiting for him. His heart sped up at the thought. Even if he did feel drained and weak, the thought of her, waiting and smiling, expectant, made him feel suddenly light-headed.

Kuro walked around the front of the house and moved through the side gate, heading toward the back. He passed into the garden through the dirt path and looked up, eager to see her again.

In the middle of the garden, in the grass, Caroline had placed a blanket. She sat there now, her legs drawn to her side. She had loosely braided her hair, and it hung over her shoulder in a thick cord. She wore her gardening overalls, her hat discarded nearby. She was beaming with excitement, waving to him, inviting him over.

Kuro came to a sudden halt, his blood freezing with numb horror, as he stared at the figure who sat beside her.

A black and solemn silence stretched between them, and then a low, familiar voice, dangerous with its calm insinuation, greeted him.

"Hello, Kuro," Jaden said, his smile cold. "We've been waiting for you."

Acknowledgments

If you haunted fictionpress.net in 2002, you might have been the first to read about the black *kitsune* Kuro, who emerged from the forest to find Caroline on top of her barn, gun in hand. You might already know his true name (it hasn't changed, like so much of this story has), but *ssh* – don't tell anyone. True names are powerful things.

After I came out of adolescence, in a fit of embarrassment, I deleted all my juvenile short stories: they were the early dreams of a young and eager mind, and adulthood had taught me that the world was filled with writers *much* better than I would ever be, and so the best and most sensible thing I could do was scrub anything I ever wrote out of existence.

But Kuro (and all the rest of the lives he would touch, the stories yet to come), remained in my mind. I turned my short story into a bad novel and gave it to a good friend to read as a present, and I hoped to have it published someday. What writer doesn't?

It didn't work out; my manuscript began to gather its first of many layers of dust.

And then in 2011 I stumbled upon a post to the tvtropes forum. The user 'zerky' was looking for a short story she had read years ago, a story she "loved to death" and "wanted to re-read."

It was the story of a *kitsune* named Kuro; zerky went on to describe the initial short story in lengthy detail, and I felt my heart race: there had been someone – *one single person* – who not only read my story, but loved it enough to shout into the vastness of the Internet for help finding it again.

Whenever I thought about leaving this story to gather its dust, whenever I thought again about the *thousands* of writers who have more talent in a single finger than I have in all the best of my thoughts combined, I would open my writing journal; I had printed out zerky's post and taped it inside.

I would remind myself that I had an audience of one, somewhere out there.

Years passed, and then the pandemic happened, and in possession of a safe home and a secure job in a time of massive societal upheaval and cultural trauma, I was one of the *incredibly privileged* individuals who had a space and now time to pursue their own creative outlets. So many others were not so fortunate; so many others sacrificed their lives to keep us safe. I would be remiss not to acknowledge that.

But during those years, I wrote, and wrote, and wrote.

Kuro's story grew into an entire series of novels, and I discovered that after holding him in my mind for *twenty years*, I once more had the brazen courage and lack of good sense I had when I first shared his story, and therefore, it was time to share it again. I hope you'll go along with him on his journey; his world is so much bigger than Kuro could ever imagine – bigger even than Jaden could dare to dream...and there are so many other little foxes waiting to meet you, just a book or two away.

My favorites are yet to come.

So: zerky, if this story finds you, I hope that despite the changes wrought by time, you'll still enjoy it. Thank you for inspiring me to put this story out into the world.

And finally, no acknowledgement would be complete without a gracious 'thank you' to my husband, whose unwavering support, confidence, and enthusiastic encouragement helped bring this project to life. You are, and will always be, the best part of my life, and the better half of me.

KEEP READING

For an excerpt from the second book in the Color By Numbers series by Danielle Thompson: A Splash of Burgundy

J aden was dressed impeccably, pressed blue pants and a white Oxford button down, looking for all the world like a graduate student fresh from campus. He sat coolly relaxed, one leg bent, one stretched out before him, his unblinking gaze fixed on Kuro.

A pleasant smile graced his lips, almost boyish in its easy charm, but Kuro knew the shape of that particular mask: his stare – the intensity of it, the slightest furrowing of his brow – told him that beneath the surface of his congeniality lay a serpent that could strike at any moment. He raised a teacup to his lips and sipped it placidly, and Kuro watched his eyes narrow over the rim of the cup, an unspoken warning to him not to react.

Caroline's delighted voice cut through his horror.

"*Kuro!* Come on!"

He tried to regulate his breathing, but his heart was pounding in his chest. He took one wooden step forward, then another.

Jaden set the teacup down, nodding. He leaned back on one hand; the palm was casually splayed open on the ground, the edge of his fingertips almost touching Caroline. It was a deliberate, slow placement; he need only move in one practiced, swift motion, and Caroline would be at his mercy.

Kuro had no idea what the demon was doing there, how he had found her, or why they were in the garden together.

A worse fear twisted in his gut: he had no idea what Jaden had told her.

Jaden gestured to the edge of the blanket. "Sit down, Kuro." Kuro could hear the iron in that tone, the command layered just under the pleasantry.

He did as he was told, slowly, his limbs stiff. From the corner of his eye, he saw the subtle shift in Caroline's expression; she sensed something was wrong, and her gaze moved back and forth between them, her smile faltering.

Jaden picked up the cup again and had another sip, draining it. He looked down at the empty porcelain in mild disapproval. "You never told Caroline about me, Kuro." He cast an apologetic look at Caroline; the hand that was much, much too close to her now lifted and passed over his heart, as though the thought hurt him, and a dramatic, playful sigh escaped him. "I'm wounded."

Caroline's mood lifted again, reassembling itself; she laughed, but she glanced again at Kuro, puzzled by his reaction. His fists were clenched against his legs, the knuckles white, fingers trembling. He became aware that a muscle in his face was twitching.

"...So you've met." He was unable to hide the tremor in his voice. He cleared his throat, wrestling with himself to regain his composure; he didn't want to frighten Caroline or provoke Jaden into any violent impulse. "How long have you been here?"

"A few hours, actually." Jaden's bland smile tugged into a smirk. "You know, when I showed up...she thought I was *you*."

Kuro winced. The demon had annunciated each word with a pointed accusation that only he could hear, intimations of consequences yet to come; with Caroline looking at Kuro now, she couldn't see the way Jaden's eyes had gone cold with consternation.

"Feral went wild," she said. "I thought you came back, so I went outside...and your friend was here. He asked if I had seen anyone who looked like you. I said no, but he said he was sure you told him to meet him here."

"Which you did," Jaden said. His hand returned to the blanket, once more much too casually near to Caroline's thigh; he relaxed his weight against it and lifted his index finger, tapping it slowly. *Meaningfully.* "Remember?"

Kuro nodded, sick.

"And Feral wouldn't calm down...I haven't seen him like that since the night I met you, and I thought..." Caroline played with the end of her braid and shrugged. "I thought, well, this might be a little bold, but since you'd never mentioned having any *human* friends...I asked him if he was a *kitsune*, too."

All at once, it felt like his heart forgot how to beat. The color drained from him, his breath catching in his throat. Jaden's smile stretched into a grin.

"Imagine my surprise," he said, his voice untroubled, cool in his detachment. "Naturally, I told her 'no.'" His words were measured, perfectly amicable, but Kuro licked his lips, fighting against panic. "But then she told me, if I *was*...what was it you said? Ah, that's right. She told me I didn't need to be afraid, because she already *knew all about us.*" He propped his elbow on his knee, resting his cheek against his fist as if he was recounting an extraordinarily boring story. "And then I was just too curious, because your scent was just about everywhere, and here was this young woman who knew about *kitsune,* and I thought...well, *this* is certainly interesting."

He didn't sound interested in the least.

"Kuro, you didn't tell me there was another one of your kind here." Kuro turned to look at her; it took a force of will to drag his eyes away from Jaden. He could feel the hurt hidden under her excitement, and at the edges of her soul, someone else...someone creeping, *touching*. He whipped his gaze around and glared at Jaden, but the demon only shrugged.

"I only just came down from the mountains a few days ago," Jaden lied smoothly. "You mustn't blame him. He's thoughtless sometimes, but he would *never* deceive someone – especially not a friend." The words were a fast dagger thrown straight to Kuro's heart. He swallowed. "Like I was telling you earlier, I've known Kuro for a long, *long* time."

Caroline set a cup in front of him. For the first time, Kuro noticed that there was a teapot on the blanket and a small tray of cookies, lemon wedges, and sugar cubes. His mind began to pick up on other details: if Jaden intended to threaten Caroline, he had yet to do it, nor did she anticipate it. This was no hostage situation.

Inexplicably, this was afternoon tea.

He looked up to find Jaden's stare on him once more. "Have a drink, Kuro," he suggested in that low voice of his that expected obedience. "You look like you need one."

She poured him a cup, and a light curl of steam rose from it. He didn't touch it; he couldn't risk taking his eyes off Jaden again. It felt like someone else spoke when he heard himself ask, "What have you been talking about?"

Jaden held out his cup with polite expectation; Caroline refilled it. They looked almost like lovers in the easy way they lounged, the way she poured him tea. "Well, I told her how I ran into you a few days ago, and you told me I could find you here...but, we've mostly been discussing books."

Kuro fought the urge to lunge at him. The *holy dark* was surging inside of him, and with an effort, he did his best to suppress the tide, a metallic taste in his mouth. "Books?"

"Jaden's a great reader," Caroline said. She sounded impressed. "You seem so different from each other."

Jaden let out a short bark of laughter. "And to think, we've grown up with each other, but yes...we're very different, in some ways. In others...not so much. I'd like to think we've rubbed off on one another; we've been together practically since birth."

Caroline drew back in surprise. "I didn't know that. Kuro hasn't told me much about his life in the mountains."

"Well, I'm sure you'll have plenty of time to talk." Jaden reached forward and plucked a slice of lemon from a tray, setting it down in the tea. "As for me, I have to admit, this is all so very...*new*, this talking to a human...but not *as* a human. Not quite." He took a long sip, a playful grin sneaking across his features. His eyes sparkled with a light that Kuro decidedly did not like. "I've been enjoying it *thoroughly*."

He would, Kuro thought; undoubtedly he was loving the attention of this wholly novel experience, if Jaden was indeed capable of enjoying anything.

A stiff silence suddenly invaded the space; Caroline looked from one to the other, trying to understand the growing tension that she could no longer deny. Her soul had that rattling quality to it that it got just before she began to talk too much from nerves...

and Jaden was staring at her, smirking, enjoying her growing anxiety.

"Jaden won't show me what he really looks like," Caroline blurted suddenly.

Kuro's blood was boiling; he wanted to punch that look of smug satisfaction right off of Jaden's face. "Did you ask him to?"

"I did." Caroline's tone was apologetic. "I just...I was so excited. I had to ask."

"I'm not holding your curiosity against you," Jaden said. He finished his drink again and set it down. "You'll just have to excuse me; I'm shyer than Kuro...but I think, as we get to know each other more – and we will," he added, shooting Kuro a look, "I may warm up to the idea."

Kuro stood at once, knocking his teacup over.

Jaden looked at the spill, frowning. "That was rude, Kuro."

"We actually have to be going." He reached down and yanked Jaden to his feet, his hand closing around his forearm with a vice-like grip.

Caroline stood, confused. "But you just got here."

"I'll be back."

"It was nice meeting you...Caroline," Jaden said, and he dipped his head in a deferential goodbye. Behind them, Caroline watched them go, and Kuro could feel the sudden wave of uncertainty and suspicion in her soul.

Kuro didn't let go of him until he was certain he had dragged Jaden at least half a mile into the woods. Only then did he release him, furious and hissing.

"What do you think you're doing!?"

Jaden straightened his sleeve. "Kuro." He tugged at the other one, satisfied that they were even, and when he spoke, his voice was icy. "I'm going to give you one warning to change your tone with me. Do you understand?"

Kuro did and didn't care. He sprung forward, grabbed Jaden by the collar of his shirt, and slammed him against the base of a pine tree. Jaden reached up, glaring, and grabbed him by both hands. For one painful moment, his fingers were replaced by claws, and they pierced the flesh in his arms. Kuro let go and stepped back just before he could draw blood, and Jaden was fully human again, pushing his hair out of his face, glaring at him. There was an emotion very near to hatred in his eyes.

"You *lied* to me, Kuro." The air crackled with the sound of a tail snapping behind him, and Jaden stepped forward, fists clenched. "That girl has a *dog*. You were attacked by a *dog*."

Kuro slowed his breathing, navigating his thoughts. "Yes. Her dog attacked me. You're right. I lied."

Jaden opened and closed his hands slowly, flexing. "And the hunting accident. Is that true? Or was *she* the one who shot you?"

Kuro stared him down, finding the will to lie again. He knew Jaden would not be very kind to the person who shot him; sheer necessity gave his words a bold truthfulness that his previous lies had lacked. "It was a hunting accident, just like I told you. I had to hide – I crawled into her barn, and her dog found and attacked me."

"And you didn't give yourself those sutures. I let that lie go – oh, don't look so surprised Kuro, you're as transparent as glass. The moment you suggested you did a *multi-step process* requiring *patience* and *research*, I knew you were lying. I assume she did those?"

It would be easier to tell the truth rather than keep track of more lies. Kuro shook his head, inwardly seething. "No. She called a friend over, and he helped me." He took a moment to focus his thoughts in an effort to get a handle on the situation. "Jaden, I'm sorry – I didn't mean to lie to you, it's just..."

"What?" Jaden sneered at him. "She's pretty, Kuro – in a country kind of way. You think I wouldn't understand?"

No, he thought. He didn't think he'd understand *at all*.

"You were hurt; she helped you, and you wanted to keep her all to yourself. That's *fine*, Kuro. I don't care. You've always been more sentimental than I am. I think you're an absolute, goddamn *fool* for telling her you're a *kitsune,* for *showing* her what you look like..." He took a deep breath. "I can't believe you would do that. And she seems to have accepted it *remarkably* well... Does she know you're the one in the paper?"

He nodded. Jaden snorted. "And does she think you're the one who did the killings?"

"...No."

Jaden considered this for a moment. "...That's why you didn't tell her about me. You didn't want her to know about your involvement."

I wasn't involved! He wanted to rage, but he clamped down on the thought, swallowing it. He was *complicit,* he knew. That was bad enough. "What did you tell her, Jaden?" His voice was shaking again. "What did you talk about before I got there? Don't lie to me."

"*Books.*" Jaden turned on him in a rage. "We talked about you for the first thirty minutes, but despite what you might think, you're not that interesting." He stalked away in a fury then came back, shoving him. "You showed her what you *look like,* you *idiot!* What's your plan when for you're done and you're ready to move on?"

Kuro stumbled backward, gathering himself. "When I'm done...?"

Jaden gestured inarticulately, rolling his eyes. "What's your goal here, Kuro? You've never shown interest in humans before. What do you *want* from her? A warm bed, a hot meal, a quick fuck?"

Kuro's fists bunched to strike, but he restrained himself with every ounce of his will. He could have throttled him for that last comment, but Jaden stood before him now looking genuinely interested and mildly perplexed.

His mind wheeled, searching for an answer, but he didn't know. There had to be something he could say, something to convince Jaden to lose interest in her and leave her alone. *And what if he doesn't?* What if he kept coming back, what if he threatened her...? He thought of that girl in the car, saw the blood again, and shuddered.

He couldn't let him do that to Caroline.

ABOUT THE AUTHOR

Danielle Thompson likes a strong cup of coffee in the morning and a stronger cup of tea in the afternoon. Born and educated in the United States, Danielle spends most of her time trying to find her cat, a Somali named Moxie, who is inevitably never where she should be.

A Black and Solemn Silence is her first published novel, and the first in the *Color by Numbers* series.

For more information, follow her on Instagram at @author.danielle.thompson or visit her Web site at www.writer-daniellethompson.com.